A NOVEL

PIECE OF MY HEART

PENELOPE TREE

MOONFLOWER

Published by Moonflower Publishing Ltd.
www.MoonflowerBooks.co.uk

1 2 3 4 5 6 7 8 9 10

Copyright © Penelope Tree 2024

ISBN: 978-1919618791

Cover design by Jasmine Aurora

Cover image and interior images of Penelope Tree used
with kind permission from © David Bailey

Printed and bound in Great Britain by Clays Ltd, Elcograf S.p.A.
Suffolk, UK

Moonflower Publishing Registered Office: 303 The Pillbox, 115 Coventry
Road, London E2 6GG, United Kingdom

MOONFLOWER

"...to arrive where we started
And know the place for the first time."
Little Gidding – T.S. Eliot

For Paloma and Michael, and for DJKR

ONE

Kathmandu, August 1973

I dreamed I was asleep in my old bedroom at Thurston, with Violet curled up by my feet and early morning sun flooding through a gap in the curtains. Then the smell of musty sheets and the steady *drip drip* of water falling onto the wooden floor reminded me how far I was from home.

When I opened my eyes, it was still dark. Outside, the rain was bucketing down so hard even the street dogs were quiet for once. This wasn't polite English rain – it was a roar of falling water, a constant, endless deluge. The damp of the Nepalese monsoon seemed to seep through the walls into my bones.

Too wide awake to sleep, I lit the paraffin lamp and reached for my notebook.

I'd discovered by then that it helped me to write. Some nights I'd sit for hours doing nothing but describing my surroundings in as much detail as possible, down to the black furry patches of damp on the wall by the window, the sound of my next-door neighbour hoiking up phlegm and spitting it out, and the view across the street to the rooftops, slick and shining in the rain.

The leak in the sitting room ceiling is precariously close to the overhead light, I wrote. *Little hope of getting it fixed. Aju doesn't speak much English, and he pretends to understand even less.*

Still, apart from these minor hitches, the flat was cushy by local standards. As well as the bed, there was a desk, a small table and three rickety chairs, a thick-pile Tibetan rug and, most crucially, a sit-down lavatory, rather than the usual squatting pan. The American engineer I'd sublet it from had left behind stacks of American crime novels, erotic thrillers and, oddly, *The Teachings Of Don Juan: A Yaqui Way of Knowledge.* Though power outages were frequent, when the electricity was on the overhead fan in the bedroom was a godsend.

If I had to wait out the monsoon, this wasn't a bad place. Though I felt more at home in the small Tibetan hamlet a few miles out of town, the road through the paddy fields was currently impassable, and I didn't want to be stuck without access to a telex machine. I'd been assigned by *Now!* magazine back in London to write weekly pieces about my life in Nepal, but I'd arrived at the same time as the monsoon and been trapped in town ever since. This was my first writing job and I didn't want to blow it. The small fee I received had paid for the flat, as well as all my meals, taxis and those crucial vodka and tonics at the Yak 'n' Yeti bar in the Royal Hotel.

Apart from my weekly deadline, I had few obligations. For the first time in my life I was free to do whatever I wanted. Which usually meant venturing out to explore the town in the early morning and evenings, when the rain let up and the humidity became almost bearable.

After several cups of *chai* and a *sei roti*, I'd return home, mud splattered and sweat soaked, to write. It had been the same weekly routine since I'd landed here three months ago.

The actual writing had been easier on the road. All I'd had to do was observe my fellow passengers and describe their reactions to the dire situations in which we found ourselves. The more extreme the experience, the better the copy. So far, I'd missed only one deadline. And I'd more than made up for it the following week when I described in graphic detail what it was like to have dysentery on a long-haul bus trip.

We'd been struck down in Pakistan. There were ten of us passengers – including three couples who, as the journey progressed, were navigating various stages of breaking up: a silent Dutch aid worker; an Aussie surfer with hair down to his waist; Roger, who'd recently dropped out of Edinburgh Uni; and a heartsick English girl – me.

What began as mild nausea and stomach cramps soon escalated to the moment when half a dozen of us were violently expelling the contents of our stomachs from both ends, within a few feet of one another, in a recently planted field with no trees or bushes to hide behind. We had to repeat the same hideous scenario several times in the same day. The stomach cramps were so bad I was actively praying for my life to end. Someone spread the rumour that the water tank was contaminated and perhaps it was true, because everyone except Max, the driver, fell ill. It was bad enough that we had to stop at a hostel for a few days to recover.

Max had seen it all before and knew exactly what to do. There weren't enough antibiotics to go around so he fed the rest of us a mixture of salt and sugar in boiled water, followed by opium in black tea. Once we could hold it down, things started to improve. Though we were all constipated for the next three weeks, we were perfectly happy to sit in the bus for hours at a time, gazing out of the window in a drugged stupor.

There was no mystery where the opium came from. Roger, the most astute one of us all, had figured out early on that the baggage hold on the bus had a false panel and extended much further back than it appeared. Which explained why canny old Max from Hackney Wick was such a fascist when it came to restricting our personal luggage. He had travelled the overland route many times. Wherever we went, border officials waved us through without delay. The fact that Max was risking our long-term freedom as well as his own didn't appear to bother him in the least.

As a result of Max's odd detours to remote locations in Afghanistan, followed by the dysentery saga in Pakistan, we had arrived in Kathmandu three weeks later than scheduled. By then, I was exhausted and emaciated, but elated to have made it – until I discovered the friends I had planned to meet had already left the country, and I would need to wait out the monsoon alone.

Roger chuckled when I told him the news. 'Come to Thailand,' he urged. 'There's an island in the Andaman Sea where we can live on the beach for next to nothing. I'll look after you.'

He wasn't unattractive but… no. As far as my heart was concerned, ten countries, three months, and eleven thousand miles hadn't changed a thing.

Alone in a strange place, I buried myself in my work. My editor and friend, Julius, wanted human-interest stories: 'This is Now! magazine, not National Geographic,' he shouted down a crackling long-distance line, after I had spent days writing a detailed piece about Newari architecture. So instead I described the characters I met on Freak Street where the foreign hippies – the inveterate stoners, the mountain climbers, the dharma bums, and the genuine truth seekers – met over hashish cheese toast and *bhang lassi.*

The *chai wallah* on the corner of my street spoke some English. He was the one who told me about a little girl known as a living goddess, who lived in an imposing brick palace down an alleyway in a small square. Determined to see her, I waited outside her house for days, rain or shine.

Finally, one morning, she appeared behind the latticework of a third-storey window; tiny, in a red and gold sari, her hair in a topknot, her eyes outlined heavily with black kohl, with an inscrutable expression quite at odds with her childlike features. As she glanced across to where I stood near a group of white clad pilgrims, I felt a wave of heat pass through me like an infrared beam.

Afterwards I wandered around the town for hours, feeling slightly unhinged. Layers of monsoon cloud, spectral white, on top of murky charcoal, hung over the rooftops, obscuring the view of the Himalayas. Many of the curio and statue shops were closed due to the heavy rain, and the streets had a mournful, hemmed-in feel. As I crossed Durbar Square, with its maze of ancient palaces and tiered pagodas, wraithlike figures appeared and vanished back into mist. With every step, memories from my last trip here four years earlier flooded back.

When I came across a shrine set in a massive tree trunk just after a busy intersection, I stopped in my tracks, remembering it was the domain of the toothache god. Over the years, devotees had nailed coins all over the wood and smeared layers and layers of vermilion paste over the coins. If there had ever been an actual representation of the god inside the hollow, it had long since disappeared, leaving the distinct impression of a bloodied mouth frozen in a Francis Bacon scream.

When I'd last been in Kathmandu, Ramsey had photographed this landmark from various different angles, fascinated by its ghoulish appearance. It made me shudder to look at it now.

In the days after our break-up, the physical ache of missing Ramsey had been all-consuming, and resulted in a profound sense of disconnection, even from people I loved. Months on the road had numbed me, but I soon discovered the pain had simply burrowed deeper inside.

He had taught me how to look at things, what to value, what to discard – and I had accepted his opinions as my own.

His self-belief was so potent that for years it had given me a safe harbour in which to avoid growing up. The end for us had occurred near here, in the village of

Boudhanath – though at the time I was so completely under his spell that I ignored all the signs.

That was why I had decided to return to Nepal and follow a thread of light back to the source, to try and make sense of the peculiar set of events that had occurred here four years ago. But so far, any insight had eluded me, and instead I simply felt Ramsey's absence like a bottomless chasm inside me.

So I did what I always did when I reached the same impasse. I went straight to the bar at the Royal and ordered a double vodka and tonic. It went down very well, so I had another, and another.

When I emerged from the hotel – one of the few with its own generator – the town was shrouded in darkness and it was raining again. The doorman found me a taxi and for some reason the driver insisted on dropping me off a few hundred yards from my flat. Still drunk, and soaked to the skin in seconds, I misjudged the depth of a puddle, landing face down in the mud.

I immediately burst into tears and began crying uncontrollably.

No doubt if Sunny had been there, the moment would have been comical. She would have pulled me to my feet and made me laugh. But I wasn't even sure we were still friends. She hadn't replied to any of my letters so far. The thought of losing her after everything we'd been through was unbearable.

Still shaking, I dragged myself to my feet and climbed the creaking stairs to my flat, leaving a trail of muddy footprints behind me.

In the bathroom, I stared at my reflection in the mirror. Thin strands of hair glued to my pale skin. Swollen eyes like pissholes in the snow, as Ramsey was fond of saying.

Sunny had warned me not to travel to Nepal alone. 'Not in the state you're in, Ari,' she'd said. 'You need your friends.'

Her logic was hard to argue with. I respected her opinion over everyone else's, but there were some things she would never understand.

Bone tired and shivering, I fell asleep as soon as I got into bed. There was a long blackout, and then suddenly I found myself at Thurston, with its distinct scent of beeswax, wood smoke, geranium leaves, and wet dogs. And the sounds: the crunch of gravel in the driveway as weekend guests arrived, the excited exchange of greetings in the hall, and the clink of glasses and laughter from the drawing room.

My childhood home, the one I had fled from many years before, without a backward glance.

TWO

Chatham Hall, October 1962

The first time I left home, it was to go to Chatham Hall. I was thirteen. I shared a dormitory with nine other girls. They'd all been to prep school and knew the boarding-school ropes. Within minutes they'd become fast friends and I was left on the outside, awkward, shy and missing home. I listened to them giggling, chattering away while I pretended to sleep, wishing I could acquire their communication skills by pure osmosis, but the knack eluded me.

Sometimes I heard them whispering about me and, more disconcertingly, about my parents. I could never quite catch what they were saying, until one day a girl called Lavinia Featherstone confronted me point blank in front of the others, as if she were acting on a dare.

'Is it true your parents are divorcing?'

The other girls tittered.

Her words were like a nail bomb exploding inside me. *Were* they divorcing? I thought of my father's long absences. The arguments in the drawing room.

How could this girl know more than I did about my own family? The pain brought fury.

'No, it's not true,' I hissed at her. 'Are yours?' It was a feeble response, but all I could muster.

That put an end to their questions, if not to my own.

They weren't divorcing, I assured myself. My father would have told me. Or my sister would have said something.

Still, after that I spent as little time as possible in the dorm. I was increasingly alone, in the dining hall, the classrooms and especially during Games. I tended to trip

14

over my own feet, and I couldn't catch a ball. So I was always the last to be chosen for any team.

It turned out I wasn't alone, though. There was another girl always on the side lines, also feeling left out.

Sunny had arrived at Chatham believing that boarding school was going to be like something out of *Girl's Own*, with jolly girls having midnight feasts and solving local murders. That illusion was torn away the moment she opened her mouth to speak. Not one of our schoolmates had ever heard a Lincolnshire accent before. Nor were they accustomed to such a gravelly voice on a young girl. They pretended not to understand her, joking that she was too common to warrant attention. But from the start I liked her. She was a full head shorter than me but a hundred times savvier. She could also fight ferociously, a skill she'd acquired back in Grimsby at a young age.

Becoming friends with Sunny changed everything. We laughed at the same things. She wasn't afraid of anyone, and her fearlessness made me braver.

When she told me she wanted to be a singer when she grew up, I thought she was fantasising, though I kept my doubts to myself. It was true she could play almost anything on the piano right through after just hearing it once. However, the music teacher was unimpressed because Sunny didn't know how to sight-read or play classical pieces.

Still, if anyone could do it, I thought Sunny could. She exuded confidence. When half-term came and she couldn't go up north for just a few days, I brought her home to Thurston, to meet my parents.

My father sent Reg, his chauffeur, to collect us. Reg hugged me and teased me, as he always did, about my untidiness. On the drive, I sat with Sunny in the back seat, talking away, unaware that she thought the chauffeur was my father.

When at last we drove though the iron gates and down the long drive through the parkland, she gasped when she saw the house appearing through the trees.

'Christ, Ari,' Sunny whispered. 'It's bigger than Selfridges!'

I was taken aback by her reaction. Thurston was the house I'd grown up in, so I took it for granted. It was so familiar to me.

Maud and Papa both came to greet us with the dogs, who jumped up and down making a crazy racket. After they finally calmed down, I introduced Sunny, who seemed slightly alarmed when Maud asked her real name.

Just by the way Maud took a deep drag from her cigarette holder, I knew immediately she thought Sunny was common. She ushered us quickly up the front steps. Behind us, Papa made his way more slowly, clutching onto the balustrade with one hand. He was clearly in pain, but he hated it when anyone commented, so I went back down and linked my arm though his. We didn't have to say anything. No matter how long the separation, we were instantly at home with each other.

I found Sunny in the front hall, her blue eyes huge as she took in the sheer scale of the enormous mythical paintings flanking the entrance to the inner hall, and the vast sweep of the black and white marble floor.

I was desperate to run upstairs to see Nanny in the nursery, but Maud had arranged tea for us with Miss Bolton in the drawing room, where we made awkward conversation.

Miss Bolton, my governess, barely said a hello at me. Her attention was fixed on the scones and cucumber sandwiches, which she systematically demolished.

Maud lit another cigarette and directed her attention at Sunny, as she said in her most sympathetic tone, 'Chatham must be such an enormous change for you, Christine. How are you coping?'

Sunny never used her real first name.

I shot her a mortified look. But Sunny just murmured something unintelligible, her eyes fixed on her plate.

I'd never seen her like this. She was always ready to defend herself. When girls at school teased her, she stood up to them, fists curled, shouting, 'I'm proud of my dad for making his own money. It's far cleverer than just inheriting it.' Nobody but Sunny could make inheritance sound like such a dirty word.

Now, though, she looked intimidated. Her already small frame seemed to shrink even further.

Maud, who valued fluent conversation above almost everything else, blew out a stream of smoke.

'Is the food absolutely disgusting at school?' Papa inquired, with a knowing glint.

'Foul,' I confirmed. I glanced over at Sunny for agreement, but she avoided my eyes.

'Really, Serena, I do think Cook could do better than to give us a two-day old cake,' complained Miss Bolton.

Sunny looked confused.

'Serena's her real name,' I whispered, lips hardly moving. 'It's just the family

16

who call her Maud.'

Rupert had come up with the nickname when he was about five, after an outspoken cartoon character in the *Daily Express* called Maudie Littlehampton, with whom he was obsessed. Our Maud was so unlike a Mum, a Mummy, or even a mother, that we all fell into using the nickname.

Maud took another drag on her cigarette, eyeing Papa meaningfully through a cloud of smoke. 'We've got a houseful of guests arriving any minute, and Mrs Philpott has her hands full,' she said, barely glancing at Miss Bolton. 'I think she does a marvellous job, considering.'

'Come on, Lillian,' Papa urged Miss Bolton. 'Cheer up, we've got the old girl back at last. And her new friend. What will she be thinking of us?'

Miss Bolton eyed the cake suspiciously. By common agreement, she took her meals in her flat above the garage, so teatime was her only opportunity to do battle with Maud. I was often on her side, and she was sometimes on mine. A few weeks apart had changed our dynamic. Now that I was no longer her student, she seemed to have little interest in me, and didn't ask how it was going at school.

Actually, thanks to her, I was drowning in most of my lessons. She firmly believed that girls like me would require only a very basic knowledge of maths in later life and her overriding priorities lay in teaching the art of handwriting; French (spoken with an exaggeratedly English accent); botany; and a particularly passive-aggressive form of guerrilla warfare, which she waged against everyone on the estate, apart from my father. It was for him she had me memorise epic poems, and passages from Shakespeare every week, which I was expected to recite without faltering.

The moment Miss Bolton patted her lips with her napkin and liberation was finally in reach, Maud said she and Papa would like a quick word with me. Rather than leave Sunny alone with the dragon, I brought her into the library.

Papa stood in front of the fire looking distinctly uneasy. Maud sat on the sofa and patted the place next to her.

'Ariadne, come and sit. Christine, I think you'll find some magazines you might like to look at over there? This won't take long.'

Sunny blinked and said stiffly, 'Thank you, Miss. Please, where is the toilet?'

Maud squirmed visibly but directed Sunny down the hall.

When the three of us were alone, she stood next to Papa. She was still in her London clothes, a fitted red jacket over a white satin blouse, a red pencil skirt, patent leather pumps; her hair freshly coiffed. I noticed a pinkish blotch on her neck just above her pearls.

Something in her expression made my stomach lurch.

'You've been so grown-up the way you have settled in at Chatham and made new friends, we're awfully proud of you, aren't we, Papa?' She glanced at him but didn't wait for his answer. 'Every now and then one is required to be unselfish for the greater good – in this case one's family.'

This, I knew did not bode well.

'Now, you remember darling Minty?'

I shook my head.

'Papa's second cousin, she's stayed here often.'

I knew that was a lie.

'The poor darling is on the verge of a nervous breakdown. With three children and everything she's been through…'

'I don't understand…' I glanced at my father, but he was looking past me.

'She's simply never been able to find trustworthy help in the Midlands,' Maud said, as if this were a known fact, 'and now that you and Hen and Rupey are all off at school, we rather felt there was no reason why Nanny shouldn't take up the position. I must say she was a brick about the whole thing. She rushed off at once.'

Tears had begun pouring down my face. Maud faltered but forged though to the end. 'I thought it was better to tell you in person, rather than on the telephone. I knew you'd understand.'

Understand? I couldn't breathe.

Maud was always busy in London, and Papa was often abroad. Nanny had looked after me since I was born. She was the only one who let me be completely myself. Who loved and accepted me no matter how bad-tempered or difficult I was. I loved her dearly. Thurston was her home, just as much as it was mine.

'Now, darling, stop this,' Maud scolded as I sobbed. 'You don't want to upset your guest. Ah, look, here's Christine.' Her voice brightened as Sunny walked back into the room. 'Hello! Well done for finding your way back to us!'

As Sunny stared at her, Papa chimed in, 'Ari, there's a marvellous surprise waiting for you upstairs. Shall we go up and see?'

In a blur of anguish, I followed Maud up the two long flights of stairs to the nursery with Sunny, mute, by my side. Papa took the lift.

When we reached the top floor, Maud said, 'All right, close your eyes!'

We obeyed, walking with our arms out in front of us as she guided us down the hallway.

'You can open them now,' she instructed in a sing-song voice.

I blinked as the light momentarily blinded me. It took a few seconds to register that the cosy, cluttered nursery I had shared with Henrietta and Rupert now resembled a sitting room in a hotel. Gone were the upright piano, the shelves stacked with books, games, and jigsaw puzzles, the round table with brightly painted chairs. Gone was Nanny's favourite wing chair by the window, the faded rose-patterned carpet. The familiar scuffed light-blue walls were now a dusky shade of apricot. Stiff-backed sofas and armchairs were configured round a glass coffee table. A new carpet covered the floor.

'Awfully chic, isn't it?' my father half-asked, half-informed me.

'Frightfully grown-up!' Maud exclaimed. 'And you're the first to see it. What do you say?'

'Thank you, Maud and Papa,' I said, meekly. 'It's super.'

Papa put his arm round my shoulders and squeezed.

As soon as my parents went downstairs, I headed straight for the bathroom to wash my face. I didn't want Sunny to see me upset. She had been disparaging about girls at Chatham who went on about their nannies, so I hadn't told her about mine. I would never be able to explain how much she had meant to me.

When I came back to the room, I told Sunny, 'Let's go outside. I'll show you around.'

We changed into our jerseys and dungarees and ran down the back stairs, collecting the dogs on the way, and ran out into the fresh, cool air.

THREE

Thurston, October 1962

The flowerbeds in the garden were dying back, though a few frostbitten black roses hung on to their stalks, like tiny shrunken heads. We followed the chalk path to a small wood and up a slope onto a newly ploughed field. At its exact centre grew an ancient beech tree with a canopy that extended all the way down to the ground. The narrow passage I had cleared through the nettles and underbrush the previous summer hadn't quite grown over, and we crawled through to the enclosed and spacious chamber encircling the giant trunk.

Here I had long ago stored a rolled-up tarpaulin and a cigar box containing agate pebbles and a small blue and white china elephant. We rolled out the tarp and lay on our backs looking up through the leaves. The sun had just set, sending vivid pink streaks across the sky. Violet and Pav, my two lurchers, sniffed excitedly for rabbits around the roots as we gazed up into the twilight.

'What's up with your granny then?' Sunny asked, her voice finally returning.

'She's not my granny. Miss Bolton was our governess until we all went away to school.'

Sunny, who had gone to normal school in Grimsby before Chatham, absorbed this. 'So you had a nanny and a governess? That's mad. Just for you?'

'No, there's also Rupert and Henrietta,' I said. I didn't mention that they had both been sent to boarding schools at the age of seven. Papa had battled with Maud to keep me home until I was thirteen. He won, but at a price. As far as Rupert and Henrietta were concerned, I was horribly spoiled.

'Are they both at school now?' Sunny asked.

'Rupert's twenty-four, and Hen's twenty-two.' I picked up a piece of grass and held it between my fingers. 'She's engaged to a plonker.'

As we lay under the tree, I struggled to explain my complicated family to her.

Rupert and Hen were my half-brother and sister from Maud's first marriage. Their father had been killed in the war. They respected Papa, and were civil to him, but it was clear where their ultimate loyalty lay. We were really two separate families under the same roof.

My half-sister, Henrietta, was cut from the same cloth as Maud. She had the self-confidence I desperately lacked; she was an excellent horsewoman and shone at all kinds of sports.

Rupert, the oldest of us, had just managed to scrape through Harrow and was now working in the City. Papa once remarked that my brother was born with a whiskey and soda in his hand,

I was so much younger; it was hard to connect with them. Rupert treated me like a favoured pet, while Henrietta was tall and blonde, and wildly popular with boys. She had no time for children.

I was nothing like them. I was awkward and fearful. I loved dogs more than people and had endless strange quirks. When I was young, I'd gone through a phase of dressing up like the Virgin Mary, making little shrines in the woods, requesting a boy doll so I could wrap him in swaddling clothes and worship him in a cardboard manger.

'I'm afraid Ari is a religious fanatic,' I overheard my father say one afternoon.

Maud, the daughter of a vicar, was not amused. She never disguised the fact that she hated my oddness. And yet, in her good moments she could be wonderful. She showed me how to roll down a grassy hill, so the world spun round and round.

Once, when one of my milk teeth fell out, a circle of flowers appeared on the lawn for me from Tatiana, Queen of the Fairies.

Often, in the early evening before dinner, I would perch on Maud's four-poster bed as she sat at her dressing table in a blue silk robe, getting changed for the evening. The sweet scent of stephanotis oil from her bath lingered in the air and on winter nights a fire crackled in the hearth. Maud would address me through the mirror as she powdered her face with a soft fluffy puff, asking questions about what I'd been up to, occasionally interrupting my answers to address June, her lady's maid: 'The chartreuse silk pumps, please, and the gold evening bag. No, not the leather one, the Minaudiere.'

I watched her apply a little liquid rouge under her cheekbones, a touch of iridescent green eye shadow on her upper lids. When her *maquillage*, as she called it, was complete, Maud tilted her head like a bird, and pulled a peculiar face as she studied herself in the mirror. She dabbed Mitsouko onto her neck and wrists. And then came my favourite part. She'd produce bulging suede pouches from the dressing table drawers and I would help her decide which pieces of jewellery to wear before June helped Maud into her evening clothes. This could take some time; sometimes fifty tiny hooks were involved, especially if the dress had a corset built into it.

Even on Sunday nights when Maud and Papa dined alone, or *en famille*, as Maud referred to it, my father was always in black tie, and my mother in one of her tea gowns from Balenciaga or Balmain. 'Your father expects it of me,' she explained solemnly, when I once asked why.

Papa never tried to stand in the way of her career, and I don't think anyone could have stopped her if they tried. She loved politics and had risen quickly through the ranks of the Conservative party, a trajectory that soon found her as a personal advisor to a prominent MP in the House of Commons. Inevitably, this meant she spent Mondays through Fridays in London, where she went out every night to cocktail parties and dinners. She received admiring write-ups in newspapers and magazines, which June carefully cut out and stuck into red leather binders stacked on the long table behind the sofa in the sitting room.

Maud drove herself hard and she expected everyone around her to do the same; yet between her work, her London life and weekend parties at Thurston, she was often on edge. Then she found fault with everyone, including my father. The two of them bickered about most topics, especially about me and my education. I dreaded Sunday afternoons when the last guests left, because inevitably there was a fight or a brooding atmosphere between them.

I explained all this to Sunny as we lay beneath the tree and, to her credit, she accepted it without criticism. If anything, she seemed to find it fascinating.

'How did your mother and father meet?' she asked.

'She was working as a secretary for one of his friends in the Foreign Office. Papa met her and took her out to supper the same night. That was it, apparently; they got married six months later.'

'I'm sorry about Maud,' I added. 'The way she talks to you like you're from another planet.'

Sunny laughed. 'She's all right. Really, you should have heard the way my American family reacted the first time they heard me speak. They didn't understand a word I said when I first arrived... they just fell about laughing as soon as I opened my mouth.'

America was Sunny's trump card. Very few girls at Chatham had flown across the Atlantic and Sunny had travelled there alone last year, to visit her aunt and uncle.

I knew little about this time in her life, except that her mum had been in hospital, and her dad had sent her to stay with his brother in the States. And Sunny had loved it.

'They live near a lake big as the sea, in a white house with dark green shutters and a porch in the front and back.' A leaf drifted down, landing on her eye, and she batted it away, distractedly. 'The family joke was to make me repeat northern phrases, like "ya daft wazzack" and then fall about laughing. They said my voice sounded like I had a three pack a day habit. But they weren't being horrible like the girls at Chatham, they just thought I was a hoot. One night, Linda made me get up and sing at a Saturday night talent quest.'

'What did you sing?' I asked.

Sunny turned her head to grin at me. '"I'm Sorry" by Brenda Lee. Linda said I made people cry.'

I was fascinated, unable to imagine singing or doing anything in front of a crowd. 'Weren't you petrified?'

'At first, yes. But when I was up there on stage, something came over me. That's when I knew.' She gave me a fierce look. 'I'm going to be a singer. I just will be, Ari. I will.'

In that moment, underneath the leafy canopy, I believed her.

'Did you want to stay over there with your aunt and uncle?' I asked.

'I thought about it,' she confessed. 'They said if I wanted, I could live with them and go to school there. I would have done it, if it weren't for Mum. Even though I haven't seen much of her since I've been back, at least I know she's doing all right, and she'll be back home by Christmas, Dad promised.'

After that, the conversation faltered. I sensed that Sunny didn't want to talk about whatever was wrong with her mother. And by now it was getting dark.

We ran back down the path through the woods and stopped on the hill above the house to catch our breath while the dogs ran ahead, barking.

23

All the windows in the house were blazing, and we could see a dozen cars parked outside the east portico. As we walked down the hill, we were momentarily blinded by the headlights of a dark green Rolls Royce. It came to a stop on the far side of the turning circle, effectively blocking the exit for other cars. The doors opened, and a woman with a voice like a jackdaw tottered out on high heels leaning on the arm of her companion in black tie.

'For God's sake, Freddy, you could have dropped me orf at the steps,' the woman complained. 'This gravel is hell on my Ferragamos.'

'Do shut up, darling; your incessant moaning is intolerable,' her companion answered mildly.

They slowly climbed the stairs to the front door, where they were greeted by Giles, the footman. When he spotted us over their shoulders, he gave me a warning look.

'Let's get out of here,' I told Sunny.

Giggling wildly, we legged it all the way around the south side of the house, where we burst into the back door with the dogs at our heels, and ran down the hallway, nearly colliding with Mr Collins, the butler, who was emerging from the pantry in his tails.

'Your supper is waiting in the nursery,' Collins informed me, and Sunny burst out laughing. It was the first time I had fully understood how strange my life was compared to hers.

Collins frowned, baffled, as the two of us ran upstairs in hysterics.

When I came down the next morning, I found Papa in the dining room reading the papers. He glanced up as I walked in.

'Darling, where have you been?' he asked, setting the paper down. 'I was starting to think you were avoiding me. Where is your little friend?'

'She's still asleep,' I said, giving him a quick hug.

'I do miss you, you know. How are you, really? What do you think of your new school? Is it ghastly?' His eyes searched my face. 'You can tell me, you know.'

A few weeks earlier, I might have broken down. But I had Sunny now, and things weren't so bad.

'I dunno,' I said, taking a triangle of toast from the rack 'I hate Games. And I miss you, too.'

Papa watched me butter the toast. 'I'm glad you've made a friend. Rather odd how she has the voice of a nightclub owner, though.'

I rolled my eyes and reached for the jam.

'Her father was rather brave in the war, you know,' Papa continued. 'And he's gone on to do frightfully well in fish, apparently.' This line was delivered with a straight face, but his eyes glittered with amusement.

I stared at him. 'How do you know about Sunny's dad?'

'Oh, I made a few enquiries.' His tone was offhand but, seeing my horrified expression, he shrugged. 'Well of course I did, Lumpy. I want to know who you're bringing home. Who you spend your time with. Sunny seems perfectly charming, but I do wish you would get to know the Spencers' daughters, Anthea and Rose. And what about Charlotte Cunningham-Stuart? Such lovely girls.'

'I make friends with people I like,' I informed him.

He sighed. 'You are such an old toughie, Ari.'

After that, he changed the subject and talked about Portugal, where he was researching his new book. An endeavour which would also take him to Brazil, Goa, and Macau.

'That is, if we survive the next few weeks.'

I took a bite of toast and replied with my mouth full. 'What do you mean?'

He held up the paper. 'An American spy plane photographed Russian missiles on Cuba. The Americans have quite rightly said they'll bomb if they are not removed.'

I knew at once what that meant for us. Every Friday an airmail copy of *Life* magazine arrived at Thurston. Mainly I looked at the photographs, but recently an article had caught my eye about the crew of the Enola Gay, the plane that dropped an atom bomb on Hiroshima with a blinding flash like a trillion lightning bolts. The piece described the fire storms that pulverised thousands of Japanese civilians instantly, without a trace, or worse, burned off all their skin. I was haunted by these images and could not get them out of my mind.

'Do you think there will be a war, Papa?' I asked, inwardly panicked but determined not to show it.

'There is absolutely no way of telling,' he said, soberly. 'The trouble is the Russians are hot-headed. It's in their blood. We're in the lap of the gods.' He paused, picking up his copy of *The Times*.

'At least if there's a war, I won't have to go back to Chatham ever again,' I said.

25

Papa laughed, thinking I was joking.

'Exactly, darling and we'll all be spared having to listen to that crasher Clive bang on about the Kennedys.'

Clive was the defence minister, and one of Maud's closest friends, a frequent guest at Thurston. He'd come to the party last night and was staying for the weekend, along with a secretary and two plain-clothes detectives, who annoyed Mr Collins by eating too many biscuits and drinking tea all day in the staff dining room.

A lunch party was planned for the weekend guests and some neighbours. As Sunny and I helped Papa with the drinks, the grown-ups talked of little except the missile crisis. Even dotty old Lady Virginia was unusually serious, despite the yachting cap perched at a jaunty angle on top of her platinum bob. 'Is there nothing on the telly about it?' she said, as I handed her a Bloody Mary. '*Clive* must know what the hell is going on, but he's being uncharacteristically secretive. Where is he, Maud?'

In hushed tones, Maud informed her that Clive was about to be driven back to London to attend a meeting at Number Ten. I imagined snakes rearing up on the conference table.

'Goodness,' Lady Virginia remarked. 'Orf before lunch? It must be serious.'

Everyone knew Clive liked his food. A big sloppy mouthful of *oeufs en cocotte à la crème* never prevented him from holding forth with an opinion, either.

But Clive's expression gave nothing away as he strode purposefully down the hallway with his battered leather briefcase. Maud accompanied him to the car waiting in the drive.

Sunny and I watched from the front doorway as they talked earnestly. Finally, Clive pecked Maud on the cheek before climbing into the sleek black sedan next to his secretary.

Maud lit a cigarette with her gold lighter and placed it in her tortoiseshell holder. Then she stood in the drive, smoking, until the car disappeared round the bend.

Papa always said he was 'awfully bright', but I knew he resented Clive. And I didn't like how Clive smoked Papa's cigars without caring where his ash fell, or how he liked telling jokes, and stories about world leaders he had met, referring to them by their first names: Winston. Harold. Lyndon. Lately, he stayed at Thurston nearly every other weekend, usually holed up in Maud's sitting room. It suddenly dawned on me that Clive's staff could now be put up in the newly redecorated nursery and bedrooms while I was away at school. Papa looked sheepish when I put it to him.

'Well, you see, darling, it rather gets them out of everyone's hair. Only while you're at Chatham, of course.' He got up from the table with some difficulty. 'Why don't you find your friend and we'll go for a walk?'

Later, over spaghetti hoops and peas in the nursery, Sunny and I discussed the end of the world. All the adults had been acting so strangely. Maud was quieter and more nervy than usual, puffing away at one cigarette after another. I watched Papa closely for any signs that he might be unduly worried but he seemed, if anything, rather chipper.

'One might as well enjoy life; one never knows when it might end,' he remarked at one point.

'All right for you, David, you're in your sixties. Some of us still have things we want to do with our lives,' Maud replied, crisply.

Only Sunny remained upbeat.

'My dad says they'll sort it out. They have to. Even the Russians want their children to have a future.'

Something about her words rang true, and I felt a weight fall from my shoulders. Of course they would sort it out. They always did.

The radio was playing Little Eva's 'Locomotion', so we got up from the table and danced.

FOUR

Thurston, July 1963

Within a year, I met two people my age who would later change my life. One was Sunny. The other was Jules.

I was home from Chatham for school holidays, and I was at the drinks tray mixing a Bullshot the way Papa liked them, when there was a sudden change of temperature in the room. All the houseguests grew silent and stared at the new arrival framed in the doorway. He stood only two or three inches over five feet, his immense head made even more conspicuously large by a voluminous upsweep of silver hair and a prominent Roman nose. Even if he hadn't been deeply tanned, even if I hadn't seen his face lit to dramatic effect on so many record covers in my parents' collection, Igor Levertov had unmistakeable star presence.

Maud rushed to his side, a glass of champagne in her hand. 'What an honour, Maestro! David and I are simply delighted to welcome you as neighbours.'

A faint smile played on Levertov's lips. He turned his head slightly. 'Lady Lyttleton. May I present my wife, Cecile?'

Cecile Levertov was at least six inches taller than her husband and dressed in a smart navy-blue suit and pearls.

'And our son, Julius,' Levertov continued, motioning his child forward like he was directing a violin section. Julius executed a self-conscious bow in Maud's direction, then glanced nervously over at his father.

As a product of such physically mismatched parents, it was hardly surprising that Jules's appearance and demeanour were unusual. He reminded me of an illustration of *Struwwelpeter* in one of our old books of fairy tales.

While most public schoolboys wore their hair short, Jules's grew straight up above his broad forehead in a frizzy straw-coloured thicket. His skin was pale, his limbs gangly. He had huge feet, and the long fingers and veiny hands of a grown man. At fourteen, he was already nearly six feet tall. He blinked at us owlishly from behind thick glasses as Maud pulled me forward and introduced us.

Our conversation turned out to be stilted, to say the least. We were seated next to each other at lunch where again I struggled to find any common ground. Though he jiggled his leg under the table in the most annoying manner, Julius appeared to be listening intently to the grown-ups' conversation, which I also found tiresome.

Finally, Maud peered down the table. 'Children are excused! Ari, darling, do show Julius around the garden' she suggested, brightly.

My heart sank but I wasn't going to argue with my mother in front of guests.

'I guess you'd better come with me,' I told Julius, irritably.

As we walked out the back door and along the curved footpath, Julius was quiet. He was clearly not impressed by anything he was seeing.

Soon, I stopped trying to engage him in conversation, and we walked silently up the hill towards the kennels where the dogs were kept when we had guests. Julius watched, expressionless, as I said hello to Tobias the groundskeeper, and opened the gate to the stable kennels. As the dogs tumbled out, though, Jules's face lit up.

Soon, he was rolling on the ground with Violet and Pav, my two lurchers; Papa's golden retriever Gin, and Henrietta's pug, Sooty; bits of straw and grass sticking to his blazer as he laughed. The dogs were often cautious around strangers, but they liked Jules from the start.

As we headed for the woods, Jules astounded me by launching into a word-for-word dissection of the conversations back at the party. He was a brilliant mimic and could imitate even the most subtle mannerisms and accents with deadly accuracy.

He started with his own father, who he captured perfectly just with one arrogant flick of the head. Then he moved on to the local MP, Sir Cedric Meriwether, who, between monologues on farming subsidies, made strange sounds in his throat like a pigeon roosting. The only person at the table who escaped Jules's ridicule was my father, which was a relief. I didn't want to see Papa skewered like that.

By the time the Levertovs left, I was sorry to see Jules go.

Later, I learned Igor and Cecile had bought a house near Oxford to give Jules a base of sorts. He had been brought up in hotels and rented houses around the world, wherever his father happened to be working. Like me, he'd been tutored instead of going to school. However – as Maud pointed out, eyeballing Papa – his tutors had been a team of Oxford graduates, rather than Miss Bolton. At fourteen, Jules could speak several languages, and he played both jazz and classical piano. But I liked him because he was thoughtful, and devastatingly funny.

He never made me feel stupid. He was the only boy I knew who was gentle. We both hated sports and loved animals, and we laughed at all the same things.

Maud was delighted when I received an invitation from Cecile to join them for lunch a week later.

When Reg dropped me off at Jules's house, though, I discovered it was mostly empty. Jules explained that his father had been called to London to conduct a concert at the Albert Hall, and Cecile had gone with him.

'She's completely dominated by the Maestro, I'm afraid,' Jules said, sadly. 'She also likes to keep her eye on some of his more ardent female fans.'

Even the housekeeper was away. Jules and I were completely alone.

The housekeeper had left out a plate of cheese sandwiches, a bowl of crisps and two bottles of bitter lemon on the kitchen table, as well as a plate of chocolate biscuits wrapped in red foil.

We made awkward conversation for a while, and then Jules disappeared, returning a moment later holding a silver tray with two generous wine glasses full of sweet sherry. We clinked glasses.

'To absent parents!' Jules declared, cheerfully. 'I mean, to their absence. May it be prolonged.'

The wine took effect almost immediately and my nervousness evaporated. We were soon giddy and giggly. He told me about the geishas who had made a fuss over his father in Japan and I told him how much I loathed Chatham Hall. He dissected his father's double standards and discussed *West Side Story*, which he'd seen in New York and which was my current obsession.

After a top-up of the sherry, Jules sat down at the piano and played 'Save the Last Dance For Me'. He played beautifully but his voice was terrible, which meant I could join in without shame.

It was a relief to discover that he couldn't do everything.

We decided to catch a bus into central Oxford, about ten miles away. It was a humid July day, so we went down to the river and lay in the grass, watching the punts glide by. As we stared up into the cloudless sky, we played a game, both of us declaring one thing we liked and one thing we disliked about our lives, then switching. It started off quite mildly. He liked Stravinsky and hated Benjamin Britten. I liked olives and hated anchovies. His examples were much cleverer, but he still laughed at my choices. After a few rounds, the game became more personal. Suddenly Jules blurted out that he loved Cecile but hated Igor.

'He's a bully and a tyrant, and I loathe him,' he declared with surprising vehemence. 'Even though I concede he is possibly a genius.'

Jules's confession gave me the courage to tell him I loved Papa but 'disliked' Maud.

'She is definitely *not* a genius,' I added.

I didn't know why I'd said that. Did I really dislike my mother? I wasn't even sure I knew her.

I hated her and loved her, but above all I felt extremely anxious when we were together.

Jules also fantasised about having a different sort of family. He was disarmingly open about it.

'Having given it some thought, my father and your mother would be far better suited to each other, and so would my mother and your father. We could go to live with David and Cecile and leave Maud and Igor to run the world,' he announced, glancing at me to gauge my reaction. 'I see us in Rome in an old apartment building with a view over the rooftops, so your father could concentrate on writing his books and my mother could play piano without criticism. Don't you think, Ari? Shall we get a drink?'

Without waiting for my reply, he stood up and brushed the grass off his shorts. We walked to a little stand at the edge of the park and he bought two bottles of warm lemonade. I told him how nervous I was of returning to boarding school in September.

Jules looked solemn for a moment and then said seriously, 'There are compensations, you know. It's quite a relief to escape the parental net, but on the other hand one is somewhat cast into the lion's den. In any case, I'm told girls are more civilised than boys, so it can't be all that bad.'

By now, experience had taught me that in their own way, girls could be just as vicious as boys, but still, Jules's words made me feel a little better.

I didn't see Jules again for the rest of the summer. He and his parents travelled to Salzburg and then on to music festivals across Europe. We wrote to each other regularly. His letters were in tiny, barely legible handwriting on blue airmail aerograms that inevitably tore right down the centre of the page when I tried to open them. He wrote about everything, from diva's tantrums to *Sachertorte* to his love of Wagner. Some of his best letters were written in the voice of his father, recounting the rave reviews he was getting, and noting the famous people who thought he was marvellous.

FIVE

Alderley Edge, Cheshire, October 1964

Chatham Hall was hardly Dickensian. It was simply deadly dull. Sometimes I bit the flesh on my wrist as hard as possible just to alleviate the tedium. Days bled into weeks, weeks haemorrhaged into eons, with the passage of time marked by stodgy puddings and a chaperoned expedition on Wednesday afternoons to the newsagents in the village to buy sweets.

That year, Papa was abroad researching his book and Maud was busier than ever with her work, so I spent most school holidays with Sunny's family.

When her dad struck it rich, he'd moved the family from Grimsby to a rambling mock-Tudor mansion behind electric gates in Alderley Edge, Cheshire. Their place wasn't as big as Thurston, but there was a music room for Sunny, a billiards room, and beige wall-to-wall carpet everywhere, from the basement right up to the attic. And every single piece of furniture was brand new.

I loved it there. Not only were we allowed to take the bus into Manchester, but also Sunny's mum, Pat, cooked supper every evening and we all sat down together to eat. She'd been home from hospital for a few months and seemed very, very calm. She smiled a lot, and spent long hours at the sewing machine, making clothes for Sunny. She also loved to cook.

In contrast to Mrs Philpot's jellied mousses, soused grouse and poached fruit, Pat made roast beef and Yorkshire pudding, toad in the hole and beef burgers with chips. Puddings were heavenly: chocolate cake, treacle tart, marmalade pudding. Multiple helpings were encouraged. I was becoming resigned to being called big-boned.

The most animated I ever saw Sunny's father, Norman, was on the phone to his factory –although once, when Sunny played 'White Cliffs of Dover' on the piano, he turned red and choked up. However, Sunny told me that he dismissed out of hand her ambition to become a singer.

'He wants more for me. That's how I ended up at Chatham. Mum was dead against it, but she's useless when it comes to standing up to him. He's got a will on him, Dad. Which unfortunately for both of them I've inherited.'

Sunny's most prized possession was a portable record player. It looked like an old-fashioned make-up case covered in tweed, with red leather edges and brass hinges. It opened up to reveal a turntable. It was by far the most desirable item I had ever seen.

We spent all our pocket money on pop music, which we listened to obsessively, learning the nuances of love from the likes of Dusty Springfield, Dionne Warwick, and The Shirelles.

The release of a new Beatles album every few months provided us with fresh insights into a new way of understanding the world, and we watched *A Hard Day's Night* over and over. Fortunately for our friendship, we had very equivocally drawn a line in the sand between us by establishing that John Lennon was Sunny's and George Harrison was mine.

The best days were when we went into the city. There was excitement in the air in Manchester – change was blowing through, connecting us to all the other millions of kids our age who loved music and fashion as much as we did.

We had both turned fifteen, and we were determined to check out one of the lunchtime dances at the Manchester Palais. My parents would have been horrified, but Sunny's parents thought it was perfectly normal for us to go into town together as long as we came home by supper time. Especially after the endless restrictions at Chatham, freedom was dizzying.

Under our coats, we were dressed in our shortest minis and patterned tights and our black Mary Janes with a strap over the instep. We ran down the tree-lined street to catch the bus and the second we were in our seats, we got out our make-up bags. By the time we arrived in the city we'd transformed ourselves from schoolgirls into dolly birds with pale foundation, swooping eyeliner, and white lipstick.

In Manchester, we made for the Gay Dolphin Cafe for frothy coffee, before racing to Ralph's Records where there was a long row of listening booths. We danced in the booth and blew most of our pocket money on records. After that, we headed to our real destination.

In front of the Palais, the neon sign on the marquee drew us like a beacon:

LUNCH TIME DANCES WITH LIVE DJS WEDS AND FRI!
OCT 15 – HERMAN'S HERMITS!

The words sent a lightning bolt of adrenaline through me. This was everything I'd been hearing about on the radio. Everything I'd ever wanted to do.

All around us, kids were streaming towards the Palais from every direction. We had to get past at least thirty Rockers who were standing by their motorcycles outside the theatre, gawping at every girl going in. Sunny put on her toughest Grimsby-girl face and stared back at them with contempt. We paid our 2s/6d entrance fee and joined the rush into the cavernous foyer, where a sea of bodies throbbed with expectation.

Everyone smoked, and everyone dressed sharp.

Some groups of girls arrived with scarves over their curlers and made a beeline for the Ladies to brush out their 'dos, jostling through clusters of boys bantering with each other, while eyeballing the talent.

Inside the massive theatre hall, it was pitch black apart from the dim sparkle of a slowly revolving mirror ball and a spotlit stage where a DJ delivered a constant stream of patter.

There was a subtly menacing atmosphere in the hall. Mods in suits and Rockers in leather stood on opposite sides of the dance floor; everyone seemed wary.

The DJ stopped talking and The Supremes' 'Baby Love' began to play through the speakers. Instinctively, Sunny and I drifted towards the Mods. Almost at once, she got asked to dance by a skinny boy with long sideburns and a narrow leather tie.

As they moved onto the dance floor, he almost ignored her, eyes to the ground, grooving in his own cool world. Sunny kept looking back at me, shrugging and giggling.

When the song ended, Stan the Man, the DJ on stage, talked so fast I missed most of what he was saying, but when he shouted into the mic, 'Manchester over Liverpool, yeah?' even the Rockers screamed back 'Yeah!'

Suddenly everyone was dancing except me. Sunny broke away from her dance partner and dragged me onto the floor. We danced together until, at the other end of the hall, a commotion began.

The lights blinked on and off urgently and through the crowd we saw several boys pounding each other, before a burly group of bouncers dragged them off.

I watched wide-eyed. But nobody else seemed bothered.

'It's laike fookin' clockwork every week,' the girl next to me remarked to her friend, rolling her eyes.

But the fight didn't last long, and after that the DJ played 'Where Did Our Love Go?' and Sunny's original partner returned. They immediately fell into a clinch. As the other boys melted away, I headed to the Ladies and occupied myself backcombing my hair to make it as big as possible. I could scarcely see myself in the mirror for all the beehives.

For something to do, I joined the queue at the bar in the foyer, watching faces in the crowd. Everyone around me seemed to know each other, and there was lots of banter between cliques.

At some point a couple of the older blokes brushed past me forcefully. Because my toes were scrunched into too-small shoes, I was caught off-balance and nearly fell over backwards. Someone grabbed my shoulders just in time and righted me again.

A male voice said, 'Cheeky bastards! Are you OK?'

I looked round, embarrassed, and there he was, smiling down at me. He was the first boy who had looked at me all afternoon; except he was more a man than a boy. I insisted I was fine, but he didn't walk away.

He was neither Mod nor a Rocker and wore a black turtleneck jumper under a diamond-patterned V-neck pullover, with a thick gold bracelet on his wrist.

'I haven't seen you round here before,' he said, eyeing me with interest. 'Where you from then, luv?'

'I'm staying in Alderley Edge,' I explained, vaguely.

He smiled. 'Oh, posh bird, are we?'

'Not really,' I said, self-consciously. 'I'm staying with a friend.'

His smile broadened. 'You talk dead posh an' all. I'm Niall by the way. Mate of DJ Stan's from way back. What's your name?'

'Ari,' I said.

He laughed. 'Ari? What the hell kind of name is that?' Before I could reply, he leaned closer. 'Couldn't help noticing you standing there on your own. You're a cracker, you are.'

I blushed. I wasn't used to talking to boys at all, much less men. He had to be at least nineteen. He seemed to be making the same calculations.

'How old?' he asked, casually, turning to wave and smile at a passing friend.

'Seventeen,' I replied, certain I looked it.

His face brightened. 'I would have guessed eighteen at least. Left school, then?'

'No, one more year.' I didn't want to get too ahead of myself just in case Sunny appeared. She never lied, even to save face.

'Grand old theatre this one,' Niall said, looking around the huge, faded bar. 'Used to be a music hall in the '30s. All the greats played here – George Formby, Arthur Askey. Then it housed hundreds of folk who'd been bombed out in the war. My family lived here for three months until we were rehoused.'

He turned his head briefly. In profile, he could have been John Lennon's brother. 'I were a nipper, and it was like being at a continuous party. I missed it when we moved to a flat. So this place really is home to me, you see.' He gave me a sweeping up and down look. 'Have you been to any other gigs in Mannie?'

I shook my head. 'I've been too busy,' I said, glancing away.

'I could get you into Herman's Hermits on Friday night, you and your friend. Pete's a mate.'

I wanted to stay cool, but my jaw dropped. Sunny would cack herself when she found out.

'I'd love that,' I said.

'Let me get you a drink,' Niall said.

We fought our way through the crowd and I asked for a Tizer. Niall ordered a shandy and a packet of crisps. He opened the bag and held it out for me to take one.

'How did you meet the Hermits?' I asked casually.

'Oh, I went to school with Pete and some of the others,' Niall explained, sipping his drink. 'He and I started a band together when we were 14, but to tell you the truth he was a much better musician than me. I did National Service and was stationed in Changi. Missed out on the glamour, but I've done all right for myself.'

Maud always told us it was rude to ask someone directly what they did, unless they were American (in which case it's the first question you ask), but I was starting to believe Niall must have a job at a record company. He certainly made it seem that way.

When we finished our drinks, he took my hand and said, 'C'mon, let me introduce you to Stan.'

I should have insisted on telling Sunny where I was going. I hadn't seen her in at least fifteen minutes. But before I could say a word, we were waved through a side door by an usher who smiled and nodded at Niall. And then we were backstage.

I followed Niall down a winding network of corridors in the bowels of the theatre. Unlike the busy bar, here it was shadowy and strangely quiet. I shivered a little, wishing I'd stopped to grab Sunny.

I was always nervous, that was the problem. I could never forget myself and just have fun. I wanted to learn the knack. So I didn't object or insist on going back.

'This is the Green Room,' explained Niall, pushing open a door to reveal a dingy, low-ceilinged room that smelled of stale cigarette smoke.

There were a few chairs scattered around, and a dartboard on one wall. But the room was deserted.

'Fancy a fag?' he asked, producing a packet of Players. He put two in his mouth, lit them both and handed one to me. When I inhaled my knees nearly buckled from the head spin.

Niall's brown eyes narrowed. He seemed to miss nothing. I was sure he knew I wasn't seventeen, and I hadn't smoked much before.

'I don't see any green,' I said, hoping he would stop looking at me oddly.

'It's just a term.'

Another silence fell.

'Do you like the Yardbirds?' I tried, a bit desperate now.

He ignored me, his head cocked to the sound of footsteps pounding down the hall and a girl laughing. Then the voices faded away.

'I'll show you the headliners' dressing-room if you'd like?' Niall said, with what I was beginning to recognise as self-importance. 'It's even more of a shithole than this but all the greats have passed through it at some stage. The Beatles played here, you know.'

I agreed eagerly, hoping to find a way out of the backstage maze. But when we left the room, Niall strode down the corridor at speed, and nothing looked familiar. So I followed him, almost running, past some bongo drums and guitar stands, then up a flight of stairs.

At last we came to a scuffed door decorated with the twin masks of comedy and tragedy both grimacing. Niall opened the door, peered inside and flicked a switch. Though the rest of the room was still dark, a row of lightbulbs surrounding the big rectangular mirror flickered on.

'A lot has gone on in this room, I can tell you!' Niall remarked.

Suddenly, a chill ran through me. I didn't like Niall, and I didn't want to be here.

'Shouldn't we be joining the others soon? My friend will be wondering where I am,' I said, my voice shaking.

'She's dancing. She doesn't even know you're gone.' His tone was cool, but then his teeth flashed and he smiled, pulling one of the chairs out from under the dressing table, 'Sit yourself down here. You can imagine you're Cilla Black or sommet.'

Reluctantly I did what I was told. He pushed the chair towards the mirror, so my stomach was right up against the edge of the table. There was no choice except to look at myself. Wide saucer eyes stared back from a pale face.

'You're lucky to be in here, you know. All the girls out there would do anything to get back here.'

An edge had crept into his tone. His intent gaze was fixed on mine in the mirror.

My breath caught in my throat. I felt gripped by an unfamiliar current of energy that was nine parts revulsion and one part curiosity.

Breathing heavily, Niall put his hands on my shoulders. I tensed.

'Hey, hey, calm down and relax, baby. Look at you, sweetheart. I love a well-built bird.'

He bent down and kissed my neck, sending a shiver down my spine.

I had never kissed a boy. I wasn't prepared for the powerful charge of a grown man's touch.

Niall's hands moved down to my breasts. My mouth went desert dry.

He grasped the arms of the chair to pull it out but my feet were glued to the floor and the chair didn't move.

'Come on,' he hissed, the veins on his forehead popping.

Without warning, he grabbed my hair, yanking it so hard that my eyes watered and I lost my footing.

He swivelled the seat around so I was facing him. In one smooth move, he unzipped his trousers and shoved a hard bulbous mass of purple flesh against my mouth, holding my arms down at the same time. The accompanying toilet smell made me gag. I jerked my head to the side, and he rammed his hairy groin against the side of my cheek and ear.

At that moment, the door swung open.

Two men stepped in and stared at us.

Niall had his back to them but they must have been able to see what was happening in the mirror.

One of the men laughed harshly. He was small and slight with long hair and a narrow, pointed face.

Quickly, Niall dropped his hands from my head, whipped his penis back into his trousers and pulled up his zip.

Seeing my chance, I grabbed my bag and rushed past the two men, tugging unsuccessfully at the door handle.

They watched with amusement. 'She's a bit young, isn't she, Ni?' one of them said.

Niall, who had recovered, shrugged. 'Nah, she's seventeen. Ain'tcha, Ari?'

I couldn't look at him. The weaselly man made me stand aside and opened the door easily, with a sharp twist and pull, but he blocked me from going through.

'Please, I have to go and meet my friend,' I pleaded, fighting back tears and nausea.

'And what are you going to tell her then, darlin'?' His face wore a thin smile, but his eyes meant business.

'That I saw The Beatles dressing room.' My voice came out sounding faint and unsteady.

'You make sure that's all you say, otherwise we'll have to tell your friends about what really happened. You've got no business back here.'

I wanted to argue, tell him how he'd got it all wrong. But more than anything, I wanted out. So I nodded.

'Go on then,' the man hissed, edging forward so I had to brush past him, and squeeze sideways through the tiny opening he'd made.

'Fat cow!' Niall called out as I bolted down the narrow stairs. His words echoed in my head for days afterwards.

The ladies' toilets stank of hairspray and disinfectant, but to my relief no one else was in there. Shaking, I studied myself in the mirror. Apart from black mascara smeared under my eyes, I looked the same as always.

Sunny would be furious if she knew. She'd go straight to the police station. But as soon as her parents found out, both of us would lose whatever freedom we had. I couldn't take that risk.

The dance was ending. In the foyer, ushers stood by the front doors herding the last stragglers from the building. I saw Sunny outside, shielding her eyes in the fading afternoon light, anxiously looking up and down the street. When I caught up with her, she lost her rag.

'Where the hell have you been? I've been looking for you everywhere.'

I gave a vague shrug. 'I got asked to go backstage. It was dead grotty. I wished I'd stayed in the dance hall.'

Her eyes searched my face. 'Have you been crying?'

I forced a laugh. 'Of course not. I'm just a bit sweaty. It was hot in there.'

She didn't seem convinced, but I didn't blink.

Sunny would never know.

SIX

Chatham Hall, June 1965

A few weeks before the start of the summer holidays I was summoned to Miss Dewsnap's office and told to pack my trunk 'pronto', because a taxi was arriving to take me to Thurston. When I asked why, Dewsnap said one of my mother's colleagues at work had been taken ill, she was upset and wanted her family around her. That didn't make any sense to me.

But something was definitely wrong. For the past few months, a persistent feeling of foreboding had taken root inside me. It was connected to home. I couldn't say why, but I knew things weren't right.

Food had become my enemy. I couldn't stop eating and gained a stone in the process. Whenever we were allowed, and sometimes when we weren't, I slunk down to the village for Walls ice cream and a packet of chocolate digestives – both would be gone by the time I got back to school.

I'd had to go up a size in my school uniform. But I couldn't fight the urgent need to fill the hollowness inside me.

As a taxi waited outside, I searched the school for Sunny. She'd spent the last month rehearsing for a musical of *A Midsummer Night's Dream*. She was playing Puck.

When I finally found her, she was in full costume. She'd never looked more elven, in pointed shoes, and with her blonde wavy hair hidden beneath a green hat.

When I explained that something was wrong and I was being sent home, she hugged me, and I breathed the heady scent of Ambush.

'When are you coming back?' she asked.

'I don't know,' I said. 'Something's wrong but I don't know what. It's some sort of emergency.'

'I can't believe you'll miss it.' She gestured at her costume.

'I know. But you'll be brilliant,' I told her. And it was true. Her voice, though untrained, was astonishing, both in range and timbre. The stuffy, antediluvian music teacher had left the year before, replaced by a young woman who recognised Sunny's talent at the outset and encouraged her to join the school drama society and sing in assemblies. Having found her niche at Chatham, Sunny was happier, and although I was proud of her, I also felt increasingly left out of her life, and unable to navigate my own.

The taxi driver was uncommunicative on the three-hour journey home, but I doubt he knew anything anyway. I didn't understand why my parents hadn't sent Reg. When we reached the entrance to Thurston, two police officers were standing outside the gates, guarding them from a group of men with cameras slung over their shoulders who loitered on the road.

As I stared in astonishment, the photographers rushed to the cab and peered through the windows at me. Flashbulbs fired, blinding me.

The police waved us through. The driver put his foot on the accelerator.

My heart began to race. What had happened?

By the time we pulled up in front of the house, my dread had exploded into full-blown panic. When Papa emerged from the house, I threw myself into his arms.

He held me tight. Then he pulled back a bit so he could see my face.

'Now, Ari, darling, I'm afraid your mother has had a terrible shock.'

'What's happened?' I was shaking. 'Is it Rupert or Hen?'

'No, they're both fine,' he assured me. 'Your mother was walking across Parliament Square with Clive on their way to a meeting, and he had a heart attack.'

A wave of relief washed over me. It was only Clive. Nothing had happened to anyone I loved.

'Is he all right?' I asked, as my heart rate returned to normal.

Papa's shook his head. 'He died in the ambulance on the way to hospital. Your mother is devastated.'

I thought of the police out front. The gaggle of press photographers.

'But what…?' I began, but he didn't let me finish.

'I'm so sorry to hoick you out of school, but it's rather serious,' he said briskly. His tone made it clear he didn't welcome questions.

We were standing in the front hall, summer light flooding through the open door behind us. Crimson peonies filled a green and white china bowl on the hall table. The dogs were jumping around me, excitedly. All the familiar sights and smells of home, from the wrong end of a telescope.

Papa paused; his ear cocked toward the staircase. Then I heard it too; an unearthly wailing from the first floor. Henrietta materialised on the landing above us.

'Was that the doctor?' Catching sight of me, she said, 'Oh. It's just Ari.' Then she turned around and went back into Maud's room.

'Hen's had to take the brunt of it,' Papa said darkly, ushering me away.

In the living room, Rupert was sprawled on a chintz-covered sofa surrounded by newspapers. He forced a smile.

'Hallo, Lumpy.' He glanced at Papa and added morosely. '*The Express* has really gone to town, I'm afraid. Dempster ought to be shot.'

Papa rang the buzzer by his chair. 'It'll blow over,' he told us. 'We must batten down the hatches for a few days. And obviously don't under any circumstances speak to any of these piranhas.'

Mr Collins entered the room, his expression grave.

'Ah, there you are. A Bullshot please,' said Papa. Rupert chimed in immediately. 'Make that two.'

Collins bowed imperceptibly. Though his range of expressions was, as always, confined to subtle movements around his eyebrows and mouth, I had known him for ever and saw at once that his displeasure was acute. But, with his usual calm decorum, he collected Papa's empty coffee cup and saucer from a side table and headed back to the pantry.

The front door knocker resounded so loudly it made us all jump. 'Let's pray that's Dr Craig,' Papa said, struggling up from his armchair.

I stayed downstairs while the doctor was ushered up to my mother's room. I still didn't understand what was happening. Why was the press outside our gate? Clive hadn't died here. But I knew to keep quiet for the time being.

When the doctor had gone, Papa and I went in to see Maud.

'Ari's here to see you, darling,' he said in a kind, consoling voice.

Maud's windows overlooked a large parterre garden in the shape of two Tudor knots. Today, though, the heavy curtains were drawn, and the only visible light came from a crack under the bathroom door. It took a few moments for my eyes to adjust and make out the small shape almost enveloped by bedclothes. I sat down on the edge of the bed closest to her and tentatively put my hand on her shoulder.

'Mummy, I'm so sorry,' I said. 'Poor Clive. Poor you.'

I felt her shudder beneath my fingers.

I had never seen Maud like this. She was always impeccably groomed and in control of every situation. Her sudden vulnerability was alarming, and at the same time outrageous. Maud was married to Papa. Why was she so upset?

Papa himself didn't seem offended, but I was offended on his behalf.

Henrietta swept into the room carrying a tray with rolled linen hand towels and a white china bowl of water. She brusquely moved me out of the way, sat down where I had been and dabbed Maud's brow.

'Perhaps you'd better go now so Mummy can sleep,' she murmured.

As I left the room, it struck me that we had both called her Mummy for the first time in years.

The next few days were a blur. Maud slept most of the time but wailed pitifully when the injections wore off.

Henrietta was annoying in her new role as Florence Nightingale.

Rupert told endless bad jokes that fell flat. The dogs couldn't be walked because the police had gone and journalists kept appearing at the front and back doors. Several times, we discovered them peering through the dining-room windows.

Papa no longer watched the evening news, nor were the papers delivered. The phone seldom rang unless it was a journalist. We were marooned.

One morning, I ran downstairs to find the library door ajar and the sound of voices. I hung about outside.

'She's just not up to it, it'll be mortifying,' Henrietta was saying,

'I promise you; it will be far worse if she doesn't go,' Papa replied emphatically.

Rupert said, 'What about the damned press though? Must we all go?'

'We'll just have to present a united front and hopefully they'll stop bothering us. The trick is not to make a single comment,' Papa said. 'Give them nothing.'

'We haven't even been invited.' Henrietta sounded miserable.

'They can't turn us away. Your mother is more than entitled to attend, considering how much she has done for Clive in the last few years.'

And so, a few days later, Maud was disinterred from her bed, held steady by

Henrietta and me while June helped her into a black Balmain coat dress, sheer black tights and a black hat with a veil covering her face.

We climbed into a hired Daimler and headed to London for Clive's funeral.

Throughout the hour-long drive Maud stared blankly out the window. When we arrived, a mob of photographers descended, and the popping electronic flashes clearly disoriented her. She put her hands up in front of her face, losing her balance. Rupert and Henrietta grabbed her on either side and half-carried her down the path towards Westminster Cathedral. Inside was a huge sea of people, and a low buzz of voices.

We were ushered to our seats by a spotty youth in tails. An impenetrable wall of black-clad figures loomed in front of us, blocking the view of the altar. Our arrival caused a stir. All around, people turned to stare at us.

An old woman with a severe expression leaned forward from the aisle opposite to get a better view. A susurration spread through the crowd.

I squeezed Rupert's hand and tried to avoid touching Henrietta, whose lips were pursed together in fury.

'God, poor Mummy,' she hissed to Rupert. 'This is frightful.'

But Maud was in her own world and seemed unaware of all of it.

A few deep chords rumbled through the cathedral, then the choir rose and sang, 'When I Survey the Wondrous Cross'.

A rotund minister in white and gold brocade walked slowly up the aisle. Behind him came a half dozen young men in tails, trembling under the weight of Clive's coffin and three enormous pyramids of white flowers that sat on top of it. As they staggered by, Maud's knees gave, and she sat down.

Papa continued to stand, mouthing the words of the hymn, looking very ill, as if at any moment he too might collapse.

The minister intoned, 'I am the resurrection and the life, saith the Lord: he that believeth in me, though he were dead, yet shall he live and whosoever liveth and believeth in me shall never die…'

Maud stifled a sob, which was nonetheless loud enough to draw attention from everyone in the pews around us. Papa's features remained impassive.

'Ari, I'm losing the circulation in my arm,' Rupert whispered as I clutched him tightly.

The minister was sonorously chanting:

'…I commend unto You thy servant Clive, beloved husband of Margaret, doting father of Peter and William…'

Alarmed, I sat bolt upright. Margaret, Peter, William… what? No one had ever mentioned them before. None of them ever accompanied Clive to Thurston.

The funeral seemed to take a lifetime. When it was finally over, Clive's coffin teetered past us on the shoulders of his pallbearers. Behind it, a bird-like middle-aged woman was pushed in a wheelchair by a young man around Rupert's age. Next to him, walked a tall handsome boy, a more angular version of Clive.

As he passed our pew, he glanced over at us, an expression of pure loathing on his face. I felt my cheeks turn crimson.

Maud, sitting forward with her head bowed, didn't look at him, nor did Papa. But Henrietta, Rupert and I stared back at him silently while the grieving family moved on.

SEVEN

Chatham Hall, September 1965

When the autumn term began, Sunny arrived back at school with her hair teased into a beehive, a small white velveteen bow stuck on the crown. Within a few hours she was forced back into plaits by our housemistress. But they couldn't do much about the fact that Sunny now needed a D-cup bra and had a compact little hourglass figure that defied the school uniform. I had grown six inches in a year and towered over her, but I was virtually the same width from my neck to my toes, like a giant caterpillar.

We'd been trapped at Thurston all summer – afraid to go anywhere or do anything. The press were finally bored of us, but Maud hadn't wanted to be seen in public. With little else to do, I'd eaten my way through the long, hot months.

Maud had rallied over time. She still took Dr Craig's sedatives every day, but she'd gradually recovered some of her equanimity. Sometimes she joined us at meals, though it was hardly a relaxing experience.

One sticky afternoon as we'd sat in the living room, Maud's attention had suddenly fixed on my legs.

'Darling, I'm rather worried about your knees.'

I'd looked down at myself, puzzled. 'What do you mean?'

'How do I put this? If you must wear shorts, then you really have to do some more exercise.' Maud told me, bluntly. 'You can't go around looking like that.'

I had never given my knees much thought, but when I looked at them now I saw she was right – they were hideous; puce jellies, covered in bramble scratches and purple bruises.

After that, I'd stopped wearing shorts. But shorts weren't the problem.

Back at school, the boys from the village who hung around the newsagents waiting for Chatham girls didn't look twice at me, except to ask where my friend Sunny was.

I didn't care. I didn't care. I really didn't care.

Superficially sympathetic, Sunny was too excited about her summer in America to pay much attention to my burgeoning self-loathing. She'd had her first kiss with a boy called Skip in his pick-up truck; not a great success, since she'd cut her tongue on his braces, but thrilling all the same. I heard every last detail about her American friends; what they ate, what they talked about, what they did for fun, and it sounded like heaven.

Most girls thrived at Chatham, they cheered on the lacrosse team at inter-school matches, they won prizes for excellence. Part of me wanted to be like them, but a much darker current ran in my veins. I woke up each morning with a leaden weight in my stomach that became heavier as the day progressed.

For me, Sunday was by far the most depressing day of the week. There was compulsory chapel in the morning, followed by a designated hour to write a letter home, which then had to be scrutinised and approved by our housemistress before the envelope was sealed. Next there was 'free time' which in fact was anything but free. After lunch, we were all required to get some fresh air. Usually Sunny and I went off to hide out in the lean-to we'd built in the woods, where we would smoke the fags we'd bought in the village and which we kept buried in a tin along with a box of Swan Vestas.

Sunny was thriving. Her performance as Puck had been a *tour de force*. Nobody teased her about her accent or her father any more.

One Sunday in late autumn as we crossed the playing field towards the woods, a group of girls from the year above ours surrounded her. The previous Friday in school assembly, she had performed 'Up on the Roof' to wild applause. Now, they begged her to sing it again. With no piano accompaniment, in the middle of a field, she sang it perfectly, her rich alto wringing every drop of emotion from the words. The girls cheered and Sunny glowed.

The more adulation she received, the more I felt like a talentless nonentity. As I trailed behind the laughing, singing group, I watched my dark elongated shadow moving across the lawn and imagined myself as slender and graceful as that sylph; how my life would transform if I could only manage it.

People would notice me. I would fit in.

In the blink of an eye I made my decision.

It was surprisingly easy. Chatham food was famously bad. We compensated by buying treats in the village, which meant we lived on cakes, crisps and sweets. I gave up all of that. At the same time, I adopted the art of looking as if I was eating normally by filling my plate with boiled vegetables, taking small bites and chewing very thoroughly, like Miss Bolton.

I was always hungry; but hunger was a reminder that I had a secret and, as my body began to change, the secret became increasingly pleasurable.

I had never put my mind to anything before. Now I discovered willpower.

Quite soon, I could feel a difference in the way my clothes fit; changes no one else would notice for months. Heating at Chatham was more or less non-existent, so during winter everyone wore multiple layers. When I went home for the Christmas holidays, everyone in the family was too preoccupied to see the changes. Papa was about to have a hip replacement, and Maud was distracted with her work.

Maud had always watched her weight, and everyone else's too, but a strong instinct told me to not draw attention to myself. So, I moved the food about on my plate, and fed as much as I could to the dogs under the table. I was permanently light-headed but I considered that proof the diet was working. I didn't mind the gnawing hunger, I clung to it. Nearly every night, I dreamed of course after course of delicious dishes and woke feeling sick with guilt.

By February, my experiment had become an obsession, and still no one had noticed, though the games mistress expressed surprise when she saw me running back and forth on the sports field one afternoon.

I laughed and said I had promised my dad that I'd get fit for our Hadrian's Wall walk over the summer. I had no idea where the lie came from. Lies slipped out so easily nowadays. I was starting to enjoy them.

My collarbones had begun to protrude through my flesh, and the top of my thighs no longer touched when I walked. I was thrilled. I had achieved something measurable. It was a relief when my periods stopped.

The only negative, as far as I was concerned, was that I was always cold. Thurston was huge and hard to heat, and I shivered despite many layers of clothing, and turned blue on walks with Pav and Violet. Even layered in sweaters and tights, I was constantly frozen.

The only time I felt truly warm was in a hot bath so, when I was home, I took baths constantly.

One night when my parents were out for dinner, I filled the bath and slipped beneath the water, letting out a sigh as the warmth seeped into my bones.

I was almost asleep when I heard Maud's horrified voice: 'My god, Ari, what's happened to you?'

I'd forgotten to lock the door. She stood in the doorway in evening clothes, her mouth 'O' shaped as she stared at my naked body.

Sitting up abruptly, I hugged my knees to my chest in an attempt to hide the evidence of months of not eating.

'Nothing happened,' I told her, calmly.

'Ari, you're a bag of bones.' There was shock in Maud's voice, and something close to rage.

She stood watching as I clambered self-consciously out of the bath and wrapped myself in a towel.

I made up as many excuses as I could summon. I told her I had stopped eating rubbish, and 'the weight just fell off me'. That we were being forced to exercise more. School food was too awful to eat. It just happened.

But her lips were tight. 'I'll call Dr Craig in the morning,' she announced.

'I'm fine,' I insisted, shivering inside the towel. 'It really isn't a big thing.' But I was secretly delighted she had finally noticed.

In truth, I thought of very little except what I had to eat yesterday, what I might eat today, and how many calories were in every mouthful I consumed. It was exhilarating to have won control over my body at last.

The next morning, when I bumped into him on the stairs, Rupert said, 'Come clean, Lumpy, how much have you lost?'

Clearly Maud hadn't wasted any time spreading the news.

I skipped down a few steps and said, 'Oh, I don't know. A stone and a half, something like that.'

It was two stone eight, actually; I knew it down to the last ounce.

'That's appalling, Lumpy, I won't even be able to call you Lumpy any more.' He laughed, but there was a hint of respect in his tone.

Later that day after Dr Craig had given me a clean bill of health, I could hear my father shouting down the phone at Miss Dewsnap back at Chatham Hall.

'You have a duty of care, dammit! I could get you up for gross negligence.'

He threatened to withdraw me from school, but Dewsnap managed to persuade

51

him that it would be a terrible idea, just before O-Levels.

When I returned to Chatham, the school nurse's assistant was obliged to sit with me during meals and make sure I'd eaten.

But it didn't take long to work out ways to outsmart her. There was no way I was going to not be thin. Life was already rewarding me for starving myself.

EIGHT

Chatham Hall, June 1966

That summer, Sunny and I were both expelled from Chatham.

It started innocently enough. When Sunny was home for the Easter holidays, she entered a contest she'd seen on the back of a cereal box. The prize was two tickets to a live filming of *Top of the Pops* at the BBC Television Centre in London.

She'd almost forgotten about it when, months later, her mother forwarded her a letter with the opening line: 'You're a WINNER!'

Sunny ran to find me, her face alight with excitement.

After we'd screamed and jumped up and down, though, the reality of the situation hit us. The broadcast was being filmed in London, during term time, on a school night.

'Oh god,' Sunny said, all the joy leaving her face. 'We can't go.'

We both knew there was no way we would ever get permission.

But we also knew there was no way we could pass up this opportunity. This was our favourite TV show, with actual pop stars. We could be close enough to touch them.

There had to be a way.

For years, I'd been replicating my mother's handwriting on notes to get out of sports days, and I kept a sheaf of Smythson's headed notepaper tucked away in my bedside table. In Miss Bolton's view, beautiful handwriting was by far the most useful life skill one could possibly acquire, and we'd spent hours copying techniques, from old English manuscripts to my parents' individual styles, an exercise she maintained was good preparation for developing a 'unique hand'. In this way, over time, I had become quite proficient at the art of forgery.

In the library that week when we were meant to be composing our history essays, Sunny and I worked on the wording of a letter requesting the headmistress's permission to take us out of school on a Thursday night to see Laurence Olivier in *Richard III* in the West End. 'I consider this to be a once-in-a-lifetime learning opportunity,' 'Maud' asserted, very firmly. When we were satisfied, we walked to the village and sent it to Jules, who duly posted the letter to Chatham from Oxfordshire.

A few days later we were called into Dewsnap's office and granted permission to go to the theatre in London, as long as we were back in time for our first lesson the following morning.

'I assume you'll be staying at your parents' flat?' she enquired, and I nodded my head silently, too excited to trust my voice.

In truth we had no idea where we would spend the night, but that didn't matter. We'd sleep at the train station if it was our only option.

Maud often sent a local taxi to drop me off and collect me from school, so no one raised an eyebrow when a Maidstone taxi – ordered by our co-conspirator Jules from his college in Cambridge – arrived to take Sunny and me to the train station on the afternoon of the show.

As the grim façade of Chatham Hall disappeared behind us, Sunny declared, 'This is the greatest day of my life.'

It was good to see her smiling again. Her mother's increasingly erratic behaviour on her last visit home had Sunny deeply concerned.

'Laurence Olivier awaits,' I exclaimed, with a theatrical flourish.

We paid for the train tickets out of my allowance, which had accumulated dramatically now that I no longer ate sweets.

The journey was consumed with the serious task of making up our faces, including cutting up false eyelashes and sticking individual strands on our top and bottom lids with lash glue, while accusing one another of hogging the only hand mirror.

By the time we disembarked in London, we both looked at least three years older. We changed into our minis and strappy shoes in the Victoria Station lavatory, stuffing our uniforms and school brogues into a bag and hiring a locker for two shillings so we didn't have to take it with us.

Then, in a state of heightened excitement bordering on hysteria, we took a black cab to Shepherd's Bush, where we joined the queue outside the BBC studios.

By then, we had hardly any cash left. It hadn't occurred to me to take the Tube to save money. When we were in London, Maud always either had a chauffeur-driven car or a taxi. However, any anxiety regarding mundane matters such as how we were going to get back to the station vanished when the doors opened and we were shepherded inside, along with a noisy throng of glamorous older teenagers.

Awestruck, we took in the scene; the vast expanse of scuffed vinyl flooring, the black ceiling crisscrossed with dolly tracks, and bright spotlights trained on the small stage, where a few technicians were running around checking mikes and cables. Most of the crowd dashed straight towards the dance space, but Sunny and I planned to avoid the camera since everyone at Chatham watched *Top of the Pops*.

So when Tony Blackburn stepped on stage and the audience erupted, we hid at the back of the crowd. After his usual spiel, he announced, 'A very special group of lads has made history this week, skipping all ninety-nine positions in the top 100 to reach Number One in the charts. We'll leave you guessing who they are until the very end. But first... Here's this week's number ten: Dusty Springfield!'

Sunny spun around to look at me, her eyes enormous. Dusty Springfield was her favourite singer on the planet.

When Dusty stepped out onto the stage in a slinky sequin evening dress to the floor and a platinum bouffant, I screamed along with the others. But then she began singing 'You Don't Have to Say You Love Me' so compellingly, in her distinctive throaty alto, that we all stood spellbound.

Next to me, Sunny was drinking in every word, every note, in a blissful trance. After the second chorus she edged towards the stage to get a closer look at her idol. I ran after her and pulled her back into the shadows. But as soon as The Mamas and The Papas came on to sing 'Monday, Monday', I lost her completely. She raced into the crowd at the edge of the stage, and after that there was no getting her back. I caught a brief glimpse of her gazing reverentially at the band on the stage, before she disappeared into the crowd.

A rush of panic surged through me, but there wasn't much time to think further because now the Troggs were on, blasting out 'Wild Thing' and a tall, beautiful boy came out of nowhere and asked me to dance. I still wasn't used to male attention and before I could talk myself out of it, I said yes.

He turned out to be an amazing dancer and, even if we couldn't bring ourselves to look each other in the eyes, there was a definite spark between us. After a few minutes we drifted closer to the stage. I kept my head down, hoping my long hair and altered appearance would render me unrecognisable. Every time the camera came near me, I spun around so only my back was visible.

Across the dance floor I spotted Sunny really going for it, tossing her head about so her hair flew, her hips and shoulders shimmying so fast her body was a blur. Even if I'd wanted to, there was no way I could pull her away, surrounded as she was by a clutch of boys dancing in a protective semi-circle around her, as if they knew she was a star in the making.

Suddenly, with knife-edge clarity, I understood that not only was the world opening up for both of us, but that we had to claim our places in it quickly, before the opportunity evaporated.

Then the lights went out and, for a few moments, the atmosphere of expectancy was so intense I was breathless. I forgot all about the cameras. I *had* to know what was happening next.

A single spotlight came on, beaming down on an angelic boy with a golden halo of hair and heavy bags under his eyes. Cross-legged on a white disc that seemed to be hovering in the air, he was cradling a sitar in his lap. At the sight of him, all hell broke loose. Girls screamed. Boys rushed the stage. Another spotlight beamed down on Keith playing a flamenco-inspired intro, while Brian smiled down from his solitary cylinder of white light. There was a momentary pause, then three more spotlights beamed down into the darkness where the rest of the Rolling Stones each appeared inside their own shafts of light, and Charlie Watts pounded out the insistent rhythm of 'Paint It Black'. Mick Jagger, menacing and sinuous, writhed across the stage snarling out the lyrics with magnificent contempt.

It was a glorious moment, and my eyes were closed in beatific ecstasy when, unbeknownst to me, the massive studio camera zeroed in for a close-up, before panning back for a full-length shot that included my dance partner, both of us caught in the grip of frenzy as the song climaxed. Nor was I able to catch Sunny's far more impressive dance performance, also captured on celluloid – although we heard a great deal about it afterwards.

In retrospect, I would have given anything to be a fly on the wall back at our dorm where our housemistress, Miss Wright, and thirty girls were sitting in front of the television. It would have been worth all the nightmares we subsequently endured just to witness their shock as we danced across that screen.

Unfortunately, Miss Wright quickly recovered her wits and alerted Dewsnap. At that moment our fate was set. But in London, we had no idea of the commotion we were causing back at Chatham Hall.

When the show was over and the lights came on, Sunny and I found each other in the crowd. Our ears were ringing, we were dazed and elated, and somehow we knew that our lives would never be the same again – though not for the reasons we thought

Our little problem – having next to no money and a long night ahead of us – was resolved when we were surrounded by several boys, all keen for us to join them for a drink and more dancing. We demurred at first, then accepted. After all, it was hours until the first train.

We took the Tube with them to Soho. One of the boys handed me a token. I stared at it blankly, wondering at first if it was a coin. When he realised I didn't know how to use it, he was astounded.

'How can you have never been on the Tube before?' he asked.

'Posh birds don't take the Tube, you plonker,' another boy said, shoving him.

Soon they were play-fighting and we were forgotten.

By the time we reached the club it was crowded and hot, and the atmosphere was not at all like the BBC studio. Everyone was much older. After an hour of dancing, and fending off some proper creeps, Sunny drew me aside and whispered, 'I think we should go.'

Relieved, I agreed. Seeing so many Nialls under one roof had triggered panic in me. We made our escape and ran down Brewer Street laughing, slightly hysterically.

The fresh air felt cool and clean against our skin after the smoky, sweaty room, and we took deep breaths. Penniless by this stage, we had no choice but to walk to the station. Luckily a map at a bus stop showed us the general direction.

It was eleven o'clock, but the streets were just as crowded as they had been when we first arrived that afternoon. People poured out of theatres and pubs and queued outside nightclubs and taxi ranks. Crowds clustered at corners, waiting for the chance to cross. London at night was the most alive place I'd ever been. I wanted to plunge into it, like a pearl diver.

We floated through Trafalgar Square, down the Mall to Buckingham Palace and on to Victoria Station, making plans for our future lives, exhilarated and excited. Everything seemed possible.

The train station was largely empty as we retrieved our bags and began looking for a bench where we could wait until the first trains in the morning. Most were already occupied by sleeping people doing the same thing.

'Over there,' Sunny said, pointing at an empty bench near the ticket office.

We were racing over to claim it, giggling wildly, when two police officers stepped in front of us. We skidded to a stop.

'Pardon me, miss,' the taller one said to me, in a voice that did not sound apologetic. 'Are you Ariadne Lyttleton?'

I was caught so off-guard, for a moment I couldn't speak.

Finally, I nodded, my throat too dry for words.

He reached for my elbow. 'We'd like you to come with us.'

Ten minutes later, we were heading back to Chatham in the back of a police car. The officers, none too impressed at being tasked with driving two underage runaways back to boarding school, told us that we'd been seen on television by someone at our school, who had contacted our families. He didn't need to say more. I could guess the rest. Maud would have called her friend, the Home Secretary, and our descriptions would have been shared with all the bobbies on the beat in central London.

The journey took over an hour, and we spent it huddled in the back seat, barely speaking. I felt strangely removed from the scene, as if I were watching everything unfold from a distance.

We arrived at Chatham to behold the figure of Dewsnap looming darkly at the front door, her features contorted with rage. Countless pairs of eyes peered down at us from every window in the building, as we emerged from the police car in our flimsy minis and climbed the steps to meet our fate.

We were separated, interrogated, and summarily expelled.

Sunny was devastated. She knew how much her father would mind. And also, I think she loved Chatham.

For my part, I was quietly elated.

I was free. And I'd decided where I wanted to live. As soon as I was old enough, I was going to move to London. And never look back.

NINE

Thurston, July 1966

Four weeks later, I woke to the sound of shouting and hammering. Peering out of the window, I saw several men struggling to put up a large blue-and-white striped marquee on the south lawn. Henrietta and Simon's engagement party was imminent.

Down in the staff quarters, Mr Collins was fielding a large delivery from Berry Bros. Crates of wine, champagne, spirits, and soft drinks had been stacked outside the kitchen and pantry, as well as inside the staff dining hall and Mr Collins's own office.

I took an armful of letters and parcels from him and sorted through them.

Somewhere near the bottom of the stack was a letter in a large brown envelope, addressed to me in a rounded hand I knew as well as my own.

It was from Sunny. I hadn't heard from her since we left Chatham, even though I'd written to her three times.

I tore open the brown envelope eagerly.

Dearest Ari,

You won't in a million years guess where I am at the moment – London!

I've run away from home and I'm never going back. Actually, I can't go back even if I want to. Dad was so mardy about me getting kicked out he didn't speak on the drive home from Chatham, then I found out Mam was back in hospital again which he's been keeping from me for weeks. He went on like everyone had let him down, and I felt so guilty and upset. He was going to send me to a crammer, but I couldn't face it. So I packed a bag and legged it early one morning.

I made it to the King's Road and blew nearly my last few bob on a sandwich and a coffee in a café. There was a bunch of Aussies raving on at the table next to me and when they saw my guitar we got talking. I told them I had nowhere to go, so they invited me back to their flat. I've been staying with them ever since. They helped me get a job waitressing and I've even done a few auditions. I don't miss home. London is the best thing that ever happened to me. You have to get down here, Ari.

Please write and tell me what's been happening with you. There is no phone where I am. I hope you're okay. Your mum must have been livid!

Love, Sunny xoxo

P.S. Flat 2, 34 Queen's Gate Terrace, London, SW7

P.P.S. Get here if you can.

I could no longer hear the clatter in the kitchen. Everything faded away as I absorbed this electrifying new information.

Sunny was the most independent, brave person I'd ever known, but still I was stunned she had managed to strike out on her own without any support from her father, financially or otherwise. I took the dogs out for a long walk around the lake to think about it.

Not for the first time, I felt left behind by her. It was if she was racing ahead into adulthood, and I was too afraid to make a move.

When I got back to the house, a stout woman in a tweed suit, pearls and a pillbox hat was in the front hall, admonishing two young employees as they put the finishing touches on a vast flower arrangement.

'Give those flowers some room to breathe, for heaven's sake. Now take out a few peonies and fill in the gaps with Queen Anne's lace and raspberry foliage. Keep it light and frothy.'

Her assistants tried to keep up, working with nervous, darting movements.

As I walked towards the stairs, a curious figure in a navy-blue caftan and embroidered leather slippers emerged from the guest bathroom, mopping his brow, on top of which sat an ill-fitting toupée.

'Constance, dear,' he said, 'if you keep on persecuting the help, they may well mutiny and then you'll be left plucking hedgerows on your tod.'

The woman glared.

'Nonsense, Humphrey. My pupils know how frightfully lucky they are. Isn't that true, girls?'

'You can always come and work for me instead,' said Humphrey, addressing the girls, who were observing this back and forth like soldiers in the middle of a field as shots flew over their heads.

Then he fixed his large pop-eyes on me.

'And who might you be, dear?'

'I'm Ari.'

He peered at me with new interest. 'Oh, yes, the black sheep! I've heard about you.' Turning, with a sweep of his caftan, he motioned for me to follow. 'Come and see what we've been up to in the Quong Room, dear.'

As we walked down the long gallery, he lowered his voice to a stage whisper.

'What a palaver! Your sister's hubby-to-be is a bit naff, isn't he? I smell *dinari* in the air. Can't be any other reason. I don't usually do this sort of thing, you know, but your mother begged me. Regretting it now, of course.'

'Everyone always does,' I assured him.

His mouth pursed approvingly. 'Oh, I knew I would like you.'

When he opened the last door at the end of the hall, I gasped.

Humphrey stood back, spreading his arms. 'Fantabulosa, *n'est ce pas?*'

The cavernous ballroom glowed in cream and gold, with a chinoiserie mirror at either end, both reflecting a vast eighteenth-century crystal chandelier in the centre of the ceiling. It had been transformed with silver and gold *trompe l'oeil* foliage on the walls and ceiling. What could have been garish was executed with such throwaway flair and artistry that I could only stare in astonishment. The grand French doors opened out into the recently erected marquee, which, in contrast to the glimmering ballroom, was bare and empty, apart from three morose figures huddled round a ladder drinking tea in a cloud of cigarette smoke.

'Ari, meet the girls,' he said, indicating each one with a dramatic gesture. 'There's Dutch Doris, Toni Palone, and Curious George.'

The first two could have been Chatham Hall dinner ladies in trousers, while George was reptilian, with slicked-back peroxide blond hair hanging below his collar, and his shirt unbuttoned to reveal a heavily tattooed barrel chest.

They glanced over at me with disinterest.

Humphrey turned to me. 'Ari, darling. What are you up to for the rest of the day?'

'Nothing. Actually, I'd love to help you if I could?'

He beamed.

But it wasn't long before he realised I was hopeless when it came to cutting out branches and leaves, something he and the girls did effortlessly, without even using a template. They did have need of an assistant who knew the house, however, so I was relegated to finding tools, making tea, and listening to them gossip and bicker incessantly.

Later in the day, Humphrey took delivery of scores of dead trees from some black-fingered nursery, which we spray-painted silver and gold. The following morning, they were to be strung with fairy lights and assembled in the marquee to give the impression, as Humphrey kept saying, of a 'shimmering glade'.

'All must be ready in time for Cecilia's arrival,' said Humphrey, his head cocked to one side and his mouth pursed. 'Mrs Beaton loves a bit of *zhooosh*.'

It took me a moment to understand what he was saying. 'Cecil Beaton is coming here?'

I had pored over Beaton's photographs many times in his books and diaries, and heard my parents' friends talk about him endlessly.

Humphrey gave me an arch look. 'Didn't you know? He's photographing your sister for *Vogue* tomorrow.'

Humphrey turned to Doris. 'Cecil should do Ari at the same time, don't you think?' Without waiting for an answer, he looked back at me approvingly. 'You're like a little woodland nymph, dear. He'll adore you.'

Soon after Humphrey and his crew left that evening for their hotel in Oxford, Maud arrived home with Henrietta and Simon in tow.

I'd barely seen my mother since I'd been expelled. It was the busiest period of the London social season, and Parliament was still in session. It had been a brief stay of execution.

On my way to the ballroom early the next morning, Maud materialised in the hallway like a ghastly apparition and frogmarched me into her sitting room, where she announced that I was being sent to a school in Switzerland. I was expected to join their summer programme, in three weeks' time.

When I tried to protest, she cut me off curtly.

'I'm sorry, but we've had enough of your nonsense, Ariadne. It's time for you to grow up.' The cold finality in her voice stopped me short.

'Anyway,' she continued, 'I expect you'll adore Les Cimes. Henrietta was frightfully envious when she heard you were going. I know at first it might be daunting to go to school so far away, but you'll be home every holiday, and I expect soon you'll make marvellous new friends.'

Her words were almost reasonable but her eyes were stony, and I felt her simmering rage inside my own gut.

It was pointless to argue. But as she filled me in on the details of her plans for me, my dreams of visiting Sunny abruptly ended.

The phone rang, interrupting her monologue, and she snatched it up. There was a brief silence while she listened intently, and then she exploded: 'What do you mean, Cecil's stuck in Gander? For god's sake, this is too bad, Miss Miller. No, I have not heard of the other man; who is he?' There was a pause while Maud lit a cigarette with an impatient flick of her Dunhill lighter. Exhaling a stream of smoke, she waved me away.

As I left, she was saying, 'I don't like the sound of him. I want Henrietta to look *pretty*, not like a ghastly shop girl on the King's Road. I find this untenable.'

Depressed at the thought of mournful Alpine eyries, I ran upstairs to pour my heart out to Sunny in a long letter.

'It's all over. Finished,' I wrote gloomily. 'Before I even get to finishing school.'

By the time I returned to the marquee in mid-afternoon, the gold and silver trees had been electrified and were being planted in groves around the periphery. A new, dramatically striking, tree chandelier hung from the roof canopy.

Humphrey stood on a steep ladder fixing it in place.

'Cecil Beaton's not coming after all,' I announced, pleased to have some gossip to pass on. 'He's in Gander or something.'

He glanced down at me. 'That's ancient news, dear. They've sent darling Bill Ramsey instead, and your mother is livid. You know who Ramsey is, don't you?'

Humphrey climbed down to join me, his face flushed with effort. I shook my head.

'Bill is only the best photographer of his generation, dear, and he oozes sex appeal. Anyway, the *Vogue* team arrived at lunchtime and it's been rather a disaster. They put your sister in a transparent dress – well, it *is* St Laurent, dear. I got a peek at it, and it looks absolutely divine. But your mother placed an immediate call to *Vogue* and spat the dummy.' He lowered his voice, 'I think your sister's rather keen on Ramsey. Anyway, now Henrietta's been put in a tweed suit by Hardy Amies. The poor girl looks exactly like Unity Mitford. It's just not Ramsey's kind of thing, so now she's in a terrible strop. The lines to *Vogue*'s offices must be melting.'

I skulked off to make tea, hoping to spot Bill at work, but the only person I could find was the dreaded Simon, Hen's betrothed. He was sitting in Papa's chair in the drawing room, cocooned behind the *Financial Times*. I coughed loudly.

'Oh, hallo, Ari,' he said, looking up. 'I heard from your ma that you're off to Switzerland, soon. Lucky you.'

'Yes, lucky me. Where's Henrietta?'

'I think they're down by the stables,' said Simon, returning to his paper.

After I had delivered a tray of tea and biscuits to the Quong Room, I pleaded with Humphrey to accompany me to the stable yard.

'Please, Humphrey. I've never seen a fashion shoot before. Just for ten minutes?'

He fluttered his hands. 'Why can't you go on your tod? I'm in a lather trying to get finished.'

I told him Maud was lurking about and I needed a minder.

He sighed. 'All right, come along. You can take a short fag break, girls!' he called out to his team.

'I don't do short fags,' Doris informed him, peevishly. 'Only *looong* ones.'

Humphrey and I walked down the drive to the stables, his long silk robe blowing in the warm breeze, while I bounced eagerly at his side.

When I first set eyes on Bill Ramsey, he was standing on top of a mounting block, scowling. Pancho, my sister's bay gelding, was being uncooperative.

'He's not accustomed to being ridden side-saddle.' Henrietta said, apologetically, reins tight, heels dug into her horse's ribs.

She was dressed in a frilly white blouse, a long black skirt and smart boots. A tricorn hat was perched on her smooth, blonde hair. She looked very pretty, but I thought she seemed uncharacteristically nervous.

'You're supposed to be an Olympic rider,' Ramsey reminded her, as the horse fidgeted and threw his head up and down violently, while prancing sideways.

'Pancho, stop it,' hissed Henrietta, tightening the reins.

A delicate-boned boy passed another camera up to Ramsey, who was staring intently at Henrietta through the viewfinder.

Perhaps it was the equine setting, but Ramsey instantly reminded me of Popcorn, our ungovernable old Shetland pony, with his sturdy body and unruly black hair. I found his high-pitched voice curious and endearing. His facial expressions were fluid and ever-changing, ranging between impatient, amused, focused and bored in a matter of seconds. I couldn't keep my eyes off him.

Unaware of our presence, Ramsey continued to shout commands.

'What's your name again? Oh yeah, Henrietta. Smile, girl! That's better. I'd like you to… Ooh yes, keep looking at me like that. Yes, yes… that's great. I know all about girls and their horses. Chin up… keep your eyes open. Shit. Can't that animal just stay still for a minute? Now lean back with one hand on his bum, give me that sexy look. Like that, but try to make it look natural.'

When Henrietta and the fashion editor disappeared into the tack room to change for the next shot, Ramsey stepped down from the block and handed his camera to his assistant. As he walked towards us, his hand shading his eyes against the afternoon sunshine, his serious expression softened into delight when he saw Humphrey.

'Hello, you old poofter!' he exclaimed, pulling Humphrey into a warm hug. 'Thank god you're here.'

Humphrey stroked his shoulder. 'It looked fantabulosa, dear. Like a glorious Velazquez.'

'Well, at least it made her look as good she's ever going to look with that chin.'

Just then, Ramsey switched his gaze to me. A bolt of electricity shot up my spine. I suddenly couldn't breathe.

'Who's this, then?' he murmured.

'Isn't she divine?' Humphrey turned to me. 'This is Ari, the black sheep, dear. Henrietta's younger sister.'

'Don't tell me the woman in the house back there is your mother.' Ramsey threw his head back and laughed. 'My condolences.'

I blinked at him, speechless, my cheeks burning.

'Listen, black sheep, I need your help. I want to find a location that looks a bit, you know, Burne-Jones kind of moody,' he told me. 'The light is good right now – we need to move fast before we lose it.'

'What about the temple on the other side of the lake?' I suggested, my mouth so dry I could hardly get the words out.

'I dunno,' Ramsey said, gazing at me intently. 'Can you show me?'

Humphrey stepped back. 'Sorry to disappoint, but I must scarper back to the salt mines. Come and see us when you're finished, Ramsey.'

'Not if that dragon's around I won't,' Ramsey said.

Humphrey wandered off and Ramsey turned his undivided attention to me.

'Which way, girl?

I pointed toward the lake, and we headed down a path.

'You don't look anything like your sister or mother,' he told me. 'Perhaps you're a hospital switch. That happens a lot, you know.'

I explained that Hen and I had different fathers.

While we walked, he lobbed one question after another at me. How old was I? Why wasn't I in school?

When I told him I'd been expelled, he just nodded. 'Good for you. School's a waste of time. I left at thirteen, before they could indoctrinate me.'

I confided that my parents were sending me to school in Switzerland, and that I was dreading it.

'That's easy,' he said, without missing a beat. 'Don't go. They can't make you. You're about to be seventeen. You can leave home legally; did you know that?'

I shook my head. I had no idea.

'Well,' Ramsey slung his camera over his shoulder. 'Now you know. What would you do instead?'

'I'd go to London. Live with my best friend. Get a job.'

I hadn't really thought any of this through, but as soon as I said it, I knew it was exactly what I wanted to do.

I pointed to where the folly on the other side of the lake was now visible between the trees.

'I could help you get a job in fashion. I know a lot of people.' Ramsey said, somewhat offhandedly. He studied the lake. 'Is there a rowboat we could use?'

I said nothing, but my heart had begun to race. This was no accident. Cecil Beaton cancelling, Ramsey coming instead. All was not lost – London was still a possibility.

We went back to collect equipment and soon Henrietta made her way down the grassy slope, glorious in a low-cut pale chiffon evening dress. She held the long skirt high, so that her horsewoman's legs were exposed. She was flanked by Tommy, Ramsey's assistant, and the fashion editor, who carried a hairbrush in one hand and a make-up bag in another.

Henrietta gave me an irritated look. 'What are you doing here, Lumpy?'

But at just that moment, Ramsey, who was standing in the bulrushes, a cigarette dangling from the corner of his mouth, glanced over at me.

'Hey, Ari, could you run back to the house and find some cushions and blankets to line the dinghy?'

I took off like a shot. As I ran, I could feel Henrietta's eyes on my back.

By the time I returned, Henrietta was arranged in the boat with Ramsey shooting her from above. He barely glanced up as I joined them.

I couldn't prise myself away. I was fascinated by every detail of the shoot. Unfortunately, Ramsey's focus was so fixed on his work, he barely seemed to notice me. It felt as if he'd forgotten our conversation from earlier.

Afterwards, when all the camera equipment, garment bags of clothes and make-up cases had been packed up in the back of the estate car, and the *Vogue* team was about to drive away, Ramsey hugged Humphrey goodbye, and then walked over to where I stood alone on the front steps. He slipped a scrap of paper into my hand with the deftness of a magician.

Leaning forward, he whispered, 'Look me up when you get to London, yeah? Bye, girl.'

I waited until I was alone before carefully unfolding the paper.

In thick block letters sloping downwards he'd written RAMSEY and, underneath, the number PRIMROSE 7221.

TEN

Thurston, July 1966

The party, in the end, was a huge success. Humphrey spontaneously draped a length of gold lamé around my torso, fashioned a crown of silver leaves for my hair, then insisted I attend on his arm. He proceeded to introduce me to everyone he knew, which was basically everyone there. To my surprise and delight, I received endless compliments and attention. His friends seemed to enjoy the story of my dismissal from Chatham and one of them, an artist, asked to paint my portrait.

Maud cornered me the moment Humphrey went off to the khazi. 'You should be ashamed of yourself,' she hissed, 'selfishly grabbing the attention for yourself on your sister's big day.' I sensed the green monster behind her words, but they stung me deeply in any case. I slunk off to bed feeling miserable.

Soon afterwards, Julius wrote to me from London, telling me about his summer job – the assistant to an editor in a famous publishing house. I was so envious. He was out every evening and described in amusing detail the wildly diverse social circles – high and low – in which he was travelling. He also dropped a bomb in his postscript: 'Word has it that Maud is seeing a Conservative MP – another one! As if Clive wasn't ghastly enough. Though this one isn't married, which I suppose shows some kind of progress.'

The scales fell from my eyes. I suddenly understood what I had refused to take on board for so long. Maud had been in love with Clive. Poor Papa. I ran to my hideout in the beech tree and cried with shame for him; for us both. I had no sympathy for Maud; a more honourable person would have left, I reasoned, rather than continue the charade and make her husband look like a fool. Papa's good manners and loyalty

68

clearly prevented him from making a scene. No wonder he was spending so much time away from England.

Much later on, Julius told me that by divulging the truth about Maud, he had intended to give me a bargaining chip, so I could fight my corner and insist on going to school in London.

Yet as soon as I saw her arriving home for the weekend, I knew I would never find the courage to confront her. Vast primeval creatures swam about in the shadowy depths beneath us. Why risk disturbing them? It seemed far wiser to swim close to the shore and avoid potentially explosive subjects. Nevertheless the overwhelming desire to live my own life was becoming increasingly urgent.

Just after my seventeenth birthday, my father headed to Lisbon to work on a book about Portuguese gardens. His publishers had given him another short deadline, so he was obliged to go quickly, seeing that Damiano, the photographer with whom he always collaborated, was only available during July and August.

'Buck up, Lumpy,' my father told me the morning he left. 'You might like this school more than you think.'

But neither of us believed that.

The house felt very empty without him. Miss Bolton was grumpier than ever. I agonised over saying goodbye to the dogs, and ate as little as possible to numb my fears about Les Cimes. Maud had intimated that the school would be closely monitoring my food intake and take 'necessary measures' if I lost more weight when I got there. I spent the time poring over my parents' collection of photographic books by Avedon, Penn, Cecil Beaton and Cartier-Bresson, as well as many others. Now that I'd met Ramsey, discovering as much as I could about photography was a way of feeling closer to him.

On the day of my flight to Geneva, Reg drove me to London to pick up Maud, who insisted on seeing me off at the airport. Reg complained that the logistics didn't make sense, especially as the roads were particularly congested because the Queen was holding a garden party at Buckingham Palace. It was a blistering hot day to spend hours in the traffic.

When we finally reached Parliament Square, Maud was waiting for us outside the House of Commons. She was in a white linen summer dress with a black patent leather belt that highlighted her trim figure, a three-strand pearl necklace, and black pumps with white leather piping. In the crook of one arm she held an alligator handbag with a gold clasp. In her other hand she carried a black Dunhill briefcase Papa had given her for Christmas a few years before.

As she climbed in, she was uncharacteristically cheerful. 'Hello, Ari. Don't you look smart? Come sit in the back with me, darling.'

I'd dressed in a matching navy-blue jacket and pleated skirt and pulled my hair back into a ponytail. One thing I hadn't wanted to do today was argue about my appearance. Maud seemed to pick up on my willingness to acquiesce to her.

'I'm so sorry I've been too busy to help you this week. But I hear you've been frightfully grown-up and organised your own packing.' She smoothed a strand of hair out of my face. 'Ari, I know you've been unhappy lately, but honestly darling, this school will mark the start of the most marvellous time in your life. Goodness, at your age, I could only dream of travelling to Europe.'

I glanced out of the window. We were passing a leafy park, where scores of scantily-clad Londoners were sunbathing on the grass or lolling about on striped deck chairs. I felt as if I were on a tumbril, headed for the big chop, with time for a reprieve fast running out.

Maud glanced at her watch. 'Reg, could you put on the radio? Mr Wilson is being interviewed at 11:30.' She gave me an apologetic look. 'I really must listen to this, darling, it's about the frightful wage freeze.'

On came her glasses and her frown. She loathed Harold Wilson.

I pulled *Melody Maker* out of my satchel and studied the headline.

'Cream: Sweet and Sour Rock 'n' Roll – A thunder of blues in a London church hall complete with Brownies and caretakers was the bizarre setting for the first tentative creations of the Cream – Britain's most exciting new group, featuring star instrumentalists, Jack Bruce, Ginger Baker, and Eric Clapton.'

And they expected me to exchange London for Grindelwald?

As soon as the interview was over, the radio was switched off and Maud disappeared behind the *Daily Telegraph*. Now that she was completely hidden, I plucked up the courage to ask if she was going home after she dropped me off. It was Friday, after all.

My armpits prickled with apprehension.

'Yes, darling, why? Have you forgotten something?' She lowered the paper, peering at me over the rim of her glasses.

'We're having house guests, aren't we?' I persisted, knowing very well this was the case. Collins had fielded endless deliveries from the fishmonger, the wine merchant and the butcher. Mrs Philpot had been busy prepping summer puddings and cold soups, as she always did before a house party, and the gardener had brought in baskets of roses and sweet peas.

'Oh, nothing too gala, just a few colleagues staying until Sunday,' Maud told me.

'Who's coming?' I persisted.

'The usual suspects... you know, the Fischers, Michael Doonan, the Carringtons.' She made an airy gesture.

'And Charles Morgan?' I asked. I'd pumped Julius for his name on a recent phone call.

Maud didn't miss a beat.

'Yes, of course. We're all on the same committee.'

Whatever that meant. The atmosphere became dead still. I was sitting by the door closest to the curb, gazing into a Harvey Nichols window where, on the hottest day of the year, six mannequins, all replicas of Twiggy, were dancing around a Mini Minor, in brightly coloured coats and boots, while autumn leaves in dayglo colours swirled around them. The traffic lights at the corner had turned green at least three times and we still weren't moving.

I turned back to Maud. A strange calm had descended on me. There really was nothing to lose.

'I'm not going to Switzerland.'

Maud opened her mouth to talk but I didn't give her the chance. 'I know all about what you've been up to behind Papa's back; everyone does. Do what you want but leave me alone. I have a legal right to live my own life. Goodbye!'

I'd opened the door by the time she found her voice.

'Ari, for god's sake...'

I gave her one last look – the *Telegraph* had tumbled to the floor. Then I grabbed my satchel, jumped out and, with all my strength, slammed the door behind me. I leapt onto the curb and darted across the pavement into Harvey Nichols where a uniformed doorman pulled open the heavy glass door to usher me in.

Over my shoulder, I caught an almost comical glimpse of Maud shouting at me through the car window before I escaped into the cosmetics hall.

After a few minutes had elapsed, I fled the store through a side entrance, ran a few yards towards the Underground sign and down the steps to the Tube.

By the time I reached the ticket office, I was perspiring and breathless. My hands trembled so hard, buying a ticket seemed to take forever.

As I'd only travelled on the Tube once or twice in my life, it occurred to me I had no real idea where I was heading. I only knew I needed to keep going.

On the steep escalators down to the Piccadilly line, I gripped the handrail hard. The flickering yellow light, the oppressive heat, and the stench of a hundred years of human sweat made my stomach lurch as I got on a train headed to Cockfosters.

Cockfosters. It might just as well have been Vladivostok.

The train juddered and screeched and travelled at such speed between stations that sudden disaster seemed inevitable, and yet everyone around me appeared resigned, even bored. Five or six stations later, as passengers got on and off, my heart finally stopped racing.

I took a seat and clutched my satchel to my chest. Inside was my passport, a tartan purse containing twenty-five pounds, the slip of paper from Ramsey with his telephone number, and Sunny's letter.

A few days before, I had looked up Queen's Gate Terrace, SW7 in Reg's *A-Z*. After a long perusal of the Tube map on the wall above the carriage door, I realised I was heading in exactly the opposite direction.

At the next stop, I got out and walked across the platform for the westbound train to Gloucester Road.

As I waited for the train to arrive, my paranoia was overtaken by sudden elation.

I'd done it. I'd broken free at last.

ELEVEN

London, July 1966

'Who are you, darls?'

The girl at the door had Asian features and spoke with a broad Australian accent. Her black hair hung down to her waist, and she wore a breathtakingly short patchwork miniskirt, with a white halter top and red cat's eye glasses.

I tried to look over her shoulder but could see nothing but a scuffed staircase. 'Is Sunny around?'

The woman shook her head. 'She's at work.'

I hesitated. I had nowhere else to go. 'Can I… can I please wait for her inside?'

She looked me up and down with a hint of exasperation. 'Not *another* runaway. Look, darls, you can come up and wait for Sunny but you can't stay. We're chokka, it's all getting completely out of hand.'

She held open the door for me and motioned me in.

'Thank you so much,' I said, weak with relief. 'I'll stay out of your way.'

'How old are you? You can't be more than seventeen,' she guessed, examining my face. 'You'll be popular here, I warn you. I'm Cindy, by the way.'

'I'm Ari.'

A large pink and purple poster of a moustachioed Mona Lisa surrounded by bananas and swirling patterns hung on the wall opposite the front door, near a mirror from a fun fair that twisted and distorted my image. To the left were double doors, open just a crack. From inside the room came the sound of '19th Nervous Breakdown', blasting. Cindy barged straight in.

The French windows were wide open but the room smelled of cloyingly sweet joss sticks. No one looked up as we entered, not the man hunched over, drawing on the long wooden table, nor the barefoot girls cross-legged on a wooden day bed on the other side of the room. Facing them, seemingly oblivious to the loud music, a wiry man perched on the edge of his seat, talking rapidly, waving his arms. He had long dark hair, a large, sensuous mouth and a slightly simian quality about him that I immediately liked.

'This is Ari, a friend of Sunny's,' Cindy shouted over the music. One of the two women glanced up and smiled at me before turning her attention back to her friends.

Cindy disappeared without a word, so I found an empty stool at the table and sat down, awkwardly.

The room was large and had once been quite grand, but the twenty-foot ceiling's ornate plasterwork had huge brown stains, and the scuffed parquet floor was daubed with splashes of paint. In sections, the wood was almost completely worn away.

Now that I was here, I didn't know what to do. I felt horribly naff in my neat navy suit and ponytail.

'Are you someone's chick, or a plant from the vice squad?' the artist muttered, without looking up from his drawing.

He spoke softly, and I couldn't hear what he was saying over the music, so I kept asking, 'What?'

He repeated the question in the same flat tone.

'Neither. I'm just waiting for Sunny to come home from work,' I said, primly.

He grunted in reply.

The song changed and 'As Tears Go By' began to play. The artist lit another Gitane from a packet at his elbow. The overflowing ashtray next to him smouldered with cigarette ends that hadn't been properly stubbed out. He was surrounded by detritus – grotty mugs, various tubes of paint, pens, pencils, wood shavings and paintbrushes soaking in a jar of muddy water.

Cindy reappeared with two mugs of tea and handed one to me. 'Here. You look like you need this,' she said.

'Thank you,' I said, my voice barely above a whisper.

'Marianne Faithfull was in the shop yesterday and bought loads of my gear,' Cindy said. 'White nightdresses, satin slips, and a military jacket with gold frogging from Russia or somewhere. So it's off to the markets at dawn tomorrow to replenish the stocks. Jesus, Ritchie, you're like bloody Pigpen.' She eyed the artist with distaste.

'You've always been a bourgeoise chick at heart,' Ritchie muttered out of the corner of his mouth.

'Lucky for you, otherwise you'd be living in a complete sty,' Cindy replied.

She took a sip of tea and turned her attention to me.

'How did you land here, darls?'

I told her that Sunny and I had been expelled from school together a few weeks before. Glancing around, I embellished the story a bit. 'My parents were furious and they just threw me out. Sunny told me to find her.'

Cindy watched me with knowing eyes. 'I hope the fuzz aren't going to come looking for you. That's the last thing we need.'

'They won't,' I promised. 'Nobody knows I'm here.'

'Well, that's something anyway,' she said.

'You did the right thing by getting out. It's your life.' For the first time the artist looked at me. He had unnervingly direct blue eyes. 'I'm Ritchie, by the way.'

Cindy introduced me to the others one by one.

Rob and Sarah were friendly, but the other woman, Carolyn, visibly annoyed at the interruption, yawned theatrically and began reading a magazine. She was a few years older than the others, her sour face framed by a spiky tangle of dark brown hair.

'Ari's another runaway!' Cindy announced.

'In that suit?' Carolyn sniggered, and I flushed crimson.

Sarah looked concerned and asked if I had somewhere to stay.

'Not here, darls. I've already told her,' Cindy interjected firmly. 'There's eight already, not counting everyone else in London who crashes here when they're in a fix. The plumbing is about to give up the ghost.'

'Then we'll really be in the shit,' said Robbie.

'I plan to get a job as soon as possible, and I can pay something up front,' I pleaded.

'Got a fiver on ya?' Robbie asked. I nodded warily.

'Far as I'm concerned, you're in. Welcome to the Consulate. Who says we can't be bought?' Before I could ascertain whether he was serious, he pointed over my shoulder. 'Your mate's arrived.'

I swivelled round to see Sunny, standing in the doorway.

'Ari!' she cried.

I ran across to her. We hugged for a long time. I'd never been so happy to see anyone in my life.

Behind us I heard Rob say to Ritchie, 'This is your dream come true, isn't it, Ritchie? Though they might be a little too old for you.'

I begged Sunny to lend me one of the new outfits that she'd scored from Cindy in exchange for minding her stall on Portobello Road. We were completely different sizes, but I found a striped T-shirt with long sleeves, and some denim overalls with a bib that she said made her look fat, and shook out my hair. It wasn't a look I would have chosen.

'Appalachia meets the King's Road,' Ritchie remarked, when he saw me. Still, it was a transformation of sorts, and I felt instantly liberated from my schoolgirl yoke.

Then Sunny and I headed out to a café on Gloucester Road where we ordered eggs, fried tomatoes and beans on toast. The food tasted like freedom, and I devoured every scrap on my plate without even a twinge of guilt.

When I told her about my quick flit to freedom through Harvey Nichols beauty halls, Sunny laughed so hard everyone turned to stare at us. 'Did you buy some eyeliner while you were at it?' she cackled. Then a thoughtful expression came over her face.

'You should write a postcard to your parents and let them know you're all right,' she advised. 'Tell them you want to take some time out to work, and you might go back to school in a few months. Sound as reasonable and practical as possible.'

I searched her face. 'Is that what you did?'

'No, but that's because I know my dad won't try to find me. Your parents might.'

She had a point. Maud was very capable of hiring private detectives.

'And you really don't mind if I crash in your room?' I asked.

'Nah, I'm actually relieved. Those Aussie geezers are full-on.'

'Don't worry, I can cope.' Ever since vile Niall I was confident that I now knew how to shut down interested blokes before they even got started.

'But have you seen the bathroom yet?'

I made a face. 'Yup.'

'Yeah, well, wait until you see the kitchen. At least the rent is cheap as chips.'

When we returned to the flat, it was heaving with people talking, smoking, drinking, laughing. In the kitchen, I found Cindy snogging a bare-chested man who wore a woman's shawl wrapped around his waist.

'It's like this every night,' Sunny informed me as she led the way through the crowd, pausing to fill two paper cups from one of several bottles of wine left amid the bottles of turpentine, linseed oil, and overflowing ashtrays.

We bumped into Robbie, with Sarah at his side. She was fine boned and ethereal, with tawny hair and perfect skin. I instantly longed to be her.

'As you can see, we're now running a creche around here,' was how Robbie introduced us to his friends.

There was a lot of talk about *Gondwana*, the underground magazine that Rob and Ritchie were launching in the autumn. Rob said it was going to be the clarion call for a 'profound political, sexual, and cultural revolution'.

'I have no doubt how the establishment will react but if they try to shut us down, they'll have our entire generation to contend with,' he said, confidently. Everyone at the party seemed to be contributing to the first issue in some way.

'Do you write?' Sarah asked me.

'Only a diary.'

'Well, keep it hidden otherwise Rob'll publish it,' she said.

I stuck close to Sunny. Though she was generally outgoing and friendly, she never gave away too much of herself, and men seemed to adore her. I couldn't put my finger on exactly how but it seemed as if she had become an adult in the few weeks since she'd left Chatham. I suddenly realised what a disadvantage it was to have been cossetted all my life. Everyone at the Consulate was bursting with creativity, ideas and radical opinions. Sunny at least played guitar and wrote songs, and she was practical. It had to be faced, I had very little going for me. Still, I smiled and chatted and got sent up a lot. If Maud taught me nothing else, it was how to make polite conversation. But here, any social conventions were frowned on in favour of outrageous directness, and a kind of ping-pong spontaneity that made my head spin. After a few glasses of wine, I staggered up the hall and collapsed on Sunny's mattress. It had been a very long day.

Sunny's room was a tiny space at the back of the flat. There was just enough room for a double mattress, a lamp, a small rail of clothes, and a broken rattan chair holding a pile of magazines and 45s. The window was curiously high off the ground, facing a bleak internal courtyard.

On that first night, I was so exhausted I slept for over twelve hours straight.

By morning, sharing such a small space seemed quite normal, like being back in the dorm at Chatham.

Over mugs of strong sweet tea, Sunny revealed that she now had a boyfriend, Eddie.

'I can't wait for you to meet him,' she enthused. 'He'll love you.'

My heart sank, just a little, but I forced a note of enthusiasm.

'What's he like? How did you meet him?' I asked, envisaging Sunny with Terence Stamp at the very least.

'He's so cool. We met in the Troubadour on an open mic night. I played a couple of songs and he dug them, and we started chatting and that was it.' She wrapped her arms around her knees and squeezed them. 'All I know, is we're meant to be together. He's staying in Margate right now. His uncle is a window cleaner – he fell off a scaffold and Eddie's filling in for him for a few weeks, but he'll be back soon. He's got plans to manage me.'

I tried to look pleased. Though Eddie didn't sound very glamorous, she'd stolen a move, and I wasn't nearly ready to catch up with her.

'So, what's it like, then?' I asked.

Sunny looked vague. 'What, sex? A bit hit and miss at first, but it gets better. Why, is there anyone you've got your eye on?'

My thoughts immediately turned to Ramsey, as they often did, but there was no point in even mentioning him. I'd read in the *Daily Mail* that he was married to a beautiful Italian actress.

'No,' I replied gloomily.

After breakfast, I put Sunny's overalls back on and we walked to Kensington High Street where I bought a facecloth, some Pears soap, a toothbrush and toothpaste, and two packets of knickers, but it wasn't a relaxing expedition; I saw Maud in the face of every well-dressed middle-aged woman. Paranoia even prevented me from making a pilgrimage to Biba, just a few streets away.

So instead, I took Sunny's advice and posted a card to my parents, telling them I was safe, and that I wasn't going home.

Shortly after we got back to the Consulate, Sunny left for work. I suddenly felt completely at sea and too shy to venture into the front room where Ritchie was again working. But I needn't have worried. Cindy, back from her trip to the flea market, appeared in the doorway of my room and ordered me to help her clean up the flat.

Looking like Rosie the Riveter in her baggy blue overalls and a print scarf tied around her head, she attacked the daunting task with grim determination, cleaning around Ritchie as if he were a waxwork, sweeping, vacuuming, disinfecting, all the time shouting instructions at me. She was a whirlwind, and I loved her determination.

At Thurston, I didn't even make my own bed. I'd never wiped down a kitchen counter in my life. Cindy must have seen immediately that I'd never had to clean before. But she didn't comment on my inability to wield a broom with any skill, she simply showed me how to use a dustpan and moved on.

'This is real life, darls, you might as well get used to it,' she admonished, when I baulked at cleaning the toilet.

I wanted to be friends with her, so I held my breath and did it.

When we'd finished, I surveyed the spotless flat with unexpected pride. Cindy looked at me.

'Right,' she said, rubbing her hands. 'Now, let's find you something else to wear.'

Her room was shrouded in darkness, but it smelled sweeter than the rest of the flat. When she switched on a lamp, the soft pink light revealed racks and racks of clothes.

Exquisite sequinned and cut velvet dresses, gold lamé trouser suits, embroidered Spanish shawls, shimmering miniskirts, ruffled silk shirts in every colour, satin tea gowns, summer frocks and black lace cocktail dresses hung suspended from floor to ceiling across three walls on a complicated pulley system. Scarves, belts, Fair Isle jumpers and ethnic jewellery tumbled out of drawers.

'What is this?' I asked, awestruck, looking around the treasure trove.

'This is my business, darls,' she explained, touching a sequinned sleeve. 'I've been selling vintage clothes at Portobello Market for the last year, and now I've signed a lease on a shop in the Chelsea Antiques Market. Everything's crammed in here until I get the keys.'

She held up a simple yellow shift.

'I think this will really suit you. Why don't you try it on?'

Too excited to feel shy, I stripped down to my knickers and pulled the dress on over my head. Cindy looked at me for a moment, then dug through a basket and fished out a wide belt with a round buckle, which she fastened round my hips. My school brogues rather ruined the look, however, so Cindy rooted around until she found some strappy snakeskin shoes with low heels, in my size.

We surveyed the result in the mirror.

'It's all about the cut, darls. You look divine,' Cindy declared, in her usual self-assured manner. I usually hated my appearance; my big nose and bad skin. But there was no denying that the deceptively simple design of Cindy's dress made me look older, taller, thinner.

'You could be a model, Ari. You know that?' she said. 'You've got the perfect model's body, anyway. Let me introduce you to a friend of mine who runs an agency.'

I didn't want to show how thrilled I was in case Cindy was winding me up. But she seemed genuinely enthused. I soon realised that even though she took no prisoners and could be devastatingly frank, if she liked you, she would do anything to help you survive. Especially if you were willing to haul racks of clothes across London and tackle grotty bathrooms.

True to her word, a few days later, Cindy did my make-up and dressed me in a short white broderie anglaise shift with bell sleeves and low silver pumps from her collection and took me to her friend's agency on the King's Road. As we walked down the street, I noticed for the first time in my life men turning to stare at me. I took this as a good sign.

Cindy's friend, Felicity Prescott, was in her mid-forties with an authoritative air and a trendy Vidal Sassoon haircut.

'This is the girl I told you about,' Cindy said.

The agent looked me over with a professional's scepticism. 'Hmm. Nice straight hair. Good height. No need to lose any weight. The nose could be a problem. And the skin. Might be worth doing something about those spots.'

She paused, tapping her chin with a long, perfect nail. 'We'll have to get you working with a photographer to get a portfolio together. That will cost about £100. If the shots turn out OK, we can get you some go-sees. That's the best I can do.'

My heart fell. I didn't have a hundred pounds. But, a second later, it occurred to me that I did know a photographer.

It took a few days to pluck up the courage to call Bill Ramsey. Despite thinking about him constantly, I hadn't spoken to him since that afternoon at Thurston, though I'd gazed many times at his phone number on the crumpled scrap of paper, debating whether to call him. Finally, one sweltering afternoon, I made my way to the call box down the road, my heart pounding. I placed a threepence in the slot and dialled his number.

A woman with icicles in her voice answered. When I asked for Ramsey, she told me he was away and didn't volunteer any further information. I hung up quickly and fled the stifling phone box. Obviously, I had let a foolish fantasy take over at a desperate moment. As if he would ever want to photograph me anyway!

I was going to have to find another way.

TWELVE

London, September 1966

By the end of summer I had acquired a job in a shop and settled into London life. After that one attempt to call Ramsey, I'd given up any hope of modelling. I had to be practical. I didn't think I looked like a model, even though I was skinny enough. Models were perfect. I definitely wasn't.

Giving up was not in Cindy's nature, however. One day in mid-September, I arrived home after work and found her in the sitting room with a stranger. Not wanting to intrude, I headed straight to the kitchen.

Moments later she appeared at the door of the kitchen and hissed urgently, 'Put on the Bird Dog trouser suit and come to the sitting room. There's a photographer with me and he needs to see you.'

There was no question of disobeying that tone. I raced to my room and changed into the dark blue velvet suit, raked a brush through my long hair, and strolled into the sitting room.

'This is Antoine,' Cindy said, stretching out her arm to the man next to her. 'He's a photographer, visiting from Paris. I've been telling him all about you.'

In a crumpled shirt, long unwashed hair and a Gitane hanging from an obstinate-looking mouth, Antoine was a virtual caricature. As I said hello, his small, quick eyes assessed me.

'Yes,' he said, in a thick, French accent, as if someone had asked him a silent question. 'I like.'

He guided me to the window, produced a camera and began taking pictures. As he worked, he didn't utter a word, pausing only to angle my chin with his hand.

I'd learned French in school, but I knew better than to try and speak it with an actual Frenchman. It would be too mortifying. Best to say nothing. So instead we worked in silence.

The session took just ten minutes. When he finished, he kissed both my cheeks rather vaguely and went off with Cindy. And that was that. I took off the trouser suit and put my jeans back on.

When Cindy returned, she was in a state of high excitement. She told me, 'Antoine Boucher is a legend in fashion. He's working on a commission from the *Sunday Times* and he's insisting that I style the clothes instead of their usual fashion editor. He's so in demand, they're going to let him have his way. And – he wants you to be the model, darls. I told you everyone would get sick of dolly birds sooner or later.'

She beamed at me. 'Out of all the girls, he's chosen you.'

The shoot took place in a bombed-out mansion in the East End. The blast had torn the facade clean off the building, so it now resembled a giant ruined dolls' house. Piles of rubble and rubbish covered the grounds while, upstairs, remnants of a rose-patterned wallpaper clung to the plaster in the bedrooms. Outlines of fireplaces and pipes that had long since been pulled out for scrap were visible on the walls, along with layers of graffiti. Miraculously, some of the roof was still intact, which explained why the house had not simply rotted into a heap.

A chain link fence surrounded the property. A sign reading: *Danger – Trespassers Will Be Prosecuted* was mounted at the entrance. Antoine did not consider this a problem and directed us to climb over the barricade.

'Do we have permission to be here?' I asked Cindy.

'Probably not; but look at it.' She studied the ruins with awe. 'What a setting.'

Antoine's point-blank refusal to even attempt to speak any English other than yes or no, combined with his fearsome reputation, gave him such an air of authority that even the editor of the *Sunday Times Magazine* couldn't stand up to him. She'd wanted Celia Hammond for the shoot – Celia was everywhere that year; on every magazine cover.

But Antoine refused to consider it.

'He told her it was you or nobody,' Cindy told me, as we followed Antoine over the fence.

This revelation filled me with a mixture of excitement and terror. What if I let Antoine down after he'd championed me?

It was six in the morning. Antoine thought the cold, early morning light was best for the mood he was trying to create.

Now that we were here, he seemed happier, occasionally turning to smile at me as he nimbly prowled around the ruins working out his shots.

In the car, I wriggled into the first outfit – a full-length white crepe halter neck dress, with a long, bare back.

There was a chill in the air and my teeth chattered as Cindy tucked a shawl round me and swept my hair into a classic French twist. She clipped white dangly earrings on my earlobes.

Following her instructions, I had already applied a pale foundation and drawn exaggerated eyelashes on under my eyes with dark brown pencil. When I was ready, she stood back to survey her work.

'My god, you look like a ghost bride,' she said, pleased.

It was just before seven when Antoine led me carefully across the mounds of rubble into the damaged house. Without a word he pointed to where he wanted me to stand.

As soon as he started shooting, an almost telepathic communication developed between us. It seemed to me that he wanted a certain atmosphere of longing in the shot. Longing was something I knew all about.

'Yes,' he muttered to himself as he shot. 'Yes.'

He directed me to lie in an 'S' shape on a slope of rubble in one of the ground floor rooms. After some time, he looked up from the camera and said, '*Très, très bien! Fait ques'que tu veux, maintenant.*'

I undulated on the rocks, aware that the white dress was suffering, and sharp stones were digging into my skin. The image in my mind was of a girl dressed to meet her lover during the Blitz. The force of a sudden explosion a few metres away from the house terminated her life so abruptly that she had no idea that she was dead.

Antoine's response was immediate. He was animated, excited.

'*Cindeee*,' he crowed, when we returned to the car so I could change into the next outfit. '*Vous avez trouvé une vrai gemme ici.*'

When we prepared for the next shot, Cindy eyed the state of the Ossie Clark dress nervously as she dabbed astringent on my grazed back. There was so much adrenaline coursing through my body that I didn't register either cold or pain.

This must be what love feels like, I thought. Too wonderful to question.

We completed two more shots on the ground floor, and one in the hallway with the ruined staircase behind me. By now, Antoine was like an old friend, and I wanted to give him my best. For once, I could use my emotions in a way that was useful to someone. Everything I did seemed to be just what he was after.

When I'd changed into the last outfit in the series, Antoine smiled gravely and pointed to the second storey of the ruined house, making a gesture as if to say, 'Are you game?'

God, yes, I was game – until I saw the stairs up close. Held up by little more than a few stones, they were virtually collapsing.

Fully aware of the sign out front, and the dangers it warned about, I hesitated.

Antoine went up first, testing each step as he climbed. When he reached the top, he gestured for me to keep to one side of the stairs. As I followed behind in a virtually transparent long chiffon dress, I heard Antoine's assistant mutter to himself, 'This is mad.'

But I wanted to show everyone I was worthy of their faith in me. So I climbed. The steps creaked loudly, shivering beneath me, but they held.

When I reached the top, I exhaled, clenching and unclenching my hands as the tension left my shoulders. However, Antoine still wasn't done.

I watched, aghast, as he made his way to the centre of the destroyed front bedroom, moving like a tightrope walker, stepping only where floor joists bisected the supporting beams and pausing for a minute or two after each step.

On the ground below, Cindy stood gazing up at us with her hands covering her mouth, as Antoine carefully retraced his steps and gave me a confident nod.

'*Seulement pour cinq minutes*,' he said, holding up five fingers.

I couldn't see how it made any difference whether it was five minutes or two hours. It was the journey to and from the spot he wanted that would kill me.

But it was too late to say no.

I held my skirt in one hand as I followed the path he had taken, focussing on one step at a time, while imagining I was as weightless as a ghost, balancing perfectly on my toes.

By the time I reached the centre, Antoine had already gone back down the stairs. He was standing on a concrete girder below me, his telephoto lens glinting in the sunlight.

The floor beneath me seemed to sway with my every breath, as I stood straight with my head in profile and one arm bent behind me, afraid to move much at all.

I turned to glance at Antoine. That was when I saw a police car coming to a stop on the street in front of the ruined building.

I hissed, 'Police' at the trio below me, but they couldn't hear. I pointed hard at the street behind them.

Cindy turned around and froze. Two police officers were walking towards her.

I stood on the first floor watching the scene, the floor shifting gently beneath me, as they argued.

Finally, I tiptoed cautiously back along the joists, holding my breath. That was when I heard one of the coppers say furiously, 'Where the bleeding hell is she going?'

'I'm coming down to you,' I called.

Seconds later, I heard a crash on the stairs.

I inched my way to the staircase, to find one of the policemen sitting with his trouser leg rolled up, examining a long cut on his leg. His colleague barked into his radio and glared at me.

'Don't you bloody move,' he warned.

I stayed at the top in the dust until a new unit of police dressed in black gear appeared, and brought me down via a contraption of ladders and ropes.

By now, a large audience of amused bystanders had gathered on the pavement.

Pandering to the crowd, the sturdiest officer insisted on carrying me across the rubble to the street. The gathered group cheered.

But my relief at surviving the decrepit building was short lived. We were all ordered into a police van and driven to Bethnal Green station for questioning. I spent hours in a funky corridor, waiting to be questioned. When the police found out I was a model, and not involved in planning the shoot, they lost interest in me.

Antoine and Cindy were both charged with trespassing and damaging private property. The police had threatened to impound the film from the day's shoot, but by this time Antoine had been in touch with someone from the magazine who sent a solicitor.

Finally, we were allowed to leave with the film in hand.

Back at the Consulate, Cindy and I surveyed the state of the dresses. They all needed dry-cleaning and two of them were damaged. 'If the *Sunday Times* don't use those photos, Ossie will never forgive me,' Cindy said gloomily, as we sat on the balcony wrapped in blankets, drinking black tea laced with whiskey.

Autumn was in the air; the expansive summer mood we had enjoyed for so long was fast evaporating. Though the shoot had ended calamitously, I felt curiously upbeat about the day's work, having found something to give at last.

THIRTEEN

London, September 1966

The following Sunday, Cindy woke me at seven. 'The pictures ran,' she shouted.

We threw on clothes and dashed down to the newsagents, snatching up copies of *The Times* and flicking through the magazine before we'd even paid.

The full-page images were arresting. I stared at the photos of myself, draped across rocks, my skin milk white in the morning light, my eyes staring at the grey sky, and I knew my life was about to change.

I didn't look like me. I looked like... a professional model. A real model. All long legs and huge dark eyes, slim arms extended.

Cindy had tears in her eyes when she turned to me and said, 'Darls, I think Antoine has made the most important leap in fashion photography since Avedon's work with Suzy Parker in the '50's.'

I laughed. She was always so dramatic. But anyone could see the photographs were startlingly original and stood out from the page. I had to hand it to Antoine. For once I was happy with the way I looked.

Reactions were mixed amongst my housemates. Later, when they all surfaced, Robbie said I looked like a china doll dug up from a grave. Carolyn sniffily said that the pictures were sexist and demeaning. Of course, Sunny and Sarah thought they were brilliant and went out to buy a bottle of Lambrusco so we could celebrate.

Since we didn't have a phone, there was not much outside feedback at first. So, I had no idea that the pictures were causing some ripples. It was the era of the dolly bird – bright mini-skirts and happy, healthy models cavorting on bikes or dancing for the camera. Antoine's dramatic photos bucked the trend, and it turned out that some of the more conservative elements in the media didn't like it. The *Daily Mail* suggested there was something intrinsically perverse about the photos. It was rumoured that Antoine's former girlfriend, a Czech model, had killed herself. Now he had his claws into a young English ingenue.

I discovered from the King's Road bush telegraph that some people had found the pictures offensive, as if Antoine had somehow trivialised the Blitz by using a World War II bomb site as a backdrop for expensive clothes.

It had already occurred to me that Maud read *The Times* every day.

A few days after the story appeared, the headline of Nigel Dempster's column in the *Daily Express* read: 'Row over shock pics of peer's daughter', along with a distorted account of our arrest at the ruined house. I was identified as 'The Hon. Ariadne Lyttleton, daughter of Viscountess Lyttleton, prominent Conservative Party socialite and power broker'.

Feeling I had little choice, I went down to the phone box on the corner and called home.

Mr Collins answered. It was wonderful to hear his familiar, stern voice. 'Col, it's Ari,' I said. 'How are you?'

The long silence that followed was the only indication that I'd shocked him.

'I'm very well, thank you.'

I found myself smiling at his stiff tone and continued; 'Is Papa there?'

'Just one moment.' He sounded relieved to be able to pass me to someone else.

My father abruptly came on the line.

'Ari, thank heavens. I've never been so worried in my life.'

'I'm perfectly safe,' I assured him. 'I saw the story in the *Express*, and I just wanted to make sure you weren't upset. I know how you feel about Dempster.'

'The man's a monster,' he announced, without hesitation. 'But why on earth are you in the *Times*, darling, lying on stones?'

'It was a modelling job. I got paid,' I said.

'One shouldn't do everything one can be paid for,' he said, sharply.

'It was a good job. Papa, I don't want to fight...' I began, but before I could finish, he exploded in a sudden rage.

'Have you gone quite mad? You have no idea how much we worried about you, Ariadne. How dare you disappear like that? It was unbelievably selfish. Anything could have happened! I haven't slept properly in months.'

Pangs of guilt engulfed me. I'd dreaded this moment for so long, and now here it was.

Luckily, I'd had months to decide what to say. 'I wrote to you the day I got to London to tell you I was safe,' I reminded him. 'I'm sorry if you were worried but you should have stuck up for me over Switzerland. I never would have left if you and Maud had allowed me to go to a normal school. Any school would have done. Now it's too late.'

I drew a breath, fighting a tide of anger. 'I know it wasn't you. It was Maud. She was dying to get rid of me. And she succeeded.'

'Ari, she loves you,' he said weakly. 'She just has trouble expressing it.'

Before I could call him out on that lie, he continued briskly, 'Look, darling, the good news is she's caved in and has given her permission for you to attend a crammer in Oxford. Crowne and Holt. We just want you to come home.'

Clown and Dolt, the last refuge for parents with dim children.

I bit my lip and sighed.

'Look,' I said. 'I have a place to live, a job, and friends. I'm happy for the first time in years. I'm not going back to school.'

'Darling, I beg you to listen to me. If you don't finish your education, you'll regret it your whole life.'

I simply didn't believe him. My father had been born in the Victorian era when there were still no cars on the road, just horses and carts. One of his earliest memories was the stench of seasick bears languishing in the hold of his father's yacht on the journey across the Baltic from St Petersburg during an expedition to collect animals for the London Zoo.

'I'll make a bargain with you,' I said. 'If I can't support myself for the next six months, I'll come home and go back to school. Agreed?'

He tried his best to change my mind, but in the end, he agreed.

We moved onto the subject of Henrietta's wedding ('Mummy's already frothing at the mouth about it and it's eight months away') and his planned trip to Angkor Wat and the Far East, for a new project.

When I hung up, I felt lighter. I missed him, but reasoned it was he who had trained me to handle long separations from him in the first place. It wasn't as if he was home alone twiddling his thumbs waiting for me.

When I returned to the Consulate, I found Cindy lurking impatiently by the door.

'Felicity sent a message. She wants to see you again, darls. They're mad about the photographs at the agency.'

When we arrived at the agency on the King's Road, it was very different from the last visit. This time, Felicity and her partner Jude met us at the door, all smiles and hugs.

Felicity beamed at me, her perfect brown bob swinging as she gestured. 'We've been talking about signing you since July, haven't we Jude? We've just been so snowed under. Can I get you a coffee? A sticky bun?'

It turned out that not only did they want to represent me, but they also offered to finance my portfolio up front – no mention of reimbursing the costs. They told me they'd set me up with their most experienced booker, and make sure I got tons of work. And a place to live as well. So I signed the contract on the spot.

'I told you this would happen, darls,' Cindy said smugly, when we were back on the street. 'You know I'm never wrong.'

FOURTEEN

London, November 1966

Sunny and I left the Consulate on the same rainy day in late October. She moved in with her boyfriend in a tiny flat in Elm Park Gardens in South Kensington. I took a room in a little mews house in Fulham, which I shared with three Scandinavian models: Anna, Solveig, and Gunilla. My new place was clean and orderly. The second I walked in, I missed the chaos of the Consulate and my mad Aussie flatmates. The room I was assigned was box-like, but it was all mine. Despite my loneliness, I relished the privacy – until I realised an interconnecting door from our front hallway led into Felicity's house, where she lived with her accountant husband and their ten-year-old daughter.

Felicity had a habit of appearing in our apartment without warning.

'Making certain ve don't have men here,' Anna explained darkly. 'And liking to know vat ve are eating.'

Some men, as it transpired though, were considered fine.

On my first weekend in the house, the other three models lounged about all day with their hair in rollers, watching cartoons on television, painting their nails. On Saturday night, the rollers came out, the crochet minis went on, and a parade of men with sports cars called in to collect the three for dinner and dancing at Annabel's. Felicity, it turned out, regularly arranged dates for them with eligible wealthy bachelors, as part of her service as an agent.

After a few weeks, she tried her dating game on me, matching me up with a suitable 'young man'. He turned out to be nearly forty with a considerable paunch. A tense dinner at Alvaro's ensued, where he banged on about his responsibilities and his success. When he asked how I saw the future, I quoted Robbie: 'I believe the ruling class will be overthrown by 1970.'

That brought a brisk end to a tedious evening.

I yearned for my old housemates, their humour, and the constant stream of interesting people who flowed through the Consulate. At least there was a telephone in the new place, so I could call Julius at Cambridge.

He often came to London, where he stayed in South Kensington with a well-known actress in her late sixties, Dame Hermione Eyre, who had taken quite a shine to him, introducing him to all her friends. On nights when he wasn't required to escort her to the theatre or a party, he would take me on long walks along the Thames towpath and to dinner in candlelit bistros on the King's Road.

He was proud of me for striking out on my own but warned me modelling was a short career.

'There aren't any old models,' he pointed out. 'Or even middle-aged ones. Make your money while you can and be ready for whatever comes next.'

I didn't really pay much attention. Middle-age was a hundred years away. I was just getting started.

Living with three professional models was an eye-opener. They worked long hours and returned home most nights to a dinner of cottage cheese on Ryvita in front of the telly. It was disconcerting to see how disciplined they were. I didn't feel like I shared that dedication.

The problem was I didn't have much work yet. I was constantly told I looked weird, like an alien. I didn't even have a good tear sheet, despite several attempts. Felicity's stable of groovy young photographers either attempted to make me look like a dolly bird or a sophisticate – neither look suited me. The pictures they took were unusable.

When I was sent to try out for a commercial at one of the top advertising agencies, my audition ended with an executive calling Felicity to berate her for wasting their time. Apparently, I wasn't considered sexy.

I wanted to crawl under a table. But when I told her about it later, Alice, my booker, was undaunted.

'Look, love,' she said, 'it's just business. It's not personal. You might do better in Europe. We should send you to Paris.'

Sunny was having better luck. One of her demos had been noticed by a record company, and she was in the studio cutting a single of a song she'd written, 'Bedroom

Eyes'. I was thrilled for her.

Whenever we spoke, I could hear the excitement in her voice and it left me feeling hollow. I longed to know what success felt like.

As weeks passed, a sense of inertia and failure threatened to drag me down. I spent more time alone in the flat, smoking endless cigarettes and trying to decide what to do with my life. One day, as I turned the pages of *Vogue*, the phone rang.

A familiar voice at the other end trilled, 'Ari, poppet, how are you? It's Henrietta!' I hadn't spoken to my sister since I jumped out of Maud's car in July.

'Uh… hello,' I said, after a brief, startled hesitation. 'How…?'

'David gave me your number,' she said brightly. 'I've been dying to tell you I've got a flat in London now,' she continued. 'I'd love it if you'd come and have a drink with me tomorrow. I haven't seen you in ages.'

Caught off guard and unable to quickly summon an excuse, I found myself reluctantly agreeing.

Two days later, I climbed to the top floor of an Edwardian mansion block overlooking Redcliffe Square. When I reached the landing, Henrietta was standing at her door in her coat. Her blonde hair was hidden under a silk scarf, her cheeks flushed. It struck me that I could see Maud in the shape of her face.

'Oh, darling Lumpy, look at you!' she exclaimed with uncharacteristic enthusiasm. I'd borrowed a crimson St Laurent trouser suit from Anna, hoping to appear prosperous.

She kissed my cheeks, her skin cool against mine. 'I only just got in from work and I'm afraid the place is in absolute chaos.'

'It's lovely,' I said.

In fact, the flat was beautiful, with huge windows overlooking the square, five storeys down. But it was the flat of a middle-aged woman, filled with china knick-knacks and silver framed photographs. The chintz sofa covers matched the curtains.

I could see Maud in that, too. In fact, this might as well have been my mother's flat.

I studied Henrietta's large collection of embossed invitations propped on either side of the mantelpiece, rivalling Maud's. Her life looked so organised, full of grand friends with accounts at Smythson's.

Henrietta poured us both glasses of wine and we sat down in the living room.

'Is this Simon's flat?' I asked.

Henrietta flushed slightly. 'Actually, David and Mummy sweetly gave it to me. House prices are shooting up, it just seemed sensible to buy rather than waste all that money on rent. Besides Rupes has his own flat, it only seemed fair.'

Fair? I bit back a sardonic laugh and changed the subject.

'What did you want to meet about? You said you had something to tell me.'

'Oh yes.' Henrietta lit a cigarette. 'I was just wondering, are you coming home for Christmas?'

'Probably not. I've got to go to Paris.' The lie came to me easily, and I was sure my tone sounded convincing.

'For a modelling job? At Christmas?' Henrietta's eyebrows rose.

'Yes, I've got this job for *Marie Claire* and then I've been invited to stay with friends in a houseboat on the Seine.' I kept my tone casual, almost bored, but I longed for it to be true.

Henrietta stubbed out her cigarette in a white china ashtray shaped like a butterfly. Then she said sharply, 'Honestly Ari, don't you have the first clue about how much it would mean to Mummy and David if you were at home for Christmas? I do think they have been absolute *saints* letting you go off by yourself for six months. The least you could do is come back for a day.'

I glared at her. 'If Maud enlisted you to get me home, I'm telling you right now I can't. I'm too busy, and I can't afford to take time off.'

From the direction of the hall, there was the unmistakable sound of a key turning in a lock. Suddenly I knew why Hen had been so insistent that I come here tonight.

'What have you done?' I hissed at Hen, whose face had gone completely blank.

Maud appeared in the sitting room doorway in her sable coat. She flashed a radiant smile and stretched her arms out towards me, her gold bracelets rattling.

'Darling. What a joy to see you.' She looked so happy that for a second I was thrown.

'Come and give Mummy a hug. I've missed you terribly.' There was nothing angry in her tone. No resentment or fury.

Hesitantly, I got up and submitted to the familiar 'A'-shaped clinch; our shoulders and arms thrust forward for a brief squeeze; our torsos separated. I breathed in the familiar mix of Mitsouko and Dunhill Menthols.

'Drink, Mummy?' Henrietta had already risen.

'Thank you, darling.' Maud stepped back from me. 'Longing for a drink. What a day. Endless meetings. I've been going since dawn.'

Henrietta took her coat and briefcase and disappeared into the hall.

'Isn't Henny's flat divine, Ari? You should have seen it before the renovations.' Maud dropped onto the sofa. 'I don't know how she managed it all as well as her job. Yes, we're talking about you, darling,' she said as Henrietta reappeared, carrying a glass of Chablis, and a dish of cheese straws on a tray which she set on the glass coffee table between stacks of *Tatler* and *Country Life*.

I was feeling quite drunk but accepted a refill when Henrietta offered; alcohol was the only way I was going to get through this. I gave Hen an accusing glare as she filled my glass, but she refused to meet my gaze.

Maud turned towards me. 'Ari, darling! How are you?'

'I'm fine,' I said. Henrietta and Maud glanced at each other. 'It's going well,' I added, needlessly.

Silence again.

'Now, do you have a plan B?' Maud asked, after a deep pull on her cigarette holder. 'I mean if it doesn't work out? The fashion world is so famously fickle. Heaven knows, you're frightfully attractive, darling, but I'm not sure that you're truly model material.'

If I'd had any hope that the tension between us would have eased in the months I'd been away, it faded in that moment.

Her mannerisms were repellent. The way she pursed her lips when she was concentrating on saying something unpleasant. Her emphasis on certain words. That famous smile. I hated all of it. I wanted to love her, but I couldn't.

It was pointless to try to tell her about my friends or what I had done in the last few months, she would have diminished all of it. Besides, I had achieved nothing, and was barely keeping my head above water. And yet. I had been free to breathe my own oxygen for the first time in years, and that was close enough to happiness for me.

'I don't have a plan B,' I told her. 'I've got an agent, and I'm going out for jobs. I've got a good place to stay.'

'Really?' Maud gave me a cool, knowing look. 'Because I'm told by everyone that you're struggling. And I honestly think for all our sakes it is time to put all the silliness behind you and take stock of your life before it's too late. Crowne and Bolt are eager to have you.'

I started at her, too shocked to speak. Who was 'everyone'? Who had she been speaking to? Paranoia gripped me. Was it Felicity? Jules? Who could be blabbing?

'I don't know what you're talking about,' I said, attempting to appear unmoved.

'There's no need to lie.' Henrietta gave me a pitying look. 'We're family. We can help you.'

'Yes, darling,' Maud cooed, a hint of acid in her tone. 'All we ask is that you give up this nonsense. It's not good for you. You're so pale and your bones are sticking out everywhere.'

I felt a little frisson of triumph as she gestured to my knees, visible beneath my mini-skirt.

'You can't keep starving yourself like this, it's dangerous, don't you see? Your father is beside himself with worry.'

I needed a moment to think.

'Where's the loo?' I enquired.

The dragonflies on Henrietta's wallpaper were pulsating as I passed through her bedroom; not a good sign. I turned on the light in the bathroom and locked the door. To stop myself from spinning out, I stared at a set of faded botanical prints grouped in two rows on either side of the sink, forcing myself to study the ferns.

Over the low whirring of the extractor fan, another sound, higher pitched, rose and fell abruptly, a long way off in the distance. I strained to hear it, but there was silence for a few moments before it started up again. A radiator hissing. Or sounds from a TV next door?

I washed my hands, then closed the bathroom door behind me, taking several deep breaths. Now the fan was switched off, the high-pitched frequency that had sounded so far away in the bathroom was much louder. Shocked, I hung back in Hen's bedroom, listening through the door.

'*Shh,* Mummy, *shh*, don't upset yourself like this, it's not good for you. You'll make yourself ill again,' Henrietta was pleading.

A strangled scream ensued, followed by ever more frantic sobs. 'I don't deserve this!'

Through the partly open door, I caught a glimpse of Maud, with her hands over her ears and a frantic, panic-stricken expression on her face, pacing up and down, in and out of view. She had been mildly upset when I left the room, now only minutes later she had become frenzied, wailing in the same ghostly pitch as when she was in mourning for Clive. Her world seemed to have collapsed in a matter of minutes. I had to escape before mine did too.

As I ran for the front door, she delivered her final devastating blow. 'You're killing him… don't you understand… you're killing your father!'

I felt like screaming at her, 'What do you know about my father's feelings? They never bothered you when you were with Clive!' but instead, I fled onto the landing, leaping down four flights of stairs, arriving in the entrance hall just as an elderly couple was coming through the front door. I pushed past them into the rainy street.

It was a blustery night. Raindrops swirled wildly in the headlights of cars and in the long beams of light cast by the streetlamps. I took a deep breath of the cold, damp air.

I walked for at least an hour in the rain trying to calm myself down. Maud's histrionics were no less terrifying just because she had the emotional range of a four-year-old. She was still my mother, and a part of me suspected she was right; that I was a selfish monster, bound to fail at everything. But I was determined to prove her wrong, whatever the cost.

My Biba coat was cool rather than warm, and I shivered as I crossed Old Brompton Road, past the red brick mansion blocks at the top of Earls Court, the crowded Aussie pubs, and the string of seedy convenience stores nearer the Tube station. Christmas lights were twinkling everywhere, and the shop windows were stuffed with Santas and elves, but for the first time London appeared to me like a bleak, impenetrable fortress.

By the time I got home, I was soaked through and exhausted. The wine had worn off and my head pounded as I stripped off my clothes and climbed into bed, tumbling immediately into a torrent of unhappy dreams.

I didn't know how much time had passed before someone was pounding on my door.

'Ari? Hello?' It was Anna's voice.

Disoriented, I looked up to see her standing by my bed with Solveig, my other housemate. The curlers in their hair made their heads look enormous.

'Are you OK?' Anna inquired, 'Dere vas veird noise from your room and ve vere concerned.'

'I'm sorry. I must have had a bad dream,' I said, blinking groggily at them. 'W– what time is it?

The sky was still inky black through the rain-spattered skylight. It had to be night time still.

'Ten-tirty,' came the soft sing-song answer. 'Ve saw your coat in the hall and this message from Felicity on the table for you. Here…'

Even through scrunched-up eyes I could tell Anna was excited as she delivered the note into my outstretched hand.

I reached out to the bedside table, switched on the light and read, 'The editor of *Vogue*, Beatrix Miller, has asked to see you at 11am tomorrow. 5th Floor Vogue House, Hanover Sq. W1. Make sure you dress appropriately. Get a good night's sleep. Good luck – Felicity.'

I stared at the note for some time, aware that my hand was shaking. Solveig and Anna stood over me, watching me absorb this information. Even in rollers and pyjamas, they were both so strikingly beautiful. I couldn't hold a candle to them. Maud had been right; I should cut my losses and go home.

'Why are you crying, Ari? This is good news,' Solveig said. She sat down on my bed and stroked my hair. No one had done that for a while. Unable to get any words out, I shook my head.

Anna came back into the room with a mug of cocoa, which she handed me. 'Drink dis before it gets cold,' she whispered.

As I sipped, they chatted away, about work, mostly. If they were trying to distract me, it worked, and I found myself laughing when they joked about a randy art director they'd worked with who had hit on them both.

Before long, I was telling them how scared I was. How many rejections I'd had already, and how I felt like I was letting everyone down. My face would be swollen tomorrow after such deep crying, it would be pointless to show up at *Vogue*.

'The thing is, all I know about modelling is how to apply make-up and stay thin,' I said. 'And if I don't learn how to do this, I think I'm going to fail completely.'

The two of them exchanged a glance, and something unspoken passed between them.

Anna spoke first. 'Solveig and me, ve vill help you. You vill be beautiful. But you must start now.'

She left the room, and I heard the bath taps running. A cloud of pine essence wafted down the hallway.

While I lay soaking, Anna brought me a cold towel to put over my face, and after five minutes, replaced it with another one. When I got out of the bath, my eyes were still bloodshot, so they produced a bottle of blue eye-drops from France. 'Model's secret veapon!' she informed me. 'During Paris Collections, especially.'

Within seconds, the whites of my eyes went from Schiaparelli pink to the colour of snowdrops. Afterwards, Solveig gave me some special oil from Morocco to comb through in my hair and yogurt from the fridge to slather on my face. Then she painted my nails.

In her pyjamas, with no make-up and her hair tied back, Solveig looked like a nondescript schoolgirl, though her skin was flawless, and she had the kind of symmetrical features that made her face particularly photogenic. I distrusted most other girls, especially the pretty ones. Solveig and Anna took me by surprise. Casual observation and undeniable envy had made me think they were humourless simpletons with icy blood running through their veins. It turned out they were different to English girls in that everyday kindness was second nature to them; perhaps because they had never been to boarding school. They enjoyed the process of preparing for work, and made it seem fun rather than boring or fraught with anxiety.

When we were done with the masks and treatments, they gave me a small pink pill and a glass of water.

'You sleep,' Anna told me, as she left my room. 'Then you start again.'

FIFTEEN

London, November 1966

The reception area at Vogue House was surprisingly fusty. I had imagined marble staircases and six-foot vases of flowers. The reality was much less intimidating. A scuffed parquet floor and the faint whiff of mildew were the main things I noticed when I walked in from the cold. An expressionless security officer cast a jaundiced eye over me from behind the front desk, before laboriously examining several typewritten pages of names until he found mine.

The lift took forever to go up three floors, and by the time the door rolled open, I was shaking with anxiety.

Upstairs, racks of clothes lined the edges of the open-plan room, and framed covers of back issues covered the walls. I paused at the top of the stairs, braced to meet a stereotypical dragon of a fashion editor. Instead, a smiling young woman appeared to greet me.

'Hi, Ari,' she said, as if we were old friends. 'I'm Sophie. We'd like to start by trying a few pieces on you, if that's OK?'

She was only a few years older than me, friendly and distinctly unintimidating. I liked her instantly.

She took me to an office where another rack of clothes waited for us.

'There are so many things I want you to try, but I think this one in particular would be perfect on you.'

Sophie held up a dark purple velvet shift with starched white collar and cuffs. It had a hint of a school-marm about it, but also an indecently short skirt. 'You can wear it with these, I think,' she added, handing me charcoal-patterned tights.

I was learning not to be self-conscious about taking my clothes off in front of strangers, so I stripped off my dress and draped it over a chair.

'Gosh, you're so enviably tall and slim,' Sophie observed, with a sigh. 'I'm always on a diet, but even if I lost a stone, I'd never have a figure like yours.'

'Oh, it's only because I run everywhere; it keeps my weight down,' I told her. A well-trodden lie.

When I pulled the dress on and straightened it, she drew in a delighted breath.

'It looks fab on you. Just, wow.' She clapped her hands. 'I knew it would work. Right. Now I want you to try another one…'

I tried on outfit after outfit. Everything she gave me fitted as if it had been made for me. It didn't occur to me at the time that this was because Sophie was such a brilliant fashion editor, she had spent days working out the right look for the shoot.

When I'd tried on the last outfit, Sophie leaned back against her desk, smiling at me. 'You know, I had a hunch when I saw Antoine Boucher's pictures of you in the *Sunday Times* that you would be perfect for this story. Keep on what you are wearing, and let's go meet Miss Miller. I want her to see you in person.'

Bea Miller was famous in London fashion for her exacting standards and perfect eye. So my heart was stuttering as we walked down the corridor to a door, painted high-gloss racing green. Perhaps sensing my sudden panic, Sophie gave me a reassuring smile before knocking.

Inside, most of the lights were out. I stuck close to Sophie as we crossed a vast darkened chamber to where Miss Miller stood behind a desk. A light box covered with photographic negatives lit up her face from below. In its pale glow I could see her honey-blonde hair was piled on top of her head, and the plump hand she extended across the desk had sharp nails lacquered blood red. She had an intelligent, thoughtful face, with a touch of the headmistress about her.

She deftly lit up a Rothmans with the gold lighter on her desk and exhaled deeply.

'So, this is Ariadne,' she said, exhaling a stream of smoke. 'It would be nice to see you properly. I do apologise for the Stygian darkness – we're working on layouts for the March issue.' She glanced past me. 'Minnie? Open the blinds, will you?'

A young girl in a yellow wool trouser suit put down her pad and pencil and hurried to the windows. Soon, bright winter sunlight flooded the room.

'We featured your sister in the October issue. You're not much like her, are you?' said Miss Miller. 'I would never have guessed you were related.'

'Who's this then?' came a reedy voice from behind me. I turned around.

Bill Ramsey was sitting cross-legged on the floor in the corner, a sea of photocopied photographs spread out in front of him.

When our eyes met, he scrambled to his feet.

'I know you.' His eyes searched my face. 'Something to do with horses, no?'

I laughed and shook my head, aware that the air around us appeared to be rippling like water. Since I'd thought of him every single day since Henrietta's photo shoot, his actual presence was extremely unsettling.

'Where have you been?' he asked. 'I thought you were going to call?'

Ramsey stared at me closely, without embarrassment, and I gazed back at him as steadily as I could, considering the sudden surge of energy coursing through my system.

'When are we shooting?' he asked Miss Miller without taking his eyes off me. 'She'll do, by the way.'

The editor looked from him to me, her expression knowing and not necessarily approving.

'We're scheduled for Monday afternoon.' She paused before saying, firmly, 'Now listen, Bill Ramsey, you need to be gentle with Ari. She's young and hasn't had much experience.'

'Yeah?' said Ramsey, his eyes boring into mine. 'How old are you, girl?'

I found my voice again. 'Seventeen.'

Ramsey laughed derisively. 'At your age I'd already been out of school and working for years. I knew much more about the world then than I do now. It's lucky I found you now before you start developing bad habits with terrible photographers.'

'Her only proper shoot so far was that Boucher spread,' Bea continued, with resolute determination. 'So, go easy.'

Ramsey snorted derisively. 'Boucher... another pretentious git posing as an artist. He had a cheek, going down the East End without my permission.'

'If you are only allowed to shoot pictures in the place you grew up, I'd better cancel your upcoming jobs in Paris and Milan,' Miss Miller told him crisply. 'For Monday's shoot, Sophie found a marvellous location – a beautifully renovated barge down in Cheyne Walk.'

'What? No, Bea. You must be mad,' Ramsey told her. 'I'll shoot Ari in the studio. The clothes are a bit boring, but this is Vogue; what can you do?'

He looked down at his watch. 'I've got to go. I'm shooting Albert Finney in half an hour.'

My heart sank. Now he was finally in front of me, his sudden departure was devastating.

He was halfway across the room when he turned. 'I'll see you Monday, girl. Be good. And if you can't be good, be careful. And if you can't be careful, name it after me.' He threw back his head and chortled loudly.

Then he left, and all the oxygen went with him.

That night, I had dinner with Sunny and Eddie in their flat.

Sunny's first single had been released the previous week and was getting serious radio play. As soon as I walked in, she threw her arms around me.

'We're number 43 in the charts!' she announced. 'This is a celebration.'

We went into the kitchen, where Eddie popped the cork on a bottle of Moët & Chandon and poured three glasses.

'I've heard "Bedroom Eyes" on Radio Luxembourg quite a few times in the last week,' I told her, taking a sip. 'It's already playing in my head, driving me mad.'

'You have to come if we get invited on *Top of the Pops*. Imagine how they'd react at Chatham.'

'There'd be a mutiny.'

'If Dewsnap hadn't been such a cow, we wouldn't be here now. So I'm dead grateful to her, personally.'

I clinked glasses with her. 'I'm thrilled for you, Sun.'

Her face was glowing with happiness. 'Come in and sit down.'

Things had changed in their flat since my last visit. There was a plush sofa in the living room, and a glass-topped coffee table.

'The record company gave me an advance,' Sunny explained.

'Just don't let Ritchie see all this. He'll call in the Bolsheviks,' I said, as we sank into the red velvet cushions.

I gave her an only slightly edited version of my news, although her enthusiasm evaporated when I mentioned Ramsey.

'Ari, you know he's married,' she said.

I shrugged. What did that matter? I'd put the icy voice on the phone out of my mind long ago.

'I'm only working with him, not shagging him.'

Sunny gave me a cool glare. 'Do you think I'm thick? I didn't live in the same tiny space with you for three months and not pick up on how you constantly dropped his name in random conversations!'

Embarrassed, I smiled at her. 'Oh god, did I? But, Sunny, he's unlike anyone I've ever met.'

'And he's so old.' Sunny continued. 'He's already been married twice, and he's had a million girlfriends.'

I wanted to say, 'Probably because he hasn't found the right one.'

But not wanting to jinx my chances, I shut up.

SIXTEEN

London, November 1966

Ramsey's studio was a cave of matte black, apart from a white paper backdrop on the central wall that extended several feet along the floor. I perched on an unusual, delicate high-backed chair in the centre of the paper runner, as the hairdresser Gavin put the finishing touches to my hair and Ramsey's assistant, Tommy, fiddled with the lights.

Down at the other end of the room a series of colour prints of Iris Freeman was propped up against the wall. The slight bags under her luminous blue eyes suggested that she had more interesting things to do than sleep at night.

Ramsey followed my gaze. 'Yeah. Iris: beautiful, no? I've never met anyone who is more loved by the camera. Though she's beginning to look a bit tired lately. I mean she's getting on, she's nearly twenty-five.' The way he said it did make her sound ancient.

Seated on a stool behind the camera, he studied me dispassionately, as if I were an insect under a microscope.

I remembered that piercing look of his from the day he visited Thurston. Determined not to be intimidated, I stared back, unblinking. After a second, he nodded, as if satisfied.

'Right. Thanks Gavin. She's ready.' He picked up the camera and began giving orders. 'Sit facing me, leaning forward. That's it. Careful with that chair, it's a signed Charles Henry Macintosh.'

Just like that, the moment had arrived. Everyone else stepped back. Sophie stood by the rack of clothes. Gavin waited just out of camera-view. Tommy fiddled with the lenses.

I sat stiffly, my chin tilted up.

Working with Antoine Boucher had been very different. We had dreamed up a story together without even exchanging words. Perhaps it had been a fluke, magicked up by the dramatic location, but the photographs had real atmosphere.

Here in the studio, where the focus was so much more intense, I knew that even small gestures and expressions could look overly theatrical and absurd. But I soon discovered that Ramsey was more directive than Antoine had been, to the point of wanting to control my every tiny movement.

I felt frustrated and awkward. Nothing I did seemed to please him.

Ramsey frowned into the viewfinder of his Rolleiflex and barked orders at me, as my face reddened.

'What's going on, kid?' he demanded after a few minutes. 'Why are you so uptight? I thought you were meant to be this free spirit?'

'I would be if you let me,' I snapped back.

Ramsey laughed and ducked behind the camera again.

Click... Click... Click...

'Much better,' he said. 'I've woken you up finally. Move your chin a little to the left. That's it. Perfect!'

He looked up from the camera again, 'It's looking a bit forced. Try sitting the way you would at home. Yeah, slouch. Great.'

But the moment of approval was too brief, and soon Ramsey's dark mood returned. Sophie and Gavin were constantly interrupting the flow of the shoot in order to fix my hair or powder my nose. Ramsey put up with it for a while but suddenly he flipped and threw them both out of the studio. Then he banished Tommy to the darkroom.

I blinked at him, intimidated for the first time.

'My bite is worse than my bark,' he said, scowling. 'Actually, this mess is your fault for not doing exactly as I say.'

I cleared my throat. 'Is this a Ruth Etting record you're playing?'

He gave me a surprised glance. 'Yeah, you know her? No one else seems to. There's something touching about her voice.'

He picked up the camera. 'I hate pop music,' he added, turning up the volume on the gramophone with his free hand. 'Now, OK. Give me that look of yours again.'

I tilted my head. 'What look?'

'That fuck-me look.'

I blushed and I felt my mouth twitching.

He put his head back and laughed like a macaw. And then, a minute later, he was glowering like he hated me.

'I think we got something good today,' Ramsey told me as he set his cameras on a table. 'You've got potential, you know. Sometimes you look like you're from outer space, sometimes like a Disney character.'

'Thanks,' I said. 'I think.'

He smiled and grabbed my hand.

'I've been meaning to ask,' he said, lowering his voice. 'Have you got a boyfriend?'

I shook my head.

'Why not?'

My mouth went dry.

'I haven't met anyone I want to be with,' I said, after a pause that lasted too long.

'Until now,' he said softly, his gaze locked on mine.

It was a joke. It had to be. But my body was blazing.

Then he disappeared upstairs to his living quarters, and seconds later, Bob Dylan was blasting through the walls.

I'd been dismissed.

Downstairs in the office, Dani, Ramsey's secretary, called a taxi to collect Gavin, Sophie and me.

The office walls were covered in framed black and white photographs from his book, *Sixties Unbound*. These included the famous moody shots of the Rolling Stones at Stonehenge. Iris, again, in an evening dress, dancing with Fred Astaire. Agneta Luzzatto, smiling seductively in a marble bath full of spaghetti, her nipples poking through the strands.

'That one was taken at the Hassler in Rome,' Tommy told me, when he saw me looking at it. 'The staff used every pan in the kitchen to cook all the pasta at five in the morning before the breakfast orders started coming in. First the chef made the mistake of adding tomato sauce, which looked like blood clots in the photograph. So they had to do it all over again using just plain spaghetti with olive oil.'

The phone rang, and Dani picked it up. She listened for a minute and then said, 'Ramsey's in India most of January. He has a few time slots in April when he might be able to come to New York. After that, he's booked through June.'

Just then Ramsey appeared at the door, brandishing some contact sheets. He handed them to Sophie. 'Look at these.'

She flipped through them quickly, and then lifted her eyes to meet mine, and gave me a delighted nod. 'They're great.'

'They're more than great,' he corrected. 'They're brilliant. I knew it.' He turned to me. 'Listen, Ari, I need your help. Do you mind staying here for an hour or two?'

My heart began to race. 'Sure,' I said, as casually as I could.

Sophie looked concerned, but before she could speak, Ramsey grabbed my wrist and pulled me close to him. 'She'll be fine. I'll bring her back in one piece.'

I saw Gavin exchange a glance with Sophie, but by then Ramsey was hurrying me away up the stairs.

'What's going on?' I asked, as we arrived in Ramsey's living quarters.

'I've got an idea,' he told me without breaking his stride. 'If it works, they'll pay you, of course. And it will work.'

A few minutes later I was sprawled on a Persian rug in Ramsey's black sitting room, sipping champagne. On various perches, four solemn boys in their late teens with long straggly hair and tight bellbottoms were arrayed around me. Ramsey stood on a ladder above us, shooting the scene.

'Come on, boys,' he cajoled, 'this is your bloody album cover, not mine. Try to look lively. What's the name of the single again? 'A Whiter Shade of Pale'? That's fitting.' Ramsey laughed.

Click... Click... Click...

In between shots, I glanced around. Ramsey's sitting room was crammed full of paintings, photographs, tribal masks, ethnic textiles. The overall effect might have been overwhelming if there hadn't been a thirties-style mirror covering one entire wall, making the room seem twice its actual size. In front of the mirror, on a broad table covered with a cobalt-blue cut-velvet cloth, a collection of old stone and bronze statues of Hindu gods, goddesses and Buddhas flanked small gold-framed head shots of Iris Freeman, Agneta Luzzato, and Liz Watson, the model in a recent *Vogue* spread, like deities on an altar.

The album cover shoot only lasted an hour. As soon as Ramsey put the camera down, the band said their goodbyes and were off downstairs into a waiting Daimler.

Ramsey took my hand and pulled me up from where I was sitting the floor. For the second time today, he looked pleased.

'You were great, darling, thank you,' he told me, as he poured another glass of champagne. 'You have such expressive eyes. Everything you did today looked fucking fantastic. *Vogue* will be happy. The band will be happy. Great work, girl.'

He sat down next to me on the chesterfield, so close the sides of our legs were touching. So close I felt dizzy.

He handed me the champagne and poured himself a neat whiskey from the bottle on the coffee table in front of us. 'I could make you as big as Iris, you know that? People might have laughed at you ten years ago, but you are perfect for now.'

'Come on,' I said, doubtfully.

'No, really,' he insisted. 'The English rose is over. The girl next door is too. It's time for something cooler; quirkier.' He took my hand. 'Will you work with me?'

I nodded, attempting to appear calm.

I wanted to say more. 'I think you're a genius. I think I'm in love with you and I have been ever since I met you.' But I didn't dare. And yet, I got the feeling he knew.

His fingers threaded through mine. I felt sick with desire, and a certain amount of dread.

I don't know what I expected – for him to kiss me, I suppose. Instead, he glanced at his watch.

'Shit. I'm going to be late for dinner. You'll need a lift, won't you? Listen, I'll drop you off at a taxi rank on the way. Is that OK?'

Deflated, I dropped his hand.

'Sure, that'd be great,' I said, tonelessly.

A few minutes later we were gliding noiselessly down Baker Street in his Rolls.

'Are you a Buddhist or a Hindu?' I asked breaking several minutes of excruciating silence.

'No, I'm not into any religion, I just like the art. You can buy great stuff in India for nothing. You should come with me some time.'

Come with him? It was the kind of thing people said to be nice. Though 'nice' was hardly a Ramsey trait.

With his eyes still on the road, Ramsey reached out for my hand and squeezed it hard. Ever since the incident with Niall, whenever I got close to a man, disgust and fear overwhelmed me. Now, while there was still fear, for the first time, love and desire were stronger. With slow deliberation, I pulled his hand up to my lips, and kissed the middle of his palm, inhaling the strangely familiar smell of his skin.

Ramsey turned the wheel hard, veering into a side street. As soon as the car stopped moving, he pulled me into his arms.

I had pushed down every kind of hunger for so long, now my desire for him was so ferocious that there was nothing else in the world, and where we were didn't matter.

My dress was unzipped and half off when he suddenly stopped.

'Ari, listen. I can't do this. Not now. You're so beautiful... But I promised to meet someone.'

I recoiled but he held me tightly.

'No, listen. We broke up but she's still in love with me. I don't want to hurt her more than I have.'

'Your wife?' I said, confused.

'Oh no,' he said. 'That's been over for years. This is someone else. Liz.'

He was being honourable, telling me the truth. It was physically painful to disengage from him, but I could wait.

He dropped me off at a taxi rank outside the Connaught Hotel and pressed a fiver into my hand to cover the fare.

'I'm sorry I can't take you all the way home, but I'm late. I'll call you soon, yeah?'

I watched as his car turned into Mount Street towards Berkeley Square and disappeared into the night.

Two weeks passed. Felicity told me *Vogue* loved the photos, and that the band was using the image taken that day on the cover of their single. But there was no word from Ramsey. I was sick with anxiety. Had I said the wrong thing? Done the wrong thing? Been too forward? Too weird? Was it the person he'd gone to meet that night – the one who wasn't his wife?

The one thing I would not do was phone him. I'd rather be alone forever than appear as needy as I felt. Instead I mooned about, reading poetry – 'The Wasteland' by Eliot spoke to me, even though I had no idea what any of it meant – and eating as little as possible to try and numb my feelings. Sometimes I hung out with Anna and Solveig, who were sweet to me, and never asked questions.

Sunny, on the other hand, was in the middle of a whirlwind of press and TV appearances. The one time I visited her, she was too distracted to talk. She wore a brand-new bright blue and white shift from Tuffin and Foale with black tights and slightly naff white vinyl boots, which she managed to pull off. A mountain of backpacks and drum and guitar cases was piled in the hall, and there was a smell of bacon frying in the kitchen. Sunny's mum, Pat – recently discharged from hospital and now staying with Sunny and Eddie – was making lunch. Two members of the Knee Tremblers, Sunny's new band, were sprawled out on the sofa in the sitting room smoking a joint and staring at the BBC test card, badly hung over from a gig the night before in Brighton.

'Eddie just heard… we've leapfrogged 24 places in a week to number 11,' she screeched.

She grabbed me and I mustered just enough energy to jump up and down with her like we were thirteen-year-olds. The band members put their hands over their ears and groaned. I resisted the bacon butty that Pat tried to press on me, and soon left to wander around the bleak December streets on my own.

At last the phone rang. On the other end came a clipped, but friendly female voice.

'This is Dani calling from Bill Ramsey's office. I have Ramsey on the line for you.'

The phone clicked. My heart stopped for a few moments, then jackhammered.

'Ari, listen, kid – can you meet me in Paris in two days? I've got a couple of jobs to do there, and you'd be perfect for them. For *Elle* and French *Vogue*, on the 22nd and 23rd. Don't get your hopes up for millions, magazines are all fucking cheap. But there's nothing wrong with a free trip to Paris. And we could have dinner on the 22nd, yeah?'

I tried to sound offhand, but my voice was shaking when I replied: 'Sure. That'd be great.'

I had no idea if Ramsey was pleased or not, because Dani came back on and said she would call Felicity to make the necessary arrangements.

Back in my room, I stared at the unmade bed, the clothes strewn across the floor and the sunless sky through the dormer window. Nothing had changed, and everything had changed. Euphoria was heady, blissful, but also slightly alarming; like being driven by a crazy person in a fast car.

SEVENTEEN

Paris, December 1966

The *Elle* studio in Paris was full of people desperate to leave on their Christmas breaks. Simone, the senior *Elle* Magazine fashion editor had six outfits to shoot and a mutiny on her hands. She looked me up and down. 'You are *Rrrramsey*'s model?' she asked, with apparent incredulity.

Then she delivered the devastating news; Ramsey had been delayed in Italy due to a snowstorm in the Alps. Naff *yé-yé* music was playing through the speakers in the dressing room. I sat in front of a big garishly lit mirror while the hairdresser singed my hair with hot tongs.

It was all very impersonal but, now that I was working, I found I could take refuge in a neutral place – like an inner bus station – where nothing bothered me; not even Ramsey's absence.

Then Simone announced they couldn't wait any longer, and that Antoine Boucher, who lived nearby, was on his way to take over the shoot. Antoine appeared, dressed like a vagabond, and carrying a bottle of champagne. I was pleased to see him and we had a laugh about our visit to the police station a few months back.

Later on, after we'd completed a couple of shots outside in the falling snow, Antoine looked at me through narrowed eyes.

'*Que prends-tu? Pourquoi tu n'est pas froid?*'

I just laughed. 'We English are tough. You discovered that on our first shoot.'

Unconvinced, he pulled me back into the warmth of the studio and draped a coat across my shoulders. '*Non. Tu es amoureux,*' he guessed, with disapproval.

I flushed crimson and denied I was in love with anyone. But Antoine teased and cajoled until Simone mentioned that Ramsey had been meant to do this shoot.

Antoine put two and two together.

'*Non*, darling, *pas lui*,' he said, shaking his head. '*Tout le monde dit que je suis mauvais, mais Ramsey est un espèce de con. Vraiment.*'

'Steady on, Antoine. Nothing has happened, anyway,' I insisted.

But he wouldn't give up. I ducked his advice and dodged his questions until finally he said, revealing he knew more English than I thought; '*Bien sur*, you fuck who you want, Ari, but Ramsey is not a good man to love. *Retourne a l'école* and learn to do something useful.'

'You sound like my mother.'

'*Pas de tout... Ce n'est pas le morale, c'est la sagesse!*'

His warning sent a chill through me. But Antoine seemed to believe he'd done his part and, after that, he dropped the subject and focused on his work.

By the time we finished, it was dark outside, and the ground was thick with snow.

When he left, Antoine kissed both my cheeks. Taking a small Leica out of his pocket, he asked if he could take a candid photograph of me. 'Later, when it's over with that *espèce de merde*, I will send you the photo from today to remind you what you were before.'

With that, he walked out into the snow.

Of course he was jealous, I reasoned. Antoine was a good photographer but not in the same league as Ramsey.

As the taxi took me to my hotel, I stared out the window, lost in thought. I liked Antoine. I trusted him. His judgement mattered to me. But he was clearly wrong about Ramsey.

Felicity had booked me into a Left Bank hotel called L'Alcyone. According to her, all the models stayed there when they were in Paris, so I envisaged something glamorous, with Perspex and white leather interiors. What I actually found was a battered sign and a shabby lobby with an unmanned front desk. When the concierge finally appeared a few long minutes after I rang the bell, she looked annoyed at being disturbed.

She gave me the key to a third-floor room, which had peeling, nicotine-stained wallpaper and a tiny bathroom behind a flimsy PVC partition.

I put my bag down and surveyed the sagging bed with dismay, then, after throwing on another jumper, headed straight back out into the street.

Paris was particularly beautiful covered in snow. Tiny lights, like little stars, wrapped around every naked branch of every tree in the Place des Vosges to magical effect. I suddenly felt unexpectedly homesick.

At Thurston, a ten-foot Christmas tree would be up in the front hall by now, hung with the glass decorations Papa had been collecting all his life. It was two days until Christmas Eve: preparations would be under way for that night, when guests of all ages would arrive for dinner, dressed in their best, drinking champagne while the choir from the village stood on the grand staircase to sing carols.

For the first time, I wondered if I'd made a mistake coming to Paris instead of going home.

As I sat alone in an almost empty café, picking at a plate of crudités with my coat draped over my shoulders, it occurred to me that if I went to the airport now, I could request a seat on a plane to London early the next morning, and be home before everyone woke up. The idea was almost unbearably tempting.

But I'd agreed to do this shoot, and I was going to finish it.

When I returned to L'Alcyone, shaking snow from my hair, the concierge handed me a message from French *Vogue*. I was to be at the studio early the next morning for make-up and hair.

I lay down on the lumpy bed again and stared at the damp patches on the wallpaper, trying to forget Antoine's parting words.

'You come in alone, and you go out alone, so you might as well get used to it,' Jules had commented, rather brutally, when I confessed to feeling lonely after moving into the models' house. This wasn't exactly loneliness, though. I didn't usually mind my own company. I simply felt I would never be complete until I was with Ramsey. Sometimes there was a kind of deep pleasure associated with longing for him, but tonight it was excruciating.

Awake most of the night with turbulent thoughts, I managed to get to sleep at dawn and slept through my alarm. So I was already panicking about being late, and slightly hysterical, by the time the taxi arrived the next morning.

French *Vogue* was hidden away in a maze of back streets. It turned out the taxi driver had never been there. We both scanned the buildings for any sign of it and he was fuming when eventually I spied a tarnished bronze plaque next to an unprepossessing door.

On the other side of it, I found a cobblestone courtyard and a lovely eighteenth-century *hôtel particulier* with pale blue shutters and an ancient bare vine crisscrossing the façade. On the main boulevards the previous night's snowfall had already been churned into slush, but here it was still pristine and half a foot deep on the windowsills and dark green hedges.

I was absurdly late by now, and the receptionist pointed me to the stairs. '*Vite, vite! Monsieur* wants to see you *immediatement.*'

I assumed she meant another photographer and felt sick with disappointment. But when I reached the landing, breathless from anxiety, the door swung open and Bill Ramsey was looking at me sternly, dark shadows under his eyes.

'Ramsey!' Sudden joy flooded my body with sunlight.

'You're late… again! Unprofessional bird! I was on time; and I had to drive all the way from Milan on freezing bloody roads. We have four hours to shoot before I fly back to London. No seats on later planes. Fucking Christmas!'

I just beamed at him.

Ramsey turned and shouted over his shoulder: 'Françoise, get Ari ready, toot sweet. Tell the hairdresser not to mess around.' He glanced back at me, all business. 'I hope the studio assistant knows what he's doing because it's obvious no one else here does.'

In the dressing room, a row of futuristic mini dresses and trouser suits hung on a rack. Cut from a new space-age cloth that didn't crease, the sleeveless dresses had matching jackets in primary colours, like egg-yolk yellow and emergency red. One dress was like an erotic space suit, with two huge portholes cut out down each side. We were in such a rush there was no time to think about it. While I drew exaggerated eyelashes under my bottom lid in brown pencil once again, the hairdresser pinned up my hair and eased a white Dynel wig onto my head, blunt cut in a bob. I looked in the mirror and thought, you can be whoever you want. After so many years of self-consciousness, it felt as though the only way through this was to gather everything I had ever felt inside and give it to the camera, no holds barred. Look at him directly. Be a leopard, not a spaniel.

I zipped up my white boots and headed to the studio.

As I walked in, Ramsey was lighting one cigarette with the butt of another. He gave my outfit a dubious look. 'White plastic boots. Only a Frenchman could have come up with those.'

'*Alors, simplement, c'est le futur,*' Françoise the stylist told him.

Ramsey picked up a camera and studied me through the lens. 'It's funny how everyone thinks the future will be streamlined, when actually it's much more likely people will be wearing rags and cardboard on their feet,' he said.

'What do you mean?' I asked.

'I mean when there are too many people in the world and not enough food or resources to go round. It's going to happen, you know. You and I'll probably be dead by then, but our children's children will look at *Vogue* pages, if any survive that aren't being used for toilet paper, the way we look at illuminated manuscripts. So, we better make 'em good, even if they are only fucking fashion photographs.' He pointed. 'See that mark? I want you to run from left to right and jump in the air when you get to it... No! I said left to right! I thought you were meant to be intelligent!'

I ran, and I jumped. Over and over again.

There was so much adrenaline in my system that with every jump, I managed to soar a couple of inches higher. The PE teacher at Chatham would have been astonished.

'You know how to get up there, but you land like a baby hippo,' Ramsey observed, 'The whole studio shakes.'

But he had the shot, and I could tell he was pleased. Françoise removed the wig and brushed my hair straight, touching up my powder. The next few outfits were successively more revealing until we got to the porthole dress. There was no getting away from it, jumping in that dress was going to be tricky. I didn't care about exposing my almost flat chest, but without knickers? I couldn't imagine it.

When I got back into the studio, though, instead of feeling exposed, I felt liberated, glowing inside and out. It wasn't just a crush I had on Ramsey: it was absolutely, indisputably love. I had nothing to fear. I was running, jumping, turning, effortlessly, tuning into the very moment Ramsey clicked the shutter, and trusting him to worry about how the dress fell on my body.

After a few rolls, Ramsey left his camera and came over to fix my hair, which was by now all over my face. I was already breathless from all the jumping, but when his hand brushed over my lips, I stopped breathing altogether.

He leaned closer. 'If I cancel my flight, will you spend Christmas with me?' he whispered.

I forgot about Thurston. My homesickness evaporated. My reply was instant.

'Yes.'

117

EIGHTEEN

Paris, December 1966

An hour later, Ramsey and I were sitting side by side on a banquette in an almost-empty La Coupole, drinking champagne. Neither of us had eaten all day and he had only managed two hours of sleep on the long drive from Italy. We held hands and looked into each other's eyes. Small talk seemed pointless, but the silence was too fraught with desire to be comfortable.

In any case, what to say to your lover before he has become your lover? Before you have 'lost' your virginity? There was no manual for that one. When the *soupe de poisson* arrived, neither of us could manage more than a few mouthfuls.

Ramsey threaded his fingers through mine. 'Where are you staying, Ari?'

When I told him, he looked disgusted. 'That is the most depressing hotel in Paris. Who put you there? We can stay with my French agent. It's much better than that.' He went off to make a phone call.

Now that it was dark outside, the restaurant was beginning to fill up. To be in a place without any old associations was such a relief: the warm lighting, the effects of the champagne, the low-key festive atmosphere could not have been more pleasant; cosy even. Still, I couldn't shake off the same sick feeling as before a dentist's appointment. The clock was ticking slowly and inexorably towards the moment of reckoning.

Out on the street, we stopped to kiss several times in the cold. By now I was shivering with desire, fear and cold, unable to distinguish one from the other.

Ramsey had parked a short distance away, and we drove down the Boulevard Saint-Germain under arching tiaras of Christmas lights; crossed over the black and gold waters of the Seine at the Place de la Concorde and turned up the garish Champs

Élysées, crowded with holiday revellers. At the Arc de Triomphe, there was traffic mayhem. Some cars virtually stopped in the middle of the road, causing complete chaos, other cars cut straight across our path, from both sides. Momentarily loud booms and crackling sounds rang out above us, and then silver and gold fireworks spurted out of the top of the Eiffel Tower into the night sky.

'Life imitating sex,' said Bill. 'Too bad we missed the foreplay.'

I shrank down into the seat with embarrassment.

Bertrand's house was shrouded in darkness when we pulled up outside. I was glad he wasn't there; small talk with a stranger would have been out of the question, under the circumstances. Even so, Ramsey had to fish around in the wet bushes for some time before he found the key, by which time we were both nearly frozen.

The stairs squeaked as we climbed, both unable to think of anything to say. My mouth was dry from all the champagne, and I desperately wanted to pee, but was too embarrassed to ask Ramsey where the WC was.

We were making for the top of the house, and he was a few steps ahead of me when I saw a door on the half landing that looked like it could have been a bathroom, so I darted across and turned the door handle, feeling for the light switch on the inside wall with my hand. A rustling sound followed by the most piercing screams ensued and echoed throughout the house. Horrified, I slammed the door shut at once. This did not reassure the occupant of the room, who wailed loudly in a foreign language. Ramsey came bounding down the stairs again. 'Ari, for fuck's sake, what were you doing barging into the housekeeper's room?'

He knocked on her door. 'Fatima, Bill Ramsey here. Remember? *Ami* of Bertrand. We stay upstairs tonight. Sorry to frighten you. My girlfriend is *très stupide*!' Though he smiled at me as he said it. His French was worse than Miss Bolton's.

Seconds later, a small brown-skinned woman with curly black hair appeared at the door with a blanket pulled round her, looking utterly terrified. Ramsey brandished the front door key at her, while I apologised profusely and lamely, and then ran up the stairs.

'We've been together for a few hours and it already feels like years,' Ramsey said when he appeared a few minutes later, after he had reassured Fatima – again – that all was well. He turned the light on in the landing and pointed to the bathroom.

After sitting on the loo unable to pee for some time, the only way I could relax enough to get a flow going was to run the bath. Afterwards I took off my clothes and climbed in the tub. My teeth were chattering, and I wondered if I was coming down with flu. My body felt as if it belonged to someone else. I reminded myself that Sunny had done this a while ago and had survived.

'Are you all right in there, girl?' Ramsey turned the handle, but I had locked the door. 'Won't be a minute!' I called out, as cheerfully as I could manage. I soaped my alien body all over: at least I'd be clean.

Would it hurt? Stabbing hurt or stinging hurt? Would Ramsey call a taxi to take me back to the Alcyone afterwards? The only way I could imagine surviving the first few minutes without fainting was to rustle up all my courage and move first, like a ninja. Taking several deep breaths I got out, grabbed a towel from the neatly folded pile on the shelf above the bath, and dried myself vigorously, hoping to get some circulation going. Then I wrapped the towel around my torso and unlocked the door.

The only source of light in the room came from a Moroccan table lamp next to the bed, which projected teardrops of light in a swirled pattern onto the ceiling and walls. Ramsey was standing in the darkness at the far end of the room with his back to me, naked, looking out of the window. He had only just begun to turn around when I launched myself at him from behind, dropping my towel and nearly knocking him over in the process, before covering him with kisses. There was a stunned pause before he swivelled to face me, his eyes blazing. He caught my wrists in his hands and pushed me down onto the bed.

Afterwards we lay entwined. At last, I felt relaxed about the silence between us, though a wet patch under my leg felt very wet indeed. I wasn't at all sure if Ramsey had even realised what had happened. I had moaned like a trooper throughout, having seen and heard enough sex in films and through the walls of the Consulate to at least know what passion sounded like. The thing that most excited me was having his undivided attention at last.

The sex had been OK, though obviously I had nothing to compare it to. There had been a brief sense of having a battering ram inside me, followed by an inner wall giving way and the surrender into light. Even though I still had no idea how we got there, his climax was reassuring. It clearly hadn't been terrible for him. Afterwards he held me in his arms and fell asleep immediately.

From the vantage point of his chest, in the faint glow from the lamp behind us, I could see his corduroy jeans and army-green work shirt thrown over a cane planter's chair, and his black Cuban boots lying on their sides on the Persian rug. At an oblique angle, a small slice of the night sky was visible through the window. The only sound in the room was Ramsey's breathing, though at some point church bells rang out wildly from several directions around the house and then came the burr and whizz of more fireworks.

The most remarkable discovery was the familiarity of Ramsey's body next to mine, as if we had been reunited after a long period of separation. My limbs were his limbs, his skin was my skin. It was as if, in a few brief minutes, Ramsey had exorcised all the fear and shame that had lodged in me since the horrible incident with Niall. I felt released, certain that something out of the ordinary had occurred; something that bound me to Ramsey for ever.

I was still awake a few hours later when he stirred. With a yawn, he rose and walked to the bathroom. When he came back to bed and lifted the top sheet, I saw the shock on his face when he saw the blood on the white linen.

'What's this?'

I didn't quite know how to explain. He looked at me, bewildered.

'Fucking hell! Don't tell me you're a virgin.'

'Was.'

There was a pause, and then he laughed, not unkindly. He got into bed and pulled me close.

'God, Ari. You should have told me. I had no idea. Seriously, how old are you?'

'I told you, seventeen.'

'That's old for a virgin. Anyway, I'm glad it was with me,' he said. 'I hope I didn't hurt you.'

He had a bit, but I wasn't about to admit it. Instead, I told him honestly, 'I wanted it to be you from the moment I met you.'

Soon we were making love again.

When I finally got to sleep, dawn was breaking across the sky.

The next few days were infused with a sense of soaring elation and extraordinary beauty. I remember shafts of winter sunlight falling across our bed, the deserted arcades, winter trees in the Jardin de Luxembourg; every sound, every sight, every taste we shared was subsumed into bliss.

Somewhere in a far-off universe, Maud, Papa, Violet and Pav, even Sunny existed, like pale insubstantial ghosts. Only Ramsey seemed real to me. His sturdy body, sensuous lips and sharp brown eyes that missed nothing, and which visibly softened when he looked at me.

We couldn't keep our hands off each other; we flowed into each other and filled each other up until there was nothing held back. We ordered meals in restaurants we couldn't eat, kissed in the back of cinemas and missed the film we had wanted to see; we trawled the jazz clubs in the early hours, drinking Calvados. The mere fact of being alone together in Paris in the empty days between Christmas and New Year intensified our feelings.

It had become clear to me why people went on so much about sex and love. For me, life made sense at last.

I had punished my body for so long: starved it; cursed it. And now love released me from a cage of self-hatred.

I never told Bill what had happened in Manchester to scare me off love and sex for so long. That day lurked in a dark warren of corridors and dressing rooms in a rotting building in my mind. Even though he did ask about my past. He found my virginity a source of fascination.

'Did no boy ever try to fuck you?' he asked one day.

'Not really,' I said. 'When I was growing up, I went to an all-girls school. I didn't really know any boys except for Julius and he was backwards like me.'

His brow creased. 'Do you mean sexually repressed?'

'Would you call me sexually repressed?' I climbed into his lap and kissed him passionately. 'The thing is, whenever I fancied someone in the past, they never seemed to fancy me and vice versa. And then I met you.'

He ran his hands down the straight lines of my body. 'God, if only I had known it in that stable yard.'

I smiled. 'You were too busy coming on to my sister.'

'Oh, that was just a bit of fun. I could tell she was a goer. Besides, you were a bit young for me then. Seventeen is much more reasonable than sixteen.'

I didn't mention the age gap between us. I liked the fact he was older. It meant so much that he wanted to be with me when he could have had anyone.

Everything was perfect, until the thirtieth of December, when Dani, Ramsey's secretary, phoned.

Ramsey was on the phone a long time. When he came upstairs his expression was dark.

When I asked what was wrong, he just said, 'Let's go get something to eat.'

We headed to Le Bar des Théâtres on foot, our collars turned up against the biting wind; the kind that gives you earache and makes your eyes water.

We sat at a table by the window, which was fogged with condensation and cigarette smoke. Ramsey ordered Irish coffee without cream, *oeufs au plat* and *pommes frites*. I ordered coffee.

When the waiter had gone, Ramsey cleared his throat. 'You know how I told you I was booked through April? Jobs for English, French and American *Vogue* in India, and New Zealand? Well, I have to go back to London to get ready. Day after tomorrow.'

'Can I go with you?' I asked, hopelessly.

He stirred his coffee, avoiding my eyes. 'It's difficult. All the fittings have been done on the model. She's been booked for months.'

'Liz?'

He tensed. 'Yes, but listen, Ari, it really is over between her and me. The night I dropped you off at the Connaught, I told her the truth; that I'd met someone. But I can't let her down when it comes to these jobs. She needs the money. I promised her.'

I saw that. I also knew how beautiful Liz was.

Ramsey took my hands in his. 'I want you to live with me as soon as I get back. Will you promise me to wait and not go off with anyone else? I have never been so in love with anyone. I'm going to do my best work with you. I love you and I would never do anything to hurt you.'

You are hurting me now, I thought, but it was too uncool to say so.

NINETEEN

London, New Year 1967

As our time together dwindled, I became obsessed with Ramsey's impending absence. Not just because of who he was going to be with, but also due to all the ways he could possibly be killed or injured. A plane crash in the Himalayas was my principal recurring fantasy: it played on a loop in my head with all the details of his red blood seeping out into white snow, body parts scattered over the mountainside.

When we said goodbye at Orly airport, I finally confessed my fears.

Ramsey found it funny.

'Don't be silly, I won't die, I have far too much to do.'

This was cold comfort, but I almost believed him.

A few hours after he'd gone, I flew back to London alone.

Ramsey and I had decided – or rather Ramsey had insisted – that it would be better not to try to speak on the telephone while he was away. The lines from India were famously bad and international calls were ridiculously expensive.

'Besides, phones always fuck up relationships,' he added.

I wondered how I would get through two months without him.

London was grey and cold. And my life felt hollow without Ramsey in it. I tried to focus on work. According to Felicity, both the *Elle* and French *Vogue* shoots had gone down well with the editors. Which was funny, in a way, because I was so broke I hardly had enough money for a bus fare. The problem was the Paris photos wouldn't appear for months. It felt as if my entire life had been put on hold.

Meanwhile, Sunny's single 'Bedroom Eyes' was charting at No. 3 after her *Top of the Pops* triumph. The tabloids loved her. She was the bouncy, bubbly, fresh young face of pop.

Her humble beginnings were perfect fan fodder. She was portrayed in the press as the unspoiled, working-class girl from Grimsby who overcame all odds to become a singer. Very little was ever mentioned about her dad's success, the move to Alderley Edge, or being expelled from a posh girls' school. She did, however, always refer to her trip to America, and how influenced she had been by Brenda Lee, The Ronettes and Stevie Wonder.

The ultimate proof of Sunny's rising star came when a photograph was published of her drinking tea with John Lennon and Paul McCartney. It had been snapped at a café on Savile Row when The Beatles tried to convince her to join their new record label.

She desperately wanted to sign with them, but Eddie was more cautious, 'You'll get buried under their fame,' he warned her.

I thought he was mad. How could anyone not want to be part of The Beatles' label? But Sunny always gave into him, and this was no exception. She turned the offer down.

We still had a shorthand that cut through the bullshit, though I was careful not to give away my mixed feelings about Eddie. At least he was one hundred per cent on her side. But he was possessive of her in a way that was exceedingly tiresome at times.

By now it was impossible to walk down the street with Sunny as she was constantly stopped and hassled for autographs. Only when Eddie went off to a football match could we sneak out on our own, usually to Alvaro's for lunch where she was fawned over by the *maître d'*. One day, over *insalata tricolore* and a bottle of Valpolicella, I blurted out nearly everything that had happened in Paris – including the mortifying scene after my first night with Ramsey when his manager Bertrand appeared in the bedroom the next morning with a stack of neatly folded clean sheets and wished me a happy Christmas.

Sunny squawked with laughter.

Even though she clearly didn't entirely approve of Ramsey, we were much more on an even footing now that I too finally had a boyfriend. Though Sunny no longer confided much about her sex life, she did mention a slimy DJ on *Top of the Pops* had put his hand up her skirt when the lights went off, just before she was about to go on.

'He caught me so completely by surprise I didn't have time to react. I had to perform a minute later! I was beside myself, though I didn't tell Eddie in case he killed the bloke. But I stormed into the little shite's dressing room and told him off right to his face. He just laughed and made out I was loopy, and he hadn't done anything.'

Then, as an afterthought she added, 'It's such a strange coincidence, Ari. Do you remember that lunchtime dance we went to at the Mannie Palais years ago? It was the same DJ, the one who was up on stage that day.'

I shuddered and pushed my plate of pasta away.

When I got home, I found a message on my bed. Four go-sees had been lined up for the following week, and more were being arranged. The magazine editors were back from their holiday breaks, and word about the shoots I'd done with Ramsey had finally begun to spread. By February, I was working nearly as much as Solveig and Anna.

Not every go-see was a pleasant experience. Once, at an advertising agency off Tottenham Court Road, I was told to put on a tiny bikini and then ordered to stand in front of a group of men, turning a slow circle so they could eye me from all directions. One of them muttered audibly, 'I asked for a pretty girl. This one's too scrawny by half. Get your gear on, darling, thanks. Next!'

When I complained to Felicity, she shrugged. 'That's ad agencies for you. We're talking about a bunch of philistines here. I'm afraid you'll have to get used to this sort of thing if you work in this business.'

There was the raft of groovy photographers with studios in Chelsea who treated every shoot as an opportunity to party, with spliffs circulating and bottles of cheap white wine flowing in the dressing room. Every model I knew had been propositioned or groped by these dickbrains. Sometimes more pressure was applied, especially if the photographer had forked out for dinner or a club, but I was very upfront about being spoken for, so nothing too sinister happened.

I wasn't very popular as a result, but I suspect it was also because of my chronic shyness. I envied girls like Sunny, who was always herself in every situation, and knew how to chat and get on with everyone. I could never work out what to say until I got to know a person well, and in the insane dazzle of nightly parties, gallery openings, restaurant and club life, it was easy to get lost. There were so many intersecting cliques of friends and subcultures, none of which I really fitted into.

The only tribe I really felt at home with were the Aussies at the Consulate, who I still visited when I had time. The first edition of *Gondwanda* had finally been published, and copies were now being hawked by enthusiastic young recruits in every hippie hub between Chelsea and Notting Hill.

The counterculture paper was a sensation from the start, expounding the joys of free love, and the liberal use of weed and hallucinogens; its unique look entirely down to Ritchie's warped imagination and visual genius. His illustrations and drawings covered every inch of paper, including the copy. As a result it wasn't always easy to decipher the articles; it helped to get high to read them.

Robbie was rushed off his feet getting the second issue into shape, so the Consulate was even more chaotic than ever, but everyone was always friendly and welcoming. Except Steven, who, with brutally direct Aussie candour, accused Sunny and me of having become too fucking mainstream and bourgeoise. The worst insult imaginable.

I also had Anna and Solveig, of course; the polar opposites of the Aussies. They were solidly reliable and kind, at a time when I felt the ground beneath my feet was constantly shifting.

One weekend when Anna was working in Paris, Felicity arranged for Solveig to go out with a rich punter connected with Formula One. Soly wasn't particularly keen, but still, she put on the glitz just in case. When she emerged from her bedroom thirty minutes later, her blonde hair was swept up off her face in a French twist and she wore a sophisticated black lace dress from Cindy's treasure trove in the Chelsea Antique market. I was awed by her transformation from fresh country girl into an updated version of Grace Kelly.

The balding middle-aged man who appeared on our doorstep at seven o'clock didn't seem as impressed by Solveig's extraordinary beauty as he should have been.

'All right, darlin'?' he said, coolly looking her up and down before checking out our flat, as if he were casing it.

He struck me as humourless and condescending, but Soly didn't appear to notice. He was exactly the kind of sleazy rich fool who showered Felicity with flowers and crates of champagne in exchange for access to her girls. I gathered they were off to a party at the Playboy Club on Park Lane and then to Aspinall's afterwards.

The next day was Saturday, and I slept in, failing to register when Solveig didn't come home that night. Only when I caught sight of her slinking through the front door at midday, still in evening clothes, with her hair loose and straggly, did alarm bells start ringing. I called out but she went straight to her room. Soon I heard the bath running, and the smell of pine essence filled the house. When she emerged from the bathroom some time later, I found her in the kitchen with a towel turban on her head, running ice cubes over her face and eyes. She was trembling so violently her teeth were chattering.

'Soly.' I stared at her. 'What happened?'

She shook her head, her blue eyes filling with tears.

I put my arms around her and asked again. By now she was crying so hard it was some time before she could speak,

When she finally stopped, I made her a cup of tea and toast and led her to the living room. I wrapped a blanket around her on the sofa. Only then did she speak, her voice husky and low.

'After the party we went somewhere in Mayfair, to a private gambling club on the top floor of a house, with his friends. I was very tired. It was three in the morning, and I wanted to get a taxi home, but Guy said, 'Just one more glass of champagne; I'll drive you home.' So, I agreed.' She looked at me. 'That's the last thing I remember. I woke up in a bed. My clothes were on floor and my head hurting so bad.'

When she came to, the only person in the flat was an intimidating bouncer who spoke no English and seemed keen for her to leave.

I kept my hand on her arm and tried to find the right words.

'Are there any marks on your body? Are you sore…?'

She looked down at the floor, tears streaming.

Jumping up from the sofa, I started for the door.

Solveig looked up at me. 'Where are you going?'

'To get Felicity.'

'No, please. I don't want her knowing this,' she insisted, wide-eyed with alarm.

'She has to know. Her bloody friend did this. And you need to see a doctor.'

'Ari, no! You don't understand.' Solveig looked panic stricken. 'Felicity could drop me if she finds out. She will blame me. You can't tell her, please.'

Solveig described how her parents were struggling to run a small farm, how, after only two years on Felicity's books she had made enough money from modelling to buy her family a decent house and send her little sister to college.

'If I tell my mum, it would make trouble with Felicity. If I tell Felicity, she will make trouble with that man. I don't want.'

It was so easy to get a bad reputation. So easy for things to be twisted and word to spread about a 'difficult' model. Work could disappear as easily it arrived. It sickened me that she felt so trapped, but I didn't want to make things worse so I backed down about telling anyone. Though I did make her promise to come with me to the doctor the next day.

All the models and actresses in London went to Dr Redfield. He was a fixture on the Chelsea restaurant and party scene, so it seemed natural. He was a *bon vivant*, known to be remarkably generous when it came to writing prescriptions. Cindy told me she once went to his office complaining of depression and the doctor offered her a whiskey and soda.

Solveig was terrified about discussing what had happened to her – Dr Redfield was friends with Felicity. She needn't have worried. It took only moments for Dr Redfield to figure it out.

'I'm very sorry to hear this. There's no need to get your gear off. I propose you start on these right away,' he said, cheerfully, passing a packet of birth control pills across his desk to a visibly relieved Solveig. He explained that she should take several at first – just in case. And after that, one a day.

At that moment, though, Dr Redfield turned to me. 'I expect you could use some of these too, Ari,' he said, blithely. 'Right you are. If either of you miss your periods in the next month, come back and see me. I can arrange a safe termination without any difficulty. But take those pills and you'll probably never need one. Give my best to Felicity, won't you?'

TWENTY

London, April 1967

The phone in the model house rang at eight in the morning. When no one else answered it, I kicked off the eiderdown, stumbled into the corridor and picked up the receiver.

'Hello?' My voice was hoarse with sleep. The shoot the day before had gone very late.

'Is that you, Ari?'

I blinked the sleep from my eyes, trying to focus. 'Yes…?'

'It's Ramsey. Remember me?'

I kept my tone cool. 'I'm sorry. What was that name again?'

He laughed. 'Do you still love me?'

'Unfortunately, yes.' I was wide awake now.

'Good. I'm sorry I'm late. I had to stop in New York on the way back from New Zealand. Nightmare. I missed you, darling, every second.'

Late. That was one way of putting it. He'd been due back in March. I should have demanded more of an explanation, but I was too overjoyed to hear from him. Why play games when you truly love someone?

'I missed you, too,' I said, on the edge of tears.

'I was serious when I said I wanted us to live together.' There was an undercurrent of urgency in his voice. 'Pack your things. I'll be over to get you in an hour.'

After throwing everything into a couple of holdalls and tidying the room, I ran to wake Solveig and Anna and tell them what was happening.

'Right now?' Solveig sat up in bed, her blonde hair in a tangle, her expression stricken. 'You're really going?'

Somewhat annoyed by her lack of enthusiasm, I dumped my bags in the hall and knocked on the internal door to Felicity's house, finding my agent in the kitchen, drinking tea, newspapers spread out around her.

'Sorry to bother you,' I said, airily. 'I just wanted you to know I'm moving out. Thank you for everything.'

'What...?' She stared at me, her teacup in mid-air. 'I beg your pardon? Where are you going?'

'Primrose Hill,' I said.

Her forehead crinkled. 'I don't understand what you're saying, Ari. What do you mean?'

Behind me, there was a loud knock on the door. I glanced over my shoulder. 'I've got to run. I'll call you tomorrow and give you my new address.'

I dashed back into our side of the house, but Felicity followed close on my heels. She was right behind me when I opened the door.

Ramsey's eyes swivelled from my face to hers, and his expression hardened. 'Hello, you old bag,' he said, mildly, as if he had been expecting to see her.

'Oh, I think I understand.' Felicity said, stepping in front of me. She was small, but fierce. 'You're not taking her, Bill. She's only seventeen.'

'I don't think this is any of your business,' Ramsey said firmly. 'Ready, Ari?'

I tried to scuttle past Felicity, but she barred my way with an outstretched arm, while attempting to slam the door shut with her other hand. But Ramsey was too quick for her and managed to get the toe of his Cuban boot inside first. He pushed the door wide open with his foot and walked inside so swiftly that Felicity was obliged to take a few steps back, colliding with me.

'This is simply not on, Ramsey,' she said, raising her voice. 'I promised her parents she'd be looked after...'

Ramsey laughed and grabbed me by the hand. 'You should all be relieved I'm not a Rolling Stone,' he told Felicity. 'And, by the way, I'll make sure she'll be looked after. She's going to be the next Iris.'

Felicity said coldly, 'I doubt that very much.'

But Ramsey had already grabbed my bags from the hallway, and we ran to where his car was parked. Before I had a chance to catch my breath, he kissed me passionately against the car door. It was like returning home. All my fears vanished as we drove down the King's Road towards Sloane Square.

*

If I expected to wake up and gently take in my new surroundings, I was wrong. By ten the next morning we were back in the car on our way to collect Francis, a journalist from *The Times*, before heading down to the East End to meet the Kray twins. I had never heard of them but didn't want to sound stupid, so I kept quiet.

We had been making up for lost time most of the night, and though Ramsey was reasonably chirpy, I was bunging on the concealer under my eyes and getting my words all mixed up.

Francis, the writer, turned out to be lovely, with a friendly horse's face and camp mannerisms. I sat in the back seat so he and Ramsey could discuss their tactics. Meanwhile I gazed blearily out the window, trying to catch what they were saying, but with Billie Holliday turned up loud on the back speakers, eavesdropping was difficult. Her mournful voice infused the drive, as all signs of spring – well-advanced in North London – gradually vanished in the absence of any trees or green parks the further east we travelled. It was like the old Pathé newsreels, a world of sepia high streets, with covered markets, Victorian town halls and betting shops. Here and there, a few drab residential tower blocks had sprung up out of a vast maze of narrow two-storey terrace houses that covered the landscape in every direction.

'Yeah, this is near where I grew up,' Ramsey said, parking the car outside a big old pub with a faded sign, depicting two crossed keys. 'My mum still lives round the corner. Nothing much has changed. It's all controlled by the Krays. I was lucky to escape.'

Outside the entrance of the building a couple of muscley yobs stood chatting. Bill grabbed his camera bags from the boot.

'Cheers, Billy,' one of them said casually as we passed.

Ramsey took my hand. 'Just do what I say when we get inside, yeah?' he whispered. 'I should have told you to cover up a bit,' he added, looking down at my skimpy skirt. 'They're very old-fashioned down here.'

I nodded blankly.

The stench of stale beer and cigarette smoke hit us when we came through the door of the pub. As Ramsey, Francis and I walked to the bar, the crowd parted to let us through, and the buzz of voices subsided into silence. Ramsey squeezed my hand.

'I'll have a double Teachers please,' Francis said to the woman behind the bar. 'What would you like, Ari?'

'Bitter lemon, please?'

'We don't do bitter lemon down 'ere, miss; you can 'ave lemonade,' came the brusque reply.

Ramsey ordered a Coke. Francis took out his wallet to pay, when a voice behind us said, 'It's all right, Enid, it's on me.'

We all swivelled around to see a tall, sturdy man in a dark suit and tie. He had a well-oiled mini-pompadour, and a curious set of what looked like double eyebrows over a pair of intensely alert eyes that belied his stiff smile.

'All right, Billy?' He stepped forward and hugged Ramsey, who suddenly seemed like a small boy in contrast.

'Reg, thanks for meeting us,' Ramsey said. 'This is Ari. And Francis.'

Reg turned, looking at me seriously. 'Nice to make your acquaintance. Thanks for coming all the way down to our neck of the woods. What say Albert here takes you up the stairs to meet the rest of the birds? Fearne'll look after ya.'

My heart sank. But Ramsey said. 'Yeah, good idea.'

A huge slab of granite in the form of a man motioned for me to follow him. Upstairs, through a frosted glass saloon door marked 'Ladies Lounge', a cluster of women at the bar stopped talking and turned to look at me. It was like the first day of school except everyone was smoking.

'What's yours, then, love?' said a woman with fluffy bleached blonde hair.

'I'm sorry?' I asked, my voice barely above a whisper.

She smiled, her expression friendly. 'What would you like to drink? I'm 'aving a shandy, but you can 'ave cherry brandy, or whatever you'd like.'

'Oh. I'll have a shandy too, please.'

I sat down with three other women and almost immediately our drinks arrived.

''ow long have you been going out with Billy, then?' one enquired.

'Since Christmas.'

'Oh that's lovely.' She cast a sly smile at the woman next to her. ''E gets around, that one. Each time he comes in with a different bird, dunnee?' She gave a shrill laugh. 'That's Bill for you, though. 'E's got a reputation to live up to.'

The others tittered, and I smiled anxiously and took a sip of my drink.

'Are you Fearne?' I asked, grasping at conversational straws. 'I like your dress.'

Fearne was wearing a low-cut form-fitting dress that accentuated her impressive cleavage, even though the skirt came down to her knees.

'At least it covers me privates,' she said, with a reproachful glance at my bare thighs.

'Oh god, sorry,' I said, tugging at my skirt.

'I thought per-aps you'd been in a dither when you got dressed this morning and forgot you only had yer top on.' The women burst into laughter.

Colour crept up my neck.

The woman next to me patted my arm. 'Don't mind us, we're only having a bit of fun.'

'Cheers,' I said, clinking glasses with Fearne and each of her friends, who no longer seemed as bored as when I first walked in.

It turned out Fearne wasn't the boss's girlfriend.

'Nah, lovey. Not me.' She dropped her voice and whispered, 'His wife topped herself a few months after they married. She was only twenty-four. Lovely girl. Don't say I told you.'

I was shocked and cast around desperately for a less delicate line of conversation.

'And Ronnie... is he married?' I inquired of Reg's brother.

Fearne and the other women tittered.

'Where do you come from then, bleedin' Mars?' Fearne said, staring at me with outright disbelief.

'I'm actually from the countryside near Oxford,' I said.

'Oh yeah? Never been,' said Fearne, in a tone that indicated she'd never go there or anywhere else outside the East End unless forced.

It was teatime when Ramsey finally came up to get me. He put his arm around me as we walked back to the Rolls, waving at Francis, who was catching a lift back to Fleet Street on the back of a motorbike with one of Ronnie Kray's minders. He looked both thrilled and terrified as he sailed past us.

'How'd you get on?' Ramsey asked, opening the door for me.

'Let's go *home*,' I told him.

TWENTY-ONE

London, July 1967

It shouldn't have worked, but it did. After the strange start, Ramsey and I wheeled blissfully about in the thermals together. Icarus's fate, which had made quite an impression when I read the Greek myths with Miss Bolton, never even occurred to me. Why would it, when for the first time, I had found my true place in the world? Every morning I woke up in his arms feeling his love transforming me, light radiating from my skin and my eyes. I'd never felt beautiful before, but now I did. The photos from the Paris shoot came out, and I was suddenly besieged with offers of work.

I no longer skipped meals, and even took pride in a slightly more rounded figure. Ramsey and I travelled constantly, to location shoots in Scotland, Hydra and Turkey, to the collections in Paris and Milan for numerous fashion magazines. Everywhere we went, we were treated like stars; celestial twins.

Our schedule varied greatly according to jobs and travel; no day was ever the same. His assistants Dani and Tommy were constants, coming into work every weekday, making sure everything ran like clockwork.

Ramsey's house was on four levels – a kitchen and dining room in the basement, his studio on the first floor with a model's dressing room on the half landing above it, and his private quarters on the top two floors. When Ramsey was working, if I was off, I could relax in the privacy of the flat, knowing he was nearby. I felt safe and at home in his world, and though it was very much his world, everyone accepted me as part of it.

The only bit of the house I avoided from day one was the garden; a dank ghetto of cages for up to sixty parrots. Unsurprisingly, they seemed miserable, far from their native habitats. Birds had been Ramsey's hobby since he was a child, but he was usually too busy to spend much time with them. Dani ended up cleaning out the cages and removing any corpses. Even after catching bird flu, Ramsey could not be persuaded to give them up.

Julius stayed with us for a few days during his summer holidays, intending to write an article for *Punch*; not that he got much writing or anything else done. The volume of traffic through the house at all hours of the day and night was endlessly distracting. No matter how late we'd been out the previous evening, Ramsey was up early and looking through contact sheets, ready to bark orders at Dani as soon as she arrived.

By mid-morning the doorbell was ringing, heralding the arrival of editors, models, hairdressers, and couriers dropping off clothes for the shoot, or sealed boxes of colour prints from Soho Darkrooms. Most days after work, Tommy, Dani, and whoever Ramsey invited from the shoot all congregated in the sitting room for drinks. Then we'd head out to meet friends or clients in restaurants and clubs.

After a few days of this routine, Jules, a seasoned drinker, complained he needed a liver transplant. Unfortunately, he didn't get on well with Ramsey. The two of them each had strongly held opinions, and they frequently argued late into the night. Ramsey could be childish and insulting if he felt like he wasn't winning, and I found my loyalties torn.

On the morning before he left to stay with his parents, Jules invited me to join him on a walk around the neighbourhood, and on the way back, he pointed out a small house. 'Did you know that's where Sylvia Plath died?'

'Who's that?' I asked.

Jules told me about the American poet, and her doomed love for Ted Hughes. How their relationship turned into a battleground, with Hughes controlling her, and Plath fighting for air, until finally she gave up the struggle.

'Another casualty of misplaced love for an absolute shit.' He gave me a direct look. 'And it could have been completely avoided if only she'd had a sense of her own worth.'

I knew he was hinting at something, but he couldn't be talking about Ramsey. Our relationship was completely relaxed and equal.

'I don't understand what this has to do with me,' I said, annoyed with him for implying otherwise.

'You don't see it? Ari, he tells you what to do. He's mean to your friends; he pushes you around. And you let him.' His blue-grey eyes were stormy. 'You can't be happy living like that.'

He was seething, and I put it down to jealousy. It was the first time I'd had a boyfriend since I met him. He was used to having me all to himself. Now he had to share me.

But Jules had always been the one person in my life who saw all the angles. He was, I knew, a genius. He didn't have a hot temper. He had a maddening ability to simply observe and report the truth.

Ramsey was consistently affectionate towards me, but his mood could turn ominously dark without warning. If it happened while he was working, everyone would try to propitiate him, but inevitably he would explode at someone. He could be shockingly hurtful; he had an instinct for the jugular. I soon learned that any intervention on my part would just make matters much worse – and yet, as a bystander, I often felt like his accomplice. He always drummed into me, Dani and Tommy the importance of loyalty above all else, and since we all accepted his commandments as irrefutable, we learned to live with the discomfort of witnessing the carnage. Sometimes Dani got it in the neck, and Tommy often suffered too, but they never seemed to hold it against Ramsey; in fact they both idolised him.

I alone seemed to be exempt from Bill's wrath. Which was comforting in a way, but uncomfortable as well. As time passed, he grew fiercely protective of me, and that could be problematic. He didn't like me working with other photographers.

Felicity, who rarely mentioned Ramsey to me in our conversations but still represented me as my agent, sometimes booked me with other photographers. But Ramsey hated the photographs even the best photographers took of me.

'You're wasting your time,' he'd tell me, throwing down a contact sheet with contempt. 'You're getting over-exposed. You have to think these things through. It all matters.'

When Felicity tried to persuade me to fly to New York for a sitting with Richard Avedon, Ramsey talked me out of it.

'They're only interested in you because of the work we're doing together. Let's face it, they wouldn't be calling if it weren't for me,' he said. 'And since I can photograph you better than any of them, why bother?'

He paused, as if a thought had just occurred to him. 'Actually, there's no point giving an agency twenty per cent of your earnings. Dani can take your bookings from now on and you can keep the whole fee. It's not like Felicity does much to help you these days. You're the star. People come to you.'

I protested that it wasn't strictly true, Felicity got me great bookings still, with top magazines. 'She looks out for me,' I said.

But Ramsey wouldn't hear of it. He was incredibly convincing, and gradually my arguments dried up. Felicity was a difficult person to like, and our relationship had been tense since I left the model house. It wasn't hard to twist things around until I believed I didn't need an agent any more.

The next day I wrote to her and severed our business arrangement. The very basic contract between us had expired, so there were no legal blocks, but she called me in a rage.

'You're making a mistake you'll regret for the rest of your life,' she warned. 'You should never trust your boyfriend to run your career. You need an independent person to tell you the truth.'

I didn't back down. The decision was made. When I told Ramsey about it later, he laughed. 'Good riddance to that silly old bag.'

He was particularly chuffed because our work together was attracting a lot of attention. In June *Vogue*, there was a massive spread with ten pages of Ramsey's photographs of me and an effusive article titled 'The Face of '67'. However, at the same time, Miss Miller told us my look was still not considered commercial enough to rate a *Vogue* cover. Bill berated the management for being so slow to catch up with the editorial department, but they wouldn't budge.

Dani had to get another telephone installed in order to keep up with the calls from magazines trying to book me, and journalists seeking interviews.

The papers made much of our story: East End boy turns posh teen into top model, a kind of reverse *Pygmalion*. I was certain my success had everything to do with Ramsey and the transformative effect his love had on me.

Because we were all so busy, it had taken some months to get Sunny and Eddie over to the house. I did prepare Sunny, which was lucky because Ramsey chafed at her mercilessly at the beginning. He started off telling her he hated pop music, and implying she was only a flash in the pan, and would never compare to Ella Fitzgerald, or even Dusty Springfield for that matter.

Used to being the only girl around bossy men, Sun held her ground and, what was more, sent Ramsey up so hilariously that he ended up liking her and even offered to shoot her next album cover.

Eddie, however, was clearly threatened by Ramsey's teasing. He was used to being dominant, and when he realised he was no match for Ramsey, he became defensive and arrogant. This was a fatal error on his part, because it brought Ramsey's inner Rottweiler snarling to the surface. Sunny and I managed to avert the crisis with our double act about getting expelled from Chatham and our early days living with the Aussies and everyone ended up laughing.

But the next day when I spoke to Sunny, she sounded distant. Eventually she told me she had been disturbed by the glamorous mugshots of Ramsey's exes so prominently displayed in the sitting room.

'I mean, it's an insult to you, Ari. Why should you have to put up with that lot putting the evil eye on you all the time?'

'They don't bother me a bit,' I insisted vehemently.

I wasn't overly fond of Eddie either, but I'd done my best to get along with him for Sunny's sake. She'd been there for me when I was down, but now that I was in love and getting work, resentment was creeping into our relationship on both sides. Living on the other side of London from each other, having such different lives and lovers meant our friendship could go on ice for a while without there seeming to be a rift between us. I was too caught up with Ramsey to miss her, though when I saw her picture in the paper or heard her on the radio, instead of feeling proud, I felt a twinge of something uncomfortably close to jealousy.

On weekends when Ramsey didn't have to work, we rarely left the house, pottering about in bathrobes and making love in the afternoon, most often in the small guest room at the top of the house. Afterwards we lay in each other's arms in silence, watching patterns of sunlight and shadows dance across the walls. At those times, a mix of joy and sadness filled me. Knowing these moments could never be held onto made them unbearably poignant. Did Ramsey feel the same? He must have, because he often said, 'Tell me you won't leave me ever.'

'Don't be daft.'

'Say it.'

'Of course I'll never leave you,' I laughed, kissing him.

Next door to the little bedroom was a long narrow room with good light and a sloping roof which Ramsey used as a painting studio. While he messed about, experimenting, I stayed in bed reading. There wasn't any need to talk. Ramsey always kept half his mind on work. Sometimes he seemed far away as a result. As long as we were physically close, nothing else mattered.

TWENTY-TWO

Thurston, July 1967

The park at Thurston had never looked more beautiful than it did on the sunny Friday afternoon in July when Ramsey and I drove through the gates in his Morgan. Less than two years had passed since I had jumped ship and it had been the best time of my life. It was especially gratifying to have disproved all Maud's dire predictions. I felt my decision to miss conventional schooling was justified, since I was learning so much from Ramsey and making a small fortune at the same time.

Ramsey had been uncharacteristically silent throughout the drive from London. When I asked if he was nervous, he bristled.

'Why should I be nervous? Fuck them if they don't like me,' he snapped, as we hurtled inexorably towards the place I once called home.

I couldn't blame him; I was anxious, too. I looked forward to seeing my father again, but not Maud. Every encounter with my mother ended in rancour. And nothing had happened to make me think this time would be different. I hadn't spoken to her since I'd fled Henrietta's flat the Christmas before last, and I didn't particularly want to talk to her now.

Through the long dappled avenue of oak trees we caught a glimpse of the lake glittering in afternoon sun, the sloping emerald lawn, and then the serene and immense façade of Thurston loomed in front of us. My heart skipped several beats.

The visit had not been my idea. Papa had written to say he hadn't been well and missed me terribly. Now that the dust had settled, wasn't it time for a reunion?

He added that 'everyone' was keen to welcome Ramsey into the family. When I related this, much to my surprise Ramsey agreed to come along. He'd heard so much about my father, not just from me but Humphrey and others too. I was relieved not to have to face Maud alone.

Moments after we pulled up in the driveway, the front door opened and Maud, Henrietta, Simon and Rupert all rushed down the steps beaming, while Papa hobbled down behind them. Ramsey and I hoisted ourselves out of the Morgan's low seats and were immediately assaulted by joyful dogs and hugs and everyone talking over one another. Ramsey looked stunned. It was such an unexpected display of family solidarity that, to my utter surprise, I burst into tears. Papa's long embrace undid me further. 'Darling,' he said softly, 'At last!'

I breathed in his distinctive smell of pipe smoke and Trumper's Extract of Limes, and immediately felt reassured.

Over his shoulder I saw Maud with her most charming smile, graciously greeting Ramsey, who appeared thoroughly disarmed. Rupert insisted on carrying our bags inside.

Maud led the way into the sitting room. The sash windows were wide open onto the lawn where an alfresco tea table was laid.

When Papa asked, 'Would you prefer tea or a drink after that nightmare journey?' and Ramsey replied, 'Both,' everyone laughed.

The awkwardness I had anticipated didn't arise, except when Henrietta said in a loud voice, 'Thank heavens you've put on a bit of weight since I last saw you, Lumpy.'

My cheeks burned. I had been eating more and worrying about it less but any comment about my weight triggered instant anxiety. I countered it by asking about her rescheduled wedding plans, which in turn made her blush. She had postponed the wedding until the following year, because she wanted to focus on her career for a little longer, before getting tied down. I could only imagine the meltdown that Maud must have had at the time – but, I supposed, it paled into insignificance in comparison with my own life choices.

An awkward silence followed, broken by the welcome arrival of Mr Collins with a tray of Bellinis. Papa raised his glass to Bill, welcoming him to Thurston. Even Miss Bolton was in a good mood for once, though she couldn't bring herself to even glance at Ramsey.

Afterwards, Papa showed Ramsey around the garden. Papa was limping quite noticeably, but full of enthusiasm, as he showed us the newly renovated greenhouse with its rare orchids and tropical plants, grown from cuttings brought back from trips to the Far East and Brazil. Ramsey loved it and took endless photographs.

I could tell my father was pleased. I wanted to hug Ramsey. He was at his best that afternoon. Polite, interested, and witty. Even my mother appeared to be charmed by him.

Only when we went upstairs to dress for dinner did I discover that Maud had put Ramsey and me in separate bedrooms. I was irritated, but Ramsey thought it was funny. He found the prospect of tiptoeing down the corridor to my room rather titillating.

We bathed together in the enormous claw-foot nursery tub, before dressing for dinner.

'I was expecting your mother to be a bitch, but she's actually been great,' Ramsey commented as he combed his hair. 'Maybe you were just a rotten teenager.'

I was in such a good mood that I laughed. It was true, she'd been almost kind today. Perhaps she was coming round, proud of me at last.

Downstairs, there was more champagne before we moved into the dining room where the crystal and silver glimmered in the candlelight.

Outside, a crescent moon and one or two stars were visible above the lake.

'Damn,' I heard Papa mutter under his breath, deeply superstitious about seeing the new moon through glass.

Maud seated us with her usual unequivocal certainty. She wore an intricately-embroidered gold caftan belted at the waist, with gold pumps. Her ash-blonde hair rose like a soufflé, six inches off the crown of her head.

Mr C served the *oeufs en gelée* in individual ramekins, along with a basket brimming with hot buttered toast and water biscuits. I glanced at Ramsey, who had been placed on Maud's right. He was telling her about the time he photographed Winston Churchill with his pet canary on his shoulder.

She clapped her hands appreciatively. 'What a marvellous story, Bill. Weren't you fortunate to have met Sir Winston? A memory to cherish and pass onto your grandchildren.'

I hoped Ramsey wasn't going to tell her how much he loathed children, but he seemed perfectly relaxed, and smiled back at her.

I sat between Simon and my father, with Henrietta on Papa's right. Rupert had earlier informed me in a quick aside that Hen and Simon had been having difficulties since she'd postponed the wedding. 'Henbag is very keen on sticking with her job in PR as she seems to be moving swiftly up the ranks. She's not Maud's daughter for nothing.'

Simon droned on to me about the servant problem in Scotland. Rupert chimed in occasionally with a non-sequitur about someone at his bank, in a feeble attempt to change the subject.

My father squeezed my hand under the table conspiratorially.

'Where are you off to next?' I asked him.

He tapped his left side. 'After the book on Brazil comes out in September, I'm going into hospital for another hip replacement.' He gave a rueful smile. 'I've been in rather a lot of pain.'

'Oh, Papa…'

'I'm getting old, Lumpy,' he said. His tone was light but tinged with melancholy. I held back my tears, but only just. In order to lead the life I wanted, I'd missed two years with my father. It was my only regret, but it was a big one.

Across the table, my mother shot me a brief, steely look that sent a chill through me. That single glance told me she had not forgiven me for anything. So what was all this about?

Still, nothing untoward occurred. Dinner went without incident. Afterwards, Simon and Rupert cornered Ramsey over the brandy, and they talked about cars for hours. Ramsey looked as if he was enjoying this. Every time he spoke, he elicited a chorus of laughter. I hadn't realised he could fit in so easily. It was both pleasing and disturbing to discover that he was more comfortable at Thurston than I was.

We made love that night in my bed and slept entwined as we always did.

Everyone was hungover the next morning. Breakfast was laid out as usual in silver domed chafing dishes on the sideboard in the dining room. It was miles from our usual morning routine – cigarettes and coffee on the way to the studio, or rushing through an airport to catch an early plane.

'I could get used to this,' Ramsey declared, dishing scrambled eggs onto his plate.

My father and Ramsey chatted away and, afterwards, Ramsey flipped through his books, enthusing about Damiano's photographs.

'Architectural photographs are usually boring, but these have real atmosphere,' Ramsey said.

'He's bright as a button, your young man, isn't he?' Papa remarked when Ramsey was out of earshot. I thought I would burst from pride. I don't think my father had ever given me a compliment that meant more. I linked my arm through his and hugged him.

However, later that afternoon, we were soundly beaten at croquet by Henrietta and Simon, which irritated Ramsey, even though he had never played before. His mood began to darken, especially when he heard that several other guests were coming to dinner, and he would need to wear a dinner jacket.

Rupert lent him one of his spares, but since Bill was a few inches shorter than my brother, he looked like a child playing dress-up. I suppose I shouldn't have laughed. June kindly rough-hemmed the trousers and pressed them, and by the time we went downstairs, everything seemed fine.

Mr Collins met us in the hall with a tray of White Ladies before we joined the others. A couple of sips reactivated all the alcohol from the night before, so that we were both reeling by the time we entered the sitting room. Maud gave out an excited cry of 'Darlings!' when she saw us, and linked arms with Ramsey, taking him to meet the new arrivals.

'This is Lord and Lady Blantyre, Bill. We're awfully lucky to have them as our close neighbours. Peggy and Ralph, this is the talented Bill Ramsey, I'm sure you've seen his marvellous photographs of Ari in *Vogue*.'

Unlikely, I thought, as the couple in question gazed at Ramsey with a noticeable lack of enthusiasm.

Ramsey said very little. When the tour was complete, he came over to where my father and I stood near the open doors. 'Trial by fire, I'm afraid, Bill,' said Papa, jovially. 'Do have another White Lady before we go in.'

There were twenty at dinner that night – modest by Thurston standards. Ramsey and I were placed on opposite ends of the same side of the table. He was between Henrietta and Lady Blantyre, but they all seemed to be getting on so, through a swirling vortex of cocktails and wine, I concentrated on my own neighbours, a racehorse trainer and a landowner.

Afterwards, when we left the men to their brandy in the dining room, Henrietta joined me upstairs in what had once been the nursery. I sat on the window seat with Violet and Pav at my feet and she told me about her job at a top PR firm.

'So where are you off to in August?' she asked, as she applied a pale pink lipstick.

145

'Nowhere, I hope,' I said. When she gave me a puzzled look, I explained. 'Bill doesn't really do holidays. We travel all the time, so it's rather nice to stay home if ever there's a free moment.'

'You must watch he doesn't get bored,' Henrietta warned, powdering her nose. 'Especially since there must be no shortage of models throwing themselves at him, I imagine.'

'We have quite a deep bond, actually,' I retorted, bristling.

'Nonetheless,' she said. 'He's still a man, isn't he?' She snapped her compact shut and changed the subject. 'Shall we play charades tonight when the older guests have left? Maudie is keen, you know what a frustrated thespian she is.'

After some of the older guests had departed and Papa had escaped upstairs to bed, Henrietta efficiently divided the rest of us up into groups. I was on Simon's team, while Ramsey and Maud were on Henrietta's.

Ramsey had only reluctantly agreed to join in and was perched uncomfortably on the edge of the sofa where his other teammates were all squashed together, gabbling away.

'Have you played charades before, Ramsey?' Simon asked, passing him a large brandy.

'No, I hate games,' Ramsey replied.

Everyone seemed to find this amusing.

Ralph Blantyre was the first up. He took a piece of paper from the basket and attempted to act out *In Cold Blood*, which took our team some time to guess.

As she sat down, Maud leaned across her neighbour, Beth Mitchelmore, and in a stage whisper directed at Ramsey, she said, '*In Cold Blood* is an altogether new genre. They call it a non-fiction novel.'

'I see,' Ramsey replied, ice in his voice.

'Come on everyone, it's our turn!' Simon was next and the team quickly guessed *A Man for All Seasons,* to a shower of applause.

Again, Maud turned to Ramsey and said, 'It's a marvellous film. All about conscience and the importance of sticking to one's principles.'

'Yeah. I know the bloke who wrote it.' Ramsey fixed her with a steady look, but her attention was already elsewhere.

My brother pulled off an unexpected star turn acting out *Splendour in the Grass* but by then Ramsey had gone ominously still, an uncomfortable half-smile on his face. There was nothing I could do, though, as I was next.

On my slip of paper was written *After Many a Summer Dies the Swan*. I went completely blank and stood twiddling my hair, trying to work out what the hell to do. I stumbled through each word and it took my team for ever to work out the line.

Humiliated, I slunk back to my seat.

'That poor swan died a horrid death,' someone said, *sotto voce*.

Maud leaned over, and in her most kindly tone, as if she were informing a backward six-year-old, addressed Ramsey, '*After Many a Summer Dies the Swan* is a famous line from a poem by Tennyson.'

'Aldous Huxley filched it as a title for one of his books, though, didn't he?' Ramsey replied, through clenched teeth.

'Imagine you knowing that.' Maud took a drag from her cigarette holder.

The air in the room shimmered with sudden tension. Henrietta, who had been chattering away, fell silent as Ramsey's head pivoted slowly towards Maud.

There wasn't time to intervene. Everything happened so fast.

'Who do you think you are, you condescending cunt?' Ramsey enquired, almost casually. She drew a sharp breath, but he didn't wait for her to speak. 'At least I got where I am through my talent and hard work. All you did was marry a rich man and now you think you're better than everyone.' He studied my mother with unbridled contempt.

The room fell absolutely silent, everyone frozen to the spot like Scott and his team of Antarctic explorers.

Maud's face hardened.

'How dare you speak to me like this?' she said, her voice shaking. 'And in my own house!'

'It's time you heard the truth,' said Ramsey getting up. 'It's all hidden beneath the surface. But you're a viper. I feel quite sorry for David. He deserves better. But he's made his bed, I suppose.'

Ramsey was already out the door when, winded by shock, I struggled to my feet and followed, not daring to look back.

All the way up three flights of stairs, I could feel the furious eyes of the Lyttleton ancestors glaring down at us. Violet and Pav, having bounded ahead, waited for us on the top landing wagging their tails. I wondered how Papa would take it when he woke up in the morning. Though I loathed Maud more than ever, it hadn't been enjoyable to watch her total annihilation.

There was no discussion, no argument. We both knew what had to happen. Grimly we threw our belongings into bags. I grabbed a few books from the shelves and a framed photo of Papa and me. Between Ramsey and Maud, the choice was simple, though it meant giving up everything else connected with home.

Violet whimpered as she watched us pack, and Pav curled up on top of my bag when my back was turned.

'Ramsey, please can we take them with us? I can't leave them here now.'

He nodded unenthusiastically. 'All right, but they're your responsibility.' He tilted his head towards the door to indicate it was time to go.

We escaped down the back stairs. The lights were off in the kitchen and pantry. I inhaled the lingering scent of boot polish and chicken stock for one last time, and followed Ramsey and the dogs out the back door.

TWENTY-THREE

New York, August 1967

In the aftermath of the traumatic weekend at Thurston I poured all my energy into work. I said yes to every job, filling my days with photo shoots and interviews. Violet and Pav seemed lost in their new home and slunk around in dark corners, looking miserable. When I had time, I took them for long walks on Primrose Hill and Regent's Park, but I was often away. Sometimes Ramsey and I talked about buying a cottage in the country, but we were too busy to even get out of town and look.

In light of Henrietta's comments about my weight, I found a doctor in Harley Street to help me shed the extra pounds and suppress my now almost bottomless appetite. Dr Crooke offered injections that could speed a slow metabolism and supply the body with vitamins. I went in several times a week. The nurse would administer the jab straight through my tights into my behind. Almost every girl I knew went to Crooky; the waiting room was buzzing. I soon lost all the extra weight I'd put on, and coincidentally found I could get so much more done. Miracle!

Just when work was winding down for the summer, the editor of American *Vogue*, Diana Vreeland, called Ramsey and summoned us both to New York. 'I hear you've done it again, Bill,' she roared down the crackling wire. 'Discovered a new girl for a new era. I knew her father before the War. Divine man…! If you live long enough, you find everything comes full circle. Now listen up, buddy boy,' she told him. 'I want an updated version of the photographs you did of Iris five years ago… but instead of teddy bears, we have some great New York artists lined up for the story with Ariadne. Andy, Bob Rauschenberg, and Roy Lichtenstein. Are you up for it?'

Ramsey smiled into the phone. 'Of course I'm up for it, Vreeland. What do you think?'

'I think you'd better come here quickly before those boys all head off to wherever the hell they go in August.'

We arrived in sweltering Manhattan the following week. The next morning I went straight to Mrs Vreeland's office on the 29th floor of the Graybar building.

The room was lacquered scarlet, though two whole walls were covered with cork, onto which were pinned a dazzling assortment of images clipped from magazines and newspapers. Notably, there was Maria Callas, her eyes brimming with vengeful fury, spewing lava from her open mouth. Next to her, Arab stallions galloped across a desert, while the legendary model Vivara smouldered in a black fur cape outside a yurt in Mongolia.

Like the images, Mrs Vreeland was mesmerising. She didn't look or sound like anyone else I had ever met. She used theatrical gestures and exaggerated expressions, like a New York cab driver combined with a marchioness, yet she still managed to be a straight shooter at the same time.

It was one o'clock in the afternoon. We were sitting on either side of a card table. In front of her, on an immaculate white plate, was a peanut butter sandwich on white bread, cut diagonally into two triangles. Next to it, a highball glass contained a finger of neat Scotch. She ignored both and kept her gaze on me.

'I wanted to meet you first, without the divine Ramsey,' she said. 'It was just sort of a feeling, if you get my drift, that you and I have plenty to say to one another.' She closed her eyes tight and smiled at me disarmingly. 'Though his work is not exactly my cup of tea, as soon as I laid eyes on Boucher's pictures, I understood at once there was something going on in your head; call it an inner life, hmm?' She tapped her forehead with her long red nails, before launching into an epic monologue.

'Of course, it is essential to have an inner life when one is growing up. Without it I wouldn't be sitting here with you today. None of this was a given—'

She made a dramatic sweeping movement to indicate her palatial corner office, with its panoramic views of silvery skyscrapers shrouded in thick smog. 'Was I a dreamer when I was your age?' she asked me, without waiting for a reply. 'You bet I was! And, by the way, I had absolutely not one skerrick of interest in school! It all could have gone terribly wrong, except I discovered dancing. When I tell you I loved dancing, I mean dancing is the *only* thing I ever wanted to do! Ballet, flamenco, modern, tap. Day and night! I knew I had a spark, and I simply thought, I'm going to have the most marvellous life imaginable, and to hell with what my mother or anyone else thinks.'

She paused to light a cigarette. I was spellbound by her story, and amazed she took the trouble to share it with me.

'And Ramsey is only the most attractive man in the world,' Diana continued. 'Of course, I can see exactly why he went for you. No dust on old Ramsey!'

She explained that all the top American designers had been commissioned to create one-off designs for the shoot. Each dress would subtly reference a particular artist's work.

As if on cue, an assistant rattled in with a rack of clothes unlike anything I'd ever seen before.

'They're a bit of all right, dontcha think?' Diana exclaimed. 'Would you mind trying them?'

I stripped down to my knickers and stepped into the first garment, a one-shouldered Bill Blass evening dress in midnight blue.

As soon as I pulled it on, Mrs Vreeland beamed at me. 'You look like a million bucks, Ari darling!' She summoned the assistant with a snap of her fingers. 'Arlene, I want you to take down a letter. Now. This minute! Let's keep the show on the road!' Without a pause, she dictated,

'Dearest Bill, Ariadne Lyttleton is standing right here in front of me wearing your divine creation, and all I can say is, though we are doing a story on arrivistes like Andy and Roy, you are the real artist here. Love, Diana.'

When her assistants had left, she looked at me thoughtfully. 'Arrrriadne darling, for these photographs I want you to become something of a muse to each of these fellows. I don't mean in the old-fashioned sense, as if you were in their thrall, I mean, give 'em something to think about!'

I nodded sagely, as if I knew exactly what she meant.

Two hours later Ramsey and I arrived at Andy Warhol's studio. Warhol was there, working alongside a shirtless male assistant, rolling paint on a huge silkscreen on the floor, while people wandered in and out of the room talking loudly, in a disconnected manner, as if they were in a play. I felt dizzy with adrenaline and jetlag.

Andy smiled up at us in a bewildered way as if he had forgotten we were coming. After a brief hello he got on with his work, leaving us to figure out what to do.

While the fashion editor, Polly, and the hairdresser, Ara Gallant, sought a quiet

151

corner in which to get me ready, I watched Ramsey check out a blonde Morticia Addams with high cheekbones who was wafting through the studio in a full-length form-fitting black dress.

'That's Nico,' said Andy, appearing behind us. 'She's kind of a Nazi.'

I found Andy's anaemic presence quite alien until I glanced down and noticed his hands. They were the exquisite hands of an artist; large, fine, and so sensitive they could have been sculpted by Michelangelo. As a mirror into his soul, they were far more expressive than his eyes.

Getting ready for the shot took hours, because Ara's elaborate frizzy white wigs had a life of their own and had to be tamed. Once the wig was securely pinned to my scalp, I felt completely transformed. My self-consciousness receded, which was fortunate because many more outrageous players had arrived to join the party, and the Factory became a heaving mass of highly competitive performers.

Since Andy clearly did not possess Prussian army-officer qualities, Ramsey took charge. He did the only thing he could, which was to include as many Factory personalities as would fit in the shot and photograph us all from a ladder. An aggressive Irish-American filmmaker with a lisp and a machine gun-like laugh recorded the scene on video. Ramsey ordered me to lean up against Andy in the foreground of the shot. I did as I was told, although I sensed this not only made Andy a bit uneasy, but also enraged his protégées.

'How come that English chick gets to stand next to Andy?'

'She's not even pretty.'

'How much are we getting paid for this?'

Finally, the video director shouted, 'None of you are getting paid for this. Is that clear? You want your picture in *Vogue*? Then shut up.'

There were some muted grumbles, but no one budged.

Soon, though, a catfight broke out between two of the drag queens, and Joe Dalessandro's new-born baby began to wail. As we posed, a little slip of a girl danced around us, flicking glitter and confetti like a little pixie.

Later, we all decamped to Max's Kansas City. I sat between Andy and Ramsey and listened as they discussed movies. Or rather, Ramsey talked, and Andy murmured, 'Oh wow, yeah, *riiiight.*' He seemed affectless, almost bored, but I soon realised it was his way of making people so nervous they would talk even more and tell him everything.

When Ramsey got up to buy cigarettes, Andy turned his attention to me. 'Do you know any of the Royals?'

I shook my head.

'That's too bad, I just love the Queen. I wish we had one here, instead of these boring transvestites. I mean, just look at this,' he said, indicating the table-hopping collection of freaks and radical shit-stirrers circling like crazed bees around us, hoping to be noticed.

Ramsey was gone for a long time. When he returned, he didn't meet my eye. I noticed Nico slinking into the crowd around the bar and I knew at once something had happened between them.

I glared at her, hoping I didn't look as insecure and jealous as I felt.

Over the next week, we were on location every day with the other artists in the feature and hung out every single night at Max's or Elaine's. *Sgt Pepper* was still playing everywhere, especially 'A Day in the Life'.

At one point we went to a Stones concert with Mrs Vreeland.

'Musicians are changing everything. Soon your generation will be running the world.' she said with a characteristic flourish.

'It's not just music, for God's sake,' said Ramsey, as we headed back uptown in a taxi. 'It's photography, art and films too. We're experiencing one of those peak waves in time. All these people around us think just because they're riding on the crest that it's going to be like this for ever, but I've got news for them. It's not that easy. And when the wave breaks, I'll still be working.'

On Monday morning a huge bouquet of fire lilies arrived at our hotel with a typed note from Diana Vreeland, signed in green ink. I could almost hear her dictating it.

Bill and Ari,

You have done the most marvellous job with the Artists feature.

I'm not making myself clear at all.

Ariadne looks RAVISHING, and Bill, your photographs are a TOUR DE FORCE.

The story will open the October book.

Once again, the English have triumphed!

This is just the beginning.

Diana

The phone rang incessantly. We were invited to appear on television chat shows. We were invited to lunch, dinner and breakfast with people we didn't know. There were requests for interviews with the *New York Post, Women's Wear Daily* and the *Style* section of the *New York Times*. Ramsey turned almost all the invitations down.

'It's always best to play hard to get in New York,' he told me. 'What is it that Vreeland always says? 'Elegance is refusal'? It makes them determined to book you at any price.'

One day, Ramsey had a meeting scheduled with an ad agency, and made it clear he wanted to go alone. By that stage, we had not been apart for more than a few minutes in weeks. With him away, I found it impossible to relax. I didn't want to leave the hotel and I didn't want to stay inside it.

I tried reading the Tom Wolfe book everyone was talking about, but my eyes bounced off the page. The phone rang every few minutes, but Ramsey had instructed me not to pick up. He said I should let the hotel operator take a message in case I said the wrong thing to a journalist or a magazine editor.

I took a shower instead, catching a glimpse of my naked body in the bathroom mirror. A new obsession with American food was taking its toll.

To my horror, this was later confirmed.

I had been on my way to the Metropolitan Museum and made the fatal error of walking up Madison Avenue. On the corner of 67th street was a shop called Paraphernalia, with a live go-go girl in a pink bikini dancing in a cage in the window, a fixed smile on her face. Behind her, an industrial fan blew her hair about wildly.

Inside, the store was a vast cool white space with a black rubber floor, and two levels connected by a walkway. On each floor was one single rack with about ten pieces of clothing.

I chose a pink paisley bell bottom trouser suit and a bubble coat in bright yellow fake fur, and several psychedelic print dresses to try on. New clothes meant a fresh chance to become a better version of myself. But then there was the confrontation with the uncomfortable reality of my flabby naked body. The clothes were cut very small. I sucked in my stomach and struggled with zips and buttons. I was heading back to Dr Crooke the second we landed at Heathrow. I was no-one unless I was thin.

Buying the clothes in the smallest size would be an incentive to stay skinny. Proof that I'd succeeded.

'Wow,' said the salesgirl when I took them to the till, giving me the quick up and down. 'Wait, you're Ariadne, right? I wasn't sure it was you at first, you look kind of different from your photographs!'

It was the first time I had been recognised as a model, and I felt a mixture of pride and shame. Pride because a stranger knew me from my work, and shame because I obviously didn't measure up to her expectations.

I emerged from the store onto the blisteringly hot street with two huge shopping bags. Some of the tension had been eased by spending almost everything I'd made in the last month all at once. I felt momentarily calm.

When I returned to the hotel room to discover Ramsey still wasn't back, the internal voices returned with a vengeance. They criticised every move I made and poisoned every thought. The clothes I'd bought had been a waste. Ramsey was gone because I was annoying, stupid, and fat; why would he want to be with me anyway?

When he was around, the voices receded. He was so sure of himself, sure enough for both of us. He made me feel secure. Without him, panic and doubt overwhelmed me until I couldn't breathe.

TWENTY-FOUR

London, April 1968

One warm spring afternoon, I received a call from Jules inviting me to join him for lunch the following day. I hadn't seen him in months. He avoided coming to our house, and I couldn't blame him for that. Ramsey was intimidated by Julius and it made him jealous and spiteful.

When we met at Chez Victor in Soho, I was astonished to find that Jules had transformed himself from a bookish, tweed-loving aesthete into a flamboyant hippie. Gone were the well-cut tweed suits and bow ties, replaced by red velvet bell-bottom trousers, high-heeled boots, a tattered brocade waistcoat, and an unstructured navy-blue jacket with gold piping. Around his neck were several mismatched scarves. Both his hair and beard were long and luxuriant and covered most of his face.

Though the overall look was distinctly eccentric, it seemed to me that he had suddenly become extremely attractive.

'My god, Jules,' I exclaimed, hugging him. 'What happened? Have you joined the cast of *Hair*?'

'Well, darling, last term was rather insane. Editing *Varsity* sort of took over from everything else, and, well… let's order.' He waved for a waiter. 'You look cadaverous, Ari, you must be so pleased. Still, I think you should eat something before someone places coins on your eyes. Apparently, the cassoulet is delicious today.'

I wrinkled my nose. 'No thanks.' My eyes skimmed the menu in search of a low-calorie alternative. 'Dover sole and lettuce salad, please.'

When the waiter had gone, I turned my full attention on Jules. 'So, what does the Maestro think of your new look?'

He ignored that and leaned forward eagerly. 'Listen, my darling, I've been offered the chance to edit a weekly magazine in London. I'm going to take it.'

I stared at him. 'Are you saying you're going to drop out of Cambridge? After all those lectures on education you've given me over the years?'

'The thing is,' Jules said, 'either I stay there and become a serious academic, writing books about obscure philosophers, or I take a chance and do something more adventurous.' He gave me a faint half-smile. 'I guess you could say I was inspired by you.'

I knew better than to show how pleased I was.

'A rival to *Gondwanda*?'

'Ha, no! It will, at the very least, be readable!' he smiled. 'A comprehensive weekly guide to events in London, but with reviews, opinion pieces and counterculture influences. We've produced a prototype, and on the strength of that a publisher I know is going to fund the first ten issues.'

He paused, choosing his words carefully. 'Ari, I thought perhaps you might like to come and work for us. You can write about fashion or whatever you want. I'd love having your voice in the magazine.'

Whatever I had expected, it wasn't this. I stared at him, too caught off guard to come up with a good excuse.

'I don't want to write about fashion,' I said, quickly. 'I can't think of anything that would interest me less. Besides, there are already tons of guides to London out there. What's the point of another one?

'Thanks, Ari.' Jules looked genuinely hurt. 'I thought you of all people would understand, but you're sounding exactly like my parents. And if you really hate fashion so much, how come you spend all your time in that frankly benighted world? This publication is not just a whimsical idea, I've thought it through and it's going to be a huge success. I am just giving you a chance to opt in at the start.'

'It sounds great, but I honestly don't have time,' I said. 'I'm really busy right now – Ramsey has my schedule fully booked.'

'Ramsey does, does he?' Julius said, with more than just a hint of unpleasantness.

'Jules, don't,' I said. 'Ramsey takes care of me.'

He fell silent, watching me with an intensity that made me squirm.

'Remember what I told you about modelling,' he said, after a long pause. 'It will eat you alive and spit you out. You've done well so far but that business doesn't really love anyone. If you don't write for me, please write for someone else. You can do it,

Ari, I know you can.'

I felt suddenly very cross with him. I felt he was willing me to fail. Why couldn't he just be happy for me?

'I know you see it as the ultimate in romantic gestures, but loving someone with no holds barred is the ultimate turn-off, especially for a man like Ramsey.'

'How would you know when you've never been in love, Julius?' I shot back. It was a low blow, but true.

'If it means giving up my identity, then I don't want to fall in love. Ari, I miss your old defiant self. When we were growing up, you were funny and rude, but at least you were your own person. Now you're turning into a doormat. I don't get it.'

I glanced at my watch. No point in taking this any further. I'd forgotten how acerbic and unkind Julius could be.

'Sorry, I'd love to stay and chat but I've got to get home to pack; Bill and I are flying to Rome this evening.'

Jules studied me for a long second, and then turned to wave a waiter over with the flick of his wrist.

All the way home I thought of his expression – the long sorrowful look he'd given me. As if he could see things I couldn't.

But I didn't let myself think about it for long. Everything was going too well. The dogs seemed happier, now that we had hired a minder to take them on long walks every day. Work was plentiful. We never stopped travelling. We were out nearly every night. Our friends were actors, directors, artists, designers, photographers, models, musicians, writers, impresarios, and fortune hunters.

Apart from craving more time alone with Ramsey, I'd never been happier.

TWENTY-FIVE

Paris, May 1968

Ramsey and I returned to Paris in early May. There were new green leaves on the trees, the days were warm and the nights balmy: a songwriter's dream, or a lover's. On the face of it, the city had never looked more beautiful. But the combination of pollen and spring fever in the air didn't sit well with a niggling unease in the pit of my stomach. Events were flying by too fast, and there was no time to digest them.

We were staying at the Crillon Hotel, for the publication of a new magazine. *Ecume de Mer* was the brainchild of French journalist Mireille de Latour, known for her avant-garde perspective on fashion and the arts. It was funded by her German industrialist lover, and the inaugural issue was rumoured to have cost a fortune.

The cover shoot had taken place in a film studio outside Madrid, where I was styled by Salvador Dali as a dystopian Aphrodite rising out of an atomic mushroom cloud. Ramsey thought the cover would look better in black and white, but Mireille insisted on colour. An unholy row ensued. Mireille got her way, but on the understanding there would be many more *Ecume de Mer* assignments in the pipeline for Ramsey. However, we'd not yet been paid for the cover we'd already completed.

At least we were invited to the launch party. The cream of fashion royalty had travelled from all corners of Europe for the five-day extravaganza of cocktail parties, dinners in magnificent palaces, and fireworks over the Seine. Rivers of vintage Pol Roger champagne flowed through every event.

Since the magazine was paying all our expenses, we were expected to give interviews to the press in return, but at the last moment, Ramsey was hired to do a shoot for *Elle*. So the interviews fell to me. There were dozens of them. I worked out a few clever answers (or so I imagined) with carefully formulated views on artists, designers, lipstick colours; interjected with just the right amount of self-deprecating humour, so as not to appear as hollow as I felt.

Unfortunately, I didn't have the right clothes, shoes, jewellery or accessories for a five-day fashion event. In London, most girls I knew dressed in a mix of antique market finds, charity-shop bargains, and the odd Ossie Clark extravagance. But the raggle-taggle look did not translate well next to the well-groomed Europeans who lived in French and Italian couture and jewellery. They were another breed; massively rich, beautiful, well-travelled, and multilingual; probably exactly the kind of people who would have been my classmates at the Swiss finishing school had I not bolted.

It irked me that Ramsey appeared to be in his element around them, but on second thoughts it made perfect sense. At home he got a lot of very nasty press coverage, while in Europe he was considered an artist. As a result, he could get away with almost anything, including being very rude to Mireille.

I on the other hand felt closely scrutinised, expected to dress in a new outfit and be camera-ready at every event, and I just didn't have the will or the means, so I knew I would never fit in. But we still had to attend the festivities as part of the deal.

We drank steadily to get through the long evenings, which often began at 6 p.m. and inevitably went on until two or three in the morning. Mornings were nauseous, anxiety-ridden blurs where only a top-up of alcohol at lunchtime could ease the malaise. So it was hardly surprising that the gulf between Ramsey and me had widened. His long unexplained absences became more frequent. The more I tried to stay close to him, the further he pulled away, and seemed to prefer hanging out with the rat pack of young photographers from mostly aristocratic backgrounds who idolised him.

One night after an *intime* but disconnected dinner for thirty given by the model Seraphine, St Laurent's bubbly muse, we headed to New Jimmy's as usual. Regine, the hostess, greeted us with her usual weary charm and a special hug for Ramsey, for whom she clearly had a soft spot. The best tables with the choicest view of the dance floor had been reserved for our party. Waiters brought more ice-buckets of champagne.

Ramsey wandered away almost immediately, and I was determined not to follow him.

For a while I was distracted by a tall, handsome Dutch boy called Maurice who was part of the inner circle of young bachelor photographers. He was sweet and sensitive, very different to the usual brash European set. Over the din we discussed our dogs and the books we were reading. When I told him I found *Magister Ludi* by Hermann Hesse impenetrable, he recounted the plot.

Next time I looked around at Ramsey, he was in deep conversation with a girl who had recently appeared on the scene. Some models seemed as if they had just hatched right out of an egg, but Ilya had a knowing look and she certainly seemed to know how to relate to Ramsey. She was quite dashing, in thigh-high musketeer boots and suede shorts, with an oversized billowing white shirt. Her legs were toned, tanned and very long, and she had a wicked laugh. I didn't like the way they looked at each other.

As if lost in the spectacle of the dancing bodies, I gazed straight ahead but my attention was focused on Ramsey and Ilya. At that exact moment I heard Ramsey, very coolly and calmly, telling Ilya how he longed to fuck her. And she was gazing back at him, eyes sparkling, smiling, not saying anything.

An emotion of such violent intensity filled my body that I was not sure how I could contain it. I wanted to jump out of my skin. I could have lifted the back of a car up on two wheels or smashed my fist through a plate glass window without feeling pain.

And because of the circumstances, because we were surrounded by thirty rapacious gossips who would have liked nothing more than to witness a screaming fight between a model and a famous photographer, I just sat there.

Out of nowhere, I found myself thinking about Jules begging me to work for him, and I wondered if he somehow knew this would happen.

One thing was certain: nothing could ever be the same between me and Ramsey ever again. It had been done so casually, so gratuitously, as if the bond we shared had no value. Bill could take me or leave me, but Jules was right – in the fashion world I was nothing without Ramsey.

The bodies swaying on the dance floor seemed as insubstantial and hollow as straw, blowing about in a thick fog of cigarette smoke and pounding cretinous music.

Finally, I managed to stand up, and pull on the sleeve of Ramsey's jacket.

'We have to go,' I said. My voice came out sounding disembodied but urgent. 'Right now.'

Ilya blinked at me with amused innocence. I stared back at her with utter loathing.

'What's going on?' Ramsey asked when we were out on the street, the noise of the party behind us. 'I was quite enjoying that.'

I burst into angry tears and began punching him in the chest with both fists. 'How could you do that? Proposition another woman while you're sitting right next to me? You're a fucking monster!'

Ramsey calmly caught my wrists with one hand and held them together at chest height in a vice-like grip.

'You must be mad, or hard of hearing,' he said. 'We were talking about films. She's a bright bird but I don't fancy her. Will you please stop hitting me?'

Still holding my wrists, he calmly searched for the car keys in his pocket with his free hand.

I wrenched myself away. He let go of me in the same instant, and I went flying backwards, only just managing to save myself from falling to the pavement.

The urgent wailing of police sirens in the distance somehow intensified my fury. I looked around for something to throw at him as a group of people walked towards us.

'Will you get the fuck into the car?' Ramsey hissed.

Reluctantly, I obeyed, slamming the door, even more furious that he had grabbed the high moral ground.

As he pulled out of the side street and onto Avenue Montparnasse, Ramsey drove much too fast, but I didn't care if we crashed. In fact I would have welcomed a decisive ending to the torrent of unbearable pain coursing through my body. I hated him. But most of all I hated myself for losing him. Because I was losing him, without a doubt.

There were few other cars on the road, but plenty of people about. We had to avoid a pack of boys running down the Boulevard St Germain, shouting, as if they were being chased by bulls in Pamplona. It was so different to London, where even on balmy spring nights like this one, the streets were dead by eleven o'clock.

'I thought you loved me,' I sobbed, burying my face in my hands.

Ramsey sighed. 'I do love you, you mad bitch. You're poisoning everything with your jealousy. And I have no idea why. Do you know how ugly it makes you?'

Yes, because I knew how ugly I felt inside. How pathetic, and how vicious. I felt nothing but contempt for the happy idiot I had been just a few months ago.

When I didn't speak, Ramsey lit a cigarette with a furious click of his lighter and blew out a long stream of smoke. 'I thought you'd be grateful that I put myself out on a limb for you. I gave you something to be proud of, but all I've done is create a

162

fucking Frankenstein's monster.'

His words lacerated me. All I wanted to do was to get back to the hotel and throw up. Empty the sewer of acid champagne and all the bullshit I had been spouting recently. I longed to be numb again.

We turned down a narrow winding street towards the river and suddenly explosions of brilliant light flared against the sky as fireworks went off a few streets away, accompanied by what sounded like firecrackers. Then more sirens, near and far, wailing ominously.

It occurred to me that the group of boys we'd seen running down the street earlier must have been celebrating something, the end of exams, maybe. Perhaps their exuberance had turned nasty, like it sometimes did with English football fans. I soon forgot about them, however, because we were crossing the Concorde Bridge over to the Right Bank with the intent to inflict as much pain as possible on each other, hurling every insult we had.

Not long ago, Paris had been a glorious backdrop to our love affair. Now I positively loathed the place, with its golden monuments and smell of piss everywhere.

Somehow, we made it back to the hotel. When we pulled up, the night manager was standing by the revolving doors inside the lobby, with an expression of clear concern on his face.

'*Monsieur Rrramzay, j'espère que vous n'étiez pas dérangé par le petit problème?*'
I hope you weren't bothered by the little problem? What little problem?

'Thanks mate, we're fine,' Ramsey told him brusquely, hurrying me through the lobby.

In the lift, we were silent, neither of us in the mood to discuss what the concierge might have meant.

As soon as we got to the room the gloves were off again.

'It turns out, you're exactly like your mother,' Ramsey sniped, and then locked himself in the bathroom. There was a brief silence before I heard the sudden swoosh of water hitting the marble floor of the shower.

Incensed, I flung open the doors to the walk-in cupboard off the tiny foyer, gathered up one of each of Ramsey's five pairs of shoes in my left arm, crossed the bedroom and prised open the handle to the French windows. Then I flung each shoe over the balcony with all my strength. It was incredibly satisfying. Our room overlooked an interior courtyard, so I vaguely knew there was a small chance of killing someone but, in the moment, I wasn't sure I much cared.

After that, I found my suitcase in the dressing room, threw it on the bed and started packing. I had no idea where I could go at three in the morning, but I'd work it out later.

However, when Ramsey emerged from the bathroom in a white towelling robe and saw what I was doing, to my intense surprise he collapsed into a heap onto the bed and burst into tears. I'd never seen him cry before.

The sight of him lying there, with tears cascading down his cheeks like a helpless child, was unbearable.

Of course he still loved me. Perhaps I'd misheard the conversation with Ilya, and this fight had all been down to my own paranoia. Of course, he was justifiably angry with me. What a fool I'd been, getting everything wrong, as usual. And now, somehow, I had to fix it.

Through my own tears I told him quietly how sorry I was. We fell into each other's arms. In minutes the suitcase was upside down on the floor and Ramsey was fast asleep. Savouring the warmth of his body, I stayed awake for hours, silently vowing never again to be so mistrusting.

At dawn, I disentangled myself from him, threw on some clothes and raced down to the lobby. The door to the courtyard was locked, and there was some confusion among the hotel staff about who had the key. While I was waiting around, the concierge mentioned something about the disturbance in the night. He spoke in English but having not quite understood him, I went into a spin. Had there been complaints from the neighbours?

'Perhaps you are unaware,' he continued, politely, 'but there was a very serious demonstration last night. Left-wing students protesting in solidarity with the workers. Many people have been hurt and taken to hospital, and it is still going on. *Je suis desolé,*' he added apologetically, as if it were his fault.

I was relieved, though I still didn't quite understand. The key was found, I retrieved the shoes, and returned to the room before Ramsey woke.

It was only later that day, when we couldn't get a taxi to go to the airport, that we heard about the disturbance and how widely spread it was becoming; not just in Paris but in other French cities too. Still later, we realised that after leaving the nightclub we had driven through some of the worst of the riots, but we were so caught up in our own drama that we hadn't even noticed.

TWENTY-SIX

London, November 1969

My star was on the wane. It had faded gradually at first.

Now months went by when I had no work at all. Ramsey was still busy, of course, but his clients were no longer so receptive when he suggested I should be the model. I was worried but told myself it wasn't unusual. When I lived in the model house my flatmates often endured weeks when nothing much happened before work picked up again. I tried to follow the same healthy regimes as they would in these circumstances, but I ended up smoking pot all day and watching endless black and white movies on the telly.

Then one day, American *Vogue* phoned. Diana Vreeland was planning an extensive fashion and travel feature on Nepal, paid for by Royal Nepalese Airways and Air India, and she wanted Ramsey to take the photographs. It was a big deal – the cover and eighteen pages featuring top European couturiers. It was all designed to evoke, as Mrs Vreeland put it, 'a secret world of opulence and luxury which no one in *Amerrrrica* has any idea about'.

Ramsey said all the right things on the phone, but when he hung up, he laughed, 'I have no idea what she's talking about. Nepal is one of the poorest countries in the world. But I'm not about to tell her that.'

I begged Ramsey to push for me to be the model. To his credit, he must have done, because a few days later Mrs Vreeland phoned and asked to speak to me directly.

'Darling Ari, the art spread and the Paris photos you did were a bit of all right. If it were up to me, I'd use nobody except you. But the executives here... darling, they don't think your looks are commercial enough to carry such an important story.'

She spoke with her usual enthusiasm but I detected a new hint of distance in her voice.

Ramsey, who'd been listening in, grabbed the phone from my hand. 'The story is supposed to be about the exotic, for fuck's sake, give her a chance,' Ramsey fumed. 'Ari's perfect for it. What do they want? Another conventional blonde?'

'I'll do everything I can, kiddos,' Diana said. 'I adore you both.'

Ramsey complained bitterly about her choices but he privately he let me know he wasn't so sure I could pull it off either. Late nights and eating out all the time had taken a toll on my weight and my skin.

The book Ramsey had been working on for months, *Sixties Saraband*, had just been published. It received mixed reviews, but it raised his profile further, and he was very much in the spotlight again. He felt it was good exposure for the book to accept every party, TV appearance and dinner invitation that came his way. It wasn't because he craved acceptance; just the contrary. He wanted to sell as many copies as possible by exploiting the controversy surrounding his work. He liked nothing more than attacking Establishment figures, especially if he smelled a whiff of hypocrisy in the air. I loved him for it, but I also felt terrible when he hurt people who didn't deserve it. His Rottweiler instincts didn't make our social life very relaxing but, on the other hand, I admired the way he refused to bow to social expectations. He was the opposite of my parents in every way. People admired him for his honesty, but he didn't have many close friends.

But then, my own friends had drifted away too.

I rarely saw Sunny these days. She was always on tour or having dinner with journalist or a Bee Gee. And just as he predicted, Julius's new magazine had been an instant hit, so his deadlines prevented any kind of social life, unless he was schmoozing.

On the rare occasions Papa was in London, I met up with him for lunch, but essentially Ramsey was my entire world.

Since the Paris nightmare, we had been closer, but lately, imperceptibly, something between us had changed again. As we drove down the King's Road, he ogled girls walking by ('I'm only looking. Who knows? One of them could be the new Iris.' 'I thought *I* was the new Iris.' Silence).

It was unreasonable to make a fuss, but I hoped the trip to Nepal would be my chance to shine, once again, in his eyes. I stopped drinking, lived on apples and cottage cheese for a month, and went out to the library to do research on different looks, as the *Vogue* budget for the shoot did not include a hairdresser or a make-up artist. I paid hairdresser Duane Scott to match hairpieces to my hair and teach me how to use them. I tried out exotic make-up looks, and Ramsey's assistant, Tommy, took a series of pictures to show how versatile I could be. I made sure to embody Diana Vreeland's ultimate fantasy image of a gypsy girl who happened to have a wardrobe the size and scope of Barbra Streisand's.

My efforts were rewarded. To my huge relief *Vogue* gave me the thumbs up – but with the proviso that another model was also to be featured in the story. When I heard it was Vivara, I was shaken. She was six foot two, and so extraordinary she needed only one name. She came from a family of Hungarian aristocrats, and was more snow leopard than girl, with a feral intensity that leaped off the page. But for some reason Ramsey was not so keen on her, which I suspected had a great deal to do with her indifferent, rather haughty attitude towards him.

I was almost sure that Vivara wasn't going to make problems between me and Ramsey. However, when it came to her work, she was a goddess, and she transformed fashion stories into art pages. Next to her it would be difficult to shine, but I was determined at least to hold my own.

More challenging than Vivara, in Ramsey's opinion, was *Vogue*'s decision to send the fashion editor Chisie Pennington to Nepal on the shoot.

'Are you mad, you old bat?' he barked down the phone at Mrs Vreeland, sailing closer to the wind than anyone else dared. 'You can't saddle me with her. Send anyone but Chisie.'

'Oh, Ramsey darling, she's a marvellous editor,' Mrs Vreeland replied mildly. 'The best there is. Don't make this difficult, ducky.'

There was a warning in that last line, but Ramsey doubled down. 'That woman hates leaving Park Avenue, let alone America. She's terrified of germs and has no sense of humour. Travelling in the East with her is going to be a nightmare.'

Mrs Vreeland was unwavering. Perhaps she knew Chisie would stand up to Ramsey. Someone had to.

Once the team was finally agreed, things moved quickly. Within a week, travel was arranged, assistants were booked, equipment was boxed and labelled for the flight.

When I climbed into the taxi to the airport, I was already tense. After months of wondering if my career was over, I was about to embark on the most important shoot I'd ever done, one that could change my fortune, and bring me back to the very top. My inner voices were reasonably optimistic that I could achieve this goal.

We caused a small riot in customs at Delhi airport when Ramsey, Chisie, Tommy and I arrived at five in the morning with dozens of cases of clothes and camera equipment. The customs officer took an instant dislike to Ramsey. We waited around for hours while she meticulously searched everything, including the linings of all forty-three bags. Then she impounded the cameras because we didn't have the proper receipts for them. The CEO of the airline had to untangle the mess; by which time Ramsey was seething.

Exhausted, we boarded an ancient DC-3 for the flight to Kathmandu. I curled up in my seat and tried to sleep, but it soon became clear that sleep wasn't an option.

An hour after we left Delhi, we hit thick cloud and turbulence. The plane bounced around as if it were made of balsa wood. When the cloud momentarily cleared, we could see that we were not flying above the Himalayas, but *through* the Himalayas. Gigantic mountain peaks jutted up through the filmy haze all around us.

I clung to the armrests, whimpering, but Ramsey barely lifted his eyes from his book.

'It's only turbulence,' he said, calmly. 'The pilots have flown this route hundreds of times.'

The Nepali cabin crew seemed similarly unperturbed, even though they occasionally had to clutch onto the backs of our seats in order to stop themselves from being flung down the aisle like rag dolls when the plane suddenly dropped hundreds of feet or soared upwards unexpectedly.

When there was a brief respite, I picked up my guidebook again.

'*The importance placed on preserving human life at all costs is essentially a Western preoccupation, whereas from a Hindu perspective, birth and death are regarded as merely illusory phenomena of an ongoing continuum in an infinite cycle of lifetimes…*'

There was no question in my mind that such a philosophy was bound to affect aircraft maintenance standards. And how could this ancient plane possibly withstand being tossed around so violently by the elements?

A collective sigh of relief registered throughout the cabin when the flight attendants came round with soft drinks and bottles of Kingfisher beer. I drained my bottle within twenty seconds and asked for another.

About fifteen minutes later I glanced across the aisle at Chisie, at the precise moment when the boy next to her threw up violently into his cupped hands. As vomit spewed between his fingers, Chisie leaped out of her seat and lunged away, pausing only to rescue her red T. Anthony make-up case from the torrent. When she stood up, I saw her linen trouser suit was covered in brown and orange flecks.

Tommy, who was sitting nearby, watched all this with a look of amused horror. Ramsey laughed when he realised what was happening, but not for long.

The stench penetrated every molecule of air in the cabin as Chisie staggered up the aisle and disappeared into the tiny bathroom next to the galley, and the now grim-faced stewardesses tried to clean up the youth. But they had little time to do it. As the plane started juddering, more people began throwing up.

Chisie was in the toilet for so long that I became concerned. At this point, other desperate passengers were hammering at the door. When she finally emerged, she looked so haggard that I couldn't help but feel very sorry for her. She slumped down on a jump seat reserved for the cabin crew and dropped her head to her hands.

Eventually, there was another rapid torrent of unintelligible words over the loudspeakers just before the aircraft began an alarmingly swift descent through the swirling clouds, causing extreme pressure in my eardrums. The plane's engines appeared to stall, and we free-fell for a few seconds before, with a roar, they kicked in again, only partially drowning out a dissonant concert of screams inside the cabin, including my own.

Ramsey, still infuriatingly calm, prised my fingers from the armrest and squeezed my hand. 'Don't worry, it was only an air pocket, Ari.'

Before long, we emerged from underneath the cloud blanket and, now that we had our bearings, it became evident we were descending at a normal rate. The town below us was shining darkly, in the midst of a rain shower. But to the west, the sky was clear, a deep shade of cobalt, and the mid-afternoon sun was blazing down on the snowy mountain range ringing the entire perimeter of the horizon. My fear dissolved into awe.

It is possible that a huge sense of relief at just being alive may have played some part in my instant love for Nepal, but there were many other reasons too. Everyone was kind to us. When we left the plane, the air was soft and sweet – though perhaps even a sewer might have smelled delicious after the malodorous silver cylinder from which we had just disembarked.

Horse-drawn carriages and brightly painted rickshaws waited on the tarmac to take passengers to hotels, but we were met by a guide sent to us by the tourist board. Manju, an eager moustachioed man of about thirty, wore pointed winkle-pickers and rolled his head from side to side whenever he was addressed. He pointed to two large jeeps which were ours for the duration of the shoot.

Ramsey looked doubtfully at our huge stack of equipment. 'We might need a bus, Mango.'

We divided into two groups – Tommy and Chisie in one Jeep, and Ramsey and I with Manju in the other. The equipment was stacked to the roof in both.

The main road into town was little more than a dirt track pocked with deep potholes and framed by luminous green paddy fields that stretched across the valley floor and terraced the distant hillsides. Pink and ochre mud houses punctuated the landscape in bright bursts. These dwellings gradually gave way to small villages, where clusters of men crouched on their haunches, sharing roll-ups in shop doorways.

Eventually we hit the outskirts of Kathmandu and were confronted by a hectic sprawl of newly built concrete two and three-storey buildings that appeared to be already falling down. At the sight of them, Ramsey became downcast, but he perked up when we entered the old part of town. Here, narrow winding streets took us past innumerable shrines and pagoda-roofed temples. Traditional brick houses had ornately carved wooden doors and windows. It was four o'clock in the afternoon and the streets were crowded with pedestrians, children in school uniforms, market stalls, bicycles, buses, a few cows and masses of dogs, all roughly of the same breed with yellow coats and tails curved like question marks above their backs. Large lorries stacked high with hay and timber lumbered past, stirring up clouds of dust. (Later, Tommy reported that in the back of their Jeep, Chisie stared bleakly out of the window the whole time, holding a silk Hermes scarf sprayed with Miss Dior over her nose and mouth.)

Finally, we turned onto a wide boulevard divided by a riot of pink and purple bougainvillea and drove along it for a few minutes, until we came to a small driveway leading to a palatial white building with tall columns.

A swarm of bellboys ran down for our bags. We climbed red-carpeted steps to an enormous atrium-style lobby with glittering chandeliers and a grand staircase.

A beaming square-faced man in a striped shirt and black horn-rimmed glasses strode across to greet us, flanked on either side by servants in white uniforms with gold buttons and scarlet sashes, like beauty queens. He introduced himself as Boris Lissanevitch. He spoke English perfectly, with only a hint of a Russian accent.

'Anyone who survives the flight into Kathmandu deserves a stiff drink!' he announced, snapping his fingers. Tall glasses of iced orange juice with vodka and mint were brought in on silver trays.

Boris explained that he would assist us with everything we needed. 'If you want to buy something, let me help. If you want to arrange a thing, I will make it perfect for you.'

When he noticed Chisie was wavering on her feet, he took us up to our rooms.

Ramsey and I were given a suite the size of a dance hall, with a mahogany four-poster bed, and windows opening onto a balcony overlooking a huge garden with a lawn.

Our forty-three bags of clothes, accessories and camera equipment were assigned a room of their own.

Chisie disappeared into her quarters and locked the door.

We had arrived in heaven.

TWENTY-SEVEN

Nepal, November 1969

As soon as we'd changed our clothes, Ramsey announced that he was going out scouting for locations.

I was tired from the trip and longing for dinner followed by a bath and bed, but I wouldn't pass up this chance. 'I'll come too,' I said.

As soon as we were in a taxi heading for Durbar Square, I felt wide awake again.

It wasn't only the black silhouettes of the tiered pagoda roofs against the luminous sky, nor the stone tigers and elephants on either side of the stairs guarding the entrance to the old Royal Palace, or even the cross-current whiffs of sandalwood incense and smoking chilli oil from the street stalls around the periphery of the square. It wasn't even because the snow on the distant mountains was turning the colour of peach ice cream as the sun sank behind the Himalayas. The real reason I was so happy was because Ramsey and I were alone at long last.

Back home, we were never truly alone. When there were big shoots in progress, Ramsey's assistants were often still in the house at midnight. Even on quiet days, there were models knocking at the door, all made up and using every seductive trick going to get Ramsey to look at their books, and hopefully get him to do a test shot. If they succeeded it meant the ominous closing of the studio door, sometimes for hours, no question of disturbing him.

Usually, I would be posted upstairs with the art directors and advertising stooges, who would hang out drinking for hours, hoping to snare a model or meet a celebrity. Ramsey saw their presence as good for business, even though he could barely tolerate most of them.

Then there were the journalists, the film producers and other photographers.

Sometimes they brought their girlfriends, but nearly all of them were on the lookout for young models. It was my job to stay with them and keep them happy. I would fall into bed at around two in the morning, often before Ramsey had finished work. In the morning, he would be downstairs in the office by the time I woke up.

Early on in our relationship we'd often been alone. Now those moments were so rare, I sometimes wondered if he actively avoided being alone with me. I told myself this was paranoia, but our relationship had definitely changed.

We explored a crumbling seventeenth-century royal palace and visited several temples, then browsed the brightly lit shops that ringed the main square, each packed to the rafters with bronze Buddha statues, deities with several heads and arms and eyes, offering bowls made from human skulls and statues of naked female goddesses triumphantly holding up freshly severed heads.

Ramsey began haggling with a beady-eyed shopkeeper. An hour and about a dozen cups of tea later we were still there. The statue Ramsey wanted depicted a kind of grimacing hell-creature in a garland of flames.

'Why that one?' I asked, surprised

'Who knew that Buddhists were so ferocious?' he replied, admiringly.

But as the haggling stretched on, my weariness returned with a vengeance. I could hardly keep my eyes open.

'Let's go back to the hotel for dinner,' I pleaded. 'Boris said he could advise us about things to buy, get us good deals. We can come back here anytime.'

The shopkeeper's face fell when we said goodbye, and he promptly offered Ramsey a large discount. Soon he was wrapping up the statue in newspaper after Ramsey handed him a fistful of rupiahs.

Back at the hotel, we saw none of our crew in the lobby, so we went straight into dinner.

Once a grand ballroom, the dining room at the Royal could have easily seated two hundred people. Apart from a group of bearded Scandinavian climbers, however, we were the only other guests. Several waiters hovered eagerly around our table. Two monumental Victorian chandeliers hung from an elaborately moulded ceiling high above us. A slight but unmistakable smell of drains wafted in through the windows.

We ordered Tibetan dumplings with chilli sauce and beer, our legs entwined under the table. Ramsey seemed contented, not distracted and restless the way he often was at home. For once, we didn't even talk about work. He told me stories about when he was a boy, when the highlight of the week was going to the cinema on Saturday morning. At the beginning of the war he was evacuated to the countryside to stay with a family he had never met. It had not been a success. Two weeks later, after setting fire to a barn, six-year-old Ramsey was put on a train back to London, to endure the Blitz with the rest of his family.

'I hated the countryside. Because I grew up in the war, it seemed normal to sleep in the Underground like everyone else on my street, and to see houses that had been standing the day before lying in a heap of rubble. It never occurred to me that it might happen to us.'

'Is it disturbing when you think about it?'

'Nah, of course not!'

He still talked about buying a house in the country, so we could get out of London more often, just the two of us, so he would have time to mess about with painting and silk-screening.

Glancing at me, he smiled. 'As far from Thurston as possible, don't worry…'

My spirits soared. I wasn't losing him after all. Travelling must have cleared his mind, made him remember why we were together in the first place.

Still, I didn't want to show too much enthusiasm. Experience had taught me that if he felt I was trying to pin him down he would head rapidly in the opposite direction.

We finished off the dumplings and beer, not the lightest of combinations, just as Boris appeared at our table to say hello.

'Boris,' Ramsey said, leaning back in his chair, 'we met your wife in the lobby earlier. She's beautiful. How did you manage that?'

'You should talk, Bill.' Boris smiled at me. I could tell he had fallen for Ramsey in the way that men with healthy-sized egos frequently did. Ramsey tested them, pushing them to the limit of how much teasing they could withstand, but he liked Boris's refusal to get riled, as well as his prodigious energy.

Because of Boris's conviction that tourism would one day flourish in Nepal, every single stick of furniture in the hotel, and all the sheets, towels, kitchen equipment, glasses and plates had been carried from Calcutta on the backs of Sherpas, before a road between the two countries had even existed. It had only been fifteen years since the first tourists started coming to the valley, and it was partly due to Boris's vision, for better or worse.

He invited us to have a drink with him after dinner at the casino he owned next door to the hotel. To my surprise, Ramsey agreed. We'd spent two days travelling, and we had a 5.30 a.m. start the next day, but he was in a fantastic mood and wanted to pump Boris for more inside information about locations.

However, when we arrived, the casino was over air-conditioned and noisy, with Englebert Humperdinck crooning 'The Last Dance' over the sound system. We sat on a dark red velvet banquette with Boris, who insisted we drink whiskey to counteract any travel bugs we might have picked up. He promised us a tour of the Royal Palace, and a tiger shoot, but Ramsey wasn't impressed. He preferred more unusual backdrops – old walls with Nepalese graffiti, for example, though he was also aware that American *Vogue* wanted a grander look, so he was going to have to strike a balance.

We were just about to leave when an Asian Adonis came over to our table. He was much taller than most Nepalis, with abundant brush-cut black hair and eyelids tilting upwards at the sides. He was turned out in a knee-length tartan dressing-gown type garment belted at his hips, beige woollen knee socks, neatly folded over, and well-polished English brogues.

I was rendered speechless. Boris introduced him as Samdhup Dorjee, the *maître d'* of the casino.

'Please, call me Sami,' he said.

He sat down at our table and offered us Benson and Hedges cigarettes from a gold case, lighting them with an Asprey lighter. 'I hear you had an appalling journey.' He smiled at me, as if I had suffered the most. 'I hope we can make up for it, somehow.'

He radiated confidence and sensuous worldliness. I was dazzled.

'Where the hell are you from?' asked Ramsey, studying his extraordinary features.

'My brother was Prime Minister of Bhutan, a hereditary post, with his own army. A few years ago, he was ambushed and assassinated. It was a great shame, because he was a hero to many, not a reprobate like me.'

He smiled at me, causing a considerable disturbance to my equilibrium.

'I succeeded him, but because of internal politics, I was soon forced into exile, along with the officers in our army. We came to Nepal with little more than the shirts on our backs.' He gestured at our host. 'Boris was very kind. He said, 'I've heard all about your wild days at Annabel's in London when you were supposedly studying. You must have learned something during that time. Come work for me."

Boris beamed. 'My hunch paid off. He has made a great success.'

Sami continued, 'I was fortunate to have my brother's army, a group of men I could absolutely trust. They are now the croupiers and the security here when things get a little rough.'

A waiter appeared and Boris tried to convince us to have another shot of whisky, but Ramsey at last refused.

'I need three hours of sleep if I'm going to get anything done tomorrow,' he said, pushing back his chair. 'But thank you for everything. Both of you.'

As we walked up the grand stairs to our suite, the hotel was silent. He took my hand. For the first time in months, I felt that everything was going to be fine again.

TWENTY-EIGHT

Kathmandu, November 1969

As Ramsey had predicted, Manju didn't have a clue what kind of locations we were looking for. Tommy, Ramsey, and I met him downstairs just after dawn, where a driver waited for us in the larger of the two Jeeps.

Vivara wasn't due for a few days, and we needed to scout for the right locations first. We drove to some dusty gardens full of municipally planted marigolds, then miles out of town on a winding dirt road to a mountain pass where, after craning our necks, we could just about glimpse Mount Everest.

'Here is very nice place, good for pictures,' Manju declared.

'This is useless, Mango,' Ramsey snarled.

Manju was shocked at Ramsey's reaction, but his locations were, without question, unworkable and we had little energy for diplomacy. We both had searing headaches from the late night and the altitude.

It fell to Tommy to explain that we were looking for a different kind of backdrop. Something more out of the ordinary. But we weren't going to find it that day. It took hours to get back to Kathmandu, by which time the sun was setting and Ramsey's bad mood had escalated into fury.

He perked up somewhat when we returned to the hotel and Sami brought his wife to meet us for a drink. Selina was half-Burmese, half-Indian, slender and regal, with stunning features.

When Ramsey asked, rather rudely, if she and Sami had an arranged marriage, she nodded, watching him cautiously.

'It must have been a relief for Sami when he lifted your veil and saw you,' Ramsey exclaimed. 'You're beautiful!'

They stayed for dinner, and again we were up drinking until very late. Selina tittered behind her hand at Ramsey's stories, her brown eyes shining. I got the impression she did not receive much attention from Sami, who talked longingly of his bachelor days in London.

Ramsey kept pushing the conversation back to potential locations. He was determined not to waste another day on a wild goose chase.

'Most people who make suggestions have no idea what I'm looking for. They think it's some kind of fucking picture-postcard background we're after, but that's the last thing I want.' He leaned forward, gesturing dismissively at the elegant dining room. 'The problem is I don't usually know what will work until I see it. And our guide has no idea how to help.'

Selina glanced at Sami. 'What about the Pashupathinath temple? It's very special.'

Sami agreed. 'She's right. If you're looking for exotic, the temple is the place.'

The next morning, we set off early. In order to get ahead of the game, Ramsey decided to shoot one or two pages on me alone without Vivara.

Ramsey and Tommy travelled in one jeep with the guide and camera equipment, while I rode with a very subdued Chisie in the other.

'You go with her, for god's sake,' Ramsey had muttered under his breath as we stood shivering outside the hotel in the cold pre-dawn air. 'If I have to be in the same car, her death will be on your hands.'

On the off chance this location worked, I had already done my hair and make-up. I went for an extreme look – lots of colour around my eyes, and exaggerated eyelashes drawn in pencil. I wore blue Pucci leggings with a swirly pattern, a matching tunic and a pair of gold-winged Mercury sandals. Not very Asian, but then we hadn't flown halfway across the world to let cultural references get in the way of showing the clothes.

The moment we stepped out of the jeep, a group of children appeared from nowhere. Two of the little girls carried babies on their hips. None wore shoes. I smiled, and they moved closer, hands extended, eyes pleading.

'Don't do that, you'll encourage them,' Chisie hissed, searching in one of the bags for her pink fringed sun umbrella. I realised I didn't have any rupiahs on me – I'd brought nothing at all except my clothes and make-up. Feebly, I apologised to the children in sign language. They stared back at me blankly.

Chisie handed me the memos Mrs Vreeland had given her back in New York; short meditations on what our team should bear in mind for each look. Under the circumstances they seemed absurd, conjuring up a luxurious vision for the shot that was a million miles from the reality in front of us.

Gazing with disgust into my hand mirror, I began to wonder if I could really pull off the story. It was far easier to disguise my flaws in a studio with proper lighting. Locations were different; you couldn't hide behind so much make-up, and the sunlight, especially at a higher altitude, was much less forgiving. The familiar insecurity returned with a vengeance, along with a slight feeling of nausea.

Chisie was not helping. As Ramsey and Tommy gathered their equipment and headed off up the hill, she nervously piled several gold chains of varying lengths around my neck, and at least a dozen Ken Lane bangles up each arm, which I knew Ramsey would hate. She was anxious about the children with their matted hair and noses running with green mucus. They'd never gone far away but had regrouped nearby, watching us.

'It's all so *filthy*,' Chisie muttered, helplessly.

Our driver Rinchen gave the children sweets and shooed them off but, like obstinate little ghosts, they simply followed us up the hill at a distance. Not long afterwards, to my delight, a family of monkeys appeared just above us on the slope. They seemed just as interested as the children and completely unimpressed when Chisie raised the sun umbrella above her head and began waving them away vigorously. Once again, Rinchen had to intervene. He didn't even have to raise his voice, since his tone carried authority. The monkeys scampered away and vanished into the woods on the ridge above us.

By the time we reached the top of the hill we were out of breath and sweaty, dragging bulging bags of clothes and make-up across scrubby grass. We caught sight of Tommy, standing in the shade of a large domed building that resembled a mausoleum. It was an ominous place with carved snakes encircling the eaves. A few hundred yards to the left a paved terrace looked out onto the temple Sami had described. There, the hill fell away, offering a glimpse of golden roof tops beyond. Seeing us approach, Tommy waved and pointed around to the other side of the building. We headed in that direction. When we turned the corner, Chisie stood frozen in her tracks.

Ramsey was sitting on some steps, talking to two men who were tending a small campfire. One was almost naked apart from an abbreviated saffron *dhoti*, his face and body smeared in white ash. His long, matted hair and beard hung in ash-covered dreads almost to his waist, and there was a red and white cross-hatched pyramid painted on his forehead. His fierce X-ray eyes bore first into Chisie, then me. His companion, in a red and saffron turban with a topknot of thick braids emerging from the peak, was no less startling. As we approached, he lit a long conical pipe with a match and took a drag. When he exhaled, most of his head disappeared in a cloud of smoke.

I realised immediately that Ramsey was hoping to use them in the shot. Standing a respectful distance from the holy men, Manju looked anxious.

'Where have you been?' Ramsey asked as we neared, the corners of his mouth turning down. 'We're losing the good light.'

A negotiation between Manju and the holy men ended with a transaction that didn't seem to make Manju particularly happy. As soon as the notes disappeared into their respective *dhotis*, Ramsey sprang to his feet and grabbed his camera.

'Ramsey, I really don't think this is appropriate,' Chisie said, clearly terrified of going anywhere near them.

As if she hadn't spoken at all, Ramsey turned to me. 'OK, darling, stand over there by the wall in the shade. That's it. Tommy? The Nikon. Chisie, Ari's nose has gone shiny, where's the powder? And will you tell the naked geezer to sit in profile? I can see his fucking balls hanging out of his *dhoti*.'

'For pity's *sake,* Ramsey,' Chisie whispered, horrified.

When the shot was lined up, I stood in the foreground leaning moodily against a wall of the mausoleum with the holy men several yards behind me, somewhat obscured by smoke from their campfire. As I lifted my eyes to the camera lens, I wondered what Mrs Vreeland would make of the picture.

Chisie was irritated. 'I really don't think those people are right for a fashion story,' she said. 'The Pucci deserves to be shown in a majestic setting, not with... vagrants.'

Our silent audience of staring children had reappeared, though perhaps because of the holy men, they kept their distance. A group of American tourists, dressed for the golf course, also drifted over to take photographs of us.

'Is that man an Aboriginal?' I heard a woman ask.

'No that's a *sadhu*, a wandering ascetic. He has given up all his worldly possessions to follow Lord Shiva,' explained their American guide.

When Ramsey was satisfied with the shot, Chisie held up a shawl to hide me from our growing audience as I changed into another evening dress.

As I pulled the dress over my head, I heard Ramsey tell Tommy he thought the Pucci was too hectic for my pale skin tone. 'But let's not worry about it now,' he concluded. 'Plenty of time at the end to reshoot on Vivara if we have to.'

And I thought it had gone well! I choked back my tears. A puffy face would mean we'd have to stop work for the day.

The next outfit was a full-length purple *crepe de chine* halter neck dress, hanging from a yoke of polished silver metal. I unpinned the hairpiece and twisted my own hair back into a low chignon. Sweat was pouring off my face and under my arms which rather ruined the overall look.

By now Ramsey was unhappy with the light; there was too much glare. But rather than waste the morning, he decided to attempt the shot using a filter. We decamped to the paved terrace overlooking the ancient and beautiful temple complex on the opposite bank of the Bagmati. Several men in sarongs were washing themselves in the slow-moving river below us, sunlight reflecting off their wet skin. A group of pilgrims garbed in white milled about on the stone steps behind them, as I reapplied my make-up.

All the visitors had attracted more monkeys. Several perched a few yards away on a wide guard rail at the edge of the lookout, waiting for tourists to give them food. Tommy watched the camera equipment like a hawk while Ramsey went off to scout for the best spot to shoot.

It wasn't easy applying false eyelashes in front of a crowd which now included children, tourists and a group of teenage boys.

Manju and Rinchen made a concerted effort to get the disparate groups to move further away, but they all crept a few paces forward whenever our backs were turned. Chisie muttered bitter complaints about the conditions as she layered multiple accessories on my body, as if I were a Christmas tree. The instant she finished, Ramsey reappeared and instructed her to take off everything except the dress and the earrings.

'Simple is much better for Ari,' he said, with a sidelong glance at me. 'She's complicated enough as it is.'

I made myself forget the comment I'd overheard earlier. Vivara would be arriving in Kathmandu later today, and I needed to make the most of this shoot and behave professionally.

It was only ten o'clock, but the sun was already so bright it was difficult not to squint. Ramsey moved me into a better spot.

'Come over into the shade of this tree,' he instructed. 'Stand at a three-quarter angle from me, look up beyond the rooftops of the temple to the pine trees in the distance, and think of something interesting. Me, for example.'

For some reason, Sami popped into my mind. He was the only man who had ever openly flirted with me in front of Ramsey.

I widened my eyes and looked straight at the camera.

'Put your hand up to your brow as if you're shielding your eyes… Yes, there. That's good.' *Snap. Snap. Snap.*

After a while I changed the pose for variety's sake, but Ramsey peered around the camera at me and said sharply, 'You've got to let me direct you; I'm trying for a geometric line here. And sorry, darling, but can you suck in your stomach? It's just because of the angle. That's good now, OK Ari, you look great.'

Even though by now the American group had departed, and none of the children or teenagers appeared to understand English, I could feel my cheeks turning red with shame. How could I have allowed this to happen? Nepali curry and beer had made my belly swell up like a balloon. I just wouldn't eat for two days, that always worked. It was a necessary sacrifice if I didn't want to look even more like a podgy midget next to Vivara. But my stomach was already grumbling from hunger. Too bloody bad. What had happened to my willpower?

As we worked, I was distracted by the sharp crackling sound of a bonfire in the distance. Clouds of dark smoke were drifting across the pagoda roof tops. I squinted to get a closer look.

'No, darling, don't move, stay looking up, up, *up!* I know it's bright but keep your eyes open at all times. That's it.'

Ramsey was shooting me from below – a notoriously unflattering angle. Serious double chin territory. I stretched my neck, pushed my shoulders down and sucked my stomach in. Who could I be now? An expression of wistful serenity seemed appropriate for a temple shot.

'Ari, look to your right,' Ramsey hissed, and I realised there was monkey action on the balustrade. A gang of them were coming into the shot. It was every photographer's dream when this kind of spontaneous event occurred.

'For fuck's sake, Tommy, quickly, load the Nikon. Ari, just stay completely still. Do we have any food for them? Chisie?'

I didn't have to turn around to realise Chisie would be stalling for time, rummaging around in the duffel bag, knowing full well she wouldn't go near the monkeys.

Tommy produced a packet of digestives from a pocket in one of the camera cases and went over to the rails to give each monkey a biscuit. Two of them immediately darted off with their loot, tails raised high in the air, but the oldest and biggest one sat just a couple of feet away, chewing, his lips moving in a funny, exaggerated way.

'Chisie, powder Ari's face,' Ramsey hissed. 'And her hair needs a bit of smoothing. Quickly, before he takes off.'

I snuck a peek at Chisie as she hovered around me, with her default expression of blank disdain. Unfortunately, she set her glasses down on the balustrade. Within a second, the monkey made a lunge for them and took off down the hill on the other side of the railing to examine his prize.

'*Nooo!* They're my only pair! I can't see without them!' Chisie wailed.

I tried, and failed, to repress the kind of wild, hysterical laughter that surfaces mainly at inappropriate moments. There was much shouting as Manju, Rinchen and some of the teenage boys yelled at the monkey in Nepali. Tommy waved the remains of the packet of biscuits around. With comic timing, the monkey dangled the glasses over a sheer drop of a few hundred feet above the river and looked back at us impudently. Ramsey was laughing too, but he managed to fire off a few snaps of the scene at the same time.

In the midst of the chaos, my eyes travelled down towards the source of all the smoke. Piles of rubbish appeared to be burning in front of the temple although, judging by all the people milling about, a ceremony seemed to be in progress. My gaze alighted on two men heaving a long bundle wrapped in white cotton on top of a pallet. They made their way slowly towards the river, followed by a small party of people who gathered while they lowered the bundle on the steps. When the white cotton shroud was removed, the corpse of a young girl was revealed; her mouth bound with a white cloth tied at the back of her head. After her feet were washed by a group of women, she was carried up the steps to a stone platform and laid down on top of a large bed of straw and kindling.

A bald man appeared on the scene, wielding a big stick. I was too far away to see his expression or what he was doing as he hovered over the body, but not long afterwards the pile of twigs was ablaze. A man, a woman and two small boys gathered at a distance watching; I assumed they were the girl's family. From my vantage point they all appeared quite dispassionate. But there was also a terrible sense of desolation about the scene, as flames began to lick the girl's body and the attendant vigorously stoked the straw underneath her with his flaming torch. Never having seen a dead body before, much less one burning on a pyre, I was profoundly shocked by the stark reality of the scene, which no one else in our party seemed to have noticed.

Moments later I was startled by a loud whoop from an unusually exuberant Chisie. Rinchen the driver had managed to scale the railings and coax the monkey into relinquishing the glasses in exchange for some bright orange sweets. Everyone clapped as he handed the glasses to Chisie, who could barely bring herself to touch them, though she did thank him.

By then Ramsey decided it was time to stop for lunch. While the team packed up, I returned to the terrace overlooking the river and temple. Thick clouds of brown smoke edged with sparks billowed furiously out of the girl's pyre, obscuring the temple behind. Her head and torso appeared to have disintegrated and the only identifiable part of her left were two thin legs, which poked down out of the straw like black twigs. The official was prodding and bashing them with his flaming stick. After a while, they snapped like dried branches, and he shovelled them into the pile of bones in the centre of the fire. The official stopped for a minute and wiped his face with his forearm. The girl's family had vanished, possibly because the heat had become too intense.

Despite the raw pathos of the scene, passers-by walked across the bridge, barely glancing at the pyre. A group of boys played in the river just below the fire. A yellow dog lay asleep on the steps nearby.

Rinchen appeared beside me. 'Miss Ari? We go now. I take your bags.' He followed my gaze to the funeral pyres.

'Holy *ghat*,' he explained. 'Burn all day; all night.'

TWENTY-NINE

Kathmandu, November 1969

That evening, following another tricky shoot in the afternoon, Boris greeted us in reception. 'Countess von Schwaben-Durneiss auf Aleinstadt arrived a couple of hours ago,' he announced, pronouncing each syllable of her name with relish. 'She's in the pool doing laps.'

Of course she was. Vivara was terrifyingly disciplined. I hadn't even considered exercise since we arrived.

'Why use one name when four will do?' muttered Ramsey. I noticed he was eyeing the pretty receptionist in a tight-fitting *salwar kurta* as she handed him our tasselled room key.

Unlike Boris, Ramsey had no time for titles.

At dinner, he was distant and uncommunicative, clearly unhappy with how the day's shoot had gone. Abandoning my earlier resolve, I drank a bottle of beer to ease my nerves. Lately, nothing flowed when Ramsey and I worked together. If I tried something different, he'd accuse me of pulling silly faces instead of doing what he asked. When I mentioned the cremation in the temple he simply said, 'That's what they do here,' and changed the subject.

Just as we were about to leave the dining room, Vivara walked in. Though she was dressed simply in a grey cashmere jumper and jeans, all the other diners turned and stared at her as she strode across the room to our table. Her tawny shoulder-length hair was dead straight, and she wore no make-up, but her honey-coloured skin brought out the luminosity of her ice-blue eyes. Her long legs were as toned as a dancer's.

When Ramsey rose to his feet and kissed her, even though she was wearing flat

185

boots, she had to bend to reach him. He flagged down a waiter and ordered a bottle of champagne, suddenly cheerful for the first time since that morning.

My heart sank. I was desperate to go to bed, but leaving Ramsey alone with Vivara was out of the question. So we sat at the table and listened as she told us about her stay in the vast palace belonging to the Maharajah of Jodhpur, and how she rode in an elephant polo team and everyone said she brought luck to them because they won.

'Well, you'd better bring some good luck to our team, darling, because we're not cutting it at the moment.' Ramsey laughed.

I looked down at my hands. I wasn't cutting it, he meant.

It turned out Vivara never touched alcohol when she was working. She was wise. I drank her share and mine too. I never could bypass the short-term solution.

It was an early call the following morning. Ramsey was testing Vivara's mettle, but she was already in the room we'd designated as the changing room when I stumbled in at five o'clock. Chisie took one look at me and handed over the Panadol and the French eyedrops. A pot of sweet chai and a plate of biscuits had been left out and I fell on them. Vivara sipped mineral water.

Chisie helped us into Yves St Laurent caftans in contrasting shades of yellow, with white silk tight-fitting shirts and leggings underneath. The colours made my pale skin look jaundiced, but Vivara was instantly transformed into the queen of the souk, with wide gold bangles showing off her perfectly toned upper arms and her tawny hair swept back off her face in the style of a sphinx.

We arrived in Durbar Square at first light, and although it was freezing and I was feeling like hell, the splendour of the temples, shrines and palaces lifted my mood. Ramsey decided he wanted Vivara and me leaning against the carved stone elephants guarding either side of the stone steps leading to the main temple. Manju informed us that every king of Nepal had been crowned here since the fourteenth century.

This morning, a toothless old man, with a couple of goats in tow, sat on his haunches smoking a chillum at the top of the steps. He looked surprised when Ramsey gave him some rupiahs to stay there.

'Ari, stand in profile, and look at Vivara. V, eyes straight at me. That's it. Wonderful. You look like an Egyptian frieze.'

It was my first opportunity to study Vivara's technique up close. I had modelled alongside other girls, even Twiggy. But Vivara was in another class. She had perfected the art of the micro expression. One moment she was a lioness basking in the sun, the next, she exuded a post-coital glow. A slight smile at the corners of her mouth hinted at a secret. She could even laugh on cue, as convincingly as if she had just heard the funniest joke in the world. Several years must have been spent in front of the mirror rehearsing all these subtle changes of expression. She knew exactly how to turn her head so the photographer could catch her best angle, no matter where the sun was positioned. I sensed Ramsey's growing admiration for her, and I could see exactly how Vivara made his work easier.

Most of Ramsey's instructions were now directed at me. In these variable conditions, every move I made seemed to cause problems. To make things worse, whenever Chisie intervened in order to adjust the way the caftans fell, or to apply a little more gold powder to our cheeks, she would tell Vivara how great she looked and ignore me completely. I felt increasingly paranoid and downcast.

Later, we returned to the hotel to shoot some pictures in the garden. Boris had recently taken delivery of two tiger cubs for his zoo, and his wife, Inger, spent hours every day feeding them formula from baby bottles. Vivara was given the honour of posing with them in a perfectly tailored St Laurent safari suit in champagne-coloured silk. I had to give Chisie credit – it was the perfect combination. There was such a resemblance between the model and the cubs no one would have been at all surprised if Vivara had started suckling them from her own teats.

Ramsey was delighted.

Then it was my turn. In a backless white satin evening dress by Balmain, I stood on the lawn trying to get close to a white peacock. He darted about nervously, refusing to spread his tail even though he had done little else since our arrival. The mosquitoes were out in full force, and my back was soon covered in red bites. It was a disaster.

When he saw how upset I was, Boris put his arm around me. This inspired Ramsey to restage the shot in the Yak 'n' Yeti bar, with Boris gazing into my eyes.

We drank several martinis in the process, and Boris told me fabulous stories about his childhood in Russia, escaping the Bolsheviks on horseback, taking up ballet in his late teens and touring Europe in the 1920's with the Ballets Russes. He had experienced war, famine, the loss of many friends and family members, but the journey had made him fearless. Or at least, this was the impression he gave.

By the time we finished, a considerable audience of Boris admirers had gathered in the bar; including the Scandi climbers who'd been in the dining room on the first night, a middle-aged Anglo-Indian couple, a grizzled group of bird watchers from

South Carolina, and of course Tommy and Chisie.

The spell was broken when Vivara appeared in the bar, sleek as a seal in black ski pants.

Immediately, the spotlight deserted us and settled on her.

'I wish to buy *Boodha* in bazaar,' she announced to Boris, oblivious of the spell she had broken. 'You know where is good shop?'

Boris said he certainly did know and offered to accompany her.

Ramsey went off with Tommy to plan the next day's shoot but, before he left, he kissed me and said, 'You did good today, girl. We got a great shot. You looked so much more natural than Vivara. Now get some sleep while I finish up. It's going to be another early start.'

All my doubts evaporated in an instant.

As soon as I got to the room, I passed out on the bed, poleaxed by the martinis and lack of sleep the previous night, too exhausted to take off the Balmain.

I fell into a swamp of dreams. In one, I stood on the deck of a sailboat holding a little girl. Behind us a group of friends were drinking and laughing in the cockpit, a smirking man sat at the helm. He wished me harm, but I was trying to ignore him. Without warning the wind changed, and the boom swung across at full speed from the other side of the boat and struck me on the side of my head. Reeling precariously close to the edge, I was aware of a pain more intense than any I had experienced before. I clutched onto the mast with my free arm and, summoning all my strength, I managed to hold on to the little girl and my balance without falling overboard.

The images dissolved into darkness, but a pounding headache remained as I awoke abruptly.

I didn't have to open my eyes to know that Ramsey's side of the bed hadn't been slept in. But there was no time to think about that, as my stomach heaved threateningly.

I stumbled across the suite, which was spinning like a fairground ride, to the bathroom. There was no time to get the Balmain off before I vomited violently, then huddled over the toilet in a dress that cost as much as a house.

When my stomach was empty, I stood with a groan, clutching the sink to hold myself up. My head throbbed with such force I could barely think but I knew I shouldn't still be wearing that dress. I tottered unsteadily back into the bedroom and tore it off, tossing it in the direction of a planter's chair where it landed briefly before sliding off onto the tiled floor. I could hear Boris's exotic birds chattering and jeering outside as I staggered back to bed and pulled the covers over my head.

Where was Ramsey?

I reminded myself that insomnia often drove him out on his own. How many times had he told me that he loved me and only me, but he needed to be left alone when he was working? He hated it when I crowded him. I closed my eyes but stayed wide awake ruminating for some time.

It was mid-morning when Ramsey returned to the room to change and take a bath. By then, I felt a little better. I'd hidden the stained dress in the back of the cupboard before soaking myself in a bath with rose oil.

'Were you sick in here?' he looked around the bathroom, wrinkling his nose.

He wasn't a picture of health either, having stayed up drinking with Boris and Inger in their apartment, before falling asleep on their sofa.

'Boris must have put away a bottle of vodka last night just by himself,' he commented. 'He's a goer.'

'And Vivara?' I asked.

He stood at the sink, his back to me. 'Oh, she wasn't there. I think she went to bed early.'

It sounded plausible. 'Who else was with you?'

The question hung in the air momentarily as Ramsey washed his face. When he straightened, he changed the subject. 'Oh, I almost forgot. Boris says we are all invited to the royal palace tonight for dinner. He's going to ask the King if I can take his picture. Otherwise, as far as I'm concerned, it's not worth the effort. But we'll have to get at least two pages done today before we can think of going.'

My gut had finally begun to settle by the time we were both dressed and ready to go.

By then, Ramsey was in a good mood again. I tried to ignore the anxiety in the pit of my stomach about his disappearance overnight. Maybe he really had slept on Boris's couch. Maybe everything was just as he'd described it.

Ramsey didn't want breakfast, so I sat alone in the vast dining room, watched over by a dozen waiters while I ate some *congee*, a kind of lightly sweetened rice pudding. It was certainly binding, like eating paper glue, but it did the trick.

With every mouthful I became more aware that Ramsey had lied to me about what had happened last night. Clearly, I would have to confront him, but when? It never seemed like the right moment.

When I bumped into Inger in the lobby after breakfast, she was as bright and efficient as ever, but there was something a little tight about her mouth. I wanted to hear her account of the evening, but she hurried away before I could find the words.

When I made it to the changing room, Vivara was already made up. She looked beautiful as always and rested. Surely she hadn't been up all night?

Chisie was in two minds about putting us in the Fortuny dresses before we reached the location. The permanent hand-pleating method used to make them had been invented by an Italian in the 1920s and kept secret for half a century. Mrs Vreeland had persuaded the Fortuny family to go into production once more as she was convinced there would be a huge market for them again.

'They'd look modern in any century!' she'd proclaimed.

As Chisie fretted that we might damage them, I said little. If she knew the condition of the white satin Balmain dress I'd worn the day before, she would have lost her mind. When she asked where it was, I told her the dress was being pressed by Inger's personal valet and would be returned this evening. Chisie was delighted, which only made me feel worse. I suspected the dress was ruined and at some point I'd have to tell the truth about what had happened. But not today.

Meanwhile, Vivara sat at the dressing table in our palatial changing room, glowing with health. From the bottom drawer of her three-tiered red leather make-up case she produced hair pieces, bobby pins and Alberto VO5 hair spray. Within minutes she had scraped her shoulder-length hair up into a knot on the top of her head, out of which cascaded a three-foot long ponytail of golden Dynel.

By the time she'd finished, Chisie had decided that dressing us on a Kathmandu street would cause chaos. So she stood on the bed and expertly eased a simple Fortuny sheath the colour of a chilly sea over Vivara's head. The dress accentuated her curves, turning her elongated gazelle body into a Brancusi sculpture. Even I was gobsmacked as the cerulean blue of Vivara's eyes seemed to adjust to match the darker shade of the fabric.

If she had grown a mermaid's tail at that point, it would not have surprised me. Envy melted away into admiration; I was simply outclassed.

Chisie put me in an ankle-length Fortuny dress the colour of turds, but with an exquisite diaphanous chiffon *djellaba* worn over it. The silk gauze material was as delicate as gossamer and had a vivid Turkish pattern of flowers and birds stencilled over it, and the hems and edges were trimmed with coral-coloured Venetian beads. It was the most extraordinary dress I'd ever worn. My eye make-up was dark and layered, and my hair teased up, like the Marchesa Casati, or so I hoped. Chisie reminded me how much the ensemble cost and how careful I had to be.

I followed Vivara across the lobby and took pleasure from seeing the eyes of staff and guests widen and their jaws fall open as we strode past them, Vivara's long ponytail swinging jauntily from side to side.

Yesterday's shoot had gone well in the end. Today's would be even better. All I had to do was put Ramsey's shenanigans out of my mind and stay focused.

THIRTY

Kathmandu, November 1969

Leaving the dusty town behind, our three-jeep convoy negotiated bumpy dirt tracks between terraced rice paddies. Overhead, voluminous black clouds scudded across the sky, although decent patches of blue were still visible behind them. Then came a dramatic flash of lightning, followed a few seconds later by earth-shaking thunder and a sudden downpour so intense we had to pull over onto the side of the road. In the space of a few minutes, the road itself became a swift moving torrent.

'It was sunny all the time you were faffing about, and now we're completely fucked for another day,' Ramsey snarled at me out of the corner of his mouth. His mood had deteriorated during the hours it had taken us to get ready.

Manju turned around from the front seat and fluttered his hands. 'No, no... is fine,' he insisted. 'This will pass.'

Unconvinced, Ramsey stared out the window in a rage. I tried not to breathe or speak in order not to annoy him further.

It was hot in the un-airconditioned Jeep, and we were all sweating profusely. I could feel the poisons from the night before seeping through my pores into the priceless Fortuny silk dress.

Fortunately, Manju was right. As suddenly as the storm had begun, it ended. The sun came out and a giant rainbow arced over a sky in which the clouds gleamed pale gold. We rolled down the windows and drank in the smell of rich, red earth. Flashes of blinding sunlight in puddles on the road, and the psychedelically green rice paddies, added to a euphoric sense of release we all felt after the downpour.

Ramsey jumped out with his Pentax and fired off a barrage of shots in every direction. Then he shaded his eyes against the light and shouted, pointing at something in the distance. I scrambled out of the Jeep and joined him on the road.

Rising out of a hilltop hamlet, in the midst of a higgledy-piggledy collection of ancient mudbrick houses, a golden spire atop a golden pyramid shimmered in the afternoon light. At the base of the pyramid, visible just above the rooftops, was a mesmerising pair of painted eyes.

'What the hell is that?' Ramsey asked.

'This is Tibetans' holy spot. Also Hindus. Very old,' Manju explained, his tone reverent.

Ramsey climbed back in the jeep and told the driver, 'Forget our plans.' He pointed at the spire. 'We're going there.'

The other two jeeps followed ours as we turned off the road onto a track that climbed up the hill. When we arrived at the village ten minutes later, we found no cars were allowed inside the old walls. We left the vehicles with their drivers in a back street and walked through an ornate wooden gate with carved dragons and snow lions that led straight into the main square, dominated by the most otherworldly structure I had ever laid eyes on.

From the ground, the *stupa* was monumental, a vast, whitewashed dome topped by the golden pyramid and spire we had seen from a distance. The body of the *stupa* rested on a series of three ascending platforms upon which thousands of tiny flames flickered. From afar we had failed to take in what we could see now – the pyramid was four sided, and enigmatic blue eyes were emblazoned on each side. Wherever we walked, we were conscious of a celestial, unearthly presence following us.

There was a festival-like atmosphere in the square surrounding the *stupa*. A profusion of white, red, yellow, blue and green prayer flags streamed in all directions from the top of the spire to the ground, where they were secured to metal posts around the base. Groups of pilgrims made their way around the platforms on narrow pathways between the candles, completing a full circuit of each level before climbing the stairs down to the next. However, most of the crowd walked around the base in a clockwise direction, chanting and singing. The older Tibetans looked as if they came from Middle Earth; tiny, with ruddy complexions, some of them stooped over or limping, but nonetheless walking with determination, and attired in a combination of dusty rags and stunning turquoise and coral jewellery.

The youngest women wore their hair in multiple plaits, fixed with turquoise and coral beads, beautiful with their high cheekbones and deep-set eyes.

We all stared at the scene, transfixed.

On Manju's recommendation, Tommy and Ramsey found a place for us to set up on a second-floor balcony used by a small restaurant, where the tables all faced one side of the *stupa*'s enigmatic azure eyes.

Chisie immediately went about organising the outfits she had chosen for the next shots and setting up an accessories table.

'Don't mess about,' Ramsey told us curtly. 'We've got to get three shots done before sunset.'

Only one other table on the balcony was occupied, by a young, hippie couple slurping bowls of noodles. The girl was tiny, a sexy confident little pocket Venus with dark skin and flashing eyes, six inches of silver bangles on her wrists and ankles, Turkish pantaloon trousers, and a skin-tight tank top.

The young man was long and lean with an impressive turban of golden dreadlocks which increased his already considerable height by at least a foot.

They watched with interest while Vivara and I retouched our make-up and Tommy loaded the cameras.

As he waited, Ramsey zoned in on the couple. 'Where do you come from, then, you two?'

'We're from San Diego.' The girl gestured at the sunlit square. 'But Nepal is our spiritual home.'

The young man tapped his chest. 'I'm Reed and this is Durga. We're Tibetan Buddhists, attending teachings here in Nepal from some of the high lamas.'

Ramsey smiled and nodded, and when they weren't paying attention, he whispered 'What are they high on?' to Tommy, who laughed quietly as he worked.

Reed had no inkling he was being teased. He explained earnestly that some of the Tibetan masters had suffered great hardships under Chinese rule. Many had been forced to flee across the Himalayas to Nepal and India, where they were now rebuilding their monasteries.

I asked Reed if the eyes on the *stupa* represented an extra-terrestrial presence.

'No way, they're the eyes of the Buddha,' he explained. 'Stylised, in the Eastern tradition, but about as human as you can get. The point is that the Buddha was not a god but a man. Some of his bones and teeth are meant to be buried inside the *stupa*, along with tons of gold, precious stones, and reams of prayers. That's what magnetises people to come here.'

I waited for Ramsey to make a joke, but he'd lost interest. 'Fascinating,' he said, in a tone that suggested he was not fascinated. 'Right. Let's get to work.'

He arranged us so I was sitting at a table opposite Vivara, playing cards, under the watchful Buddha eyes. He shot a few rolls from different angles but soon made it clear he was not happy with the set-up.

He didn't direct me as much as usual, which was a relief, though he seemed cross about everything.

After a while, he stopped for a whispered conference with Tommy, who nodded enthusiastically. 'Ari,' Ramsey said, 'could you step out of shot please?'

As I got up and walked behind the camera, he turned to Reed. 'How would you like to be photographed?'

Reed looked surprised, but shrugged. 'Sure.'

Durga clapped her hands in delight as he left her side and took my seat. I was silent, puzzled, as Chisie hovered around Reed with powder and a brush.

Looking through the viewfinder, Ramsey said, 'Yeah, that's better. You see, Ari, together, you and Viva look like fashion plates, and it just doesn't work with this location. It's much better for the whole look of the story if one of you has acquired a lover along the way. It so happens that Steve here – is that your name? No? Sorry – is a perfect match for Viva. OK, now I want you to be staring into each other's eyes, like you are about to devour each other. Don't worry, darling.' He glanced at Durga, who was beaming at her boyfriend. 'You can cry on my shoulder, if you want.'

'But what about the dress Ari is wearing? We simply MUST show it in this story,' carped Chisie.

'Later, Chisie. Don't bother me. I've finally got what I'm looking for.' Ramsey was now excited and fully engaged. I stood watching this in my forty-thousand-pound dress, my hair slowly wilting.

I turned on my heel and legged it down the stairs, nearly colliding with a waiter carrying a tray of drinks. He pointed me to the loo, but the smell of shit in the tiny bathroom made even solitary tears impossible and I left immediately, stumbling down another flight of stairs and out into the square again.

Without thinking about it, I joined the stream of Tibetans, Nepalese, and hippies circling the *stupa*. While I was dressed for the palazzo, with a painted face, big hair and a priceless frock, my state of mind had descended into hell; the only word for it. I was burning with shame, jealousy and homicidal fantasies. In order to contain them,

195

I realised I needed to move and keep moving; allow the steady stream of pilgrims to carry me along with them until I could calm down long enough to figure out a plan. And it was strangely comforting to be lost in the crowd, so I simply copied whatever everyone else was doing.

Inside the stucco wall around the *stupa*, long brass tubes embossed with Sanskrit letters revolved when they were pushed by the pilgrims as they went past, so I pushed them too. I chanted or muttered what I thought everyone else was chanting.

It took about ten minutes to complete one circuit of the *stupa*, and after several rounds, I was in a kind of pleasurable trance, about as far removed from the *Vogue* shoot as it was possible to be. So I was genuinely jolted when Tommy appeared, frantic and out of breath, with Rinchen behind him. When he spotted me, relief suffused his sweet face.

'Thank god, Ari! We've been looking for you everywhere. We're about to leave. We're going to another temple Reed recommended and we have to do it fast while the light's good. Ramsey says we don't need you for now. You can go back to the hotel. We'll do your dress on the staircase when we get back.'

I must have looked upset, because Tommy touched my shoulder in a gesture of sympathy which made me feel much worse. I heard myself stuttering, 'OK. Go! See you later.'

He ran off to join the others, and I was left with Rinchen.

I didn't want to be watching forlornly as Ramsey and the rest of the team, including Reed and Durga, disappeared through the ornamental gates. So I asked Rinchen to wait for me.

Without giving it too much thought, I joined the crowd circuiting the *stupa* again. *Put one foot in front of the other*, I told myself. *That is how you'll get through this.*

THIRTY-ONE

Kathmandu, November 1969

A party of chatty ladies in bright silk saris and *kurtas* sauntered casually along the path in front of me. They were soon overtaken by a delegation of monks wearing woollen maroon robes draped around yellow silk undergarments. A few of them were young teenagers, still gawky, constantly rearranging their robes. They were accompanied by watchful older monks with shaved heads and wire-rimmed glasses. Ten yards ahead, I spotted two wild men in white robes, and sandals, their long dreadlocks wound around the tops of their heads in a knot, a turquoise earring in one ear. Their faces were dark and leathery, as if they spent a lot of time in the sun at high altitudes. I noticed that many of the locals bowed deferentially to them as they passed.

By now it was late afternoon and the sun's bright glare was softening.

A faint drumbeat pulsed in the distance. A narrow fringe of red and green silk billowed in the breeze above the mesmerising blue eyes of the *stupa*. Coloured flags fluttered like confetti down from the spire, while several flocks of pigeons wheeled about in the sky overhead. My senses were so overwhelmed that once again I forgot everything except the scene in front of me.

The slow steady drumbeat picked up pace and became more insistent. Then came the peculiar, strangulated sound of a trumpet crossed with bagpipes. I quickened my pace and followed the raucous noise until I encountered a procession of about twenty monks in dark red robes ascending the stairs up to the *stupa*. Some of them wore tall saffron-coloured hats, like cockatoo crests, and they lined up on either side of the central steps, as if they were expecting to receive a king.

I joined the crowd below, who seemed to know what was happening, since they had all turned to look expectantly at one of the houses opposite the *stupa*. Minutes later, a cluster of monks emerged from the house and slowly made their way towards us. They were supporting another man, a striking figure at least a foot taller than the others. He was hunched over and hobbling, clearly in pain, but he smiled at each person who caught his eye and said a few words to them.

It was hard to see through the crowds, so I slipped through the gates and ran up some narrow steps to the right of the *stupa* entrance. Apart from the monks grouped on either side of the central stairs, the platforms were deserted, save for a little hut on the first platform. Here a young Tibetan man sold candles, which were little more than wicks floating in oil in little iron holders.

He waved me over. 'Hi, friend. I dig your outfit!' He spoke English with an American accent and informed me he also spoke French and German, which he had learned from the hippies, although he had never left Nepal.

As usual, I had no money on me, but he gave me six candles – he called them butter lamps – in an iron tray. When I thanked him, he smiled. 'You came on an auspicious day. A lama from Bhutan is doing a *puja* for Guru Rinpoche. You must make an offering with these lamps and say some prayers for good luck.'

He gesticulated with an upward sweep of his hand.

Following his instructions, I took my tray of votive butter candles and walked slowly around the *stupa*, carefully climbing the stairs where there were fewer people, and then heading back round to the spot where a group of monks were now setting up a small table with statues and objects that looked like strangely-shaped iced cakes. They had placed a thick-pile Tibetan rug on the whitewashed cement, and a high-backed chair covered with red, blue and gold brocade amid the statues. A Thermos and a blue and white china cup and saucer rested on a table next to the chair. I stood a respectful distance away, looking for a spot to set down my butter lamps.

Quite a crowd had gathered and clusters of the little oil lamps flickered in rows at least six deep along the edges of the platforms and on the ledge above us. The sun had begun to set, and the sky was streaked with pink. By candlelight, the *stupa* was even more enchanting.

Finding a spot on the ledge where a few lamps had burned out, I replaced them with mine, which were still steadily burning.

As I did so, a prayer came into my head, unexpectedly: 'Teach me to overcome my jealousy.'

How I wanted that! Jealousy was ruining my life. As Jules had reminded me more than once, we are all born alone. And, like the girl on the pyre, we die alone. But for me, life wasn't worth living without Ramsey. With him I was complete; without him I was a ghost. Loving him was painful, but he gave me a reason to live.

The only hope I had of keeping Ramsey was if I could overcome my possessiveness. Other models I knew had managed it with their pop-star boyfriends. They appeared to be pioneering a new, more liberated kind of femininity. But then they usually ended up sitting alone in Tudor mansions in Kent and Surrey for much of the year, waiting for their boyfriends to come off tour. I didn't want that. I just wanted Ramsey to love me the way he used to. I wanted to be enough for him.

The old lama was tackling the second staircase with difficulty, pausing every few minutes to lean on his helper-monks and wipe his brow. When he reached the top, he stopped and flashed the most unexpectedly brilliant grin at all of us standing there. It completely transformed his face, as if his infirmities were insignificant.

With great difficulty, he prostrated himself to the brocade-covered throne three times, before sitting down on it. The monks produced a brocade headdress, which they placed on his head. Out of the throng of maroon robes, two small boy monks, both about seven or eight years old, appeared and perched on little stools placed on either side of the old man.

The crowd of Tibetans around me jostled to get near him, but I held my ground, intrigued by what was about to happen. The lama said a few words in Tibetan, and then began chanting. He had an odd voice, like an underwater swimmer releasing bubbles to the surface. 'Bub-bub-bub-bub-bub-bub-bub-bub-bub.' As he chanted, an attendant walked around the crowd waving a brass vessel of smoking incense over us.

I couldn't keep my eyes off the lama, with his long face, wide forehead, and deep-set eyes ablaze. The deference and affection his attendants showed him was met with kindness, and whenever he smiled, the lines around his eyes scrunched upwards charmingly. Within the space of a few seconds his expression changed from noble to comical to grave to fierce.

Mesmerised, I found myself studying his hands. Though they were big, like the rest of his body, his fingers were wide at the base, and gradually tapered to become slender at the tips, with long fingernails like a flamenco guitar player's. In the palm of one hand he held a bell, and in the other, a small bronze sceptre. While he chanted, he moved his hands around one another in a series of fluid gestures, like a conjurer or a dancer.

Sometimes he rang the bell and other times he put it down and took up a hand drum, which he shook with a long flourish. The two little boys at his side fascinated me, for they both had the alertness and gravitas of the older men around them, though I caught one of them sneaking curious glances at me every so often.

Just as suddenly as it had begun, the ceremony ended. The old lama emerged from his reverie, looked around at the crowd, and beamed. Whatever ritual had been performed was evidently finished. His attendant poured a cup of tea for him, and the crowd rushed forward to kneel at his feet for a blessing. He talked to them for some time.

At last, the attendant monks scurried around packing up the shrine, and gradually the crowd melted away. The two little boys got up and started a discreet game of catch. While I stood watching, night came on suddenly, accompanied by a swift drop in temperature. The flames in the butter lamps surrounding us blew horizontally in the evening breeze, first in one direction and then another. A number of them blew out completely in a sudden gust of wind. Prayer flags flapped against the ropes on which they were strung.

Aware that Rinchen must be wondering where I was by now, I looked across at the old lama and bowed self-consciously with my palms together, elbows folded against my ribs as I had seen others do. To my surprise, he responded with a little half wave and a smile. Something told me it was bad form to turn my back on him, so I continued to bow and grin while taking little steps backwards.

That was the last thing I remember before the ground suddenly flew towards me at lightning speed. A sensation of sharp icicles pressed down on the back of my legs, and then something heavy and coarse was grinding down on top of me. I couldn't scream, as I had bitten my tongue and blood was pooling in my mouth. Apart from these sensations there were no thoughts, just a vacuum. And then, quite abruptly, I was hovering above the scene, looking down at a mêlée of maroon robes thrashing a naked back, hearing the echoes of unintelligible shouting. I realised it was my body they were beating, but I was as far removed from it as I had been from the corpse on the pyre at Pashupatinath the day before. I remembered the last moment before her bed of straw was lit. She had not been trapped in her body, as I had imagined at the time. In reality her body was like a pod made of vegetable matter, just like mine, and everyone else's. And she was long gone.

THIRTY-TWO

Kathmandu, November 1969

If you stop struggling, you'll be free...

Consciousness zoomed about erratically, like a kite in the wind; my thoughts drifted by like clouds, changing shape constantly. The ties and concerns in my life were tiny figures moving about on the ground while I watched from the top of a tall building. None of it mattered any more. I could vaguely hear loud unfamiliar sounds in the distance, jostling crowds, and enormous currents of energy swirling around but they didn't affect me. Awareness of the sheer scale of space and all its infinite dimensions threatened to overwhelm me until I made myself so small that I was just a part of space itself.

There was an amorphous presence; a thick cloud of dense, ruby-red atoms hovering in the shadows. Unlike everything else in my field of vision, the red vapour remained the same shape and size. I had noticed it all along, but it had been hovering in the background, in the shadows. Now it moved slowly but purposefully in my direction and, without hesitation, dissolved into me, giving rise to a sense of completion beyond anything I had experienced, even with Ramsey. The feeling was straightforward, clear and clean, and immediately the whirling chaos dissolved and I was right back in my body.

Back in the struggle again.

I became aware that I was lying on my side, covered by a quilt, aching everywhere, with the coppery taste of blood in my mouth. Opening my eyes a crack, I saw a dimly lit room in which the walls and ceiling were painted with intricate patterns in faded red, yellow, blue and green. It hurt to look at anything for long, so I closed my eyes again. There was a burning sensation on the back of my calves, and someone was applying cooling balm onto them. Despite the pain, it didn't occur to me to be afraid. The main question in my mind was, why had I been attacked by monks? It didn't make sense.

I opened my eyes again to see yet another monk hovering over me, studying me intently. It just seemed too ridiculous to scream, anyway I couldn't find my voice, so I stared back at him. He was tall and very pale, with glasses, his brow furrowed with concern.

'How are you doing?' he said slowly, in English. 'I've brought some tea. You must be thirsty. I'm Tenzin, by the way. What's your name?'

He sounded American, and the surprise of that brought me back to my senses.

He handed me a small cup of tea. With some effort, I dragged myself up on my elbow and took a sip. It tasted salty and quite disgusting. When I looked down, I saw a pool of yellow fat lying on top of the brown milky liquid.

'Butter tea,' Tenzin explained, noting my expression. 'If you close your eyes it tastes like cream of mushroom soup.'

'Could I have some water?' My words came out jumbled as if I were drunk.

Tenzin turned and spoke in another language to the person who was dabbing salve on my legs. The woman hurried from the room.

Tenzin turned back to me. 'Do you know what happened to you?'

I shook my head.

'Your dress caught fire. The butter lamps are a menace, especially when it's so windy. It's happened before; a miracle no one has been burned alive. Lucky for you, one of the young monks noticed. He happened to be behind you, playing ball – which he shouldn't have been. He shouted to the others and a bunch of us pulled you down and smothered the fire. Whatever material your clothes were made from, it went up very fast. When you fell, your head landed on the edge of the carpet that we put down for His Holiness. It was very auspicious! You fell at the feet of the guru and then I think you fainted. Rinpoche told us specifically not to take you to hospital, but to bring you here to the monastery where we are staying.'

I blinked at him. 'Are we in Kathmandu?'

He smiled. 'We're still in Boudhanath, just a few yards away from the *stupa*. You were only out for ten minutes or so.'

'Are the burns bad?' I ventured, not wanting to move or look at them, either.

'Not too bad, considering. Not third-degree burns, anyway, but they are starting to blister. The Abbot's mother is treating them with some herbal salve. She knows what she is doing; she used to run a herbal medicine clinic back in Eastern Tibet. Much safer than the local hospital, I promise you.'

'Please say thank you for me.' I craned my neck to look over my shoulder at the figure dabbing ointment on my legs. She smiled back at me, nodding. I was so grateful there was a woman in the room. Especially when it dawned on me that I could no longer feel the silky fabric of the Fortuny against my body. The American seemed to read my mind.

'I'm afraid there's not much left of your dress,' he said, gravely. 'I'll show you later and you'll see what a lucky escape you had.'

I patted my torso under the quilt and realised I was naked. Not only had my bare flesh been exposed to god knows how many monks, but I had ruined a second couture garment in under twenty-four hours. Nice.

There was absolutely no question of facing Ramsey, and I was frightened about what might happen next. Mrs Vreeland had trusted us with that dress. It was an original piece designed in the 1920s by Mariano Fortuny himself and, consequently, irreplaceable.

With wild panic, I decided I wouldn't face any of them. I would simply never go back. I would hole up in the monastery and do a runner back to London as soon as possible – although this train of thought was halted abruptly when I remembered my passport was in Boris's safe.

The sum I was receiving for the entire shoot wouldn't cover an eighth of what the Fortuny was worth, but I could pay it off, as well as the Balmain, out of my savings. They were just clothes after all. Other things worried me more. After this there would surely be no more location trips with Ramsey. That meant the end of us. He would fall in love with an authentic beauty, who didn't need hairpieces and eyelashes and make-up to look good.

When I didn't speak, Tenzin said gently, 'Please tell me where you are staying. I want to send a message to your friends to come and collect you.'

I shook my head desperately, too weak to hold back the tears, remembering how Ramsey had pleaded with *Vogue* to let me do the story. He'd put his own reputation on the line. He'd never forgive me. Not only that but, judging from the excruciating pain in the back of my legs, I suspected there would be extensive scarring. Another nail in the coffin of my career. By then I was sobbing into the quilt.

Tenzin got up and left the room for a few minutes, returning with two aspirins and a stack of starched white linen handkerchiefs with a blue monogram MJH embroidered on each one.

With an embarrassed smile he put them down next to me, adding as explanation, 'Mom. She sent these from home. They're not much good to me here. Please take them.'

Within a matter of moments, they were soaked through with tears and snot. Tenzin told me he was going to give me privacy for a few minutes. The woman, whose name I still didn't know, patted my hand and occasionally muttered in Tibetan, as if she were soothing a small child.

I found her presence comforting. Her wide brown face and ruddy cheeks were deeply lined, and her brown eyes were cloudy with cataracts, but her hands conveyed calm and steadiness. Even though in her floor-length black dress and brightly coloured apron she was dressed similarly to the Tibetan women I had seen circling the *stupa*, she had added stylish touches; an artfully tied red scarf with frayed edges, worn like a necklace, and silver earrings the exact colour of her hair, both so lovely next to her brown skin. I noticed she was missing the ring finger and pinkie on her right hand.

Presently Tenzin appeared again, carrying a neatly folded pile of clothes.

'His Holiness would like to see you. Can you get to your feet OK? Amala will help you get dressed. These belong to her daughter.'

He handed me a shawl to wrap around myself, and I slowly rose to my feet, feeling dizzy and as if my body was not my own. Amala led me to the lavatory down a corridor. The toilet consisted of a china draining board on a small platform you stepped onto, and then squatted. It was a challenge with raw calves, but the intense need to pee and fear of falling into the stinking black drain hole kept me focused.

Back in the parlour, Amala handed me a blue silk long-sleeve shirt, with a black wool pinafore to wear over it. She laughed, because it was way too short on me, but I was in too much pain to raise more than a weak smile. Afterwards she tied a striped apron around my waist. Then she made me sit down again while she combed my hair. When Tenzin returned, he smiled at the sight of me.

'You look like a very respectable Tibetan lady.'

They'd saved my gold sandals, which looked absurd with the dress, and soon I was following him up some rickety wooden stairs.

'Who am I meeting, again?' I asked.

Tenzin's face grew serious. 'The man who was saying prayers on the *stupa* when you went up in flames. He's a reincarnate lama, known as a Rinpoche'.

'Llama as in Peru?' I asked.

'The world "lama" really just means teacher. He's called His Holiness because he's the highest of lamas, and a very great teacher.'

At the end of the corridor on the second floor was a carved wooden door. From inside came the droning *bub bub bub bub bub bub bubbubbububub*, sounding like swarns of sonorous bees. Scores of shoes lined the corridor, so I removed my sandals too. The gold glittered frivolously next to the worn fabric and leather pairs around it.

When the door opened, I was saw a large room crowded with people; some standing at the back, others sitting cross-legged on the floor facing the lama. Though it was a cold night, he was bare chested, chanting prayers on a bench covered in Tibetan rugs, surrounded by books and texts. The room was lit by candles and oil lamps and had the heavy, smoky scent of incense.

Tenzin found a wooden chair for me and placed it near the window. I had only just sat down when a woman in dusty rags entered the room carrying a small bundle. She gave it to the eldest of the two small children by her side and immediately began prostrating herself to the lama. They were all streaked in mud. The children looked famished and glassy-eyed. Tiny wails issued from the bundle. The lama smiled and gestured to the woman to come closer. He rested his hand on top of hers, while they talked. Then he produced an envelope from the pile beside him and gave it to her. She bowed low and appeared to be thanking him.

Tenzin whispered to me that they had just arrived in Boudhanath, having walked across the mountains from Tibet. The trip had taken two weeks; the baby was born in the snow on a pass. The woman's husband was in a hospital in Kathmandu recovering from having his foot amputated because of severe frostbite. I thought again of Amala's missing fingers.

Bubbubububububub. The woman stepped back and the lama said more prayers.

I had been examining him closely, and suddenly he looked straight across at me. My cheeks burned. He said something to Tenzin who translated quietly.

'It was an auspicious thing that happened today. Not just because you weren't badly hurt. I have spoken to the people in charge of maintenance at the *stupa*. Too many butter lamps everywhere and no regulation is dangerous.' The lama tapped his chest. 'Perhaps now, after what happened to you, they will realise and make some changes. So you see, you have done something positive while you've been here.'

He turned to whisper something to an attendant monk who was arranging things on the altar on the other side of the room. Then he motioned for Tenzin and me to come and sit closer to him. Tenzin translated again.

'I told His Holiness that you're from England. He was very interested. He asked, why did you come to Nepal?'

I explained that I worked as a model, and we were photographing clothes for a fashion magazine. Rinpoche's expression didn't change. I wondered if he understood. 'You see, we're advertising clothes that people buy in shops,' I explained, awkwardly. It seemed like an absurd thing to be doing.

'Like Harrods?' asked the lama in English, taking me by surprise.

'Yes!' I laughed.

He wondered where the others in my group were. When he heard they had gone to a temple, he seemed puzzled. 'For prayers?'

'No, for photographs.' Suddenly this seemed shameful, and tears began cascading down my cheeks.

The lama smiled kindly, not in the least put out. 'They will be worried about you.'

'No,' I said, miserably. 'They will be angry. It was a very expensive dress.'

He said something in Tibetan, then abruptly in English, 'How will you get back to your hotel?'

'I had a driver, but I lost him,' I said.

Tenzin intervened. 'Don't worry. This is a small village and news travels fast. Your driver is downstairs waiting for you.'

But I did not want to leave this room, so I stayed near the lama as visitors arrived and left. The two stocky men with white robes and dreadlocked topknots, who I'd noticed earlier at the *stupa*, appeared. They emanated a quiet magnetism that made me long to know more about them. I didn't feel quite the same way about the very serious Dutch woman, also in Tibetan dress, who had her own interpreter and barked a list of complicated philosophical questions at the lama. He answered her politely, in short concise sentences, quite immune to her attempts to monopolise his attention.

Shortly afterwards, the two boy monks from the *stupa* came in. They genuflected three times to the lama and then clambered up on the dais to sit on either side of him, as they had earlier. One of them had a solemn face with doleful brown eyes. He leaned into the Rinpoche's voluminous robes and shyly peered out at the gathered assembly.

The other boy sat up straight and surveyed everyone in the room with unselfconscious interest, recognising certain people and smiling at them, and exchanging a joke with a ragged man, whom he appeared to know well. When he heard the punchline, the boy burst into laughter, his shoulders shaking, and his features breaking into a kind of wild happiness that radiated light across the room. Tenzin nudged my elbow and whispered what I had already guessed 'He is the one with eagle eyes, who noticed your dress was on fire.'

At that very moment the boy looked over at us. Joining my palms together, I bowed to him and mouthed my thanks. He surveyed me with a serious, almost stern expression. Then he picked up a glass of water from the table in front of him and appeared to throw the contents at me with a quick flick.

I jumped, but then realised he had his hand over the top of the glass, so I pretended to wipe the hypothetical water off my face and body. The boy smiled, delighted.

He was certainly no ordinary child. Mischievous, certainly, but also unusually self-possessed.

But then, Tenzin got to his feet and signalled for me to follow. My audience with the lama was over. As I faced the dais, all I could say was 'thank you' to the three figures in front of me. In a strange replay of events on the *stupa*, the Rinpoche casually waved and grinned as I backed out of the room.

I retrieved my sandals and followed Tenzin down the stairs, where a shell-shocked. Rinchen was waiting. He was excited, speaking in rapid Tibetan with Tenzin, and sometimes bowing low at his answers.

'Your driver is happy to see you are all right,' Tenzin translated. 'He would have been in big trouble if anything had happened to you. And not just for that, he is also happy you met a great lama.' He handed me a jar of green-black salve that smelled powerfully medicinal. 'This is from Amala, for your burns.'

We stepped out into the square, nearly tripping over a pair of stray dogs curled up together just outside the door. It was a moonless night; a few butter lamps still flickered on the dark ledges of the *stupa*. In the shadowy light, the Buddha eyes appeared to scold me, as if I had not understood something terribly obvious that had been offered to me.

As Tenzin walked us to where the jeep was parked, I asked how he had become a monk.

He told me he left Minnesota for India to become a wandering *sadhu* and smoke as much dope as possible, but he had encountered His Holiness in a transit lounge in Delhi Airport, and immediately knew he had found his teacher. He travelled to the lama's teachings in India, Bhutan and Nepal, and eventually became his attendant.

'What's your birth name?' I asked.

'Michael Hanson.' He smiled. 'It feels strange to say it now. Like it's only vaguely familiar.'

We had reached the Jeep, but I had no desire to leave.

'How much longer will you be in Kathmandu?' he asked.

We're leaving for Pokhara tomorrow,' I told him. 'And you?'

'We're only here for a couple of months while Rinpoche looks for some land to build a monastery. Most of the time we stay in Bhutan.'

He handed me a piece of paper with an address on it. 'If you ever need to get in touch with Rinpoche… or me,' he explained, somewhat awkwardly.

As I took the paper, our fingers brushed and a current of electricity passed between us. Judging by the look on his face, it wasn't just my imagination.

My bag was sitting in the Jeep where I'd left it. Seeing it reminded me of something.

'One more thing.' I rummaged through it until I found a small model of an Air India jet. It was well made, with portholes you could look through to see the passengers and cabin crew sitting on the plane. Everyone on the *Vogue* team had been given one on the flight from London.

'Please give this to the boy monk. What is his name?'

Tenzin told me, but the long, unfamiliar Tibetan name did not register.

'He'll love this.' Tenzin grinned at the plane. 'They don't get many toys. He is a Rinpoche too, you know. In training to become a Buddhist teacher.'

Rinchen started up the engine.

'Oh, and I nearly forgot. You might want this.' Tenzin handed me a small bundle wrapped in a red cotton cloth through the window of the jeep. 'To remember us by until we meet again.'

As we drove off, I turned round and waved. Behind him, I saw the carved gate and the luminous body of the *stupa*, and caught a last glimpse of two enigmatic eyes that burned into me for a few seconds, until we turned out of the back lane and onto the pot-holed main road.

In the car, I unwrapped the bundle to find the scorched remains of the Fortuny wrapped around a tiny bronze statue of the Buddha.

THIRTY-THREE

Kathmandu, November 1969

The staff at the Royal Hotel were well-trained, so no one batted an eyelid when I returned to the hotel dressed as a Tibetan. With some trepidation, I rushed upstairs to find Ramsey. I knew he'd be furious at me for disappearing like that. But when I threw the door open, I discovered the room was empty.

Back downstairs, the receptionist informed me that Mr Ramsey and everyone from my group were attending a banquet at the palace. My heart sank to my shoes. I'd completely forgotten about the party that Boris had seemed so keen for us to attend.

My mouth dry, I asked if they'd left a message for me, but she shook her head. No messages at all.

By now it was after eleven. Far too late for me to throw on a frock and rush over there. I had no choice but to wait for everyone to return.

I asked a waiter to bring some notepaper and a pencil, as well as a beer, to the guest lounge. I sat at a desk and began writing. It had been the most extraordinary day of my life, and I didn't want to forget anything while it was still fresh in my mind.

I was so absorbed in writing, I didn't look up until I heard Ramsey's voice. 'Oh shit, typical. Look, Ari's gone native.'

I turned to see Ramsey and Boris walking in together, weaving slightly.

I held my breath in anticipation of Ramsey's fury. But to my surprise he just seemed sardonically amused.

Boris appeared much more puzzled. 'What happened to you?' he asked. 'You missed a beautiful evening. Where did you get those clothes?'

I deflected this by asking how the party had been, and they were both tipsy enough

210

not to notice. Soon they were telling me about their night.

It turned out Ramsey had also forgotten about the invitation to the palace. When the *Vogue* convoy pulled into the driveway of the Royal Hotel after the shoot, Boris was already in his dinner jacket waiting for them on the steps. They'd had ten minutes to change and rush back out.

'We were so pushed I couldn't even leave a note for you,' explained Ramsey, who never wrote notes anyway. 'But where did you go? I was worried all evening. Wasn't I, Boris?'

Boris smiled and peeled off without answering.

Ramsey was much chattier than usual but I couldn't think of anything to say. My silence seemed to make him nervous. 'I thought you must have found some good shops somewhere. I'm sorry you missed dinner. The decor was bizarre. Orange shag rugs…' He cackled. 'The Queen knew all my pictures from the time I began working for *Vogue*. She's obsessed with Elvis and told us endlessly about meeting him. The King went on about his Eton days. You'd have found it hilarious.'

I was relieved he wasn't angry, but also puzzled that my absence had raised so little concern. In fact, he seemed to have had a lovely time. I noted there was no sign of Vivara, and made myself not ask where she was.

Finally, as his stories ran out, Ramsey stopped and peered at me closely. 'What happened? You seem strange. Not yourself, somehow.'

I put down my pen and faced him. 'I'm afraid I had a bit of an accident.'

As I recounted the bare essentials of the story, excluding any mention of Tenzin, Ramsey's expression changed to one of concern. When I showed him the burns on the back of my legs, he gasped.

'Christ, Ari. I can't leave you alone for a second! We'll have to get that looked at by a doctor. You could be scarred.'

His distress seemed genuine but I wondered if he was more concerned about my use to him as a model than he was about my well-being.

Just then Boris and Inger arrived, accompanied by a waiter with a bottle of aquavit and four glasses, so Ramsey made me go through the whole story again. They were horrified. Inger disappeared to find some antiseptic burn cream. Boris vowed that he would complain to the local authorities in Boudhanath about the butter lamps. He said he felt personally responsible.

To my surprise, Ramsey didn't seem to mind about the Fortuny outfit. 'It's just another fucking frock,' he said. 'I'll talk to Vreeland about it, don't worry.' He was showing off to our hosts, but he sounded as if he meant it. Then he regaled Boris and Inger with stories of some of my more disastrous shoots, including the time I fell off a rowboat into the pond in Central Park. He didn't yet know about the Balmain, and it clearly wasn't the time to tell him.

Usually, I opened my eyes in the morning feeling as if I had a pile of rubbish over my heart, but the next morning when I woke up ready for our journey to Pokhara, I felt strangely elated. Amala's herbal salve had worked wonders on the back of my legs. Because of the pain, I'd slept on my stomach with a sheet covering only the top half of my body, and in the morning the burns were no longer weeping and the damaged skin hardening... a kind of miracle. I replayed in my head the events of the previous day, still incredulous at having survived without much worse injuries.

We were drinking coffee in the lobby while we waited for Chisie and Vivara to appear. Tommy was busy loading the camera equipment into one of the jeeps when Sami, the casino manager, came to say goodbye. Even at this early hour he emanated sexuality, in his loose tartan tunic with a crisp white silk shirt visible underneath it and a long white woollen scarf over one shoulder, draped asymmetrically across his torso and held in place at his hips by a dark brown leather belt.

The perfection was completed by his roguish laugh, which lent a hint of something risqué to his character. Even Vivara abandoned her usual regal manner and behaved like a teenage girl around him.

While the others were distracted by one of Boris's stories, Sami leaned over and whispered to me, 'I hear through the grapevine that you tried to commit *suttee* on Boudhanath *stupa*. What happened?'

His smile faded when I told him, and he grew unexpectedly grave.

'His Holiness is Bhutan's most revered Buddhist lama,' he said. 'He spent nearly thirty years in solitary retreat as a younger man. As I am not very devout,' he smiled self-effacingly, 'I don't have much to do with him, but my mother and my wife are devotees. They will be so fascinated that you met him in such strange circumstances.'

Ramsey overheard and nudged my shoulder, laughing. 'Fucking hell, Ari, don't tell me you're becoming a Buddhist now?' He put his arm around me and pulled me towards him as if I were a naughty child he was humouring.

Then his expression changed, as he looked towards the staircase and then at his watch.

'Where is that awful woman? We should be on the road by now!'

Boris sent a bus boy to investigate. Ten minutes later Chisie appeared on the stairs, uncharacteristically dishevelled and visibly cross.

'There you all are,' she fumed. 'I've been up since four o'clock. Forty-two bags to pack, some accessories and couture items missing, and no help from any of you.'

As she complained, a parade of porters staggered behind her, laden down with suitcases, hatboxes and bags.

'No help apart from the entire staff of the Royal at your disposal,' Ramsey snorted. 'C'mon, you silly old bag, get in your Jeep and stop complaining. We have a long journey ahead, and a much more basic hotel in Pokhara,' said Ramsey grimly. 'God, I'm dreading it.'

There ensued much hugging and promises of reunions with our new friends before we finally piled into the overloaded Jeeps and took off towards the shimmering Himalayas in the distance. But every step of the way, I found myself wishing I wasn't leaving at all.

THIRTY-FOUR

London, April 1970

As soon as we arrived back in London life grew busy again and, before long, it was as if Kathmandu had never happened. A clear image of Tenzin's calm face sometimes flashed across my mind as I was falling asleep, but the overall memory of that extraordinary day began to fade.

Despite Ramsey's optimism, there had been a major fuss about the two ruined dresses. Ramsey went on the counterattack but Mrs Vreeland's response to him was uncharacteristically lukewarm. Nor was she overjoyed with the photographs. The shot of Vivara with Reed the hippie didn't make the final cut, and Diana told Ramsey: 'It's rather curious, there's no languor in Ari's lips in any of the shots!'

'*Vogue* is losing whatever relevance it once had,' Ramsey fumed, slamming down the phone. 'They only care about the fucking advertisers.'

I said nothing, but I'd noticed work was not exactly flooding in for either of us – although that didn't stop Ramsey from taking delivery of a new Porsche.

It was becoming clear that the Sixties aesthetic was fading. A new generation of photographers and models were rising to the top of the heap, and *Vogue* editors were favouring clean-cut American models with a California sheen.

'I hate that healthy look,' I told Sunny. 'It's just not me.'

'It could be you, if you pulled your finger out,' was her uncharacteristically prim response.

I stopped talking to her about my career.

She also appeared unaware that London had altered. Dark clouds were massing on the horizon. I had realised it for the first time the previous year at the Stones memorial concert for Brian Jones in Hyde Park. He had been found dead at the bottom of his swimming pool, having been fired by the band he had founded on account of his prodigious consumption of drugs and alcohol. Nonetheless, the news came as a shock. Everyone had been used to Brian stumbling around town and making no sense, but no one had expected him to *die*. Mick had released thousands of white butterflies above the crowd in Brian's honour, but due to their long incarceration in cardboard boxes, most of them fell back onto the black stage in quivering death throes. Mick had no choice except to dance on their corpses.

Everything seemed somehow… over. My resolution on the *stupa* was long forgotten, and I was consumed with jealousy bordering on hatred, not only of the women Ramsey openly coveted, but also of his charm, his drive, his absolute self-assurance. It was everything I lacked, and only he could supply it for me.

Only now, he wasn't doing that any more.

In the midst of all this, Sunny announced that she was pregnant. I was devastated. It felt as if she was living a wonderful life while mine was falling to pieces.

I said all the right things, and probably smiled, but I was going through the motions. 'Another cowgirl bites the dust,' I thought, bitterly.

For some reason lost on me, she and Eddie decided to move from London to a big house in the Surrey countryside as they prepared for the arrival of the baby. Instead of occasional lunches, we now spoke on the phone once or twice a week. Sunny was sick a lot in the first six months, which meant our conversations were not long. I missed her.

One Saturday when Ramsey was away in Paris on a shoot, I met two acquaintances, Rachida and Jerome, for lunch in Chelsea. Jerome was considering me for a part in his next film, and I was excited at the prospect, partly because I was desperate for work and partly because I knew how much it would irritate Ramsey. He felt competitive towards directors and he especially loathed Jerome's arty films.

To me, filmmaking seemed so much more interesting than photography, and Jerome believed I had real potential. He'd recently made a controversial film about a group of polyamorous Wiccans living on an island off the west coast of Scotland, which had earned him a great deal of attention, despite terrible reviews.

During our lunch at the Casserole, I found his penetrating stares and long silences intimidating. He was in his late thirties, tall and thin with a craggy face, softened by an upside-down bird's nest of light brown hair. But Rachida was funny and bubbly, and by the end of our time together I found myself relaxing, and making jokes, able to be myself in a way I wasn't when Ramsey and I were together. When we said goodbye, Jerome told me he would send the script round via courier.

When I reached the house, I found my dog Pav waiting for me in the hallway. As soon as I walked in, he shot down the stairs three at a time, looking back at me, as if making sure I was following. I knew even before I saw her it was Violet.

For days she had rarely left her bed next to the stove except to stagger into the backyard where she squatted down briefly on trembling haunches before returning to the kitchen.

Her tail thumped softly when she saw me, but she didn't possess the energy to lift her head from her paws. I sank down onto the floor next to her and she gazed across at me with a plaintive, apologetic expression. In the past few days her short coat had been shedding at an unusual rate, and there were a few near-bald patches on her grey flanks. She had deteriorated so fast, and I had virtually ignored all the signs.

In a panic, I ran to the shops to buy a roast chicken, her favourite. She sniffed at the little pieces I cut up for her, then turned her head away and closed her eyes. It was a weekend, the vets were closed, though I left several desperate messages. When Ramsey called from Paris, he sounded distant and preoccupied with work and difficult clients. I cried after I put the phone down, mostly out of shame. It had suited me to have the dogs in London, but they had been so much happier running free at Thurston. Their devotion was the one constant in my life, and I had taken them entirely for granted.

I wept into her fur. 'I'm so sorry I brought you here,' I whispered. 'It was selfish but I don't know what I would have done without you.'

Pav lay down next to me, as if to show that he understood, but that only made me cry harder.

Her keen soulful eyes were now clouded over with pain and black gunk, which I wiped away with a damp cloth.

The vet, Richard, finally turned up at seven o'clock on Monday morning and examined Violet gently. When he finished, he met my eyes. 'I'm not going to lie to you. She's suffering, Ari. It's your decision but you know what I think.'

Unable to speak, I nodded my assent.

When he returned from his van with the equipment he needed, I stroked Violet's head and told her how much I loved her as Richard kneeled down and deftly inserted a needle into her back leg. Her eyes briefly widened in alarm, then her familiar loving expression became glassy and vacant.

After it was over, I scooped her up again and rocked her gently, but the warm sleek body I had stroked and held and cried into a thousand times had been entirely emptied of Violet.

As Richard packed Violet's body in his car, he warned me, 'You'll really want to pay attention to her brother now, seeing they've been together since birth. He'll need you more than ever.'

Once he had driven away, Pav and I walked up Regents Park Road in a state of shock. On that grey Monday morning I clearly saw how the life force was visible in everyone we passed, something I had never noticed before. As soon as we reached Primrose Hill, I let Pav off the lead but instead of racing off across the park as usual, he looked up at me uncertainly.

'It's OK, boy, go on,' I said, but he stayed glued to my side and didn't even bother to sniff the grass at the edge of the path. We climbed the hill and gazed out across the green expanse to the scrappy London skyline.

When he arrived home later a few days later, Ramsey cried when he saw Violet's empty bed, and he hugged me for a long time. He understood about animals; it was one of the reasons I loved him.

By then, I'd decided to take Pav back to Thurston where Tobias the groundsman would look after him. Our lives were too chaotic, and Pav deserved fresh air for his final years.

Ramsey didn't want Pav to go, but he saw my point, and agreed to take us to Thurston after he had completed a three-day shoot for British *Vogue*.

The feature was showcasing celebrities in designer gear, just for a change. It seemed as if every two minutes the doorbell rang with couriers dropping off clothes from the likes of Rive Gauche, Gina Fratini and Bill Gibb. Editors, hairdressers and make-up artists were arriving and setting up in the dressing room.

I kept Pav with me in our flat, afraid the strangers would bother him. I was worried about him. His entire demeanour had changed since Violet died. He had become withdrawn, and unusually restless. But he was also used to being at the centre of the action, and he kept trying to get out the door and see what was going on.

So I took him with me when I went downstairs to make a cup of tea. In the kitchen

I found *Vogue*'s star hairdresser Darrell sitting at the kitchen table. He kissed the air on either side of my cheeks.

'Oh, I'm so glad to see you're still with us, Ari! I didn't like to ask. Haven't seen you in ages. Where are you working these days?'

In fashion speak, that meant, 'I thought you were dead'.

I dodged the question and asked, 'Where is everyone?'

'Ramsey didn't like the make-up. They're redoing it for the third time. I had to take a breather.' He rolled his eyes and fanned the air around his face theatrically.

Through the open door of the studio, I caught a glimpse of Tommy loading cameras on a bench; a Leon Russell LP playing softly in the background.

I ran upstairs with Pav at my heels, past the dressing room and though the connecting door to our quarters. I hauled him up onto the sofa with me and picked up Jerome's script again. Unfortunately, the characters seemed on first reading to be quite one-dimensional – though perhaps he left role development up to the actors, I wondered? There were some searingly violent scenes, including the rape of my character, Missy, by an Algerian hustler.

I wasn't sure how I felt about this.

At some point the phone buzzed and Dani put through a call from Sunny. We hadn't spoken since the previous week, and I told her about Violet.

'Oh no, I'm so sorry, Ari. You must be devastated.'

'Thanks, Sun.' She had adored my dogs ever since her first visit. 'I'm taking Pav back to Thurston so he can run free again.'

'Oh but Ari, won't you miss him?'

In reality, I couldn't bear to think about it but all I said was, 'I will, but it's what's best for him.'

Before she could ask more questions, I changed the subject. 'How are you? Still puking everywhere?'

She was still puking everywhere, as it turned out, and her band was cross with her for cancelling the planned tour. Also, the builders at the new place in Surrey had found dry rot and were charging double the original quote.

I asked her to hold on while I found a cigarette. This meant scrabbling around in the bedroom and bathroom until I finally found a packet.

Downstairs, the music was blasting again; Brook Benton singing 'Rainy Night in Georgia', punctuated by frequent doorbell ringing and the sound of footsteps and voices on the stairs. Someone opened the connecting door, then closed it after a minute, causing the noise from downstairs to be amplified briefly before subsiding. I picked up the phone again.

'I had the baby and we've moved to Japan since you were gone, thank you very much,' Sunny said, dryly.

'Sorry Sun.' I took a drag. 'Where were we?'

'Oh god,' she continued, 'and did I tell you a bloody pap got into the garden last week and snapped a photo of me sunning by the pool, looking like a beached whale? It was all over the *News of the World*; did you see it?'

'You should count yourself lucky the papers are so interested,' I said, still stinging from my conversation with Darrell downstairs.

'The whole reason we moved to the country was so we wouldn't be hassled all the time,' Sunny reminded me.

'Look, I know you're a star, Sunny, you don't have to ram it down my throat.'

There was a long silence on the other end of the phone.

In a strained voice she said, 'You know what, Ari? I thought you were the one person I could talk to about anything.' She burst into tears.

Shit.

The connecting door slammed, followed by Ramsey's familiar hurried footfall on the stairs. A minute later he appeared in the living room doorway, aspirin-white.

'I'm so sorry, Sunny. I didn't mean to hurt you,' I said into the phone. 'I'll call you back.'

Still holding the phone, I stood up and edged around the coffee table towards him. 'What's happened?'

Ramsey grabbed my hands and gazed into my eyes with an unfamiliar look.

'Pavlov,' he said. 'He got out, and he's... he's been badly hurt.'

But this didn't make any sense to me.

'No, no – he's up here with me. He was just sitting beside me.' I snatched my hands away, calling, 'Pavlov!'

I rushed into the bedroom, then the bathroom. The colour of a shadow, Pav could curl up himself up into a tiny ball and virtually disappear into most backgrounds. I checked under our bed, and then ran up the stairs, three at a time, convinced he must have gone up for a quick nap on the guest room bed. Ramsey caught up with me on the third-floor landing.

'Darling, please, listen to me. He's dead.'

I shook my head hard, hair flying. Tears prickled the backs of my eyes. 'He was right here a minute ago. He's probably down in the kitchen stealing everyone's lunch.'

Ramsey shook his head gently. 'No, Ari. That's what I'm trying to tell you. Some fuckwit of an editor left the front door open for a courier. He got out and ran into the road and—'

He had to be wrong.

I tore down the stairs towards the front door but Ramsey caught up with me and pushed me into the bedroom, standing in front of the door so I couldn't get out. I hit him with my fists and screamed for him to get out of the way, but he wouldn't budge.

'Darling, I don't want you to see this. Please believe me, it was instant. He wouldn't have felt any pain.'

And now, just like that, I really was alone.

THIRTY-FIVE

World's End, August 1970

World's End was aptly named. The less affluent end of the King's Road had not a tree nor a shrub, as far as I could see. Even the weeds growing in the pavement cracks looked unhealthy. Buses farted diesel fumes that mingled with the stale smell of hot oil from a nearby fish and chip shop. One thing was certain; this stifling strip of road marked the end of the line for my starring role in Jerome's film.

On the day of my audition, the portrait of Aleister Crowley in Jerome's studio had been somewhat disquieting, with its eyes blazing psychotically, but Jerome's partner Rachida was so welcoming, and Jerome himself so encouraging, that gradually my nervousness turned into excitement. This was just what I needed to rebuild my confidence.

For the first hour or two, Jerome filmed Rachida and me rehearsing scenes, and judging from his quietly enthusiastic response, it had all gone well. Then he suggested we improvise a situation towards the end of the script in which my character loses her mind while somewhere in Morocco. I was in the midst of imploring some imaginary Berber to take me on his caravanserai into the desert, when Rachida took my hand in hers and started exploring my palm with her tongue. Then she took my middle finger in her mouth and began sucking on it, gazing at me with kohl-rimmed eyes.

There had been plenty of *kif*-fuelled sex in the script between my character and a dusky street musician, but none with Rachida, who was playing a pop star's girlfriend. Yet so badly did I want the part that my first instinct was to go with the flow. Maybe this was improv designed to test me.

I liked Rachida. She was a free spirit, as light as quicksilver; qualities both my character and I dismally lacked. As we pulled each other closer, though, I sensed a darker presence just behind me. The fine hairs on the back of my neck stood up as Jerome slipped his hands under my shirt and began roughly massaging my breasts, while vigorously pushing his erection into the small of my back.

I wrenched myself free and fled the studio to the sound of their scornful laughter, running all the way to the King's Road. As I made my way home, I wondered if Jerome had ever really considered me for the part, or if he had simply hoped I'd be gullible enough to act out his fantasies.

Even as I walked away, I could feel his malevolent energy burrowing under my skin like a hookworm. I walked faster to try and shake him out, heading around the bend into the King's Road, eyes fixed on the middle distance, legs striding purposefully, in sync with the background rhythm of the street. In the summer heat, the towering chestnut trees in Paulton Square looked parched, their leaves clinging on, yellow-brown at their edges.

The road was almost empty of cars, but there were plenty of people around – couples out strolling, a man in a dinner jacket trying to flag down a cab on the corner of Radnor Walk and a mob of braying hoorays drinking beer outside the Chelsea Potter.

I couldn't help thinking of all the times Sunny and I had walked down this road in a fever of happy anticipation when we first arrived in London. All our dreams had come true and now we were landed with them.

I arrived home as the light was fading to dusk over the railway bridge. The second I closed the front door, Tommy poked his head out of the studio and offered me a glass of wine. He seemed unusually talkative, and keen to show me photographs of his naked girlfriend, draped around the branches of a tree, like a snake. We talked about the dogs, how much we both missed them, and Ramsey's shoot with Charlotte Rampling earlier in the day. After a while, though, I felt completely drained, so I gave him a kiss and told him I had to lie down. Even then he tried to prolong the conversation, and I idly wondered if he was on speed.

When I finally got upstairs, I could hear Ramsey in the shower, so I left the bedroom door slightly ajar for him, took off my clothes and changed into my dressing gown. Before I could lie down, I heard footsteps on the creaky stairs. A moment later, Ramsey's secretary Dani tiptoed past. I flung the door wide open just to gauge her reaction, curious as to why she had been upstairs at this hour in the evening.

She visibly jumped, but soon regained her composure.

'Oh hi, Ari. I didn't know you were back. I was trying not to disturb anyone. How did the audition go?' she asked.

'It was fine, but I didn't get the part.' There was no way I was going to tell her or anyone what had actually transpired.

'Oh sweetheart, I'm sorry,' she said, reaching out to touch my arm.

I'd always liked Dani, but for some reason I didn't want her to comfort me. I changed the subject.

'How did the shoot go today?'

She made a vague gesture. 'Charlotte was lovely, but I had a horrible headache so Rams said it would be OK to lie down in the guest room, I hope you don't mind.'

'Of course not. Are you feeling better?'

Even after four years of almost daily contact, we were always polite. She nodded and mumbled something about having to run to meet her boyfriend.

She left just before Ramsey emerged from the shower.

'I told you he was a cunt,' was his reaction when I told him the reading with Jerome hadn't gone well. He poured himself a whiskey. 'A pretentious cunt at that, and his films are terrible.'

'Well, I didn't get the part so there's no need to bang on about it,' I said, annoyed.

Ramsey dropped his towel on the floor. 'I never bang on. I just tell the truth and if people can't deal with it, that's their problem.'

'Your truth and my truth don't always mesh,' I said, wondering why I was sticking up for Jerome, even indirectly. Ramsey hated being challenged and took even minor disagreements as a sign of disloyalty.

He reached for his jeans. 'It's too bad about you, Ari. You've almost got it all but somehow you just miss the mark. Maybe in your next life you'll make it.' The remark was delivered with almost casual cruelty.

I stared at him, heat rushing to my face.

He pulled on the jeans and picked up a contact sheet from the day's shoot. 'These are the best I've done lately. That bird really knows how to give, while still holding the mystery.'

'Do you fancy her?' I asked, unable to stop myself.

He squinted at me. 'Don't be ridiculous, I've known her for years.'

'That doesn't answer my question. Do you fancy her?'

The tension between us thickened. I could sense something in his body language, something I couldn't yet identify.

He dropped the contact sheet onto the bed and started putting on his shirt. 'If I wanted to fuck her, I would have done it a long time ago.'

All I wanted was for him to hug me and tell me that he loved me; that I was the only one, even if it wasn't true. More than anything, I wanted us to stop fighting.

'Ramsey?'

'What?' He didn't look up.

'Let's drive down Devon for a long weekend.'

'When do I have time to do that? Try to understand the pressure I'm under. All right for you, you're on a permanent holiday. I'm booked up until next March except for two days at Christmas.'

This was a well-trodden path of argument. I knew that the next line would be about his weekly overheads, but before he had a chance to go there, I stood up abruptly and walked out of the room.

A few days later I woke to feel hard painful lumps along my jawline on either side of my chin. They weren't like ordinary spots; more like an interconnected root system embedded below the surface of my skin. More than anything, it resembled a case of mumps. The next day there were red lumps growing under my cheeks as well as on my neck and chest.

A few days later, I was sitting in the office of Dr Hyde, a top Harley Street dermatologist. He was in his late sixties, with bushy white eyebrows and a supercilious air. As he examined my skin, he whistled tunelessly under his breath.

'I'm afraid you've got rather a serious case of cystic acne,' he informed me. 'It does occur sometimes in people your age, but I've never seen anything quite like this.'

He switched off the powerful magnifying lens and motioned sternly for me to sit down on the chair opposite his desk as he read my patient information questionnaire.

'Hmm, I see from this you're a model. Depend on your face to live, do you?'

I nodded, waiting for him to tell me what pill I could take, or cream I could use. But that wasn't at all what he was about to say.

'That's rather unfortunate. Tell me truthfully; what have you been up to, my dear?' he asked, peering at me.

'Up to?'

He made a curt gesture. 'What sort of drugs are you on? Between you and me, of course.'

'I smoke pot occasionally. That's it.'

A few lines of coke here and there was surely not worth mentioning.

He looked sceptical. 'I'm going to be frank with you. Patients who present with this sort of acute acne invariably turn out to be hard drug users.'

'I've never touched heroin,' I protested, truthfully. But he clearly didn't believe me.

I felt as if I were falling though space, with nothing to grab onto. For the past few years, my looks, and other people's reactions to my looks, had defined me. In that respect, nothing had changed.

Dr Hyde handed me a prescription for powerful antibiotics and a topical cream. 'There should be an improvement in about seven to ten days,' he said briskly. 'Whatever drugs you're using, stop. And for god's sake don't drink alcohol with the antibiotics.'

I left his office, relieved. But the medication proved useless. After ten days, the outbreak had become even more entrenched as well as itchy. It felt as if little worms were writhing beneath my skin.

I returned to Dr Hyde who tried to convince me to go into rehab.

When I refused, he informed me coolly, 'I'm afraid you'll be left with rather serious scars if we can't shift this infection.'

He prescribed another course of stronger antibiotics.

During the first few days of the outbreak, I slathered my face with heavy foundation and went out with Ramsey in the evening. But I noticed the furtive glances as people tried to work out what was wrong with my face, and gradually I stopped leaving the flat.

Ramsey was very preoccupied by work and finances, so I retreated upstairs to the third-floor guest room to spare him having to look at me. I had *One Hundred Years of Solitude* to read, plenty of magazines, and plans to write a short story. As Nanny used to say, 'It doesn't do to wallow.'

But then an arctic fog of depression rolled in on me. I couldn't see beyond a few inches in any direction and the concepts of 'up' and 'down' became meaningless. White noise drowned out human voices. Somehow, though, the numbness didn't blot out the pain. It took all my strength to heave my bones to the bathroom to pee.

There were some advantages: for instance, zero appetite, and zero energy to care about what Ramsey got up to. I needed help, but I couldn't ring Sunny as she was in the eighth month of a tricky pregnancy and had bigger things to worry about than me. So I took to my bed and stayed there.

Ramsey must have called the GP, because one afternoon Dr Rattner appeared in my room where I was curled up in bed.

After firing off a few questions that I answered in monosyllables, he prescribed tricyclic anti-depressants, and fled. When thick flecks of foam appeared at the corners of my mouth a few days later, Ramsey threw away the pills in disgust.

'Not a good look, Ari. You're turning into a zombie.'

We drove to the country and stayed in a riverside pub in Marlow. He held me close all night, but we didn't make love. I was so grateful to him for that. The warmth of his body and his familiar smell was the best medicine imaginable, especially under cover of darkness when the damage to my face was camouflaged.

I craved being close to him, but lately, Ramsey's lovemaking had felt more like a vicious attack, albeit an impersonal one, inflicted by him with theatrical intensity and only bearable if I closed my eyes and thought of Tenzin. The rarest of rare creatures... a gentle man. And clearly smarter than most, to have let go of worldly attachments before he could be destroyed by them.

After our brief stay in the country, Ramsey returned to work and the fog descended again. The poisonous magma trapped inside my skin refused to either erupt or subside, immune to the efforts of Dr Hyde and various facialists, homeopaths, naturopaths and spiritual healers.

News occasionally filtered in from the outside world; events which seemed as unreal and remote as if they had taken place in another galaxy. Jimi Hendrix choked to death on his vomit. Sunny gave birth to twins: a boy named Donovan and a girl called Delilah.

I think I sent mellow yellow flowers to the hospital; I certainly meant to.

At some point Dani informed me that Ramsey was off to Peru for *Vogue* with Tommy, Darrell and the beautiful model Radha Rogers. He'd be gone for a month.

The morning he left for the airport he came to my door and said, 'I'll be thinking of you, kid. As soon as I'm back we'll go down to Devon and look at houses, yeah?'

I didn't reply. After a while I heard the front door slam and the house was quiet. I just wanted to sleep. Without the dogs to take care of, I didn't have to get up, ever.

However, while general visibility through the fog was poor, the resident hecklers in my head demanded my full attention. They shrieked and ranted about how, with all the advantages in the world, I had still managed to mess everything up. How my life was pointless, worthless, useless and doomed. Sunny and Jules had both made it, but I had failed.

Bad skin was an obvious sign of something much uglier within, now exposed for everyone to see. The memories that surfaced from my childhood and teenage years only served to reinforce the conviction, sown by Maud, that there had always been something inherently wrong with me. At some point I remembered there was a way out of hell: starving myself muffled the hecklers and gave me back some control.

Time lumbered on with no delineation between day or night. The outside world had become an abstract concept. Dani brought me mugs of tea, for which I was grateful, and plates of brown rice and vegetables that I flushed down the toilet.

Then one day, without any warning, my father turned up.

Dani brought him upstairs. I feigned sleep, too ashamed of the state of my appearance to risk sitting up and facing him. Out of breath from three flights of stairs, he plonked heavily down onto the chair next to the bed.

'It's only me, darling,' he said, after a short silence. 'Tell me: what's going on? I can't bear to see you like this.'

His voice was so kind, and his concern so genuine that something gave way. Soon the pillow under my cheek was soaked with tears, and my shoulders were shaking uncontrollably.

'The dogs...' I sobbed.

At least this sounded plausible, as if I were a caring person, not the self-pitying monster I actually was. Without changing my position, I groped around for the tissue box on the bedside table.

'Where have you been?' I heard myself saying, and then worried it sounded reproachful.

He told me he was building a house in Grenada. 'I can't take any more winters, darling, my old bones are protesting.'

'What about Maud?' I wanted to ask if she was going with him but didn't have the strength.

'She will visit whenever she can,' came Papa's crisp reply.

That sounded pretty final to me.

The following morning, Dani knocked on my door and told me that Maud's secretary had rung to say that an appointment had been made with a Professor Kneale at the John Radcliffe Hospital in Oxford a few days hence, and would I confirm?

Of course Papa had informed Maud about my skin condition and, in her usual style, she was taking the bull by the horns. I wanted to say to go to hell. But by now the outer layer of epidermis on my face had gone reptilian rough from all the drying lotions, while underneath the stubborn ridges of poison refused to budge.

I asked Dani to call and accept the offer. At least it showed Maud cared.

Apart from a few terse birthday and Christmas phone calls, we had not spoken in two years. Perhaps this was an olive branch. At the same time I hated being beholden to her.

Like Dr Hyde, Professor Kneale was neither charming nor sympathetic, but he was a much better doctor, and he quickly identified the root of the problem: a hormonal imbalance. 'These things can be exacerbated by stress, of course,' he added.

Within a few weeks of taking the prescribed medications, my acne miraculously disappeared. However, as predicted by Dr Hyde, the prolonged period of infection left behind deep marks, poetically called ice-pick scars, in the softer regions of my face, especially my cheeks. The condition would not improve by itself, nor would the skin on my face ever be smooth again, Professor Kneale informed me; but he could offer a procedure called dermabrasion which might improve the appearance somewhat.

It involved scratching off the outer layers of the skin with a needle-like surgical instrument, then waiting for two weeks while the new skin grew back. We fixed a time for the operation in the new year.

Somehow, this changed things for me. The fog began to lift. And for the first time in a while, I felt something like hope.

THIRTY-SIX

Thurston, February 1971

My father invited me to stay at Thurston while my new face grew back. I accepted, partly because of Ramsey, and partly because, as difficult as it was to admit, I was homesick. Things with Ramsey were continuing to unravel. It was like living with a stranger.

Papa picked me up from the hospital, where I danced down the corridor with a bloody face, high as a kite from intravenous Valium, and relieved to have the operation behind me. It was just as well I was out of it, given my father's driving. He sped through a zebra crossing while a group of children were attempting to walk across it, and then he nearly ran into another car when it stopped abruptly at some traffic lights.

Though it was a grey day, the roads around Oxford seemed filled with mystery, swathed in pearly mist.

'I've always thought daffodils were rather vulgar,' Papa remarked as we passed roundabout after roundabout full of bright flowering clumps.

'But they're a good suicide deterrent before actual spring arrives,' I pointed out.

'Ha.' He smiled. 'Perhaps I've seen it all coming round again once too often. As you get older, the relentless march of seasons becomes rather tiresome, you know.'

He began telling me about Grenada and the house he was building on a wild bay.

I laughed, listening to his grand plans. 'It won't be very wild after you're through with it.'

He just shook his head, undeterred. 'Nature is invariably enhanced by marvellous architecture, darling.'

I felt oddly comfortable, sparring gently with him. As if I were still sixteen years old. As if everything that had gone down in the last five years had been nothing more than a fever dream.

He turned into the gates of Thurston rather too abruptly and managed to scrape the front bumper on the electric gate as it was opening. It had been nearly three years since Ramsey and I had escaped in the night after the disastrous charades episode, and I hadn't been back since. Now I was returning, like Frankenstein's monster, with bloody gauze wrapped round my face.

Thankfully, Maud was in London but Mr Collins was waiting for us on the steps. Outward displays of emotion had never been his forte so when he hugged me warmly, it felt like a proper homecoming.

Since my last visit, the entrance hall had been repainted a pale ochre, and the drawing room now completely redecorated, but the clean smell of geranium leaves and beeswax, and the underlying atmosphere of calm melancholy in the house was even more noticeable now there were no dogs to greet us.

Papa's Gin had long since died, and Henrietta's pugs were with her in London.

Still high from the Valium, I ran to see Reg, June and Mrs Philpott, who were having their tea in the staff dining room. They laughed when they heard about Papa's near misses on the road and if they were appalled by my appearance, they never showed it. It was a relief to be accepted back in the fold, especially when I had not been in touch with any of them for so long.

Ramsey's name went unmentioned.

Maud arrived at dusk on Friday evening and appeared in my room where I was in bed reading.

'Ari, I...' she began, but then her gaze skated across the thick brown scabs on my cheeks and her mouth fell open.

'This is ghastly for you, darling. I'm so sorry.' She spoke with surprising vehemence, emotion raw beneath the surface. 'Somehow, I feel rather responsible.'

With that, she turned on her heel and vanished.

Her admission shook me. For the first and only time since I had known her, she had almost owned up to her failings as a mother. She could have easily blamed Ramsey, or accused me of being an addict, for that matter. I had to think hard about what she'd meant. As much as I wanted to blame her for my disastrous situation, I couldn't. The life I'd chosen to ride had bucked me off, after a good run. I had no idea how to move forward, but pride stopped me from asking Maud's advice. In any case, she never revisited the conversation. At least she never said, 'I told you so'.

On the following evening I ventured downstairs for a drink with my parents, wearing a headscarf tied under my chin like an off-duty Queen. In spite of knocking back two of Mr Collins' famously potent martinis each, Maud and Papa behaved like frosty acquaintances at a formal occasion. There were so many off-limits topics that we broadly stuck to the weather and local gossip. Maud still managed to let slip that Henrietta and Simon had finally married the year before in the Ashsprington village church. Quickly glossing over this announcement, possibly because Ramsey and I had not been invited to the wedding, she moved smoothly onto other subjects. Papa avoided my eyes, and I feigned indifference. Generally speaking, however, Maud was warmer towards me in my ravaged state.

On Sunday afternoon after lunch, a sleek government car arrived and Maud was off to London with her bulging briefcase, complaining about the number of official papers she had to get through before Monday morning. Papa and I saw her off and then he went upstairs for a siesta.

Everyone who has ever been to boarding school knows that Sunday afternoons are cursed for ever afterwards. Feeling low, I made the mistake of calling Ramsey, who sounded hungover. We chatted for a while, then he said, 'Oh, I forgot to mention, I can't come and pick you up next week like we'd planned.'

'Why not?'

'I've got a job in Milan… It just came up.' His tone was overly casual.

'You're joking.'

'Don't be like that, darling. I had no choice. You know what my overheads are like. It's different for you. You'll never understand what it's like to have to work.'

My jaw tightened so much I felt the scabs crack. 'I want to work, that's why I had the operation.'

'I know.' His tone was dismissive. 'Anyway, I've accepted the job so I won't be there.'

Suddenly I didn't want to play this game.

'You don't love me any more, that's the bottom line,' I said, flatly.

'Of course I love you.' His voice softened. 'But you've got to understand the pressure I'm under.'

'You don't love me,' I said. 'And now we have to decide what to do.'

I hung up the phone before he could lie even more. I longed to believe him, and that always skewed everything.

Afterwards I sat in the drawing room, curled up on one of the chintz-covered sofas, leafing through Papa's latest book on Portuguese colonial architecture. Buffeted by the wind and the violent spattering of rain on glass, the windows rattled incessantly. The last embers of a fire still smoked in the hearth and I could easily have added more wood to get it going again, but I felt heavy, pinned down by overpowering inertia.

It was strange being back amongst all the objects and pictures I'd known all my life. After years away, everything seemed both familiar and alien at the same time. Above the chimneypiece was a large portrait of my father when he was Master of Hounds for the local hunt. Handsome in his pink coat and velvet riding hat, astride his favourite chestnut hunter, for the first time I noticed a slightly uneasy expression in his eyes, which was somewhat at odds with his otherwise assured demeanour.

A wave of nausea swept over me, and I broke out into a sweat. Abruptly, the room seemed to tilt sideways and my ears began to ring. Everything I'd been staring at, the portrait, the fireplace, the fringed shade over a Chinese porcelain lamp at the foot of the sofa, suddenly appeared nonsensical, drained of any meaning. What was I doing here?

By now, I was no stranger to these episodes. The experience typically only lasted a few seconds, but it was profoundly unsettling, as if there was nothing familiar in the world to cling to.

From the direction of the drinks tray, there came a sudden whoosh of the soda siphon. Papa was making his first whiskey and soda of the evening.

Slowly the room came back into focus.

'What are you up to, darling?' he said, ice clinking in the glass. 'Come next door and watch the news with me.'

Later, when we were eating our supper on trays in the sitting room, I asked after Rupert.

Papa looked up from his consommé, startled. 'Has no one told you?'

'Told me what?'

'Rather odd, the whole thing. I believe he accidentally drank some punch containing... what is it? Yes, LSD; at a party last summer. He was found cowering under a table by a kind gel who looked after him until the effect wore off. By then he'd fallen hook, line and sinker for her.'

I burst out laughing. 'Rupert? LSD? I don't believe it!'

'Well it's absolutely true. He's left his job at the bank and is going into business in British Guiana.'

'It's Guyana now. Why there?'

'It's where she's from.'

'What was Maud's reaction?'

'She's had to grin and bear it. Sumitra is a few years older than Rupert, and a force to be reckoned with. He seems blissfully happy.'

I raised my glass of wine. 'To the transformative powers of hallucinogens… not that I would know.'

Papa looked vague, as if he hadn't heard. Then he quickly added, 'Oh, and I forgot to mention that Damiano is staying the night on Wednesday; he's got a meeting at the Ashmolean.'

Damiano was the photographer he'd worked with for years on his architectural books. He was Portuguese, in his forties, observant and unobtrusive, but also very good company.

'Fine, but don't expect me to see him, looking like this,' I said gesturing at my scabbed face.

'Damiano is the last person who would mind.'

'Rubbish,' I said, too sharply. 'He's a photographer, for god's sake. Anyway, *I* mind.'

But I was touched, when June appeared in my room a few days later with a terracotta pot of white narcissus covered in cellophane and tied with green ribbons, from Damiano, together with a handwritten card.

I sent down a note saying I hoped to see him when I was 'better'.

A few hours later, ravenously hungry after a few puffs on a spliff, I went down the back stairs to the kitchen in search of food. It was around 9:30pm; Mrs Philpott and Collins had already washed up and gone home. I devoured some cold chicken and potatoes, then found an open bottle of red wine in the pantry and poured myself a glass.

Down the corridor, through the green baize door separating the kitchen wing from the main part of the house, came the faint but unmistakable sound of Billie Holliday singing 'Night and Day', punctuated by exuberant bursts of laughter I recognised as Damiano's.

Suddenly it seemed silly to me that I had refused to see him. It would please my father if I went in and said hello. And why not? He was a lovely man.

Mr Collins had turned out all the lights; the entrance hall and staircase were shrouded in darkness. The only source of light came from the half-open door of the drawing room.

When I reached it, I paused. It was odd to hear my father laughing with such abandon; he sounded almost like a stranger.

I peeked around the door. For once, Papa was not sitting in his usual high-backed yellow armchair. Instead he reclined on the sofa amongst the cushions. Damiano was perched sideways on the edge of the sofa, leaning forward towards Papa while he recounted a story, using expansive hand gestures. As he listened, Papa's face radiated pleasure in a way I'd rarely seen.

Damiano reached the punchline of his story, whereupon he exploded into laughter, collapsing sideways, his shoulders shaking with convulsions of laughter. At that moment, my father leaned over and kissed him tenderly on the crown of his head.

I was thunderstruck. And in an instant, I understood so much about my parents that had always baffled me. Why he didn't mind Maud's philandering. Why they spent so little time together.

I felt like a fool – and an intruder. So I tiptoed backwards very quietly and left them in peace.

THIRTY-SEVEN

London, May 1972

'Wow, you're so skinny these days! You look amazing, babe.'

'Oh, come on. I'm a mess. I just flew in last night from New York. But you look great! Where did you get those cool suede chaps?'

'Just tilt your chin up for me, Sandy? That's it, thank you. Beautiful.'

Directly below where I was sitting on the loo in Ramsey's flat, two American models and a make-up artist were getting ready for a shoot. Some acoustical quirk to do with poor insulation between the two floors made clear every word they said in the downstairs changing room.

Everyone sounded like Andy Warhol these days: *Wow, you look so great. Have you lost weight? I love your dress/hair/necklace/sweater/shoes.*

Sometimes I could hear Ramsey's voice chiming in, teasing or cajoling the models, followed by shrieks of laughter. Occasionally he yelled at the fashion editor or hairdresser for taking so long, after which there would be a brief, stunned silence followed by a flurry of activity.

Of course, I had always known the fashion business was superficial and soul-destroying, but I'd been fine with that. I hadn't realised how much I had come to depend on all the attention until it was no longer focused on me.

Ramsey had not been impressed when he'd first seen my post-op face, all those months ago, and he kept on at me to consider further work. I eventually went back to see Dr Kneale, who said another dermabrasion was possible now that we were a few months down the line, but he couldn't promise more than scant improvement.

'Worse things happen at sea,' he'd said, lightly, attempting to give me some perspective via photographs of serious burn victims he had treated. He underestimated

235

the depths of my own self-pity – though any whiff of sympathy expressed by others was mortifying.

The fashion crowd generally made it easy for me, since almost everyone I had ever worked with now avoided eye contact, or indeed any contact with me at all.

I was discovering what it was like to lose face, in the literal sense of the word.

Despite our phone conversation the year before at Thurston, I had been far too cowardly to leave Ramsey. Instead, I had discovered the joys of self-medication to numb the pain. Grass, hash, alcohol, cocaine… everything the doctors had told me to avoid, I ingested. When I was high, I didn't care any more, and it made me careless.

One weekend, I took the train from Waterloo to visit Sunny at her new place near Guildford, stopping first at Harrods to buy a giant plush lion for Donovan and a tiger for Delilah.

Sunny sent Barry to pick me up from the station in his combi van. A roadie who went back to the Knee Trembler's Maidstone days, he worked as Eddie's factotum when they weren't touring. I'd known him since Sunny first got a record deal, and we'd always had a laugh. I'd vowed to stay sober today, but as soon as I climbed in next to him I heard myself say, 'Have you got a joint?'

'Always,' he grinned, leaning sideways to rummage through the glove box as he drove and drawing out a long, six-paper joint. He lit it and passed it to me.

I took a long drag and felt my nerves relax. 'Thank you,' I said, in a puff of smoke.

We chatted for a bit, and I was relieved he didn't mention my skin.

'How's Sunny coping with the twins?' I asked.

He snorted a laugh, eyes on the road ahead. 'She's great, as long as you don't mind hearing about wind, shit, and lack of sleep all day. And whatever you do, don't get Eddie started on the subject of the renovations.'

'Thanks for the tip. I'm rather dreading it.'

Somewhere past Guildford he pulled the van over, parked on a verge and dug out a vial of white powder from his jacket pocket. 'This'll get you through today.'

For an hour or so after the toot my spirits soared, which was enough time to make all the right sounds when I met the babies; though when Sunny tried to get me to hold Deli, I just couldn't. They were adorable – fat and pink-cheeked, with matching shocks of dark hair.

Sunny was in love all over again, effortlessly breastfeeding as we chatted. Eddie stayed near her constantly, picking up one baby or the other. They were the picture of domestic bliss.

Eddie mentioned that the tour they had postponed when Sunny fell pregnant was going ahead in two months, with the twins and a nanny in tow.

'All I've got to do is write six new songs and lose a stone and a half by then,' Sunny laughed.

'I've got a few black bombers on me now and I can get more anytime, Sun,' Barry said eagerly.

'Shut up, man,' Eddie told him.

Barry just shrugged and gave me a sly glance.

I wondered if I had lost Sunny for ever.

After tea, and a chilly walk round the garden, Barry drove me back to the station. We did a couple more lines on the way, and soon I was feeling better again, especially when Barry gave me the number of his dealer in London. 'He's very reliable,' Barry said, tapping his nose.

I realised Ramsey might disapprove – but so what? If I took a small amount every day he would never know, and it might improve our relationship if I were peppier.

When the train arrived at Waterloo Station that afternoon, I couldn't face going home. Ramsey would still be working, there'd be models and fashion editors everywhere.

On a whim, I took a taxi to Cindy's shop in the Chelsea Antiques Market.

'So, your modelling career is over, darls. Now what?' Her Aussie directness contained neither Schadenfreude nor pity, so I could deal with it. She was just being practical.

But I didn't really have an answer. 'How much longer are you going to work?' I enquired. 'I'd love to get a drink.'

'Me too,' she said, grinning. She locked up and we went off to buy a bottle of Mount Gay rum and some crisps. Then we took a taxi back to her flat in a mansion block off Earls Court Road, where it transpired her boyfriend, Ryan, had been drinking wine and smoking weed with a couple of friends since early afternoon.

Ry was a good painter with Byronesque looks. He also had a Byronesque attitude and was famously moody and difficult. Today, though, he seemed unusually ebullient; albeit prone to veering off on epic conversational tangents.

As Dylan blasted away in the background, Ry and his friends were loudly debating whether to return to Australia now that there was a progressive government running the country. Ry had decided against the idea, having concluded that suburbia by the sea was still suburbia.

'Mate, you say that in May, but what about January, when we're all surfin' at Bondi and you're freezin' your arse off?' said Giorgio, a filmmaker from Melbourne.

'Yeah Ry,' echoed Leanne, Giorgio's child bride, 'London's over, haven't you heard?'

Cindy, attired in a skin-tight red silk cheongsam and made up like Anna May Wong, rolled her eyes and poured me a drink. Soon the conversation moved on to music, and Ry asked me how Sunny was doing.

I explained her career was temporarily on hold because of the twins.

'Yeah, well she's already lost her edge, or whatever edge she had. It's too bad – she has just about the best voice in the business and she's not a bad looker either, but her material is lame, man.'

I felt furiously defensive on Sunny's behalf, but Cindy gave me a warning look and I bit my tongue. I didn't want to argue. All I really wanted was to get some blow so I could feel good again.

I asked Cindy if I could use the phone to call the dealer.

Ry answered before she could. 'Call him, Ari. Get some for me.'

'Ry, we don't even have the bread to buy bread at the moment,' Cindy reminded him.

'That's OK, I'm buying,' I said quickly.

'There you go. Let's do it.' Ry rubbed his hands together, his thick, dark curls falling forward over his blue eyes.

Barry hadn't been joking about his dealer. Jimmy materialised in under twenty minutes. He was a man of few words, but what he did have was a Pan Am bag filled with individual cellophane wraps of coke.

'One hundred per cent pure, man,' he declared, scowling at me as if I'd argued with him.

I bought two so I could keep one for myself, thinking I could make it last a week.

As soon as Jimmy departed, Ry grabbed one of the packets out of my hands and started chopping lines on an old copy of *Soul on Ice*. 'Anyone gotta bill?' he asked.

I produced my last five-pound note, and it wasn't long before we had hoovered up most of the gram between five of us. This time the high was different. Unlike the euphoria I'd felt from Barry's coke, now I felt shaky and nervous, with a bad case of buyer's remorse.

'Oh shit, I think this is cut with speed,' Giorgio said, and laughed maniacally.

'Cheating bastard dealer,' Ry grumbled, unscrewing the top of the Mount Gay bottle and taking a huge swig. 'This should bring us down.'

I took a swig too, but it didn't blunt my escalating paranoia or stop my heart pounding. Everyone was moving frantically in different directions.

I went out onto the balcony and scanned the street. Everything seemed unnaturally still outside, not a car on the road nor cat on the footpath. Cindy materialised and touched my arm. 'You OK, darls?'

'I feel like we're being watched.' My voice sounded thick and strange.

'Oh Ari, you'll be right, it's just coke paranoia. It'll wear off. Come on, let's dance.'

Behind us, Ry had put on 'Superfly' at full volume and was strutting around, singing the lyrics with slightly camp gusto.

Dancing helped. As did a few more rum shots. Gradually, my anxiety started to subside. Leanne and Giorgio were dirty dancing in the far corner, while Ry, Cindy and I were spinning dervish-like across the room.

This felt good. Getting away from Ramsey was a relief. I was doing what I wanted for once, without being reined in all the time. It was exhilarating to be breaking free in the twilight on a May evening, with the long summer ahead.

Things had been bad, but I didn't have to be a model. I could dance. I'd start taking jazz dance classes in Covent Garden and soon get good enough to perform. My skin wouldn't be an issue on stage. I'd be accepted for my talent, rather than how I looked. I was becoming lighter all the time, thinking about all the endless possibilities in store for me.

Poor Sunny, stuck out in the sticks having to play grown-ups: she would have loved this impromptu party. Closing my eyes, I folded my arms behind my head, rolling my hips in slow figure eights, in sync with the music.

This was when it occurred to me that I rather fancied a joint. Singing to myself, I danced through a beaded curtain to the little alcove where earlier I'd stashed my bag in a corner. I was rifling through it for Barry's little present of some ready-made reefers when I heard a muffled bang from the hall.

I peered through the coloured curtain just in time to see five men burst in from the corridor, screaming something I couldn't hear above the music.

Two of them leaped on Ry, who swore at them, flailing his arms. Giorgio and Leanne were screaming, biting, and kicking. My blood was pumping so fast I was sure I would have a heart attack. Especially when one of the men grabbed Leanne by the shoulders and ran her hard into the nearest wall. I watched as her body went limp, and she slumped to the ground.

Cindy slammed a green vase holding yellow roses into the back of the attacker's head. When it hit the floor, shards of glass, water and flowers flew across the room.

Miraculously, in my hiding place, I still hadn't been noticed. The door from the alcove to the bedroom was ajar, so I slipped though, clutching my satchel to my chest.

The blinds were down, and the room was dark, strangely still, and smelled of stale sandalwood incense. Warily, I opened the bedroom door to find the hallway empty. I made a dash down the corridor past the kitchen to the back door and fiddled with the latch for a few seconds before it opened.

Outside on the landing, the stark reality of the situation sank in. Several uniformed policemen were charging up the stairs towards me. Someone grabbed me in a vice-like grip and a voice said, 'You're coming down to the station with us, miss.'

THIRTY-EIGHT

London, May 1972

At the police station, my bag was unceremoniously tipped upside down onto an empty desk by a uniformed officer. The heavier objects fell out first: French and English coins, purse, Zippo lighter, keys, a felt make-up pouch, a packet of Peter Stuyvesant cigarettes, a small bottle of Fracas.

To give them credit, they were thorough. Once the joints had been discovered in the cigarette packet, one of the police officers pounced on my make-up pouch and emptied it onto a different part of the desk. Finding nothing except lipstick and mascara, he then deftly turned my soft leather and canvas bag inside out, where he discovered the zipped compartment in the lining containing the folded paper with the coke inside and a plastic pill box I'd forgotten about, containing a few Drinamyl and some mandies.

'Are these yours?' he inquired, pointing to the incriminating items.

'I'd like to ring my solicitor,' I replied.

The officer rolled his eyes and proceeded to ignore my request, so I refused to answer any further questions or even give them my name. Since I'd left my heavy wallet at home, I had no form of ID on me.

'Right, she's under the influence, put her in a cell. Perhaps she'll be more cooperative after a few hours.'

Two burly officers took me into the bowels of the building and shoved me into a cell. The door clanged shut, the key turned, and I was alone.

The cell contained virtually nothing except a narrow cement block about five foot long and three feet high, presumably meant for sitting or lying down on, though you'd have to be scrunched into an awkward foetal position to do so. The only other feature was a seatless metal toilet. As evidenced by a couple of inches of blue water in the bowl, an attempt had been made to disinfect it, rather half-heartedly it seemed, because multitudinous brown specks were still embedded round the rim. There was no window, no bedding, nothing remotely humanising, only desperate marks scratched into the thin coat of yellowish paint that covered the brick walls.

Still high on coke and alcohol, I paced up and down, tearing at my hair in an effort to process the drugs and adrenaline flooding my system. I wanted to jump out of my skin; do anything to flee the reality of a situation from which there was no means of escape. Now at last I'd seen with my own eyes why the underground press was so obsessed with exposing the hypocrisy of a corrupt police force, hellbent on crushing the counterculture.

Waves of self-righteous fury kept me moving, until finally exhaustion took over and at last I fell asleep, sitting upright on the concrete bench.

When I woke, disoriented and parched, my anger had metastasised into anguish and panic. My first thought was of my father. Despite the fact I had let him down so many times over the years, he had always believed in me. Now I had gone way too far to ever be forgiven.

As for Maud, this would confirm what she had known all along – that I was useless.

And what sort of shit-storm had I unleashed on Cindy, Ry and the others? Had they been arrested as well?

I kept replaying the moments before and after the cops stormed the flat, cursing myself for disregarding my instincts and especially for imagining that I lived on such a high, hip cloud that consequences didn't apply to me.

The full horror of what I had done hit me full in the chest like a wrecking ball, crushing my lungs and heart so I could scarcely breathe. For a long time, I'd been feeling like I was falling through space. At last, I had hit the ground.

I had no idea how long I stayed sitting in the same position, staring at the wall in front of me, when I heard the sound of a key turning in a lock. The cell door opened.

A uniformed policeman, reasonably cheery, said, 'Right, miss, you've got visitors.'

Shakily, feeling as if my knees might buckle at any minute, I stood and followed him down the long bare corridor.

When we entered the room where I'd been searched many hours before, the morning light pouring in from the windows at the far end shimmered with blinding radiance.

'Ari! Over here.'

Ramsey stood in the brightest part of the room, lost in the glare.

Weeping tears of relief, I stumbled towards him. As I neared him, I saw he was wearing a purple silk shirt with a black velvet suit, utterly out of place in this square, utilitarian room. His expression was thunderous.

In a voice frigid with anger, he told me, 'I brought you a solicitor. This is – what's your name?'

'It's Patrick Huxtable. Hello, Ari.' Patrick extended his hand and took me aside.

'Mr Ramsey has posted your bail and you'll be released soon after you've been charged. The police are saying they couldn't do it last night because you were high; is that true?'

'It's a lie,' I said weakly. 'They didn't even allow me a phone call.'

'Par for the course, I'm afraid.' He glanced over my head towards the officers at the desk. 'They had no idea you had connections. We'll discuss that later. Meanwhile, don't worry, I'm here and I'll make sure you're looked after.'

The change in my treatment was dramatic. The policewoman who took my fingerprints was almost apologetic. The detectives and uniformed police were solicitous and polite.

I heard one of them whisper to another that I was 'Serena Lyttleton's daughter,' and my heart sank further. Maud was going to murder me.

I was charged with possession of cocaine, marijuana, Drinamyl and Mandrax, and ordered to appear in court the following week.

Afterwards, in a bizarre aside, Ramsey and I were asked to sign the station's visitors' book, as if we were weekend guests at a grand country house.

When we finished, Patrick shook my hand again and said he'd be in touch to discuss strategy. I told him about Cindy, and he promised to find out where she was, and make sure she was treated well.

Ramsey said nothing. He just turned and walked out the door. I followed, straight into a crowd of photographers. I shielded my face with my bag as Ramsey and I ran down the street, with half a dozen paps following on our heels, shouting.

'Ariadne! How long're you going down for?'

'Does your mum know you take drugs?'

Bile rose in my throat as I fled. I had to call Maud and my father to warn them.

'Fucking coppers must have tipped them off,' Ramsey hissed as he unlocked the door of his latest car, a Ferrari, and pushed me in.

The photographers jostled around the car windows, snapping away as I tumbled awkwardly into the low passenger seat. We zoomed off at high speed, nearly bagging a few hacks in the process. With exaggerated brio, Ramsey tailgated every car that happened to be in front of us, aggressively overtaking each one at the slightest opportunity, just missing several collisions.

Just before Oxford Street we hit heavy traffic. That was when Ramsey exploded.

'Great, Ari! Thanks, mate. Now everyone will think I'm a junkie like you. How could you be so fucking thick?'

I burst into tears and apologised profusely. 'Thank you for organising Patrick. How did you find out where I was?'

He waved one hand. 'That Aussie bird called.'

'Cindy?' I stared at him, hopefully. 'Is she OK?'

'I don't know. Dani spoke to her.' His voice was brittle. He was in no mood for chit-chat.

I fell silent again, afraid to irritate him. 'Why are you in evening clothes?' I asked, before I could stop myself.

He didn't meet my eyes. 'I went to a dinner with some poncey publisher. One of your lot. I waited for you, but you didn't show. When I got home you still weren't there, so I started calling people, trying to find you. Finally Dani got the call from your mate. Haven't had a chance to change, what with cancelling this morning's shoot and finding you a solicitor.'

Something in his tone didn't ring true. Still, I was in no position to confront him now.

Ramsey dropped me outside the house and took off again in a cloud of diesel fumes. As soon as I got through the door, I called Cindy, who was safe at home. She told me that the Flying Squad had searched their flat, and by some miracle only a few roaches had been discovered so no one had been arrested. But the police had discovered that Ry's visa had expired, and he was now facing immediate deportation.

'Well, we were looking for a sign to help us decide whether or not to go back to Sydney, and we got one,' she said, bitterly. 'London is over, darls; at least, it is for us.'

It certainly felt that way a few hours later, when the *Evening Standard* hit the newsstands. I was on the front page looking like an ancient junkie, pulled along the street by a dapper Ramsey in his glamorous evening clothes.

The headline was to the point: 'Peer's Daughter in Drugs Bust'.

There wasn't much point in reading further.

When I phoned Maud, she was apoplectic with rage, our semi-rapprochement now long forgotten. 'Have you absolutely no concern for anyone except yourself?' she demanded. 'My entire career has been jeopardised because of you. Everything I've worked for... And your poor father. This will *kill* him. He's catching a plane back from Grenada as we speak, to try and sort this out.'

'When does he arrive? I'll meet him at the airport.' I knew it was essential to get to him before she did.

Later that week I learned how the police raid had happened. Patrick told me that Jimmy the dealer had been under investigation by the police Flying Squad for weeks, and they'd chosen the very moment when he emerged from Cindy's flat to arrest him. Of course, he ratted on everyone he sold to.

'What was he charged with?' I asked.

'Possession of a Class A substance.'

'Possession? He had at least 100 grams on him, I saw them in his bag.'

Patrick said he was only arrested with a small amount. He assumed Jimmy had handed over the coke to the police, so they could sell it through their own channels.

Everyone knew about the police and their dirty deals, but it was the first time I'd seen the evidence. It wasn't a pleasant awakening, but it gave me some ballast, as well as an avenue through which to direct my self-righteous rage, which obscured another, less digestible feeling that festered inside me – a deep sense of shame.

Jules, Ritchie, and everyone from the Consulate got in touch, offering help and support. Sunny rang to make sure I was OK, but I could tell she was distracted by crawling and wakeful babies and didn't have much energy left over after months of sleepless nights.

Meanwhile on the domestic front, Ramsey continued to slowly remove himself from me, like an ocean liner receding over the horizon. All I could do was watch helplessly. He was still my home, my life. I knew every inch of his body as well as I knew my own. We had been through so much together. And when it came to practicalities, of which I knew nothing, he organised everything; or rather, Dani did. I had no inkling how to function without him. As he kept reminding me.

While I waited for the court case to be heard, I was required to appear every week at the police station, along with the other alleged offenders on remand. We were all confined to a waiting room for several hours, where after a while we began exchanging stories. The majority were young black men, who had been arrested for possession of hash or ganja, most of them unable to raise bail and obliged to languish courtesy of HM Prison Service until they were assigned a hearing. Often, they were detained for months, experiencing all the delights that prison had to offer, including some top mentoring by professional criminals.

I remembered that one of my acquaintances from the Consulate, Claudia, had started a group called Release, an organisation that helped people arrested on drug charges get good lawyers to represent them in court. I phoned her for advice, and she was as cool and helpful as I remembered. After we had spoken for some time she said, 'If you feel so strongly about the injustice of our system, come and work for us. We need help in the office.'

Out of pure self-interest I took up her offer. It was something else to focus on rather than worrying about my trial. And I had never encountered a person like Claudia. Though perfectly comfortable in every kind of social circle imaginable, she was a maverick, a law unto herself, and she truly cared about people she saw as unfairly treated by the authorities. She was also generous, fun, and articulate; the kind of woman I aspired to be.

Ramsey didn't approve, of course. Strong women were anathema to him and he made sure they knew it. But I didn't care any more what he thought. Being around Claudia was inspirational. She was undaunted by criticism and endlessly resilient. After she met Ramsey, she took me out for a coffee and told me about controlling behaviour.

'It's hard to leave such an all-consuming relationship and stand on your own feet,' she said. 'But if you ever decide you want out, I'm here.'

Still, I couldn't walk away.

Arriving home from Release early one afternoon with a headache, I found Ramsey in the living room with Jacky, the wife of one of his best friends. They both looked so guilty, I knew something had to be going on between them. Jacky was an aspiring model, fresh-faced and beautiful.

As we stared at each other, Ramsey suddenly said, 'What have you been up to, then?'

I turned and ran up to my room. He didn't follow.

I didn't know what to do. I hadn't seen him actually doing anything but I knew. I could see it in Jacky's face. Her lips were swollen from kissing him; her cheeks red from his three-day beard.

When I saw Ramsey in the kitchen later, after Jacky had left the house, he said, 'She's as thick as a brick, that one. I don't know what Frank sees in her.'

Six weeks later, my hearing came up. Coincidentally Ramsey had a big advertising job in Paris on the same day. 'Someone's got to pay your fucking legal fees, haven't they?' he said.

Papa accompanied me instead, and stoically braved the storm of paparazzi outside.

It was especially good of him, considering how furious he'd been when I met him in the Arrivals Hall at Heathrow: 'You've betrayed your family; you've betrayed me. How could you?'

I couldn't blame him.

However, after I told him everything that had happened that day, my deeply conservative father had become radicalised. From then on, he railed against the police to anyone who would listen. I had never loved him more.

In court that day, much of Patrick's defence centred around how acne had ruined my modelling career, leading to a breakdown and heavy drug use. This information was apparently gleaned from Ramsey, because nobody had told me this was the plan.

Up until that moment in the proceedings, I'd kept my eyes on my shoes, but now I looked up, startled, to find everyone in the court staring at me with ghoulish interest.

He told them I'd spent the intervening months volunteering with an organisation that provided legal aid to young offenders, and that I'd begun turning my life around.

'This situation has been a wakeup call for Miss Lyttleton,' Patrick insisted. 'I think she deserves the chance to prove she really has changed.'

Whether it was the sob story or the volunteering, I will never know. But the magistrate gave me a conditional discharge. As long as I didn't get arrested again within two years, my criminal record would be cleared.

'But don't take this for granted,' the magistrate warned. 'You'll be dealt with far more severely if you commit any further offences. I hope never to see you before this court again.'

The feeling was entirely mutual.

Papa exhaled and squeezed my hand.

Outside the court, blinded by flashbulbs, I hung on his arm while we ploughed through the photographers to a waiting car and drove back to the flat in Cadogan Square to down some neat brandy. Needless to say, the day before, Maud had flown to Washington DC on a fact-finding mission to the US Justice Department.

'Where's Damiano?' I asked, casually.

My father brightened. 'We're dining tonight at La Fontana if you'd like to join us, darling?'

'Thanks, Pa, I just want to go home to bed, but I'll come with you to the airport in the morning.'

As we sipped our drinks, I made a silent unconditional vow to never let him down again.

When he kissed me goodbye later, he said unexpectedly, 'Mark my words, darling, one day Ramsey will be an old man and you'll wonder what you ever saw in him. No matter how charming they can be, no matter how accomplished, some people are just in it for themselves. And no matter how much you love them, they are never going to change.'

I started to object, but Papa gently refused to let me. 'I just want you to make sure you live your own life, not in someone else's shadow. It's a lesson I learned far too late.'

THIRTY-NINE

London, May 1972

The next day the papers were full of mortifying details from my court appearance, about my skin and drug problems. But even more disturbing was the fact that Ramsey hadn't called from Paris to ask how the trial had gone. Dani empathised; he hadn't phoned to check in on daily business either, so he must have his hands full, she speculated. It was an unfortunate expression, but I ignored it and left to accompany Papa to the airport.

The one cheering development came in the form of an unexpected dinner invitation from Sunny. She was leaving the twins in Surrey with Eddie and her mum for the first time and staying the night in her flat in Elm Park Gardens.

I was so happy at the prospect of seeing her alone that, despite my reluctance to show my face in public, I didn't protest when she asked to meet at Meridiana, her local.

The *maître'd* had reserved her favourite table tucked away behind a column, out of sight of the other diners. She was so giddy about being out, we demolished a bottle of Soave before the food arrived. We hardly mentioned the babies, or my court case, and I was finally able to tell her about Papa and Damiano. She looked astounded and stared at me for a few long moments. 'God, Ari! I never would have guessed, but it explains so much, doesn't it? How do you feel about it?'

'I'm sad that he feels he has to hide who he is. On the other hand, it's a relief to know he has love in his life. It always seemed like he was so lonely.'

'Has it made you feel more sympathetic towards your mother? It sort of explains her behaviour in some ways...' Sunny looked uncertain. She had never been keen on Maud.

'It explains why she has lovers, I guess. Not her general unpleasantness.'

We laughed and changed the subject, riffing on music business gossip, Eddie's golf habit, annoying Knee Trembler quirks, her American cousins who had recently visited.

By the time we finished the sea bass and a second bottle of Soave, I needed the loo, which was at the back of the restaurant. As I walked unsteadily around a corner I collided with a man coming the other way.

It was Dan O'Brien. Like Ramsey, Dan was a fashion photographer from the East End. And if there was one thing I knew about him, he was an aggressive drunk. Ramsey and Dan had a complicated love–hate relationship based on shared history and professional and personal rivalry. O'Brien had always perceived me as a threat to his laddish relationship with Ramsey and there was no love lost between us. Given his close proximity to me in the narrow corridor, however, it seemed safer to be civil.

'Oh, hello, O'Brien.' I smiled weakly. 'How are you?'

He looked me up and down. 'Is Ramsey here?' His small, glittering eyes darted around the room behind me.

'No, I'm with a friend.'

'A friend, eh?' His tone made it sound filthy. 'Does Ramsey know?'

'I have no idea.' My voice cooled. 'He's in Paris, working.'

'That's not what I heard.'

He smirked at me. Then, through clenched teeth, corn-yellow from his two-pack-a-day Woodbine habit, he said, 'I hear the poor bastard has finally found a bird who won't embarrass him. That's the word on the street anyway. Now, who could that be?'

He spoke with low, gleeful malice.

I tried to reply but no words would come out.

Seeing my horrified expression, he laughed. 'Surely you're not surprised?'

He pushed past me and walked back into the restaurant. I fled into the Ladies, locking myself in a cubicle and trying to cry, but my eyes stayed dry.

So the moment had finally arrived.

I walked back to the table and calmly told Sunny what had just happened. She listened, her clear blue eyes sympathetic and patient. She seemed even less surprised than me.

'It's over, isn't it?' I said.

The roar of the restaurant faded away. It was just the two of us, in that bubble that had surrounded us since we were twelve years old.

'It's over, Ari.' Her voice was steady. 'And not before time. The man is an unbearable arsehole.'

'I know; I know.' I grimaced in assent.

'And I need to tell you something else too, not to torture you, but because…' Her voice trailed off.

'Get on with it.'

'He's been having an affair with Dani. For years.'

'Oh, come on, that's just not possible.' I tried to sound sceptical, but a strange gurgling sound came out of my mouth instead. 'How the hell would you know, anyway?'

'Her best friend Lettice, who used to work at *Vogue*…'

'Oh yes, Lettice, the soul of indiscretion.' I laughed hollowly.

'She lives in the village near us and is always dropping round.' Sunny rolled her eyes. 'She got poleaxed one night and spilled the beans. Rang up the next morning, mortified, but you can't unsay that shit.'

I was stunned. But it made perfect sense.

Dani always took on the chin the horrible things Ramsey said to her. She never complained, never stood up to him, and always made excuses for his bad temper; even to me. Though she was hardly a shy retiring type with others, she was submissive to Ramsey; indeed, worked overtime to please him. Why had I never even suspected?

'Because you're a bloody ostrich!' Sunny said.

'So why didn't you tell me?'

'I was planning to, that day you came to lunch, but you didn't seem in very good shape. Then you got busted.'

I drained my glass of Sambuca and stood up.

'What are you doing?'

'Going to ask Enzo to call a minicab. I'm going home to pack up before Dani arrives in the morning.'

The flood of adrenaline caused by Sunny's revelation had sobered me up.

Sunny motioned for the bill. 'You're not going back there alone. I'm coming with you.'

As we turned into Fitzroy Road, I half-expected all the lights to be blazing in the house, Ramsey's bags in the hall, Ella Fitzgerald on the turntable.

251

I knew exactly what he'd say: 'Hey, kid, you all right? Missed you, you know that?'

My heart lurched for a moment, and then sank again. The only visible light came from the orange streetlamp on the pavement, which bathed the house in an eerie chemical glow. I unlocked the door, switched off the alarm, and we stood in the front hall, momentarily paralyzed.

Poor Sunny was white with exhaustion. I told her to lie down on the couch in the sitting room while I packed; there was nothing she could do to help except be there. She said on the contrary, she was looking forward to finding some scissors in order to cut the right legs off all Ramsey's trousers, and the left arms off all his jackets.

It had crossed my mind to run down to the garden and free all Ramsey's miserable parrots from their cages, but on second thoughts, they probably wouldn't have stood much of a chance in Camden Town, and he'd just buy more, anyway.

Soon, my two big Globetrotter suitcases were filled with clothes and books. Perched on what I had naively imagined was my side of the bed – rather than the busy time-share it had actually turned out to be – I looked around the room that had seen so much action over the years.

For some reason, I thought of Sylvia Plath, who'd lived just a few doors away, and died there too, by her own hand, several years before. I'd read that her faithless husband had recently installed a headstone on her grave with an inscription: 'Even amidst fierce flames the golden lotus can be planted.' I had puzzled over it at the time. Now, with so much lost, I finally understood, and longed for it to be true.

'How's it going in there?' Sunny called out in a sleepy voice from the next room.

'Done! Just found my passport.'

It was nearly dawn and I wanted to be gone before first parrot screech.

Making sure that nothing was out of place, closing all the cupboards and drawers, I climbed the stairs to the third floor for the last time.

The cleaner had been. Even Ramsey's little painting studio was tidy for once. In the spare room, there was no lingering trace of either joy or heartbreak.

I found Sunny standing in the sitting room, brushing her hair vigorously and staring at Ramsey's photographic line-up of past lovers.

'Shall I throw those bitches out the window now?' she asked.

'That's the holy shrine, Sunny,' I smiled.

'Kill marks on the side of a bomber, more like it.'

252

We stood together, staring at the row of photos. The beautiful faces stared back blankly from their gilt frames.

'Guess you'd better move over, girls,' I told them.

As we dragged my bags down the stairs and out the front door into the waiting taxi, we were both laughing.

FORTY

London, October 1972

For the first few weeks, I was giddy with relief to be out from under Ramsey's critical gaze. I stayed in Sunny's flat, volunteered at Release during the day, and went out every night. I still drank too much but mostly stayed away from drugs. I also slept with a few men, an exercise in proving to myself that I was still desirable – until it dawned on me that most men would go to bed with anyone who offered, so it was hardly the ego-boosting exercise I'd hoped.

Now that there were so few distractions in my life, it had become obvious what a mournful place London really was. The liquid sunshine of the Sixties had evaporated, and the city felt like a graveyard, full of trampled souls and hungry ghosts like me. Even the Beatles had fled.

At the end of the summer, I found my own place – a rented studio flat in Earl's Court. I also underwent another dermabrasion. This time, it worked. When the scabs fell off, the worst of the craters had been smoothed out.

However, the texture of my skin was not smooth. It had the bumpy consistency of ricotta, with white interlacing marks on my cheeks where the acne had been. It was, the doctors told me, the best outcome I could expect.

'They can easily be covered up with foundation, and your skin texture may improve with time,' Dr Neale said.

It was better than it had been, but not good enough for the camera. I knew I'd never model again.

Jules took me out to dinner for a pep talk.

His hippie attire had long since been replaced by a crumpled seersucker jacket, skinny black tie and khaki trousers. Shorter hair and horn-rimmed glasses completed

254

the picture. He looked every inch the harried magazine editor.

After I finished teasing him, he said, 'I have a confession. For the last two years I've been seeing a psychoanalyst in Harley Street. Do you think it's something you might consider? Because it has really helped me.'

'You don't seem any different,' I said, rather defensively.

'Except I don't fixate on wanting to kill the Maestro any longer,' he said, with a faint smile. 'He's never going to change, so I realised changing was up to me. Despising a parent, particularly of your own sex, is famously paralysing.'

'I know what you mean,' I said, 'but Maud is the least of my problems. I need to work out what I'm going to do with my life, not rehash old grudges.'

'In that case,' he said, refilling my glass of wine, 'why don't you write that column we've been discussing for years? Look, Ari, I've kept all your letters, I know you can write. I'm willing to try if you are.'

I told him I'd think about it, although I had no intention of thinking at all.

Despite Jules's encouraging words, I had no confidence in my writing ability whatsoever. Also, I was busy with other pursuits. Like consuming as much food as possible and then violently discharging the contents of my stomach into the white porcelain.

It was not a lifestyle choice, but the only way I knew to keep overwhelming loneliness at a level I could deal with.

I missed my old life, and most of all I missed Ramsey. Despite everything, he made every other man seem tame in comparison.

When I could get out of the flat, I walked up to Kensington Gardens and through Hyde Park, down Piccadilly to Floral Street in Covent Garden to take a jazz dance class in an old condemned warehouse.

Very soon it was all too clear that I wasn't destined for the stage either, but it didn't deter me. I felt driven to perform several daily rituals; some healthier than others. The main objective of them all was to remain bone thin while avoiding hospitalisation.

I clung to my rituals and they seemed to work – until I suffered a paralysing panic attack while walking on Oxford Street one afternoon and ended up sobbing inside a phone box. That was when I finally gave in and rang Jules's psychoanalyst.

Dr McGruder turned out to be kind man in his seventies, with a gentle sense of humour. I cringed with embarrassment when I showed him the large scab caused by my teeth biting the middle knuckle of my right hand as I shoved my finger down my throat, but Dr McGruder seemed more puzzled than shocked.

When we met the following week, he announced, 'My dear, I have looked up your symptoms, and you have an illness called bulimia nervosa.'

'A little sister for anorexia,' I said, trying to lighten the mood. And Dr McGruder laughed obligingly.

The news that bulimia was a known illness removed at least a tiny particle of the shame I was feeling.

The one thing that really seemed to help was exercise. So, as well as dancing, I took to walking anywhere my feet carried me. Miles and miles every day. I'd ride the tube to a part of town I didn't know at all, explore it for hours on foot and then take the tube back home again.

At the end of the day I was so exhausted that I would tumble into bed and sleep, dreamlessly.

One afternoon in early October, I'd just emerged onto Euston Road from Russell Square, when there was a sudden thunderstorm followed by a torrential downpour. Drenched, I made a dash for King's Cross Station. After shivering by the entrance for a few minutes, it seemed clear the rain was not going to let up, so I decided to take the tube back to Earl's Court.

At King's Cross, the escalators are precipitously steep. As I clutched the moving handrail, I gazed across at the stream of people travelling in the opposite direction. In the flat fluorescent lighting, the faces rolling past looked anaemic, vacant, like a moving assembly line of the undead. Like Blake's illustrations of Dante's *Inferno*. A wave of nausea gripped me, and I broke out into a sweat, sure I was about to lose my grip and tumble headlong down the steel stairs, hitting other people on the way and causing them to fall too.

At that moment, I spotted a flash of maroon and yellow on the up escalator. Then a bare arm, the top of a shaved head and finally, directly across from me, I saw a familiar profile.

By the time I realised it was Tenzin, he had already passed behind me on his upward journey. Desperately, I turned and shouted his name.

Tenzin glanced back and our eyes met. His face brightened.

'Ari!' he called.

I gestured wildly at the top of the escalator. 'Wait for me!'

As I watched, he reached the top and disappeared from view.

By now the panic had dissolved, but my heart was still beating wildly as I reached the platform level and ran a few feet across it to leap onto the ascending escalator, taking two stairs at a time up the left side, breathless with excitement.

A few minutes before, I had been on the brink of a full-blown panic attack. Now I was flooded with... what? Elation? But my mind struggled to process this unfamiliar emotion.

When I reached the top, panting heavily, I found him standing patiently, as the crowds pushed past. He looked as calm as if he were standing at the foot of the *stupa*.

As casually as if we had seen each other the day before, he checked his watch and said, 'Do you have time for a cup of tea? I have an appointment across the road in an hour from now.'

It had stopped raining and the sky was clearing as we headed to the Lyons' Corner House across the street.

When we sat down, I said, 'What the hell are you doing here? I cannot tell you how happy I am to see you!'

A waitress in a starched white apron and cap took our order. When she'd gone, Tenzin explained. 'His Holiness has been invited to teach in London next year, so I'm scouting the venue and meeting the organisers.'

'Oh, that's wonderful! How is Rinpoche?' I asked.

'Living in a damp cave for nearly thirty years has taken its toll – but he's in great spirits. And you? How're you doing?'

The waitress appeared with our tea so there was a brief pause for some small talk. Then I took a deep breath and launched headlong into my grisly litany: heartbreak, loss, public humiliation, failure, depression – I poured it all out. For a while he listened quietly, his expression sombre. But then, to my surprise, he began laughing. And, without knowing why, I started to laugh as well.

'Don't forget, I witnessed you going up in flames on Boudhanath *stupa*,' he reminded me. 'Crazy things seem to happen to you, Ari. Even our meeting today is impossible.'

'It's true. And I'm so glad for that. But everything else is depressing,' I said, ruefully.

'Except now you are free.' He held up one hand before I could protest. 'I know you're sad, I can see it. But did you ever consider that perhaps it's the best thing that could have happened? Did you really want to be part of the fashion world forever?'

'What else is there?' I said, only half-joking.

'Well, fine, except it didn't seem to make you happy.'

No denying that.

Our eyes met and lingered. The moment soon became too intense so I quickly changed the subject. 'By the way, how is that little monk? The boy who first spotted my dress was on fire?'

Tenzin put down his teacup. 'He's almost teenager now, very bright and quite a handful. Back studying in Bhutan. He visits all the time.'

I was suddenly struck by a wholly unexpected wave of longing. 'I'd love to see him again some day.'

Tenzin shrugged. 'That's easy. His Holiness has nearly finished building the monastery near the *stupa*. There's a guest house next door. You are welcome any time. We would all be happy for you to come.' He gave me another long look. 'Will you think about it?'

A few days later, I went to see Julius at *Now!* magazine headquarters in Soho. It was after hours, and most of his staff had gone home, so Jules was less distracted than usual. He sat at his scuffed old partners desk with a vast wall of books and files behind him, a headmasterly expression on his face.

If it had been anyone else, I would have felt cowed, but I had known him too long for that.

'Is it too late to take you up on your offer?' I asked, somewhat breathlessly. 'I've got an idea – something I'd like to write about.'

Jules nodded. 'Go on.'

'You know I was in Nepal a few years ago for *Vogue*? Well, it was a turning point for me in many ways, though I didn't really understand it at the time. I thought it might be interesting to go back and explore the place further.'

I told him my interest had recently been rekindled following a chance meeting with a friend who lived there, though I didn't go into details. Mentioning that I had a crush on a monk would not have helped convince Julius to employ me.

He thought for a moment and then said, 'Why not take the overland route to Kathmandu on a hippie bus and write a column about it for us? There are a lot of armchair travellers out there.'

He got up from his chair and pulled down an atlas from the bookshelf. As soon as we began tracing routes to the East, my spirits began to soar. Belgium, Germany, Austria, Yugoslavia, Bulgaria, Turkey, Iran, Afghanistan, Pakistan, India, Nepal. I could feel the world opening up again.

Julius seemed to be equally enthused. 'You could write about whatever catches your interest in the countries you pass through, and take note of restaurants, cafés and places to stay for people on a budget. Describe what it's like for a girl to travel West to East on her own. No one has done that so far. I think it's a great idea!'

He unscrewed the lid on a bottle of Jameson's, offering me a glass. 'The main challenge will be to find a telex machine in some of these far-flung places. Because I will expect two thousand words from you every week, no matter what. We can pay 25 guineas per column and all your travel expenses.'

'Sounds good.'

He thought some more. 'In fact, start before you go. Write about packing, what you're taking, what you're leaving behind.' He paused and smiled. 'That will be a trip in itself.'

As it turned out, I stayed in England a few months longer while Papa recovered from an operation to remove his gallbladder. Once he was able to fly back to the Caribbean, in mid-March 1973, I boarded a converted double-decker bus bound for Kathmandu – a journey that took nearly three months to complete.

FORTY-ONE

Boudhanath, Nepal, September 1973

I spent that summer in Patan. Weeks went by while I waited for the monsoon rains to finally taper off. Soon, the road through the rice paddies was passable again and I heard on the Freak Street grapevine that the old Bhutanese lama and his retinue were about to return to Boudhanath for a long stay.

For Jules, I described packing up the flat and preparing to leave Patan. Under his direction, my weekly column had become more than a quirky travel guide for hip tourists. It had detailed the ups and downs of life here. How things actually worked. The hippies on Freak Street. The torrents flowing down the muddy streets on the worst days of the monsoon. The religious festivals. And my intense, crippling homesickness on the days when I felt most alone.

The column had developed a real following. On more than one occasion, I'd been stopped in coffee houses popular with travellers and asked if I was *the* Ariadne, who wrote for *Now!* magazine.

With little to do in the evenings, I also filled thirty-two exercise books, noting down everything I could recall about the last ten years. It had been a cathartic process. While attempting to avoid our unreliable parents' mistakes, Sunny and I had conjured up a vision of love based on pop songs and films we liked. Yet Sunny had converted her dreams into reality by working hard and always being true to herself – whereas I had followed a dark star and lost myself in the process.

Having not heard from her for months, I'd received two letters from Sunny in the past week. She complained that she was permanently exhausted juggling the twins and touring. However, she'd been invited to sing at a Royal Variety show in front of the Queen. She'd already planned her outfit: a white sequin boiler suit

260

with platform boots.

Once I had digested her news, I was glad I hadn't buckled and gone home. It seemed that nothing much had changed there, whereas I had gone through a testing time and more or less survived.

After so many months of introspection it came as great relief to be in a taxi heading eastwards across a narrow bridge over the Bagmati river, into the dazzling green countryside. By the end of the day I had moved into a room in the Eden guest house at the edge of the village, where the air was so crystal clear you could almost see footprints in the snow on the distant peaks.

My room opened onto a garden with hibiscus and bottlebrush shrubs, and a small café just a few yards away. The smell of the red earth after the prolonged rain, and the profusion of bees and butterflies, was enchanting – though the effect was slightly marred by the constant din coming from the building site down the road where Rinpoche's monastery was under construction.

The following week I was sitting in a crammed assembly hall at a Buddhist centre in Boudhanath. A large contingent of Westerners sat on the floor behind a row of maroon-clad monks and nuns, all of us gazing up at the old lama, who sat cross-legged on a high-backed throne covered in brocade.

He spoke in Tibetan, while next to him on a lower seat, Tenzin translated the teaching into English. Even though Tenzin's diction was perfect, I could hardly understand a word. With everyone jammed in so close together, it was uncomfortably warm in the room and my head was swimming.

The lama described smoking out bees to get honey, an ugly woman pregnant with a king, then something about a gold statue covered in rags. None of it made any sense. Glancing around the room, I found everyone else absorbed, hanging on the lama's every word. I wanted to be as entranced as they were, but my brain was fogged with endless thoughts, mostly related to feeling claustrophobic. The people on either side of me were gradually encroaching on my space and I was irritated by their reverent expressions and the wooden rosaries wound around their wrists.

I'd been waiting for months for this moment, but it had turned into a bitter disappointment.

However, I couldn't help being impressed by Tenzin's ability to translate the lama's five-minute-long expositions without faltering. I was struck by the nobility of his features, his evident grasp on the subject matter, his gentle voice and demeanour. Perhaps it was a result of living in Asia for ten years, but his ordinary native characteristics had been refined to an extremely subtle degree. Apart from a sight accent, he didn't seem American; or any particular nationality. Nor was his energy definitively masculine or feminine, yet something told me he wasn't asexual either.

Before long, I began daydreaming about what he'd be like as a lover. Certainly he'd be more sensitive than any man I had been with to date, and the absolute polar opposite of Ramsey. The connection between us was undeniable.

At that moment, Rinpoche looked up from his text and glanced over at me. As our eyes met, I felt a wave of warmth dissolve into me. All the chaotic thoughts that had been crowding my mind just stopped. I could hear Tenzin's microphone crackle as he repeated a phrase in Tibetan, and then translated into English: 'All beings possess the seed of enlightenment. Our Buddha-nature is intrinsically pure, right from the beginning. *Drima dralrung* – all stains are removeable.'

Rinpoche cleared his throat and began chanting prayers from the text, whereupon the rest of the assembled company joined in.

For the next few days I walked around in a state of unfamiliar clarity, making friends with an eclectic mix of people from all over the world who had gathered in Boudha for the teachings. On weekends we travelled to temples and power spots in the Kathmandu Valley, and stayed up late, laughing and gossiping. I began to feel at home in a way I never had anywhere else.

I loved it all so much – but after the last column I sent Julius, he accused me of being ungrounded. There was no doubt that when it came to writing about the dharma, I was way out of my depth. But I suspected the real source of my giddiness stemmed from my feelings for Tenzin, and they were spilling out onto the page and into every moment.

Just as it had been with Ramsey, I had the sense that an unseen hand was at work, bringing us together. It was fortunate that this time I had a job and had to keep functioning… at least to some extent.

So I wrote about the countryside and the *stupa*, the Tibetan refugees, as well as the expats who had found a home here, hoping it would all meet with Jules's editorial approval.

One afternoon, while I was writing on the terrace outside my room at the guesthouse, Tenzin turned up unexpectedly. I'd seen him at the lama's side, and we'd waved at each other, and held fleeting conversations at the Buddhist centre. But we hadn't had a chance to really talk.

We sat in the sun outside the café and ordered tea and biscuits, making awkward small talk, while I did my best to hide my nerves.

Tenzin told me about the two boy monks who were presently being schooled in Dehradun. 'They'll be visiting His Holiness in a couple of months,' he said, as if the thought had just occurred to him. 'Will you still be here then?'

'I'm going to do a meditation course down the road,' I replied, just as casually. 'So yes! I should still be here.'

I'd invented the course on the spur of the moment. It was true I was keen to see the boy who had saved my life and I wanted to attend as many of Rinpoche's teachings as possible, but Tenzin was the real reason I wanted to stick around. There had been so much I wanted to ask him but now he was in front of me the conversation was digressing further away from what I really cared about: him and me.

As the time passed, I grew more desperate that he'd leave and I might not get another chance to find out how he felt.

Then I heard myself ask him abruptly, 'What about you? Don't you get sick of the monastic life and your vow of celibacy? Don't you miss sex?'

I hadn't meant to ask such a personal question; it just shot out of my mouth.

He looked slightly taken aback but kept his nerve.

'Of course I miss it. But not as much as I want to be liberated.'

My heart sank. 'But don't you believe in true love?'

He looked back at me, clear-eyed. 'As far as I can see, romantic love often turns into its opposite, as you have experienced yourself. True love? Being able to love without self-interest? I'm nowhere near that,' he smiled. 'Anyhow, in a couple of weeks I'm travelling to France to start a three-year retreat, so who knows what I'll be feeling at the end of it.'

My spirits plummeted. I felt like an idiot. Had I really imagined that Tenzin loved me too? Had I truly believed he would fling off his robes and we would live happily ever after?

Tears prickled at the backs of my eyes as I stared at the ground, hoping he wouldn't notice.

Calmly, he handed me a paper napkin from the tea tray.

'I'm sorry,' I said, with a small laugh. 'I don't know what's wrong with me. It's just that during the teaching the other day... '

I broke off, unable to finish the sentence. I could feel Tenzin listening calmly, without judgement. Finally I blurted out, 'I think I fell in love with you. It was like being hit by a thunderbolt.'

'Tell me exactly what happened?' he asked gently.

After I described the sequence of events during the teaching, Tenzin laughed. 'So you were shown the nature of your mind, with all references stripped away. Great masters like Rinpoche can do that, give you a glimpse of awakening, but now it's up to you.'

'What do you mean, references?' I asked, trying to make sense of what he was telling me.

'Oh, references like your gender, race, nationality, personal history, stuff like that,' Tenzin replied. 'That's why you felt so light and clear afterwards. A fantastic experience of your true nature, but I can absolutely promise you it has nothing to do with me.'

He paused momentarily, then looked directly into my eyes.

'Ari, I know you're looking for someone to save you, but you already have everything you need... Look what you've achieved in the last few months.'

'I'm not sure a travel column is much of an achievement,' I laughed.

'No, I mean learning how to be alone. It's not easy – most people can't hack it for long. But since I last saw you in London, you've really come into your own.'

Tenzin glanced at his watch and sighed. 'I should get back to work. Will you walk with me?'

We headed through the garden gates and onto the bustling main thoroughfare, dodging motorbikes, wandering cows and rickshaws. At the bottom of the hill, the street opened out onto the wide open square with the great, circular *stupa* at the centre. High above its golden spire, a large flock of pigeons were wheeling about languidly while prayer flags crackled and whipped in the breeze.

I turned to Tenzin, who was shielding his eyes from the sun's glare as he gazed at the steady stream of pilgrims circling the *stupa*.

'May I write to you while you're on retreat?'

He looked down at me, somewhat surprised, and then smiled. 'I'd like that. I'll give you my address before I leave.'

He hugged me lightly, like a brother or a friend. Then he turned to walk away, pushing the loose end of his robe over his shoulder and giving me a quick smile.

I was grateful to him for not faltering.

I turned in the opposite direction and headed down the slope towards the *stupa*. After a few steps, I turned back for one last glance, just as Tenzin did the same.

We each lifted a hand and waved at each other.

I knew then I still loved him, yet I felt like a seal freed from a fishing net, diving into freedom.

Acknowledgements

To my friends who kept on at me to finish this book when I lost confidence along the way, I owe a special debt of gratitude; notably Paloma Fataar, Michael MacFarlane, Isabella Tree, Charlie Burrell, Julie Clarke Neville, James Sumerfield, Susanna Moore, Peter Eyre, Diana Melly, Janey Longman, James Fox, Edward St Aubyn, Alexander Vreeland, Lisa Immordino Vreeland, Janine Shultz, Emma Mahony, Jose Fonseca, Dick Kreis, Edina Ronay, Dick Polak, Julie Kavanagh, Kate McCreery, Rowan Somerville, Deborah Dorjee, Annabelle von Arnim, Noa Jones, Kfir Yfet, Jonathan Lipman, Olivia Harrison, Pedro Kujawski, and especially Dzongsar Khyentse Rinpoche.

For the indelible memories and inspiration, my thanks and love go to David Bailey, John Swannell, Jenny Kee and Verushka, and the late Jonathan Lieberson, Diana Vreeland, Boris Lissanevitch, Lendhup Dorji, Richard Neville, Martin Sharp and Michael Ramsden.

Also, I was immensely encouraged by the enthusiastic response from Sally Orson-Jones who edited an early version of the manuscript, and Diana Melly who offered good advice and important tweaks at a key moment.

Huge thanks to my steadfast agent, Jason Bartholomew at The bks Agency, whose energy, ingenuity, and excellent sense of humour I very much appreciate.

Finally, I am deeply grateful to the brilliant team at Moonflower Books; Jack Jewers, Emma Waring, Jasmine Aurora, Tory Lyne-Pirkis and especially Christi Daugherty who, with the assistance of Louise Voss, helped guide *Piece Of My Heart* into finished form.

Pagans by James Alistair Henry

OUT 24 OCTOBER 2024

SCAN ME TO FIND OUT MORE

Britain, 2023... only in this Britain, the Norman Conquest of 1066 never happened. An uneasy alliance of ancient tribes – the Celtic West, Saxon East and an independent Nordic Scotland – has formed, but the fragile peace is threatened by a series of brutal murders.

As the threat rises, Detectives Aedith and Drustan must put aside their personal differences to follow the trail, even when they uncover forces behind the killings that go deeper than they could ever have imagined.

Set in a world that's far from our own and yet captivatingly familiar, Pagans explores contemporary themes of religious conflict, nationalism and prejudice in a smart, witty and refreshingly different police procedural that keeps you guessing until the very end. Perfect for readers of Ben Aaronovitch, Neil Gaiman and Terry Prachett.

About the author

Screenwriter and editor James Alistair Henry first started writing while working as a bookseller. He joined the writing team for Channel 4's *Smack the Pony* and went on to write the BAFTA-award winning *Green Wing*, ITV comedy *Delivery Man* and cult hit *Campus* as well as episodes for smash-hit children's television shows *Bob The Builder* and *Hey Duggee*. James lives in Cornwall with his wife, a writer and medieval historian, and their two children.

MOONFLOWER

www.moonflowerbooks.co.uk

The Coming Storm by Greg Mosse

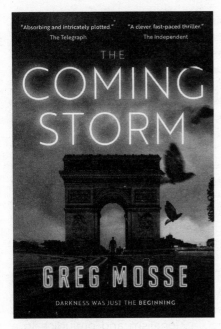

"Absorbing and intricately plotted."
The Telegraph

"A clever, fast-paced thriller."
The Independent

THE COMING STORM

GREG MOSSE

DARKNESS WAS JUST THE BEGINNING

25 APRIL 2024

**SCAN ME TO FIND
OUT MORE**

The hotly-anticipated sequel to 2022 Sunday Times Thriller of the Year The Coming Darkness sees the return of hero Alexandre Lamarque. He may have prevented the world from falling into ruin, but Alex knows his work is not done yet.

There's still a controlling intelligence out there, pulling together the strands of a new and even more destructive conspiracy. Battling with personal tragedy on one hand, and the intrusion of their new-found celebrity on the other, Alex and his allies must reunite for the fight of their lives. From the streets of Paris to the lithium mines of southern Mali, and to the mighty Aswan Dam, they come up against forces whose intentions are as devious as they are malign. Time is against them, and there's more at stake than ever.

About the author

Greg is a director, writer and writing teacher. He has lived and worked as a translator in Paris, New York, Los Angeles and Madrid. He now lives in Sussex with his wife, the novelist Kate Mosse.

"One of the best thrillers of 2022."
THE TIMES

"A clever, fast-paced thriller – an impressive debut."
INDEPENDENT

"Absorbing and intricately plotted."
THE TELEGRAPH

MOONFLOWER

www.moonflowerbooks.co.uk

The Fortunes of Olivia Richmond
by Louise Davidson

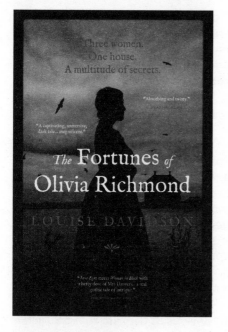

After a terrible tragedy, governess Julia Pearlie finds herself with no job, home, or references. When she's offered a position as companion to Miss Olivia Richmond, she's relieved. But Mistcoate House is full of secrets. And Julia has more than a few of her own.

As the danger grows, and the winter chill wraps around the dark woods surrounding Mistcoate, Julia will have to fight to uncover the truth, escape her past – and save herself.

Original and engrossing, this Victorian Gothic thriller is an outstanding piece of storytelling from an exciting new talent. Perfect for fans of Stacy Halls and Michelle Paver.

About the author

Louise Davidson was born in Belfast. Growing up in Northern Ireland backgrounded by the Troubles led her to develop a fascination with history, and this combined with her love of all things gothic inspired her to write her first book, a dark Victorian thriller set in a neglected and isolated mansion. Louise lives in London with her husband and step-son.

"A darkly gothic historical mystery in all the best traditions of the genre – a standout."
HELEN FIELDS, SUNDAY TIMES BESTSELLING AUTHOR

"Magnificent. Gothic writing of the most compelling kind."
MY WEEKLY

"Absorbing and twisty."
HEAT MAGAZINE

SCAN ME TO FIND OUT MORE

MOONFLOWER

www.moonflowerbooks.co.uk

The Lost Diary of Samuel Pepys
by Jack Jewers

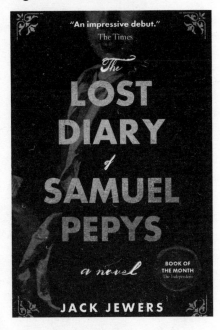

The diaries of Samuel Pepys have enthralled readers for centuries with their audacious wit, gripping detail, and racy assignations. Pepys stopped writing at the age of 36. Or did he?

This action-packed historical thriller picks up where Pepys left off as he is sent from the pleasures of his familiar London to the grimy taverns and shipyards of Portsmouth. An investigator sent by the King to look into corruption at the Royal Navy has been brutally murdered, and it's down to Pepys to find out why. But what awaits him is more dangerous than he could have imagined.

About the author

Jack Jewers is a filmmaker and writer, passionate about history. His films have been shown at dozens of international film festivals including Cannes, New York, Marseille and Dublin, and have received awards from the Royal Television Society and a BAFTA nomination. *The Lost Diary of Samuel Pepys* is his first novel.

'Book of the month... A zestful imagining.'
INDEPENDENT

'One of the best historical fiction books of the year.'
THE TIMES

'Swashbuckling action-packed drama.'
WOMAN AND HOME

SCAN ME TO FIND
OUT MORE

MOONFLOWER

www.moonflowerbooks.co.uk

About Moonflower Books

The Independent Publishing Association's Newcomer of the Year 2023, Moonflower is a young, UK-based, independent publisher. Our award-winning books are the kind that make you sit up in your seat. Books that break the mould. That are hard to categorise. In short, the kind of books that deserve your attention.

moonflowerbooks.co.uk

MOONFLOWER